MINOTAUR

BOOKS

GET A CLUE!

Be the first to hear the latest mystery book news...

With the Minotaur monthly newsletter, you'll learn about the hottest new Minotaur books, receive advance excerpts from newly published works, read exclusive original material from featured mystery writers, and be able to enter to win free books!

Sign up on the Minotaur Web site at:
www.minotaurbooks.com

Praise for Louise Penny and
THE CRUELEST MONTH

"Certain books come to mind whenever that little voice whispers in your ear 'Oh, lighten up!' . . . Louise Penny's series about the eccentric residents of a postcard-perfect town in Canada can . . . be pretty funny."
—Marilyn Stasio, *The New York Times Book Review*

"Who wouldn't be charmed by the dramas of [the Three Pines] community . . . ? Yet it is Penny's fastidious, cultured, and smart Inspector Gamache who makes *The Cruelest Month* impossible to put down."
—*People* magazine (3 1/2 stars)

"Perhaps the deftest talent to arrive since Minette Walters, Penny produces what many have tried but few have mastered: a psychologically acute cozy. If you don't give your heart to Gamache, you may have no heart to give."
—*Kirkus Reviews* (starred review)

"The thing about the Gamache novels is that while the crimes are intriguing . . . Gamache [is] completely original."
—*Booklist*

"Gamache is an engaging, modern-day Poirot . . . entertaining and thought-provoking."
—*Library Journal* (starred review)

"Expertly plotted."   —*Publishers Weekly*

"A charming oasis for the spirit . . . quirky and literate. Move over, Mitford."   —*Charlotte Observer*

MORE...

"Rich characterizations, a credible plot line, and an increasingly likable protagonist in Gamache. Add [Penny's] compassion, grace, and wisdom, and readers will rejoice in the latest entry in this stylish and sensitive series."
—*Richmond Times Dispatch*

"If you aren't familiar with . . . Gamache and the charming town of Three Pines, you are missing something wonderful in the world of mystery fiction."
—*Omaha World-Herald*

A FATAL GRACE

"This is a fine mystery in the classic Agatha Christie style and it is sure to leave fans wanting more." —*Booklist*

"A traditional and highly intelligent mystery. . . . Sure to create great reader demand for more. . . . Highly recommended." —*Library Journal* (starred review)

"Gamache is a prodigiously complicated and engaging hero, destined to become one of the classic detectives."
—*Kirkus Reviews* (starred review)

"This book is a small and perfect literary jewel. Penny is the best writer of traditional mysteries to come along in decades. I haven't read a book this beautifully written since *A Thread of Grace* by Mary Doria Russell."
—*Kingston Observer*

"Very simply, I loved this book. I expect you will, too."
—*Mystery Scene*

"The cast of *A Fatal Grace* is a marvelous mystery. . . . The plotting is intricate, the pacing perfect, the writing brilliant. . . . Ms. Penny leaves a bit of a cliffhanger for readers to ponder until the next installment. It can't come soon enough for me." —*Cozy Library*

St. Martin's Paperbacks Titles by

Louise Penny

Still Life

A Fatal Grace

THE
CRUELEST
MONTH

An Armand Gamache Novel

Louise Penny

St. Martin's Paperbacks

This is a work of fiction. All of the characters, organizations, and events portrayed in this novel are either products of the author's imagination or are used fictitiously.

THE CRUELEST MONTH

For information address St. Martin's Press, 175 Fifth Avenue, New York, NY 10010.

Library of Congress Catalog Card Number: 2007042422

ISBN: 0-312-94450-0
EAN: 978-0-312-94450-6

Printed in the United States of America

First published in Great Britain by Headline Publishing Group
St. Martin's Press hardcover edition / March 2008
St. Martin's Paperbacks edition / January 2009

St. Martin's Paperbacks are published by St. Martin's Press, 175 Fifth Avenue, New York, NY 10010.

10 9 8 7 6 5 4 3 2 1

For my brother Rob and his wonderful family,

Audi, Kim, Adam and Sarah, with love

April is the cruellest month, breeding
Lilacs out of the dead land, mixing
Memory and desire...

—T. S. Eliot, *The Waste Land*

CHAPTER 1

Kneeling in the fragrant moist grass of the village green Clara Morrow carefully hid the Easter egg and thought about raising the dead, which she planned to do right after supper. Wiping a strand of hair from her face, she smeared bits of grass, mud and some other brown stuff that might not be mud into her tangled hair. All around, villagers wandered with their baskets of brightly colored eggs, looking for the perfect hiding places. Ruth Zardo sat on the bench in the middle of the green tossing the eggs at random, though occasionally she'd haul off and peg someone in the back of the head or on the bottom. She had disconcertingly good aim for someone so old and so nuts, thought Clara.

'You going tonight?' Clara asked, trying to distract the old poet from taking aim at Monsieur Béliveau.

'Are you kidding? Live people are bad enough; why would I want to bring one back from the dead?'

With that Ruth whacked Monsieur Béliveau in the back of his head. Fortunately the village grocer was wearing a cloth cap. It was also fortunate he had great affection for the white-haired ramrod on the bench. Ruth chose her victims well. They were almost always people who cared for her.

Normally being pelted by a chocolate Easter egg wouldn't be a big deal, but these weren't chocolate. They'd made that mistake only once.

* * *

A few years earlier, when the village of Three Pines first decided to have an egg hunt on Easter Sunday, there'd been great excitement. The villagers met at Olivier's Bistro and over drinks and Brie they divvied up bags of chocolate eggs to be hidden the next day. 'Ooohs' and 'Aaaaahs' tinged with envy filled the air. Would that they were children again. But their pleasure would surely come from seeing the faces of the village children. Besides, the kids might not find them all, especially those hidden behind Olivier's bar.

'They're gorgeous.' Gabri picked up a tiny marzipan goose, delicately sculpted, then bit its head off.

'Gabri.' His partner Olivier yanked what was left of the goose from Gabri's massive hand. 'They're for the kids.'

'You just want it for yourself.' Gabri turned to Myrna and muttered so that everyone could hear, 'Great idea. Gay men offering chocolates to children. Let's alert the Moral Majority.'

Blond and bashful, Olivier blushed furiously.

Myrna smiled. She looked like a massive Easter egg herself, black and oval and wrapped in a brilliant purple and red caftan.

Most of the tiny village was at the bistro, crowded around the long bar of polished wood, though some had flopped down in the comfortable old armchairs scattered about. All for sale. Olivier's was also an antique shop. Discreet tags dangled from everything, including Gabri when he felt under-appreciated and under-applauded.

It was early April and fires crackled cheerily in the open grates, throwing warm light on the wide-plank pine floors, stained amber by time and sunlight. Waiters moved effortlessly through the beamed room, offering drinks and soft, runny Brie from Monsieur Pagé's farm. The bistro was at the heart of the old Quebec village, sitting as it did on the edge of the green. On either side of it and attached by connecting doors were the rest of the shops, hugging the village in an aged brick embrace. Monsieur Béliveau's general store, Sarah's Boulangerie, then the bistro and finally, just off that,

Myrna's Livres, Neufs et Usagés. Three craggy pine trees had stood at the far end of the green for as long as anyone remembered, like wise men who'd found what they were looking for. Outward from the village, dirt roads radiated and meandered into the mountains and forests.

But Three Pines itself was a village forgotten. Time eddied and swirled and sometimes bumped into it, but never stayed long and never left much of an impression. For hundreds of years the village had nestled in the palm of the rugged Canadian mountains, protected and hidden and rarely found except by accident. Sometimes, a weary traveler crested the hill and looking down saw, like Shangri-La, the welcoming circle of old homes. Some were weathered fieldstone built by settlers clearing the land of deeply rooted trees and back-breaking stones. Others were red brick and built by United Empire Loyalists desperate for sanctuary. And some had the swooping metal roofs of the Québécois home with their intimate gables and broad verandas. And at the far end was Olivier's Bistro, offering *café au lait* and fresh-baked croissants, conversation and company and kindness. Once found, Three Pines was never forgotten. But it was only ever found by people lost.

Myrna looked over at her friend Clara Morrow, who was sticking out her tongue. Myrna stuck hers out too. Clara rolled her eyes. Myrna rolled hers, taking a seat beside Clara on the soft sofa facing the fireplace.

'You weren't smoking garden mulch again while I was in Montreal, were you?'

'Not this time,' Clara laughed. 'You have something on your nose.'

Myrna felt around, found something and examined it. 'Mmm, it's either chocolate, or skin. Only one way to find out.'

She popped it in her mouth.

'God.' Clara winced. 'And you wonder why you're single.'

'I don't wonder.' Myrna smiled. 'I don't need a man to complete me.'

'Oh really? What about Raoul?'

'Ah, Raoul,' said Myrna dreamily. 'He was a sweet.'

'He was a gummy bear,' agreed Clara.

'He completed me,' said Myrna. 'And then some.' She patted her middle, large and generous, like the woman herself.

'Look at this.' A razor voice cut through conversation.

Ruth Zardo stood in the center of the bistro holding aloft a chocolate rabbit as though it were a grenade. It was made of rich dark chocolate, its long ears perky and alert, its face so real Clara half expected it to twitch its delicate candy whiskers. In its paws it held a basket woven from white and milk chocolate, and in that basket sat a dozen candy eggs, beautifully decorated. It was lovely and Clara prayed Ruth wasn't about to toss it at someone.

'It's a bunny rabbit,' snarled the elderly poet.

'I eat them too,' said Gabri to Myrna. 'It's a habit. A rabbit habit.'

Myrna laughed and immediately wished she hadn't. Ruth turned her glare on her.

'Ruth.' Clara stood up and approached cautiously, holding her husband Peter's Scotch as enticement. 'Let the bunny go.'

It was a sentence she'd never said before.

'It's a rabbit,' Ruth repeated as though to slow children. 'So what's it doing with these?'

She pointed to the eggs.

'Since when do rabbits have eggs?' Ruth persisted, looking at the bewildered villagers. 'Never thought of that, eh? Where did it get them? Presumably from chocolate chickens. The bunny must have stolen the eggs from candy chickens who're searching for their babies. Frantic.'

The funny thing was, as the old poet spoke Clara could actually imagine chocolate chickens running around desperate to find their eggs. Eggs stolen by the Easter bunny.

With that Ruth dropped the chocolate bunny to the floor, shattering it.

'Oh, God,' said Gabri, running to pick it up. 'That was for Olivier.'

'Really?' said Olivier, forgetting he himself had bought it.

'This is a strange holiday,' said Ruth ominously. 'I've never liked it.'

'And now it's mutual,' said Gabri, holding the fractured rabbit as though an adored and wounded child. He's so tender, thought Clara not for the first time. Gabri was so big, so overwhelming, it was easy to forget how sensitive he was. Until moments like these when he gently held a dying chocolate bunny.

'How do we celebrate Easter?' the old poet demanded, yanking Peter's Scotch from Clara and downing it. 'We hunt eggs and eat hot cross buns.'

'*Mais*, we go to St Thomas's too,' said Monsieur Béliveau.

'More people go to Sarah's Boulangerie than ever show up at church,' snapped Ruth. 'They buy pastry with an instrument of torture on it. I know you think I'm crazy, but maybe I'm the only sane one here.'

And on that disconcerting note she limped to the door, then turned back.

'Don't put those chocolate eggs out for the children. Something bad will happen.'

And like Jeremiah, the weeping prophet, she was right. Something bad did happen.

Next morning the eggs had vanished. All that could be found were wrappers. At first the villagers suspected older children, or perhaps even Ruth, had sabotaged the event.

'Look at this,' said Peter, holding up the shredded remains of a chocolate bunny box. 'Teeth marks. And claws.'

'So it was Ruth,' said Gabri, taking the box and examining it.

'See here.' Clara raced after a candy wrapper blowing across the village green. 'Look, it's all ripped apart as well.'

After spending the morning hunting Easter egg wrappers and cleaning up the mess, most villagers trudged back to Olivier's to warm themselves by the fire.

'Now, really,' said Ruth to Clara and Peter over lunch at the bistro. 'Couldn't you see that coming?'

'I admit it seems obvious,' Peter laughed, cutting into his golden *croque-monsieur*, the melted Camembert barely holding the maple-smoked ham and flaky croissant together. Around him anxious parents buzzed, trying to bribe crying children.

'Every wild animal within miles must have been in the village last night,' said Ruth, slowly swirling the ice cubes in her Scotch. 'Eating Easter eggs. Foxes, raccoons, squirrels.'

'Bears,' said Myrna, joining their table. 'Jesus, that's pretty scary. All those starving bears, rising from their dens, ravenous after hibernating all winter.'

'Imagine their surprise to find chocolate eggs and bunnies,' said Clara, between mouthfuls of creamy seafood chowder with chunks of salmon and scallops and shrimp. She took a crusty baguette and twisted off a piece, spreading it with Olivier's special sweet butter. 'The bears must have wondered what miracle had happened while they slept.'

'Not everything that rises up is a miracle,' said Ruth, lifting her eyes from the amber liquid, her lunch, and looking out the mullioned windows. 'Not everything that comes back to life is meant to. This is a strange time of year. Rain one day, snow the next. Nothing's certain. It's unpredictable.'

'Every season's unpredictable,' said Peter. 'Hurricanes in fall, snowstorms in winter.'

'But you've just proved my point,' said Ruth. 'You can name the threat. We all know what to expect in other seasons. But not spring. The worst flooding happens in spring. Forest fires, killing frosts, snowstorms and mud slides. Nature's in turmoil. Anything can happen.'

'The most achingly beautiful days happen in spring too,' said Clara.

'True, the miracle of rebirth. I hear whole religions are based on the concept. But some things are better off buried.' The old poet got up and downed her Scotch. 'It's not over yet. The bears will be back.'

'I would be too,' said Myrna, 'if I'd suddenly found a village made of chocolate.'

Clara smiled, but her eyes were on Ruth, who for once didn't radiate anger or annoyance. Instead Clara caught something far more disconcerting.

Fear.

CHAPTER 2

Ruth had been right. The bears did come back each Easter in search of chocolate eggs. Of course, they found none and after a couple of years gave up and instead stayed in the woods surrounding Three Pines. Villagers quickly learned not to go for long walks in the woods at Easter, and to never, ever get between a newborn bear cub and its mother.

It's all part of nature, Clara told herself. But a niggling worry remained. Somehow they'd brought this on themselves.

Once again Clara found herself on her hands and knees, this time with the beautiful wooden eggs they'd substituted for the real thing. That had been Hanna and Roar Parra's idea. Coming from the Czech Republic they had no mean knack with painted eggs.

Over the winter Roar whittled the wooden eggs and Hanna handed them out to anyone interested in painting them. Soon people from all over the Cantons de l'Est were taking eggs. School kids did them as art projects, parents rediscovered latent talents, grandparents painted scenes from their youth. Over the long Quebec winter they painted and on Good Friday they started hiding them. Once found the children exchanged the wooden bounty for the real thing. Or at least, the chocolate thing.

'Hey, look at this,' Clara called from beside the pond on the green. Monsieur Béliveau and Madeleine Favreau went over. Monsieur Béliveau stooped down, his long slender body almost bending double. There in the long grass was a nest of eggs.

'They're real,' he laughed, spreading the grass to show Madeleine.

'How beautiful,' said Mad, reaching out.

'*Mais, non,*' he said. 'Their mother will reject them if you touch.'

Mad quickly brought back her hand and looked at Clara with a wide open smile. Clara had always liked Madeleine, though they didn't know each other well. Mad had lived in the area for only a few years. She was some years younger than Clara and full of life. She was also a natural beauty, with short dark hair and intelligent brown eyes. She always seemed to be enjoying herself. And why not, thought Clara. After what she'd been through.

'What sort of eggs are they?' Clara asked.

Madeleine made a face and put up her hands. Not a clue.

Monsieur Béliveau again folded himself in a graceful movement. 'Not chicken. *Trop grand.* Maybe duck, or goose.'

'That would be fun,' said Madeleine. 'A little family on the green.' She turned to Clara. 'What time's the séance?'

'You're coming?' Clara was surprised though delighted. 'Hazel too?'

'No, Hazel's refused. Sophie gets home tomorrow morning and Hazel says she has to cook and clean, *mais, franchement*?' Madeleine leaned in conspiratorially, 'I think she's afraid of ghosts. Monsieur Béliveau has agreed to come.'

'We must be grateful Hazel has decided to cook instead,' said Monsieur Béliveau. 'She's made us a wonderful casserole.'

It was very like Hazel, Clara thought. Always caring for others. Clara was slightly afraid people took advantage of Hazel's generosity, especially that daughter of hers, but she also realized it was none of her business.

'But we have a great deal of work to do before dinner, *mon ami.*' Madeleine smiled radiantly at Monsieur Béliveau and touched him lightly on the shoulder. The older man smiled. He hadn't smiled a lot since his wife died, but now he did, and Clara had another reason to like Madeleine. She watched them now holding their baskets of Easter eggs and walking through the late April sunshine, the youngest and tenderest of lights falling on a young and tender relationship. Monsieur Béliveau, tall and slim and slightly stooped, seemed to have a spring in his step.

Clara stood up and stretched her forty-eight-year-old body, then glanced around. It looked like a field of der-rières. Every villager was bending over, placing eggs. Clara wished she had her sketch pad.

There was certainly nothing cool about Three Pines, nothing funky or edgy or any of the other things that had mattered to Clara when she'd graduated from art college twenty-five years ago. Nothing here was designed. Instead, the village seemed to follow the lead of the three pines on the green and simply to have grown from the earth over time.

Clara took a deep breath of the fragrant spring air and looked over at the home she shared with Peter. It was brick with a wooden porch and a fieldstone wall fronting the Commons. A path wound from their gate through some apple trees about to bloom to their front door. From there Clara's eyes wandered around the houses surrounding the Commons. Like their inhabitants, the homes of Three Pines were sturdy and shaped by their environment. They'd withstood storms and wars, loss and sorrow. And emerging from that was a community of great kindness and compassion.

Clara loved it. The houses, the shops, the village green, the perennial gardens and even the washboard roads. She loved the fact that Montreal was less than a two-hour drive away, and the American border was just down the road. But more than all of that, she loved the people who now spent this and every Good Friday hiding wooden eggs for children.

It was a late Easter, near the end of April. They weren't always so lucky with the elements. At least once the village had awoken on Easter Sunday to find a fresh dumping of heavy spring snow, burying the tender buds and painted eggs. It had often been bitterly cold and the villagers had had to duck into Olivier's Bistro every now and then for a hot cider or hot chocolate, wrapping trembling and frozen fingers around the warm and welcoming mugs.

But not today. There was a certain glory about this April day. It was a perfect Good Friday, sunny and warm. The snow had gone, even in the shadows, where it tended to linger. The grass was growing and the trees had a halo of the gentlest green. It was as though the aura of Three Pines had suddenly made itself visible. It was all golden light with shimmering green edges.

Tulip bulbs were beginning to crack through the earth and soon the village green would be awash with spring flowers, deep blue hyacinths and bluebells and gay bobbing daffodils, snowdrops and fragrant lily of the valley, filling the village with fragrance and delight.

This Good Friday Three Pines smelled of fresh earth and promise. And maybe a worm or two.

'I don't care what you say, I won't go.'

Clara heard the urgent and vicious whisper. She was crouching again, by the tall grass of the pond. She couldn't see who it was but she realized they must be just on the other side of the grass. It was a woman's voice speaking French but in a tone so strained and upset she couldn't identify her.

'It's just a séance,' a man's voice said. 'It'll be fun.'

'It's sacrilege, for Christ's sake. A séance on Good Friday?'

There was a pause. Clara was feeling uncomfortable. Not about eavesdropping, but her legs were beginning to cramp.

'Come on, Odile. You're not even religious. What can happen?'

Odile? thought Clara. The only Odile she knew was Odile Montmagny. And she was –

The woman hissed again:

> *'Each winter's frostbite and the bug*
> *That greets the spring will leave its mark,*
> *As well as sorrow on the mug*
> *Of infant, youth and patriarch.'*

Stunned silence fell.

– a really bad poet, Clara completed her thought.

Odile had spoken solemnly, as though the words conveyed something other than the talent of the poet.

'I'll look after you,' said the man. Clara now knew who he was too. Odile's boyfriend, Gilles Sandon.

'Why do you really want to go, Gilles?'

'Just for fun.'

'Is it because she'll be there?'

There was silence, except for Clara's screaming legs.

'He'll be there too, you know,' Odile pressed.

'Who?'

'You know who. Monsieur Béliveau,' said Odile. 'I have a bad feeling about this, Gilles.'

There was another pause, then Sandon spoke, his voice deep and flat as though making a huge effort to smother any emotion.

'Don't worry. I won't kill him.'

Clara had forgotten all about her legs. Kill Monsieur Béliveau? Who'd even consider such a thing? The old grocer had never even short-changed anyone. What could Gilles Sandon possibly have against him?

She heard the two walk away and straightening up with some agony Clara stared after them, Odile pear-shaped and waddling slightly, Gilles a huge teddy bear of a man, his signature red beard visible even from behind.

Clara glanced at her sweaty hands clutching the wooden Easter eggs. The cheery colors had bled into her palms.

Suddenly the séance, which had seemed an amusing idea a few days ago when Gabri had put the notice up in the bistro announcing the arrival of the famous psychic, Madame Isadore Blavatsky, now felt different. Instead of happy anticipation Clara was filled with dread.

CHAPTER 3

Madame Isadore Blavatsky wasn't herself that night. In fact, she wasn't Madame Isadore Blavatsky at all.

'Please, call me Jeanne.' The mousy woman stood in the middle of the back room at the bistro, holding out her hand. 'Jeanne Chauvet.'

'*Bonjour, Madame Chauvet.*' Clara smiled and shook the limp hand. '*Excusez-moi.*'

'Jeanne,' the woman reminded her in a voice barely audible.

Clara stepped over to Gabri who was offering a platter of smoked salmon to his guests. The room was beginning to fill up, slightly. 'Salmon?' He thrust the plate at Clara.

'Who is she?' Clara asked.

'Madame Blavatsky, the famous Hungarian psychic. Can't you just feel her energy?'

Madeleine and Monsieur Béliveau waved. Clara waved back then glanced over at Jeanne who looked as though she'd faint if someone said boo. 'I certainly feel something, young man, and it's annoyed.'

Gabri Dubeau vacillated between delight at being called 'young man' and defensiveness.

'That isn't Madame Blavatsky. She doesn't even pretend to be. Her name's Jeanne someone-or-other,' said Clara, absent-mindedly taking a piece of salmon and folding it onto a pumpernickel. 'You promised us Madame Blavatsky.'

'You don't even know who Madame Blavatsky is.'

'Well, I know who she isn't.' Clara nodded and smiled at the small, middle-aged woman standing slightly bewildered in the middle of the room.

'And would you've come if you'd known she was the psychic?' Gabri gestured with the plate toward Jeanne. A caper rolled off the end, to be lost on the rich oriental carpet.

Why do we never learn? Clara sighed to herself. Every time Gabri has a guest he organizes some outlandish event, like the time the poker champ came to stay and took all our money, or that singer who made even Ruth sound like Maria Callas. Still, horrible as these socials Gabri threw together turned out for the villagers, they must have been worse for the unsuspecting guests, roped into entertaining Three Pines when all they wanted was a quiet stay in the country.

She watched as Jeanne Chauvet gazed around the room, rubbed her hands on her polyester pants and smiled at the portrait above the roaring fireplace. Before Clara's very eyes she seemed to disappear. It was actually quite a trick, though not one that spoke highly of her psychic abilities. Clara felt badly for her. Really, what was Gabri thinking?

'What were you thinking?'

'What do you mean? She's a psychic. She told me when she booked in. True, she's not Madame Blavatsky. Or from Hungary. But she does readings.'

'Wait a minute.' Clara was getting suspicious. 'Does she even know you'd planned this evening?'

'Well, I'm sure she divined it.'

'Once people started showing up, maybe. Gabri, how could you do this to her? To us?'

'She'll be fine. Look at her. She's loosening up already.'

Myrna had fetched her a tumbler of white wine and Jeanne Chauvet was drinking as though it was water before the miracle. Myrna looked over and lifted her eyebrows at Clara. Much more of this and Myrna would have to conduct the séance.

'Séance?' Jeanne asked a minute later when Myrna asked what they could expect. 'Who's holding a séance?'

All eyes turned to Gabri, who very carefully placed the platter on a table and went over to stand beside Jeanne. Gabri's bulk and natural exuberance seemed to make the nondescript woman shrink even further until she looked like clothes on a hanger. Clara guessed she was somewhere around forty. Her hair was dull brown and looked as though she cut it herself. Her eyes were faded blue and her clothing was bargain-bin K-mart. Clara, who'd lived in poverty as an artist most of her life, recognized the signs. She wondered fleetingly why Jeanne had come to Three Pines and paid to stay at Gabri's B & B, which while not ruinous wasn't cheap either.

Jeanne no longer seemed afraid, just confused. Clara wanted to go over and put her arms round the little woman and shield her from what was coming next. She wanted to give her a good hot dinner and a warm bath and some kindness, then maybe she'd become substantial.

Clara too glanced around the room. Peter had flatly refused to come, calling it hogwash. But he'd held her hand an instant longer than necessary as she'd left, and told her to be careful. Walking under the stars round the village green to the cheery bistro Clara had smiled. Peter had been raised a strict Anglican. This sort of thing repulsed him. It also terrified him.

They'd had a small discussion over dinner, with Peter taking the predictable view that this was nuts.

'Are you calling me nuts?' Clara had asked, knowing he hadn't but loving to see him squirm. He'd raised his head, full of lush grey curls, and looked at her angrily. Tall and slender with an aquiline nose and intelligent eyes, he looked like a bank president, not an artist. And yet that was what he was. But an artist who seemed unconnected to his heart. He lived in a deeply rational world where anything unexplainable was 'nuts' or 'silly' or 'insane'. Emotions were insane. Except his love for Clara, which was complete and all-consuming.

'No, I'm calling the psychic nuts. She's a charlatan. Contacting the dead, predicting the future. Bullshit. It's the oldest game in the book.'

'Which book? The Bible?'

'Don't start with me, Clara,' Peter had warned.

'No, really. Which book talks about transformations? Of water into wine? Of bread into flesh? Or magic, like walking on water? Of parting the seas and making the blind see and the crippled walk?'

'Those were miracles, not magic.'

'Ahh.' Clara had nodded and smiled and gone back to eating.

So Clara found herself with Myrna as her date. Madeleine and Monsieur Béliveau were there, not quite holding hands but they might as well have been. His long sweater-clad arm was just touching hers, and she didn't shy away. Once again Clara was taken by how attractive Madeleine was. She was one of those women other women wanted as a best friend and men wanted as a wife.

Clara smiled at Monsieur Béliveau and blushed. Because she'd caught them in an intimate moment, seen feelings best kept private? She considered for a moment, but realized the blush had more to do with her than him. She felt differently about Monsieur Béliveau after overhearing Gilles that afternoon. The gentle grocer had gone from being a benign and kindly presence in their lives to a mystery. Clara didn't like the transformation. And she didn't like herself for being so susceptible to gossip.

Gilles Sandon stood in front of the fireplace, rubbing the warmth into the back of his substantial jeans with vigor. He was so big he almost blocked the entire hearth. Odile Montmagny brought him a glass of wine which he took absent-mindedly, preferring instead to concentrate on Monsieur Béliveau, who seemed oblivious.

Clara had always liked Odile. They were much the same age and both were in the arts, Clara a painter and Odile a poet. She claimed to be working on an epic poem, an ode to the English of Quebec, which was suspicious since she was French. Clara would never forget the reading she'd attended at the Royal Canadian Legion in St-Rémy. All sorts of local writers had been invited, including Ruth and Odile.

Ruth had read first, from her searing work, 'To the Congregation.'

> *I envy you your steady blaze*
> *Fed by the Book of Common Praise.*
> *I envy this, believe I do,*
> *That you can be, together, you,*
> *And understand you may not see*
> *That I must, on my own, be me.*

And then it had been Odile's turn. Up she'd sprung and without pause launched into her poem.

> *Spring is coming with its girth,*
> *And breezy breath of balmy warmth*
> *And burbank, bobolink, and snearth,*
> *Shall banish winter's chill and dearth,*
> *And luscious joy shall fill the earth.*

'Wonderful poem,' Clara lied, when everyone had finished and they were crowded around the bar, feeling some urgency for a drink. 'I'm just kind of curious. I've never actually heard of a snearth.'

'I made it up,' said Odile with glee. 'I needed a word to rhyme with dearth and earth.'

'Like mirth?' Ruth suggested. Clara shot her a warning look and Odile seemed to consider it.

'Not powerful enough, I'm afraid.'

'Unlike the juggernaut that is snearth,' said Ruth to Clara before turning back to Odile. 'Well, I certainly feel enriched, if not fertilized. The only poet I can think to compare you to is the great Sarah Binks.'

While Odile had never heard of Sarah Binks she knew her cultural knowledge had been stunted by an education that only admitted francophone genius. Sarah Binks, she knew, must be a very great English poet indeed. That compliment from Ruth Zardo had fueled Odile Montmagny's creativity and in quiet moments at their shop, La Maison

Biologique in St-Rémy, she'd pull out her worn and worried child's notebook to write another poem, sometimes not even pausing for inspiration.

Clara, a struggling artist herself, identified with Odile and cheered her on. Peter, of course, thought Odile was nuts. But Clara knew differently. She knew that what often distinguished great people of the arts wasn't genius, but perseverance. Odile persevered.

Eight of them had gathered in the cozy back room of the bistro to raise the dead this Good Friday, and the only question seemed to be, who would do it.

'Not me,' said Jeanne. 'I thought one of you was the psychic.'

'Gabri?' Gilles Sandon turned on their host.

'But you told me you do readings,' Gabri said to Jeanne, pleading.

'I do. Tarot cards, runes, that sort of thing. I don't contact the dead. Not often anyway.'

It's funny, Clara thought, how if you wait long enough and listen, people will say the oddest things.

'Not often?' she asked Jeanne.

'Sometimes,' Jeanne admitted, taking a small step back from Clara as though from an assault. Clara put a smile on her face and tried to appear less assertive, though a chocolate bunny would appear assertive to this woman.

'Could you do it tonight? Please?' Gabri asked. He could see his party going south fast.

Tiny, mousy, insubstantial Jeanne stood at the center of their circle. Clara saw something then, something pass over the face of this gray woman. A smile. No. A sneer.

CHAPTER 4

Hazel Smyth bustled through the comfortable, cramped house, keeping herself busy. She had a million things to do before her daughter Sophie got back from Queens University. The beds were already made with clean, crisp linens. The baked beans were slowly cooking, the bread was rising, the fridge was stocked with Sophie's favorite food. Now Hazel collapsed on the uncomfortable horsehair sofa in the living room, feeling every day of her forty-two years, and then some. The old sofa seemed to be covered in tiny needles, pricking into anything that sat on it, as though trying to repulse the weight. And yet Hazel loved it, perhaps because no one else did. She knew it was stuffed with equal parts horsehair and memories, themselves prickly at times.

'You don't still have it, Haze?' Madeleine had laughed a few years earlier, when she'd first walked into the cramped room. Hurrying over to the old sofa Madeleine had climbed right onto it, leaning over the back as though she'd forgotten how people sit, her slim bottom waving slightly at Hazel, who watched dumbfounded.

'What a riot,' came Mad's muffled voice from between the sofa and the wall. 'Remember how we used to spy on your parents from behind this?'

Hazel had forgotten that. Another memory to add to the overstuffed sofa. Suddenly there was a hoot of laughter and Madeleine, like the schoolgirl she'd once been, bounced round and sat facing Hazel, holding her hand out. Moving forward Hazel saw something in the delicate fingers. Something pristine and white. It looked like a small bleached bone. Hazel paused, a little afraid of what the sofa had produced.

'It's for you.' Madeleine carefully placed the small offering in the palm of Hazel's hand. Madeleine was beaming. There was no other word for it. A scarf covered her bald head, her eyebrows were inexpertly penciled in so she looked a little astonished. A slight bluish tinge under her eyes spoke of a tired that went beyond sleepless nights. But despite all that, Mad had beamed. And her extraordinary delight filled the drab room.

They hadn't seen each other in twenty years and while Hazel remembered each and every moment of their young friendship, she'd somehow forgotten how alive she'd felt around Madeleine. She looked down at her palm. The thing wasn't a bone, but a note, all rolled up.

'It was still in the sofa,' said Madeleine. 'Imagine that. After all these years. Waiting for us, I guess. Waiting for this moment.'

Madeleine seemed to carry magic with her, Hazel remembered. And where there was magic there were miracles.

'Where'd you find this?'

'Back there.' Mad waved her hand behind the sofa. 'Once, when you were in the bathroom, I slipped it into a little hole.'

'A little hole?'

'A little hole made by a little pen,' Madeleine's eyes sparkled as she mimicked digging and twisting a pen into the sofa, and Hazel found herself laughing. She could just see the girl tunneling away at her parents' prized possession. Madeleine was fearless. While Hazel had been the school hall monitor, Madeleine had been the one trying to sneak into class late, after grabbing a smoke in the woods.

Hazel looked down at the tiny white cylinder in her palm, unsullied by exposure to sunlight and life, swallowed by the sofa to be coughed up decades later.

Then she opened it. And she knew she'd had reason to
be afraid of the thing. For what it contained changed her
life immediately and forever. Written in round, exuberant
purple ink was a single simple sentence.

I love you.

Hazel couldn't meet Madeleine's eyes. Instead she
looked up from the tiny note and noticed that her living
room, which that morning had been so drab, was now warm
and comfortable, the washed-out colors vibrant. By the time
her eyes returned to Madeleine the miracle had happened.
One had become two.

Madeleine went back to Montreal to finish her treatments, but as soon as she could she returned to the cottage
in the countryside, surrounded by rolling hills and forests
and fields of spring flowers. Madeleine had found a home
and so had Hazel.

Now Hazel picked up her darning from the old horsehair sofa. She was worried. Worried about what was happening at the bistro.

They'd done the runes, the ancient Nordic symbols of div-
ination. According to the rune stones Clara was an ox,
Myrna a pine torch, Gabri a birch, though Clara told him
the rune said bitch.

'Well, it got that right,' said Gabri, impressed. 'And God
knows you're an ox.'

Monsieur Béliveau reached into the small wicker basket
and withdrew a stone painted with a diamond symbol.

'Marriage,' suggested Monsieur Béliveau. Madeleine
smiled but said nothing.

'No,' said Jeanne, taking the stone and examining it.
'That's the God Ing.'

'Here, let me try.' Gilles Sandon put his powerful, cal-
loused hand into the delicate basket and withdrew it, his hand
a fist. Opening it they saw a stone with the letter R. It looked
to Clara a bit like the wooden eggs they'd hidden for the children. They too had been painted with symbols. But eggs were
symbolic of life, while stones were symbolic of death.

'What does it mean?' Gilles asked.

'It means riding. Adventure, a journey,' said Jeanne, looking at Gilles. 'Often accompanied by toil. Hard work.'

'What else is new?'

Odile laughed, as did Clara. Gilles was a hard worker and his forty-five-year-old body testified to years as a lumberjack. Strong and strapping and almost always bruised.

'But,' Jeanne reached out and placed her hand over the stone still sitting in the soft center of Gilles's palm, surrounded by callus hills, 'you picked it up upside down. The R is inverted.'

Now there was silence. Gabri, who'd discovered by reading the small pamphlet on runes that his stone meant 'birch' not 'bitch,' had been arguing with Clara and threatening to cut off her supply of pâté and red wine. Now the two of them joined the others and leaned in, the circle tight and tense.

'What does that mean?' Odile asked.

'It means a difficult road ahead. It warns to be cautious.'

'And what did his mean?' Gilles pointed to Monsieur Béliveau.

'The God Ing? It means fertility, masculinity.' Jeanne smiled at the quiet, gentle grocer. 'It's also a powerful reminder to respect all that's natural.'

Gilles laughed, a petty, smug, mean little sound.

'Do Madeleine,' Myrna suggested, trying to break the tension.

'Great.' Mad reached in and withdrew a stone. 'I'm sure mine will say I'm selfish and heartless. P.' She smiled as she looked at the symbol. 'That's amazing, because I actually have to pee.'

'The P symbol means joy,' said Jeanne. 'But you know what else?'

Madeleine hesitated. As Clara watched the great energy that seemed to surround the woman appeared to dim, to diminish. It was as though she sagged for just an instant.

'It's upside down too,' said Madeleine.

* * *

Hazel's hands darned the worn socks but her mind was elsewhere. She glanced at the clock. Ten thirty. Still early, she told herself.

She wondered what was happening at the bistro over in Three Pines. Madeleine had suggested they go together, but Hazel had declined.

'Don't tell me you're scared,' Madeleine had teased.

'Of course not. It's just nonsense, a waste of time.'

'Not afraid of ghosts? So, would you move into a house next to a cemetery?'

Hazel thought about it. 'Probably not, but only because of resale.'

'Ever practical,' Madeleine laughed.

'Do you believe this woman can contact the dead?'

'I don't know,' admitted Mad. 'I honestly haven't thought about it. It just seems like fun.'

'Lots of people believe in ghosts, in haunted houses,' said Hazel. 'I was reading about one just the other day. It was in Philadelphia. A monk keeps appearing, and visitors see human shadows on the stairs and there was something else, what was it? Gave me the willies. Oh, yes. A cold spot. Right by a big wing chair and apparently everyone who sits in it dies but not before seeing the ghost of an old woman.'

'I thought you said you don't believe in ghosts.'

'I don't, but lots of people do.'

'Lots of cultures talk about spirits,' admitted Madeleine.

'But we're not talking about those, are we? I think there's a difference. A ghost is somehow malevolent, wicked. There's something vengeful and angry about a ghost. I'm not sure it's such a good idea to play around with that. And the building the bistro's in has been there for hundreds of years. Heaven knows how many people died there. No. I'll stay at home, watch a bit of TV, take a dinner next door to poor Madame Bellows. And avoid ghosts.'

Now Hazel sat in the puddle of dim light thrown from a single lamp in the living room. Remembering the conversation had left her chilled, as though a ghost had perched by her seat, creating a cold spot. She rose and turned on all the lights. But the room remained dull. Without Madeleine it seemed to wither.

The disadvantage of putting on all the lights was that she could no longer see out the window. All she saw was her own reflection. At least, she hoped it was her own reflection. There was a middle-aged woman sitting on a sofa wearing a sensible tweed skirt and an olive twinset. Around her neck was a modest set of pearls. It could have been her mother. And maybe it was.

Peter Morrow stood at the threshold of Clara's studio, peering into the darkness. He'd cleaned up the dishes, read in front of the living room fire and then, bored, had decided to go into his own studio to put in an hour or so on his latest painting. He'd walked through their kitchen to the other side of their small home, with every intention of opening his studio door and going inside.

So why was he now standing at the open door to Clara's studio?

It was dark and very quiet in there. He could feel his heart in his chest. His hands were cold and he realized he was holding his breath.

The act was so simple, mundane even.

He reached out and flicked on the overhead lights. Then he stepped in.

They sat in a circle on wooden chairs. Jeanne counted and seemed disconcerted.

'Eight is a bad number. We shouldn't be doing this.'

'What do you mean, a "bad" number?' Madeleine could feel her heart start to pound.

'It comes right after seven,' said Jeanne, as though that explained it. 'Eight forms the infinity sign.' She gestured in the air, her finger making the invisible sign. 'The energy goes round and round. No outlet. It gets angry and frustrated, and very powerful.' She'd sighed. 'This doesn't feel good at all.'

The lights were out and the only illumination came

from the fireplace as it crackled and threw uncertain light upon them. Some were in darkness, their backs to the fire; the rest looked like a series of disembodied worried faces.

'I want you all to clear your minds.' Jeanne's voice was deep and resonant. They couldn't see her face. She had her back to the fire. Clara had the impression she'd done it on purpose, but perhaps not.

'You must breathe deeply and let the anxiety and worry flow out of you. A spirit can sense energy. Any negative energy will only draw the ill-intentioned spirits. We want to fill the bistro with positive, loving kindness to attract the good spirits.'

'Fuck,' whispered Gabri. 'This was a bad idea.'

'Shut up,' hissed Myrna beside him. 'Good thoughts, asshole, and be quick about it.'

'I'm scared,' he whispered.

'Well, stop it. Go to your happy place, Gabri, your happy place,' Myrna rasped.

'This is my happy place,' snapped Gabri. 'Please, take her first, please, she's big and juicy. Please, don't take me.'

'You are a birch,' said Myrna.

'Quiet please,' said Jeanne with more authority than Clara would have guessed possible. 'If there's a sudden loud noise I want you to grab each other's hands, is that understood?'

'Why?' Gabri whispered to Odile on his other side. 'Is she expecting something bad?'

'Shhh,' said Jeanne quietly and all whispering stopped. All breathing stopped. 'They're coming.'

All hearts stopped.

Peter stepped into Clara's studio. He'd been in it hundreds of times and knew she kept the door open for a reason. She had nothing to hide. And yet for some reason he felt guilty.

Looking around rapidly he strode directly to the large easel in the center of the room. The studio smelled of oils and varnishes and wood, with a slight undertone of strong coffee. Years and years of creation and coffee had imbued this room with comforting sensations. So why was Peter terrified?

At the easel he stopped. Clara had draped a sheet over the canvas. He stood contemplating it, telling himself to leave, begging himself not to do this thing. Hardly believing what he was doing he saw his right hand reach out. Like a man who'd left his body he knew there was no controlling what was about to happen. It seemed pre-ordained.

His hand clutched the stained old sheet and yanked.

The room was silent. Clara desperately wanted to reach out and take Myrna's hand, but she dared not move. In case. In case whatever was coming would focus its attention on her.

Then she heard it. They all heard it.

Footsteps.

The turning of a doorknob.

Someone whimpered, like a frightened puppy.

Then suddenly a horrible pounding split the silence. A man yelled, Clara felt hands clutching at hers from both sides. She found them and held on for dear life, repeating over and over, 'Bless O Lord this food to our use, and ourselves to Thy service. Let us be ever mindful of the needs of others. Amen.'

'Let me in,' a voice outside their world wailed.

'Oh, God, it's an angry spirit,' said Myrna. 'It's your fault,' she said to Gabri, who was wide-eyed and terrified.

'Fuck,' wailed the disembodied voice. 'Fuuuuck.'

A window pane rattled and a horrible face appeared at the glass. The circle gasped and recoiled.

'For Christ's sake, Dorothy, I know you're in there,' screamed the voice. It wasn't what Clara had imagined would be the last words she'd hear on earth. She'd always thought they'd be, 'What were you thinking?'

Gabri rose, trembling, to his feet.

'Dear God,' he cried, making the sign of the cross with his fingers. 'It's the pre-dead.'

At the mullioned window Ruth Zardo's eyes narrowed and she gave him half a sign of the cross.

Peter stared at the work on the easel. His jaw clenched and his eyes hardened. It was worse than he'd expected, worse than he'd feared, and Peter feared big. Before him stood Clara's latest work, the one she'd soon show Denis Fortin, the influential gallery owner in Montreal. So far Clara had struggled in obscurity creating her nearly unintelligible works of art. At least, they were unintelligible to Peter.

Then suddenly out of nowhere Denis Fortin had knocked on their door. Peter was certain the distinguished dealer, with contacts throughout the art world, had come to see him. After all, he was the famous one. His excruciatingly detailed paintings sold for thousands and sat on the finest walls in Canada. Peter had naturally shown Fortin into his studio only to be politely told that his works were nice but it was actually Clara Morrow the dealer wanted to see.

Had the dealer said he wanted to turn green and fly to the moon Peter wouldn't have been more astonished. See Clara's works? What? His mind seized up and he'd stared at Fortin.

'Why?' he'd stammered. Then it was Fortin's turn to stare.

'She is Clara Morrow? The artist? A friend showed me her portfolio. Is this it?'

Fortin had taken a folio of works from his case and sure enough, there was Clara's weeping tree. Weeping words. What tree wept words? Peter had wondered when Clara had first shown him the work. And now Denis Fortin, the most prominent gallery owner in Quebec, was saying it was an impressive work of art.

'That's mine,' said Clara, trying to get between the two men.

Amazed, as though in a dream, she'd shown Fortin around her studio. And she'd described her latest work, hidden under its canvas caul. Fortin had stared at the canvas, but hadn't reached out for it, hadn't even asked for it to be removed.

'When will it be finished?'

'A few days,' said Clara, wondering where that came from.

'Shall we say the first week in May?' He'd smiled and shaken her hand with great warmth. 'I'll bring my curators so we can all decide.'

Decide?

The great Denis Fortin was coming in little over a week to see Clara's latest work. And if he liked it her career would be decided.

Now Peter stood staring at the piece.

He suddenly felt something grab him. From behind. It reached forward and right into him and took hold. Peter gasped at the pain, the searing, scalding pain of it. Tears came to his eyes as he was overcome by this wraith that had threatened all his life. That he'd hidden from as a child, that he'd run from and buried and denied. It had stalked him and finally found him. Here, in his beloved wife's studio. Standing in front of this creation of hers the terrible monster had found him.

And devoured him.

CHAPTER 5

'So what did Ruth want?' Olivier asked, as he placed single malt Scotches in front of Myrna and Gabri. Odile and Gilles had gone home but everyone else was in the bistro. Clara waved to Peter, who was shrugging out of his coat and hanging it on a peg by the door. She'd called him as soon as the séance had ended and invited him to the post-mortem.

'Well, at first we thought she was yelling "fuck,"' said Myrna, 'then we realized she was yelling "duck."'

'Duck? Really?' said Olivier, sitting on the arm of Gabri's wing chair and sipping cognac. 'Duck? Do you think she's been saying that all along?'

'And we just misheard?' asked Myrna. 'Duck off. Is that what she said to me the other day?'

'Duck you?' said Clara. 'It's possible. She is often in a fowl mood.'

Monsieur Béliveau laughed and looked over at Madeleine, pale and quiet beside him.

The fine April day had given way to a cold and damp night. It was getting on for midnight and they were the only ones in the bistro now.

'What did she want?' Peter asked.

'Help with some duck eggs. Remember the ones we found by the pond this afternoon?' said Clara, turning to Mad. 'Are you all right?'

'I'm fine.' Madeleine smiled. 'Just a little edgy.'

'I'm sorry about that,' said Jeanne. She sat on a hard chair slightly outside their circle. She'd reverted to her mousy self; all evidence of the strong, calm psychic had evaporated as soon as the lights had come on.

'Oh, no, I'm sure it's nothing to do with the séance,' Madeleine assured her. 'We had coffee after dinner and it must have had caffeine. It affects me that way.'

'*Mais, ce n'est pas possible*,' Monsieur Béliveau said. 'I'm sure it was decaf.' Though he was feeling a little edgy himself.

'What's the story with the eggs?' asked Olivier, smoothing the crease on his immaculate corduroys.

'Seems Ruth went to the pond after we'd left and picked them up,' Clara explained.

'Oh, no,' said Mad.

'Then the birds came back and wouldn't sit on the nest,' said Clara. 'Just as you predicted. So Ruth took the eggs home.'

'To eat?' asked Myrna.

'To hatch,' said Gabri, who'd gone with Clara back to Ruth's tiny house to see if they could help.

'She didn't sit on them, did she?' Myrna asked, not sure if she was amused or repulsed by the image.

'No, it was actually quite sweet. When we arrived the eggs were sitting on a soft flannel blanket in a basket. She'd put the whole lot in her oven on low.'

'Good idea,' said Peter. Like the rest, he'd have expected Ruth to devour, not save, them.

'I don't think she's had that oven on in years. Keeps saying it takes too much energy,' said Myrna.

'Well, she has it on now,' said Clara. 'Trying to hatch the ducks. Those poor parents.' She picked up her Scotch and glanced out the window to the darkness of the village green and imagined the parents sitting by the pond, at the spot where their young family had been, where their babies had sat in their little shells, trusting that Mom and Dad would keep them safe and warm. Ducks mate for life, Clara knew. That's why duck hunting season was particularly cruel. Every now and then in the fall you'd see a lone duck, quacking. Calling. Waiting for its spouse. And for the rest of its life it would wait.

Were the duck parents waiting now? Waiting for their babies to return? Did ducks believe in miracles?

'Still, it must have scared the crap out of all of you,' Olivier laughed, imagining Ruth at the window.

'Fortunately Clara here was on top of the spiritual crisis, repeating an ancient blessing,' said Gabri.

'More drinks, anyone?' Clara asked.

'Bless O Lord,' Gabri began and the others joined in, 'this food to our use, and ourselves to Thy service.'

Peter sputtered with laughter and felt Scotch dribble down his chin.

'Let us be ever mindful of the needs of others.' Peter looked her directly in her amused blue eyes.

'Amen,' they all said together, including Clara, who was herself laughing.

'You said grace?' Peter asked.

'Well, I thought I might be seeing my dinner again.'

By now everyone was laughing and even staid and proper Monsieur Béliveau was letting out a rolling, deep guffaw and wiping his eyes.

'Ruth's appearance sure put paid to the séance,' said Clara after she'd regained herself.

'I don't think we'd have been successful anyway,' said Jeanne.

'Why not?' Peter asked, curious to hear her excuse.

'I'm afraid this place is too happy,' said Jeanne to Olivier. 'I suspected as much as soon as I arrived.'

'Damn,' said Olivier. 'That can't be tolerated.'

'Then why'd you do a séance?' Peter persisted, certain he'd caught her out.

'Well, it wasn't exactly my idea. I'd planned to spend tonight here having the *linguine primavera* and reading old copies of *Country Life*. No mean spirits around.'

Jeanne looked directly at Peter, her smile fading.

'Except one,' said Monsieur Béliveau. Peter tore his eyes from Jeanne and looked at Béliveau, expecting to see the kindly grocer pointing a crooked Jacob Marley finger at him. But instead Monsieur Béliveau's hawk-like profile stared out the window.

'What do you mean?' asked Jeanne, following his gaze but seeing only the warm lights of the village homes through the lace curtains and the old leaded glass.

'Up there.' Monsieur Béliveau jerked his head. 'Beyond the village. You can't see it now unless you know what to look for.'

Clara didn't look. She knew what he was talking about and begged him, silently, to go no further.

'But it's there,' he continued, 'if you look up, on the hill overlooking the village, there's a spot that's darker than the rest.'

'What is it?' Jeanne asked.

'Evil,' said the old grocer and the room grew silent. Even the fire seemed to stop its muttering.

Jeanne went to the window and did as he instructed. She lifted her eyes from the friendly village. It took her a moment, but eventually above the lights of Three Pines she saw it, a spot darker than the night.

'The old Hadley house,' whispered Madeleine.

Jeanne turned back to the gathering, now no longer lounging comfortably with each other, but alert and tense. Myrna picked up her Scotch and took a swig.

'Why do you say it's evil?' Jeanne asked Monsieur Béliveau. 'That's quite an accusation, for a person or a place.'

'Bad things happen there,' he said simply, turning to the others for support.

'He's right,' said Gabri, taking Olivier's hand but turning to Clara and Peter. 'Should I say more?'

Clara looked to Peter who shrugged. The old Hadley house was abandoned now. Had been empty for months. But Peter knew it wasn't empty. For one thing he'd left part of himself in it. Not a hand or a nose or a foot, thank God. But things that had no substance but fantastic weight. He'd left his hope there, and trust. He'd left his faith there too. What little he had, he'd lost. There.

Peter Morrow knew the old Hadley house was wicked. It stole things. Like lives. And friends. Souls and faith. It had stolen his best friend, Ben Hadley. And the monstrosity on the hill gave back only sorrow.

Jeanne Chauvet floated back to the fire and dragged her chair closer to them so that she was finally in their circle. She placed her elbows on her thin knees and leaned forward, her eyes brighter than Clara had seen them all night.

Slowly the friends all turned to Clara, who took a deep breath. That house had haunted her ever since she'd arrived in Three Pines, a young wife to Peter, more than twenty years ago. It had haunted her and almost killed her.

'There's been a murder there, and a kidnapping. And attempted murder. And murderers have lived there.' Clara was surprised how distant this list sounded and felt.

Jeanne nodded, turning her face to the embers slowly dying in the grate.

'Balance,' she finally said. 'It makes sense.' She seemed to rouse herself and sat up straighter, as though moving into another mode. 'As soon as I arrived here in Three Pines I felt it. And I feel it tonight right here, right now.'

Monsieur Béliveau took Madeleine's hand. Peter and Clara moved closer. Olivier, Gabri and Myrna inched together. Clara closed her eyes and tried to feel whatever evil Jeanne was sensing. But she felt only –

'Peace.' Jeanne smiled a little. 'From the moment I arrived I felt great kindness here. I went into the little church, St Thomas's I think it's called, even before booking into the B & B, and sat quietly. It felt peaceful and content. This is an old village, with an old soul. I read the plaques on the walls of the church and looked at the stained glass. This village has known loss, people killed before their time, accidents, war, disease. Three Pines isn't immune to any of that. But you seem to accept it as part of life and not hang on to the bitterness. Those murders you speak of, did you know the people?'

Everyone nodded.

'And yet you don't seem bitter or bound by that horrible experience. Just the opposite. You seem happy and peaceful. Do you know why?'

They stared into the fire, into their drinks, at the floor. How do you explain happiness? Contentment?

'We let it go,' said Myrna finally.

'You let it go,' Jeanne nodded. 'But.' Now she grew very still and looked Myrna directly in the eyes. Not challenging. More imploring, almost begging Myrna to understand this next part. 'Where does it go?'

'Where does what go?' Gabri asked after a minute's silence.

Myrna whispered, 'Our sorrow. It has to go somewhere.'

'That's right.' Jeanne smiled as though to a particularly gifted pupil. 'We're energy. The brain, the heart, run by impulses. Our bodies are fueled by food that's converted into energy. That's what calories are. This,' Jeanne brought her hands up and patted her thin body, 'is the most amazing factory and it produces energy. But we're also emotional and spiritual beings and that's energy too. Auras, vibes, whatever you want to call it. When you're angry,' she turned to Peter, 'can't you feel yourself tremble?'

'I don't get angry,' he said, meeting her gaze with cold eyes. He'd had just about enough of this bullshit.

'You're angry now, I can feel it. We can all feel it.' She turned to the others, who didn't comment, out of loyalty to their friend. But they knew she was right. They could feel his rage. It radiated off him.

Peter felt set up by this shaman and betrayed by his own body.

'It's natural,' said Jeanne. 'Your body feels a strong emotion and sends out signals.'

'It's true,' Gabri said, turning to Peter apologetically. 'I can feel your anger, and I can feel that the rest of us are uncomfortable. Earlier I could feel the happiness. Everyone was relaxed. No one had to tell me. When you walk into a room full of people don't you get it immediately? You can feel whether people are happy or tense.'

Gabri looked around and everyone nodded, even Monsieur Béliveau.

'At my store you get good at reading people fast. If people are in a bad mood, or upset or might be a threat.'

'A threat? In Three Pines?' Madeleine asked.

'*Non, c'est vrai*,' the grocer admitted. 'It has never happened. But still I watch, just in case. I can tell as soon as they walk in.'

'But that's body language and familiarity,' said Peter. 'That's not energy.' He vibrated his hands in front of him and lowered his voice in a mocking tone. Monsieur Béliveau was silenced.

'You don't have to believe it,' Jeanne said. 'Most people don't.' She smiled at Peter in a way he took to be patronizing. 'Bread cast on the water,' she said unexpectedly. 'If we put angry energy out that's what we'll get back. It's pretty simple.'

Peter looked around the gathering. Everyone was listening intently to this Jeanne woman, as though they believed this crap.

'You mentioned balance,' said Myrna.

'That's right. Nature is balance. Action and reaction. Life and death. Everything's in balance. It makes sense that the old Hadley house is close to Three Pines. They balance each other.'

'What do you mean?' Madeleine asked.

'She means the old Hadley house is the dark to our light,' said Myrna.

'Three Pines is a happy place because you let your sorrow go. But it doesn't go far. Just up the hill,' said Jeanne. 'To the old Hadley house.'

Now Peter felt it. The skin on his arms contracted and his hairs stood on end. Everything he let go of had claw marks on it. And it made straight for the old Hadley house. It was full of their fear, their sorrow, their rage.

'Why don't we do a séance there?' Monsieur Béliveau asked. Everyone turned slowly to stare at him, stunned, as though the fireplace had spoken and said a most unlikely thing.

'I don't know about that.' Gabri shifted uneasily in his seat.

Instinctively they turned to Clara. Without asking for it she'd become the heart of their community. Small, middle-aged and getting a little plump, Clara was that rare combination: she was sensible and sensitive. Now she got up, grabbed a handful of cashews and what was left of her Scotch and walked to the window. Most of the lights were out around the village green. Three Pines was at rest. After a moment appreciating the peace her eyes traveled to that black hole above them. She stood for a couple of minutes, sipping and munching, and contemplating.

Was it possible the old Hadley house was full of their anger and sorrow? Was that why it attracted murderers? And ghosts?

'I think we should do it,' she said finally.

'Oh, for God's sake,' said Peter.

Clara briefly glanced out the window again.

It was time to lay the wickedness to rest.

CHAPTER 6

Monsieur Béliveau opened the car door for Madeleine.

'Are you sure I can't drive you home?'

'Oh, no, I'll be fine. My nerves are calming down,' she lied. Her heart was still racing and she was exhausted. 'You've brought me safe and sound to my car. No bears.'

He took her hand. His felt like rice paper, dry and fragile, and yet his hold was firm. 'They won't hurt you. They're only dangerous if you come between mother and cub. Be careful of that.'

'I'll mark it down. "Mustn't anger bears." Now you're sure of that?'

Monsieur Béliveau laughed. Madeleine liked the sound. She liked the man. She wondered whether she should tell him her secret. It would be a relief. She opened her mouth but closed it again. There was still such sadness in him. Such kindness. She couldn't take it away. Not yet.

'Would you come in for a coffee? I'll make sure it's decaf.'

She released her hand from his light grip.

'I must go, but I've had a lovely day,' she said, leaning in to kiss his cheek.

'Though no ghosts.' He sounded almost regretful. And he was.

He watched her red tail lights head up du Moulin, past the old Hadley house and out of sight, then turned and walked to his front door. There was a small, almost imperceptible, bounce in his step. Some tiny thing had come alive in him. Something he was sure he'd buried with his wife.

Myrna shoved a few logs into her woodstove and shut the cast-iron door. Then she walked wearily across the loft, her slippered feet shuffling on the old wooden floors, instinctively moving from one throw rug to another, as a swimmer might travel between islands, shutting lights as she went. The beamed and old brick loft slowly subsided into darkness, except the one light beside her large and welcoming bed. Myrna placed her mug of hot chocolate and plate of chocolate chip cookies on the old pine table and picked up her book. Ngaio Marsh. Myrna was re-reading the classics. Fortunately her used bookstore had no end of them. She was her own best customer. Well, she and Clara, who brought in most of the old mysteries. The hot water bottle warmed her feet and pulling the comforter up she started to read. Sipping on her chocolate and nibbling cookies she realized she'd been reading the same page for ten minutes.

Her mind was elsewhere. It was stuck in the darkness between the lights of Three Pines and the stars.

Odile placed the CD in the machine and slipped the headphones on.

She'd waited for this moment. For six days she longed for it, with increasing anxiety as the week wore on. Not that she didn't enjoy her everyday life. In fact, she was amazed by how lucky she was. That Gilles should turn to her when his marriage soured still amazed her. She'd had a crush on him through high school. Had finally found the courage to invite him to the Sadie Hawkins dance, only to be turned down. But he hadn't been cruel. Some boys were cruel, especially to girls like Odile. But not Gilles. He'd always been kind. Always smiled and said *bonjour* in the hallways, even when his friends could see.

Odile had adored him then and she adored him now.

But still, every week she longed for this moment. Every

Friday night Gilles went to bed early and she went into their modest living room in St-Rémy.

She could hear the first notes of the first song and felt her shoulders sag, letting go of the tension. She could also feel her vigilance slip. The need to watch every word, every action. She closed her eyes and took a massive gulp of red wine as a drowning man might gulp air. The bottle was half empty already and Odile worried she'd run out before the magic happened. The transformation.

After a few minutes Odile was on her feet, her eyes closed, walking across a flower-festooned stage. In Oslo. It was Oslo, wasn't it? Didn't matter.

The distinguished audience, in tie and tails and evening gowns, was on its feet. Applauding. No. Weeping.

Odile stopped part way to acknowledge their cries. She placed her hand on her breast and curtsied slightly in a gesture of immense modesty and dignity.

And then the king was presenting her with the silk sash. Tears in his eyes too.

'It gives me great pleasure, Madame Montmagny, to present you with the Nobel Prize for Poetry.'

But tonight the wild applause didn't move her, didn't wash over her and protect her from the suspicion she'd been found out for the pathetic little thing she knew herself to be. From trying to fit into a world where everyone knew the code, except her.

But Odile knew one thing no one else did. Her little secret. All those people at the séance had been afraid of evil spirits, but she knew the monster was from not the next world, but this. And Odile Montmagny knew who it was.

Hazel seemed distracted when Madeleine arrived back.

'Couldn't sleep,' said Hazel, pouring them a cup of tea. 'Expect I'm excited about Sophie coming home.'

Madeleine stirred her tea and nodded. Hazel was always a little nervous when Sophie was coming home. It disrupted the quietude of their lives. Not that Sophie was a party ani-

mal, or even loud. No, it was something else. Some tension
that suddenly appeared in their comfortable home.

'I took poor Mrs Bellows a dinner.'

'How's she doing?' Mad asked.

'Better, but her back still aches.'

'You know her husband and children should be doing
that for her.'

'But they don't,' said Hazel. She was sometimes surprised by a hard edge that appeared in Madeleine. It was
almost as though she didn't care about people.

'You're a good soul, Hazel. I hope she thanked you.'

'I'll get my reward in Heaven,' Hazel said, bringing a dramatic arm to her brow. Madeleine laughed, as did Hazel. It
was one of the many things Mad loved about Hazel. Not just
her kindness, but her refusal to take herself too seriously.

'We're having another séance.' Mad dipped her biscuit
into the tea and got the soggy and sagging cookie into her
mouth just in time. 'Sunday night.'

'Too many ghosts to deal with in one go? They had to
take shifts?'

'Too few. The psychic says the bistro's too happy.'

'Sure she didn't say gay?'

'It's possible.' Mad smiled. She knew Hazel and Gabri
were good friends and had worked on the Anglican Church
Women together for years. 'Still, no ghosts to be had. So
we're going to the old Hadley house.'

She watched Hazel over the rim of her teacup. Hazel's
eyes widened. After a moment she spoke.

'Are you sure that's wise?'

'Have you been in here?' Clara called from her studio.

Peter froze in the act of giving Lucy her goodnight dog
biscuit. Lucy's tail swished back and forth with increasing
energy, her head tilted to the side, her eyes glued to the
magical cookie as though desire alone could move objects.
If that was the case the fridge door would be permanently
open.

Clara poked her head out of her studio and looked at Peter. Though her face showed simple curiosity he felt accused. His mind raced but he knew he couldn't lie to her. Not about this, anyway.

'I went in while you were at the séance. Do you mind?'

'Mind? I'm thrilled. Did you need something?'

Should he say he needed some Cadmium Yellow? A number four brush? A ruler?

'Yes.' He went over and put his long arm round her waist. 'I needed to see your painting. I'm sorry. I should have waited until you were here and I should have asked.'

He waited to see her reaction. His heart sank. She was looking up at him, smiling.

'You really wanted to see it? Peter, that's wonderful.'

He shriveled.

'Come back in.' She took his hand and led him back to that thing in the center of the room. 'Tell me what you think.'

She whisked the sheet off the easel and there it was again.

The most beautiful painting he'd ever seen.

It was so beautiful it hurt. Yes. That was it. The pain he felt came from outside himself. Not inside. No.

'It's astonishing, Clara.' He took her hand and looked into her clear, blue eyes. 'It's the best thing you've done. I'm so proud of you.'

Clara's mouth opened but no words came out. She'd waited all her artistic life for Peter to understand, to 'get,' one of her works. To see more than paint on a canvas. To actually feel it. She knew she shouldn't care so much. Knew it was a weakness. Knew her artist friends, including Peter, said you must create for yourself and not care what anyone thinks.

And she didn't care about any one, just this one. She wanted the man who shared her soul to also share her vision. At least once. Just once. And here it was. And, blessing of blessings, it was the one painting that mattered more than any other. The one she would be showing to the most important gallery owner in Quebec in just a few days now. The one she'd poured everything into.

'But are the colors quite right?' Peter leaned into the easel then stepped back, not looking at her. 'Well, I'm sure they are. You know what you're doing.'

He kissed her and whispered, 'Congratulations,' into her ear. Then he left.

Clara stepped back and stared at the canvas. Peter was one of the most respected and successful artists in Canada. Maybe he was right. The painting looked fine to her, but still . . .

'What're you doing?' Olivier asked Gabri. It was the middle of the night and they were standing in their living room at the B & B. Olivier had reached over and felt Gabri's side of the bed cold. Now Olivier pulled the belt of his silk dressing gown tighter and through bleary eyes watched his partner.

Gabri, in rumpled pajama bottoms and slippers, was holding a croissant in his hand and seemed to be taking it for a walk round their living room.

'I'm getting rid of any evil spirits that might have followed me home from the séance.'

'With baked goods?'

'Well, we didn't have any hot cross buns, so this was the next best thing. Isn't the crescent the symbol of Islam?'

Olivier was constantly surprised by Gabri. His unexpected depth and his profound silliness. Olivier shook his head and went back to bed, trusting that in the morning all the evil spirits and the croissants would be gone.

CHAPTER 7

Easter Sunday dawned gray, but there were hopes the rain would hold off until after the Easter egg hunt. All through the church service parents ignored the minister and instead listened for drumming on the roof of St Thomas's church.

The church smelled of lily of the valley. Bunches of the tiny white bells and their vivid green leaves were placed in every pew. It was lovely.

Until little Paulette Legault launched a bouquet at Timmy Benson. Then all hell broke loose. The minister, of course, ignored it.

Kids ran up and down the short aisle, parents either trying to stop them or ignoring them. Either way the outcome was the same. The minister gave a little reading from the rite of exorcism. The congregation said Amen and everyone raced from the chapel.

A lunch was organized by the Anglican Church Women, led by Gabri, in the basement and picnic tables with red check tablecloths had been set up around the green.

'Happy hunting,' the minister shouted and waved as his car mounted du Moulin, heading for the next chapel in his next parish. He was pretty certain his little service had saved no one. But then, no one had been lost either and that was good enough.

Ruth stood on the top step of the church, balancing a plate of thick maple-cured ham sandwiches on Sarah's bread still steaming from the boulangerie, home-made potato salad with eggs and mayo, and a huge slice of sugar pie. Myrna came up beside her wearing a plank on her head scattered with books and flowers and chocolate. Villagers wandered around the green or sat at picnic tables, women in massive exuberant Easter bonnets and men trying to pretend they weren't.

Myrna stood beside Ruth, her own plate sagging under an embarrassment of food, and together they watched the hunt. Children darted around the village, shrieking and screaming with delight as they discovered the wooden eggs. Little Rose Tremblay was knocked into the pond by one of her brothers and Timmy Benson stopped to help her out. While Madame Tremblay yelled at her son Paulette Legault whacked Timmy. A sure sign of love, thought Myrna, grateful she wasn't ten any more.

'Wanna sit together?' Myrna asked.

'No I don't "wanna,"' Ruth said. 'Have to get home.'

'How're the chicks?' Myrna took no offense from Ruth; to do that would be to live in permanent offense.

'They're not chicks, they're ducks. Ducklings, I suppose.'

'Where do we get the real eggs?' Rose Tremblay stood in front of Ruth like CindyLou Who before the Grinch, holding three exquisite wooden eggs in her pudgy pink palms. For some reason the children of Three Pines always went straight to Ruth, like lemmings.

'How should I know?'

'You're the egg lady,' said Rose, wearing a soggy blanket. She looked a little, Myrna thought, like one of Ruth's precious duck eggs wrapped in her own flannel.

'Well, my eggs are at home getting warm, where you should be. But if you insist on this foolishness, go ask her for the chocolate ones.' Ruth waved her cane like a crooked wand at Clara, who was trying to make her way to a picnic table.

'But Clara has nothing to do with giving the kids their chocolate eggs,' said Myrna as little Rose took off, calling the other kids until it looked like a tornado descending on Clara.

'I know,' Ruth sneered and limped down the stairs. At the

bottom she turned and looked up at the massive black woman popping a sandwich into her mouth. 'Are you going tonight?'

'To Clara and Peter's for dinner, you mean? We all are, aren't we?'

'That's not what I mean and you know it.' The old poet didn't turn to look at the Hadley house, but Myrna knew what she meant. 'Don't do it.'

'Why not? I do rituals all the time. Remember after Jane died? All the women came, including you, and we did a ritual cleansing.'

Myrna would never forget walking round the village green with the women and the stick of smoking sage, wafting the smoke around Three Pines, to rid it of the fear and suspicions that had overtaken them.

'This is different, Myrna Landers.'

Myrna didn't realize Ruth knew her last name, or even her first. For the most part Ruth just waved and commanded.

'This isn't a ritual. This is deliberately disturbing evil. This isn't about God or the Goddess or spirits or spirituality. It's about vengeance.

> *'I was hanged for living alone,*
> *For having blue eyes and a sunburned skin,*
> *Tattered skirts, few buttons,*
> *A weedy farm in my own name,*
> *And a surefire cure for warts;*

> *'Oh, yes, and breasts,*
> *And a sweet pear hidden in my body.*
> *Whenever there's talk of demons*
> *These come in handy.*

'Don't do it, Myrna Landers. You know the difference between ritual and revenge. And so does whatever's in that house.'

'You think this is about revenge?' asked Myrna, dumbfounded.

'Of course it is. Let it be. Let whatever's in that house be.'

She jabbed her cane at it. Had it been a wand Myrna was certain a bolt would have shot from it and destroyed the brooding house on the hill. Then Ruth turned and limped home. To her eggs. To her life. And Myrna was left with the memory of Ruth's keen blue eyes, her permanently sunburned skin, her tattered skirt with its missing buttons. She watched the old woman walk back to her home with its abundance of words and weeds.

The rain held off and Easter Sunday moved along quick like a bunny. Timmy Benson found the most eggs and was awarded the giant chocolate rabbit, filled with toys. Paulette Legault stole it from him but Monsieur Béliveau made her give it back and apologize. Timmy, who could see into the future, opened the box, broke off the solid chocolate ears and gave the rest to Paulette, who punched him.

That night Peter and Clara held their annual Easter Sunday dinner. Gilles and Odile arrived with baguettes and cheese. Myrna brought a flamboyant bouquet which she placed in the center of the pine table in the kitchen. Jeanne Chauvet, the psychic, brought a small bouquet of wild flowers, picked in the meadows around Three Pines.

Sophie Smyth was there with her mother Hazel and Madeleine. She'd arrived home the day before, her small blue car filled with laundry. Now she chatted with the other guests while Hazel and Madeleine offered around their platter of shrimp.

'So you're the psychic.' Sophie took a few shrimp from her mother and dipped them in sauce.

'My name's Jeanne.'

'Like Jeanne D'Arc.' Sophie laughed. 'Joan of Arc.' It wasn't an altogether pleasant sound. 'Better watch it. You know what happened to her.'

Tall and slender, Sophie carried herself well, though with a slight slouch. Her hair was dirty blonde and shoulder length. She was, in fact, quite attractive. Still, there was something about Sophie. Something that made Jeanne back away slightly.

Monsieur Béliveau arrived just then with blueberry tarts from Sarah's Boulangerie.

Candles were lit around the country kitchen and bottles of wine were opened.

The house smelled of lamb roasting in garlic and rosemary, of new potatoes, and creamed leeks and something else.

'For God's sake, canned peas?' Clara looked in the pot Gabri and Olivier had brought.

'We took them out of the can,' said Olivier. 'What's your problem?'

'Look at them. They're disgusting.'

'I would take that as a personal insult, if I were you,' Gabri said to Monsieur Béliveau, who'd wandered over carrying a glass of wine and a piece of creamy Brie on a baguette. 'We got them at his shop.'

'Madame,' the grocer said somberly. 'Those are the finest canned peas money can buy. Le Sieur. In fact, I believe that is how they grow, right in the can. It is only the military-industrial complex that has developed the ridiculous hybrid. Peas in a pod. As though anyone would believe that. Disgusting.' Monsieur Béliveau said this with such sincerity Clara would almost have believed him, if it hadn't been for the sparkle in his eye.

Soon their plates were piled high with roasted lamb, mint sauce, and vegetables. Fresh-baked rolls steamed in baskets scattered down the table, along with butter and cheeses. The table groaned under the happy weight, as did the guests. Myrna's massive bouquet sat in the center of the table, its arms of budding branches reaching for the ceiling. Apple boughs, pussy willows, forsythia with the gentlest of yellow blooms just showing, peony tulips of vibrant pink, were planted in the earth.

'And,' said Myrna, waving her napkin like a magician, '*voilà*.' She reached into the bouquet and produced a chocolate egg. 'Enough for all of us.'

'Rebirth,' said Clara.

'But there needs to be a death first,' said Sophie, looking around with feigned innocence. 'Doesn't there?'

She sat between Madeleine and Monsieur Béliveau, taking the chair just as the grocer had reached for it. Sophie picked up the chocolate egg then placed it in front of her.

'Birth, death, rebirth,' she said wisely, as though she'd brought them a new thought, all the way from Queens University.

There was something mesmerizing about Sophie Smyth, thought Clara. Always had been. Sophie would come home from university sometimes blonde, sometimes a brilliant redhead, sometimes plump, sometimes slim, sometimes pierced, sometimes without ornamentation. You never knew what you'd find. But one thing seemed constant, thought Clara, watching the girl with the egg in front of her. She always got what she wanted. But what does she want? Clara wondered, and knew it was probably more than an Easter egg.

An hour later Peter, Ruth and Olivier watched their friends and lovers plod into the night, invisible except for their flashlights, each person a bobbing torch. At first they clumped together but as Peter watched the little orbs of light separated, became strung out, each person alone, trudging toward the dark house on the hill that seemed to be waiting for them.

Don't be such a wuss, he told himself. It's just a stupid house. What could possibly happen?

But Peter Morrow knew famous last words when he heard them.

Clara hadn't felt like this since she was a kid and would deliberately scare herself stupid by watching *The Exorcist* or going on the gargantuan roller coaster at La Ronde, slobbering and shrieking and once even wetting herself.

It was exhilarating and terrifying and mystifying at the same time. As the house got closer Clara had the oddest feeling it was approaching them rather than the other way round. She couldn't quite remember why they were doing this.

She heard shuffling behind her and voices. Fortunately she remembered Madeleine and Odile were back there, the stragglers. Clara was also happy to remember in horror films it was always the stragglers who got it first. But, if they got it, she'd be the last. She speeded up. Then slowed down, battling between wanting to survive and wanting to hear what the two women were saying to each other. After what she'd overheard while hiding Easter eggs she'd assumed Odile didn't like Mad. So what could they be talking about?

'But it's not fair,' Odile was saying. Madeleine said something though Clara couldn't make it out and if she slowed down more she'd have Madeleine's flashlight where light doesn't normally shine.

'It's taken a lot of courage for me to do this.' Odile was speaking more loudly now.

'For God's sake, Odile, don't be ridiculous,' said Madeleine, clearly and not very kindly. It was a side to Madeleine Clara had never heard before.

Clara was paying so much attention trying to eavesdrop she bumped right into a dark figure in front of her. Gilles. Then she looked up.

They were there.

CHAPTER 8

They huddled together in the cold and dark. Their flash-lights bounced wildly over the decrepit house. The 'For Sale' sign had fallen over and lay like a tombstone, nose into the soft earth. As Clara swung her torch around more decay became apparent. The house was abandoned, she knew, but she didn't think houses fell to ruin quite this fast. A few shutters were hanging loose and knocking gently against the brick. Some of the windows were broken, their glass jagged like sharpened teeth. Clara spotted something white curled up by the foundation of the house and her heart skipped a beat. Something dead, and skinned.

Reluctantly she moved down the front walk, its paving stones heaved and uneven. As she got closer she stopped and looked behind her. The rest were clustered at the road-side still.

'Come here,' she hissed.

'You talking to us?' Myrna asked, frozen. She too was staring at the patch of white curled against the base of the house.

'No one here but us chickens,' said Gabri.

'What is that?' Myrna inched down the path until she was standing next to her friend. She pointed and noticed her finger was twitching. Was her body sending out a signal? A Morse code? If so, Myrna knew what it was saying. Run.

Clara turned back to the house, took a deep breath,

blessed her food, and walked off the path. The earth was squishy underfoot and seemed to hiss at her every step. Myrna couldn't believe what Clara was doing and wanted to run forward and grab her friend back, and hold her and hug her and tell her never to do that again. Instead she just watched.

Clara approached the house and bent down. Then straightening up she walked more swiftly back to the relative safety of the walk and Myrna.

'You won't believe it, but it's snow.'

'It can't be. All the snow's long gone.'

'Not from here.' Clara dug into her pocket and withdrew a huge old-fashioned key, long and thick and heavy.

'And all this time I thought you were just glad to see me,' said Myrna.

'Har-dee-har,' Clara smiled. It felt good and she blessed Myrna for bringing her humor down this dark path with her. 'The real estate agent was all too happy to let me have it. I doubt she's shown the house in months.'

'What did you tell her?' Madeleine asked. Since Clara and Myrna were still alive the others had decided to join them.

'That we were going to summon all the demons and exorcise the house.'

'And she gave you the key?'

'Practically threw it at me.'

Clara put the key into the lock, but the door swung open. She let go and watched as the key and the doorknob disappeared into the darkness.

'Why are we doing this again?' Monsieur Béliveau whispered.

'For fun,' said Sophie.

'Not all of us,' said Jeanne and stepping around them the tiny, gray woman walked straight into the house.

One by one they entered the old Hadley house. It was colder inside than out and smelled of mold. The electricity had long since been turned off and now the circles of torchlight played on the peeling floral wallpaper, stained with damp which they all hoped was water. Emboldened by the light, as though what they held were swords, they moved deeper into the house. The floors creaked under their weight and a flutter could be heard in the distance.

'A bird, poor thing,' said Gabri. 'Trapped somewhere.'

'We need to find it,' said Madeleine.

'Are you mad?' Odile whispered.

'She's right,' said Jeanne. 'If nothing else, it's a trapped soul. We can't ignore it.'

'But suppose it isn't a bird,' Gabri whispered to Hazel, who still couldn't believe she was there.

Now they stuck together like a giant crawling insect. Multi-ped and multi-feared they moved through the dank house, pausing now and then to get their bearings.

'It's upstairs,' said Jeanne in a low voice.

'It would be,' said Gilles. 'They're never right by the door. Never in rose gardens in the summer or living in the ice cream man's truck.'

'This is like a game I used to play with Peter,' said Clara to Myrna, who really didn't care. She was trying to figure out whether, yet again, she'd be the slowest one out of there. Maybe Hazel would be slower, Myrna thought, brightening, and the demons would get her. But she'd probably put on a burst of speed if only to save her daughter. Myrna, as a psychologist, knew that mothers found amazing resources when it came to their kids.

Fucking maternal instinct, thought Myrna, screws up my life again. She stepped onto the stairs, the carpet runner worn and moth-eaten, and as she mounted one agonizing step at a time she heard the furious beating of the wings growing louder.

'Whenever we watch scary movies and people walk into a haunted house'—Clara was still talking. Good, thought Myrna. The demons will zero in on her. —'we'd play "When would you leave?" Disembodied heads floating around, screams of pain, friends disemboweled, and still they stay.'

'Are you finished?'

'I am actually.' Clara had managed to scare herself even more and wondered, if this was a movie, would Peter be screaming at the screen for her to leave.

'In there.'

'It would be,' muttered Gilles.

Jeanne was standing in front of a closed door. The only one closed on the whole floor. Now there was silence.

Suddenly there was a mad flapping of wings against the door as though the thing had flung itself against it.

Jeanne reached out but Monsieur Béliveau laid his long, slender hand on her wrist, taking her hand off the knob. Then he stepped in front of her and put his own hand on the knob.

And opened the door.

They could see nothing. Stare as they might their eyes wouldn't adjust to the darkness. But something in there found them. Not the bird, which was silent for the moment. But something else. The room produced waves of chill and riding on them was the slightest hint of perfume.

The room smelled of flowers. Fresh, spring flowers.

At the door Clara was overtaken by melancholy, a sadness that seeped from deep down into the very earth of her. She felt the sorrow of the room. The longing of the room.

Clara gasped for breath and realized she'd been holding it.

'Come on,' Jeanne whispered, her voice seeming in Clara's head, 'let's do what we came for.'

The group watched as first Jeanne then Clara stepped into the darkness. The rest followed and their flashlights soon lit the room in patches. Heavy velvet curtains hung askew at the windows. Against one wall stood a four-poster bed, still made up in cream and lace. The pillow was indented as though a head uneasily rested there.

'I know this room,' said Myrna. 'And so do you,' she said to both Clara and Gabri.

'Old Timmer Hadley's bedroom,' said Clara, amazed she hadn't recognized it. But such was the power of fear.

Clara had been in this room many times, tending to the dying old woman.

She'd hated Timmer Hadley. Hated the house. Hated the snakes she'd heard slithering in the basement. And a few years ago this house had almost killed her.

Clara felt a wave of revulsion. A desire to put a torch to this cursed place. This place that harbored all their sorrow and anger and fear, but not because it was selfless. No. The old Hadley house first bred those things, sent sorrow and terror into the world, and its progeny was simply coming home, like sons and daughters at Easter.

'Let's leave,' said Clara, turning to the door.

'We can't,' said Jeanne.

'Why not?' said Monsieur Béliveau. 'I'm with Clara. This doesn't feel good.'

'Wait,' said Gilles. The large man stood in the center of the room, his eyes closed, his bushy red beard pointing to the wall as his head tilted back. 'This is just a house,' he said at last in a voice both calm and insistent. 'It needs our help.'

'But that doesn't make sense,' said Hazel, trying to take Sophie's hand though the girl kept shaking her off. 'Is it just a house or does it need our help? It's one or the other but not both. My house never asks for help.'

'Maybe you aren't listening,' suggested Gilles.

'I want to stay,' said Sophie. 'Madeleine, what about you?'

'Can we sit down?'

'You can lie down if you like,' said Gabri, flicking his flashlight over the bed.

'No thank you, *mon beau* Gabri. Not just yet.' Madeleine smiled and the tension was broken. Without further discussion the group got to work. Chairs were brought into the bedroom and placed in a circle.

Jeanne put the bag she'd carried on one of the chairs and started unpacking while Clara and Myrna explored. They looked at the fireplace with its dark mahogany mantel and severe Victorian portrait above. The bookcase was full of leather-bound volumes from a time when people actually read them and didn't just buy them by the yard from decorators.

'I wonder where the bird is,' said Clara, reaching for the items on the dresser.

'Hiding from us, poor thing. Probably terrified,' said Myrna, pointing her flashlight into a dark corner. No bird.

'It's like a museum.' Gabri joined them and picked up a silver mirror.

'It's like a mausoleum,' said Hazel. When they turned back to the body of the room they were astonished to see the place lit by candles. There must have been twenty of them scattered around the bedroom. It glowed, but somehow the candlelight, so warm and inviting at Clara and Peter's, made a mockery of itself in this room. The darkness seemed darker and the flickering flames threw grotesque shadows against the rich wallpaper. Clara felt like dousing each candle, vanquishing the demons their own shadows created. Even her own, so familiar, was distorted and hideous.

Sitting now in the circle, her back to the open door, Clara noticed that four candles remained unlit. After each person had chosen a chair Jeanne reached into a small sack. Then she walked about their circle scattering something.

'This is now a sacred circle,' she intoned, her face alternately in shadow and light, her eyes sunken into her head so that they looked to be empty black sockets. 'This salt will bless the circle and keep all within safe.'

Clara felt Myrna's hand take hers. The only sound was the soft pelting as Jeanne scattered the salt round their circle. Clara's head was tingling, alert to any sound. The thought of a bird swooping out of the darkness, talons extended, beak open and shrieking, was freaking her out. The skin on the back of her neck was crawling.

Jeanne struck a match and Clara almost jumped out of her skin.

'The wisdom of the four corners of the earth is invited

into our sacred circle, to protect and guide us and watch over our work tonight as we cleanse this house of the spirits that are strangling it. Of the evil that's taken hold here. Of all the wickedness, the fear, the terror, the hatred that binds itself to this house. To this very room.'

'Are we having fun yet?' Gabri whispered.

Jeanne lit the candles one by one and returned to her seat, composing herself. She was the only one. Clara could feel her heart pounding and her breathing coming in short, jagged gulps. Beside her Myrna was squirming as though ants were crawling over her. All round their circle people were staring and pale. The circle might be sacred, thought Clara, but it's definitely scared. She looked round and wondered, if this was a movie and she and Peter were watching it curled up on their sofa, which of them would get it first?

Monsieur Béliveau, craven, gaunt, grieving?

Gilles Sandon, massive and strong, more at home in the woods than in a Victorian mansion?

Hazel, so kind and generous. Or was it weak? Or her daughter, insatiable Sophie?

No. Clara's gaze landed on Odile. She would be the first one lost. Poor, sweet Odile. Already lost, really. The most needy and the least missed. She was genetically designed to be eaten first. Clara felt badly for the brutality of her thoughts. She blamed the house. This house that blocked out the good and rewarded the rest.

'And now we call the dead,' said Jeanne, and Clara, who didn't think she could get more afraid, did.

'We know you're here.' Jeanne's voice was growing stronger and stranger. 'They're coming. Coming from the basement, coming from the attic. They're all around us now. They're coming down the hallway.'

And Clara was sure she could hear footsteps. Shuffling, limping footfalls on the carpet outside. She could see the Mummy, arms out, bandages filthy and rotting, shuffling toward them, along the dark and damned corridor. Why had they kept the door open?

'Be here,' Jeanne growled. 'Now!' She clapped her hands.

A shriek was heard inside the room, inside their sacred circle. Then another.

And a thud.

The dead had arrived.

CHAPTER 9

Chief Inspector Armand Gamache looked over the top of his newspaper and stole a peek at his infant granddaughter. She was sitting in the mud on the edge of Beaver Lake, sticking her filthy big toe into her mouth. Her face was covered in either mud or chocolate, or something else entirely that didn't bear thinking of.

It was Easter Monday and all of Montreal seemed to have the same idea. A morning walk around Mont Royal, to Beaver Lake at the summit. Gamache and Reine-Marie sunned themselves on one of the benches and watched as their son and his family enjoyed a last day in Montreal before flying back to Paris.

With a shriek of laughter little Florence toppled into the water.

Gamache dropped his paper and was halfway out of his seat when he felt a restraining hand.

'Daniel's there, *mon cher*. It's his job now.'

Armand stopped and watched, still poised to act. Beside him his young German shepherd, Henri, got to his feet, alert, sensing the sudden shift in mood. But sure enough Daniel laughed and scooped his tiny, dripping daughter into his large, safe arms and plunged his face into her belly making her laugh and hug her daddy's head. Gamache exhaled and turning to Reine-Marie bent down and kissed her, whispering, 'Thank you,' into the crown of her graying hair. He then reached out and smoothed his hand along Henri's flank, and kissed him too on the top of his head.

'Good boy.'

Henri, no longer able to contain himself, jumped up, his feet almost up to Gamache's shoulders.

'*Non,*' commanded Gamache. 'Down.'

Henri dropped immediately.

'Lie down.'

Henri lay down, contrite. There was no doubt who was the alpha dog.

'Good boy,' said Gamache again and gave Henri a treat.

'Good boy,' said Reine-Marie to Gamache.

'Where's my treat?'

'In a public park, *monsieur l'inspecteur*?' She looked at the other families walking leisurely through Parc Mont Royal, the beautiful mountain rising in the very center of Montreal. 'Though it probably wouldn't be the first time.'

'For me it would.' Gamache smiled and blushed a little, glad Daniel and his family couldn't hear.

'You're very sweet, in a brutish kind of way.' Reine-Marie kissed him. Gamache heard a shuffling and suddenly noticed the book section of his paper taking flight, one sheet at a time. Leaping up he lunged here and there, trying to stomp on the pages of his paper before they blew away. Florence, wrapped in a blanket now and watching this, pointed and laughed. Daniel put her on the ground and she stomped her feet as well. Gamache then exaggerated his actions until Daniel, his wife, Roslyn, and little Florence were all lifting their legs high and lunging after imaginary rogue papers, Gamache after the real thing.

'It's a good thing love is blind,' laughed Reine-Marie after Gamache returned to the bench.

'And not very bright,' agreed Gamache, squeezing her hands. 'Warm enough? Would you like a *café au lait*?'

'Actually I would.' His wife looked up from her own paper, *La Presse*.

'Here, Dad, let me help.' Daniel handed Florence to Roslyn and the two men strode off to the pavilion in the forest, not far from the lake. Joggers squelched along the trails of Mont Royal, here and there a rider appeared and disappeared through the bridle paths. It was a brilliant spring day with actual warmth in the young light.

Reine-Marie watched them go, two peas in a pod. So alike. Tall, sturdy like oaks, Daniel's brown hair just beginning to thin and Armand's almost gone on top. The sides, trim and dark, were graying. In his mid-fifties Armand Gamache held himself with ease and his son, now incredibly thirty, did too.

'Do you miss him terribly?' Roslyn sat beside her mother-in-law and looked into the comfortable, lined face. She loved Reine-Marie and had from the first dinner the older woman had prepared for her. Newly dating, Daniel had introduced her to his family. She was petrified. Not simply because even then she knew she loved him but at the thought of meeting the famous Chief Inspector Armand Gamache. His firm, fair handling of the toughest homicide cases had made him practically a legend in Quebec. She'd been raised with his face staring at her across the breakfast table as her own father read about Gamache's exploits. Gamache had aged in those pictures over the years, the hair receding and graying, the face expanding a bit. A trim moustache showed up and lines not corresponding to creases in the paper had begun to appear.

But then, unbelievably, it was time to meet the three-dimensional man.

'*Bienvenue.*' He'd smiled at her and given a little bow as he opened the door of their apartment in Outremont. 'I'm Daniel's father. Come in.'

He wore gray flannels, a comfortable cashmere cardigan, a shirt and tie for the Sunday lunch. He smelled of sandalwood and his hand felt warm and solid, like slipping into a familiar chair. She knew that hand. It belonged to Daniel as well.

That had been five years ago, and so much had happened since. They'd married, had Florence. Daniel had come home one day hopping with the news that a management company had offered him a job in Paris. Just a two-year contract, but what did she think?

She didn't have to think. Two years in Paris? They were one year into it now and loving it. But they missed their family and knew how excruciating it had been for both sets of grandparents to kiss tiny Florence goodbye at the airport. To miss her first steps and words, to miss the first teeth and her ever-changing face and moods. Roslyn had expected her own mother to be the hardest hit, but she thought perhaps Papa Armand was the worst. Her heart broke as she'd walked down the glass corridor to the plane and seen his palms pressed against the waiting room window.

But he'd said nothing. He'd been happy for them, and he'd let them know it. And he'd let them go.

'We miss you all.' Reine-Marie held her hand and smiled.

And now there was another child on the way. They'd told both sets of parents at supper on Good Friday and there'd been a roar of excitement. Her father had brought out champagne and Armand had rushed off to the store to get her some non-alcoholic apple cider and they'd toasted their great good fortune.

While they waited for their order Armand put his hand on his son's arm and guided him a little way into the pavilion, away from any onlookers. He reached into his Barbour jacket and handed Daniel an envelope.

'Dad, I don't need it,' Daniel whispered.

'Please take it.'

Daniel slipped it into his own coat. 'Thank you.'

Son hugged father, like Easter Island megaliths come together.

But Gamache hadn't moved far enough away. Someone was watching.

Roslyn and Florence had joined another young family and Daniel wandered over while Gamache subsided onto the bench again, handing his wife her coffee and picking up his paper. Reine-Marie had disappeared into the front section of *La Presse*. It was unusual for her not to greet him, but he knew that both of them often got caught up in reading. Henri was asleep in the sunlight at his feet and sipping his coffee he watched the people stroll by.

It was an exquisite day.

After a few minutes Reine-Marie lowered the newspaper. Her face was troubled. Frightened almost.

'What is it?' Gamache reached over and put his large hand on her forearm, searching her eyes.

'Did you read the paper?'

'Just the book section so far, why?'

'Is it possible to be scared to death?'

'What do you mean?'

'Apparently someone has been. Frightened to death.'

'*Mais, c'est horrible.*'

'In Three Pines.' Reine-Marie searched his face. 'In the old Hadley house.'

Armand Gamache paled.

CHAPTER 10

'Come in, Armand. *Joyeuses Pâques.*'

Superintendent Brébeuf shook hands and closed the door.

'*Et vous, mon ami.*' Gamache smiled. 'Happy Easter.'

The surprise of Reine-Marie's news had worn off. He'd read the story and just as he'd finished his cell phone had rung. It was his friend and superior at the Sûreté du Québec, Michel Brébeuf.

'A case has come up,' Brébeuf had said. 'I know Daniel and his family are with you, I'm sorry. Can you spare some time?'

It was a courtesy, Gamache knew, for his boss to ask. He could have commanded. But then the two had grown up together, been best friends forever and gone into the Sûreté together. They'd even gone after the Superintendent's job together. Brébeuf had prevailed, but it had not affected their friendship.

'They're returning to Paris tonight. Not to worry. We've had a good visit though never long enough. I'll be in shortly.'

He'd said his goodbyes to his son, his daughter-in-law and his Florence.

'I'll call later,' he said to Reine-Marie, kissing her. She waved and watched him walk purposefully to the car park, hidden by a stand of pines. She watched until he was out of sight. And still she watched.

'Have you read the papers?' Brébeuf asked, settling into the swivel chair behind his desk.

'Not so much read as chased.' He remembered trying to read, his own massive boot print on the paper. 'It's not the Three Pines case you're talking about.'

'So you have read the papers.'

'Reine-Marie pointed it out. But it said it was a natural death. Ghoulish, but natural. Was she really scared to death?'

'That's what the doctors at the Cowansville hospital said. Heart attack. But—'

'Go on.'

'You'll have to see for yourself but I hear she looked . . .' Brébeuf paused, almost embarrassed to say it, 'as though she'd seen something.'

'The paper said she'd been at a séance at the old Hadley house.'

'A séance,' Brébeuf harrumphed. 'Foolishness. I can see kids doing it, but adults? I just don't understand why anyone would waste their time with that.'

Gamache wondered why the Superintendent had come in on his day off. He couldn't remember Brébeuf discussing a case before it had even begun.

So why this one?

'It wasn't until this morning the doctor thought to have blood work done. This is what came back.'

Brébeuf handed over a sheet of paper. Gamache put on his half-moon glasses. He'd read hundreds of these and knew exactly what to look for. The toxicology report.

After a minute he lowered the paper, looking at Brébeuf over his glasses.

'Ephedra.'

'*C'est ça.*'

'But does it have to be murder?' Gamache asked, almost to himself. 'Don't people take ephedra on their own?'

'It's a banned substance,' said Brébeuf.

'True, true,' said Gamache, distracted. He was scanning the report again. After a moment he spoke. 'This is interesting. Listen to this.' He read from the report. 'The subject is five foot seven and weighs 134.7 pounds. You wouldn't

think she'd need a diet pill.' He took off his glasses and
folded them up.

'Most people don't,' said Brébeuf. 'All in their minds.'

'I wonder what she weighed a few months ago,' said
Gamache. 'Maybe this is how she got down to 135 pounds.'
Gamache tapped his glasses on the report. 'With the help
of ephedra.'

'Maybe,' agreed Brébeuf. 'It's your job to find out.'

'Murder or misadventure?' Gamache went back to the
paper in his hand, wondering what else it might yield. But
the Chief Inspector knew that paper rarely held the answers to his questions. Was it murder? Who was the killer?
Why had the killer hated or feared this woman so much he
had to take her life? Why? Why? Always the why before
the who.

No, the answers lay in flesh and blood, not in a book
and not in a report. And so often not even in things corpo-
real, but in something that couldn't be held and contained
and touched. The answers to his questions lay in the murky
past and in the emotions hidden there.

The paper in his hand would yield the facts but not the
truth. For that he had to go to Three Pines. For that he'd
have to go, yet again, into the old Hadley house.

'Who will you take on your team?' The question brought
Gamache back to his friend's office. Brébeuf had tried to
sound casual but the oddity of his query couldn't be hidden.
Never before had he questioned Armand Gamache, his chief
of homicide, about procedure and certainly not about anything as mundane as personnel assignments.

'Why do you ask?'

Brébeuf picked up a pen and tapped it rapidly on a stack
of undone paperwork.

'You know very well why I'm asking. You're the one
who brought her behavior to my attention. Are you going
to assign Agent Yvette Nichol to this case?'

There it was. The question that had hounded Gamache on
the drive from Mont Royal. Should Nichol be on the team?
Was it time? He'd actually sat in his Volvo in the near-empty

car park of Sûreté headquarters, trying to decide. But still, he was surprised his friend had asked.

'What's your advice?'

'Have you made up your mind or is there a chance I might influence you?'

Gamache laughed. They knew each other too well.

'I'll tell you, Michel, I've just about decided. But you know how much I value your opinion.'

'*Voyons*, what would you rather have right now? My opinion or a brioche?'

'A brioche,' admitted Gamache with a smile. 'But so would you.'

'*C'est la vérité*. Listen.' Brébeuf got up and came round to the other side of the desk, sitting on it and leaning down to stare at the Chief Inspector. 'To take her, well, *c'est fou*. It's nuts. I know you. You want to save her, to rehabilitate her. To turn her into a good and loyal agent. I'm right, aren't I?'

Michel Brébeuf wasn't smiling any more.

Gamache opened his mouth to speak but changed his mind. Instead he let his friend vent. And vent he did.

'One day that ego of yours'll kill you. That's all it is, you know. You pretend it's selfless, you pretend to be the great teacher, the wise and patient Armand Gamache, but you and I both know it's ego. Pride. Be careful, my friend. She's dangerous. You've said so yourself.'

Gamache could feel his heat rising and had to take a few breaths to keep his calm. To not match anger with anger. He knew Michel Brébeuf was saying this because he was the Superintendent, but also because they were friends.

'It's time the Arnot case was ended,' said Gamache firmly.

And there it was. He'd said it out loud.

Goddamned Arnot, rotting in prison but still haunting him.

'I thought so,' said Brébeuf, returning to his chair.

'Why are you here, Michel?'

'In my own office?'

Gamache was silent, watching his friend. Finally Brébeuf

leaned forward, putting his elbows on his wide desk as though he intended to crawl across and wrap himself around Gamache's head.

'I know what happened to you once in the old Hadley house. You were almost killed there—'

'It wasn't so bad.'

'Don't lie to me, Armand,' Brébeuf warned. 'I wanted to be the one to tell you about this case and see how you feel.'

Gamache was silent, deeply touched.

'There's something about the place,' he admitted after a moment. 'You've never been there, have you?'

Brébeuf shook his head.

'There's something in there. It's like a hunger, some need that has to be met. I must sound crazy.'

'I think there's a need in you that's equally destructive,' said Brébeuf. 'Your need to help people. Like Agent Nichol.'

'I don't want to help her. I want to expose her and her bosses. I believe she's working for the faction that supports Arnot. I've already told you that.'

'So fire her,' snapped Brébeuf, exasperated. 'The only reason I haven't is because you asked me not to. As a personal favor. Listen, the Arnot case will never be over. It goes too deep into the system. Every officer in the Sûreté is involved in one way or another. Most support you, you know that. But the ones who don't,' Brébeuf now raised his palms in a simple, eloquent gesture of defeat, 'they're powerful and Nichol is their eyes and ears. As long as she's near you you're in danger. They'll bring you down.'

'It works both ways, Michel,' said Gamache wearily. Talking about former Superintendent Arnot always drained him. It was, he'd thought, an old case. Long dead and buried. But now it was back. Risen. 'As long as she's close I can watch her, control what she sees and does.'

'Foolish man.' Brébeuf shook his head.

'Prideful, stubborn, arrogant man,' agreed Gamache, walking to the door.

'You may have your Nichol,' said Brébeuf, turning his back to look out the window.

'*Merci.*'

Gamache closed the door and walked to his own office to make some calls.

Alone now Superintendent Brébeuf picked up the phone and made a call of his own.

'It's Superintendent Brébeuf. You'll be getting a call soon from Chief Inspector Gamache's office. No, he doesn't suspect. He thinks the problem is Nichol.'

Brébeuf took a few deep breaths. He'd gotten to the stage where just looking at Armand Gamache made him want to retch.

Inspector Jean Guy Beauvoir drove the Volvo over the Pont Champlain spanning the St Lawrence River and onto the Eastern Townships Autoroute, heading south toward the American border. Beauvoir had suggested the chief buy an MG when his last Volvo had finally died a year or so ago, but the chief for some reason thought he was joking.

'So what's the case?'

'A woman was frightened to death last night in Three Pines,' said Gamache, watching the countryside slip by.

'*Sacré.* So what are we looking for? A ghost?'

'Closer than you might think. It happened at a séance. At the old Hadley house.'

Gamache turned to watch his young inspector's lean and handsome face. It grew even tauter, the lips compressing and growing pale.

'That fucking place,' Beauvoir said at last. 'Someone should tear it down.'

'You think the house is to blame?'

'Don't you?'

It was a strange admission for Beauvoir. Normally so rational and driven by facts, he gave no credence to things unseen, like emotions. He was the perfect complement to his boss, who, in Beauvoir's opinion, spent far too much time crawling into people's heads and hearts. Inside there lived chaos, and Beauvoir wasn't a big one for that.

But if there was ever a case for evil, in Beauvoir's experience, it was the old Hadley house. He shifted his toned body in the driver's seat, suddenly uncomfortable, and looked over at the boss. Gamache was watching him thoughtfully. They locked eyes, Gamache's steady and calm and of the deepest brown and Beauvoir's almost gray.

'Who was the victim?'

CHAPTER 11

The road to Three Pines from the autoroute was one of the most scenic, and treacherous, Gamache knew. The car shuddered and thumped and careered from pothole to pothole until both Beauvoir and Gamache felt like scrambled eggs.

'Watch out.' Gamache pointed to a massive hole in the dirt road. Avoiding it Beauvoir steered into a larger one and then the nearly new Volvo washboarded over a series of waves cut deeply into the mud.

'Any more advice?' snarled Beauvoir, his eyes pinned to the road.

'I just plan to yell "watch out" every few seconds,' said Gamache. 'Watch out.'

Sure enough an asteroid crater opened up in front of them.

'Fuck.' Beauvoir yanked the steering wheel to the side, narrowly avoiding it. 'It's as if that house doesn't want us to get to it.'

'And it's commanded the roads to open up?' Even Gamache, more than happy to entertain existential ideas, found this surprising. 'Do you think maybe it's the spring thaw?'

'Well, I suppose it could be that. Watch out.' They hit a hole and jerked forward. Lurching and swerving and swearing the two men made their slow progress deeper and deeper into the forest. The dirt road wound through pine and maple forests and along valleys and climbed the sides of small mountains. It passed streams throbbing with the spring run-off and gray lakes that had only recently lost their winter ice.

Then they arrived.

Ahead Gamache could see the familiar and strangely comforting sight of the Scene of Crime vehicles parked along the side of the road. He couldn't see the old Hadley house yet.

Beauvoir pulled the car into a spot by the abandoned mill across from the house. Opening his door Gamache was met with an aroma so sweet he had to close his eyes and pause.

Inhaling deeply he knew immediately what it was. Fresh pine. Young buds, their fragrance strong and new. He changed into rubber boots, put his Barbour field coat on over his jacket and tie and slipped a tweed cap on his head.

Still not looking at the old Hadley house, he walked instead to the brow of the hill. Beauvoir put his Italian leather jacket over his merino wool turtleneck and, scanning the results in the mirror, noticed he was closer than he appeared. After a moment's happy reflection he walked up beside Gamache until the two men stood, shoulder to shoulder, looking out over the valley.

It was Armand Gamache's favorite view. The mountains rose graciously on the far side, folding into each other, their slopes covered with a fuzz of lime green buds. He could smell not just the pine now, but the very earth, and other aromas. The musky rich scent of dried autumn leaves, the wood smoke rising from the chimneys below, and something else. He lifted his head and inhaled again, softly this time. There, below the bolder aromas, sat a subtler scent. The first of the spring flowers. The youngest and bravest of them. Gamache was reminded of the simple and dignified chapel with its white clapboard spire. It was just below him, off to the right. He'd been in St Thomas's often enough and on this fine morning knew light from an old stained glass window would be spilling onto the gleaming pews and wooden floor. The image wasn't of Christ or the lives and glorious deaths of saints, but of three young men in the Great War.

Two were in profile, marching forward. But one was looking straight at the congregation. Not accusing, not in sorrow
or fear. But with great love as though to say this was his gift
to them. Use it well.

Beneath were inscribed the names of those lost in the
wars and one more line.

They Were Our Children.

And now standing on the lip of the hill, looking into
the loveliest, gentlest village Gamache had ever seen and
smelling the brave young flowers, he wondered whether it
was always the young who were brave. And the old grew
fearful and cowardly.

Was he? He was certainly afraid to go into the monstrosity he could feel breathing on his neck. Or perhaps
that was Beauvoir. But he was afraid of something else, he
knew.

Arnot. Goddamned Arnot. And what that man was capable of even from prison. Especially from prison, where
Gamache had put him.

But even those dark thoughts evaporated before the
sight that met his eyes. How could he be fearful when faced
with this?

Three Pines lay nestled in its little valley. Wood smoke
wafted from the stone chimneys, and maples and cherry and
apple trees were in bud if not quite in bloom. People moved
here and there, some working in gardens, some pinning up
fresh laundry on their lines, some sweeping the wide and
graceful verandas. Spring cleaning. Villagers walked across
the green with canvas bags full of baguettes and other produce Gamache couldn't see but could imagine. Locally
made cheeses and pâtés, farm fresh eggs and rich aromatic
coffee beans all from the shops.

He looked at his watch. Almost noon.

Gamache had been to Three Pines on previous investi-
gations and each time he'd had the feeling he belonged. It
was a powerful feeling. After all, what else did people really want except to belong?

He longed to stride down the muddy verge, cross the

village green and open the door to Olivier's Bistro. There
he'd warm his hands by the fire, order licorice pipes and a
Cinzano. And maybe a rich pea soup. He'd read old copies
of the *Times Literary Supplement* and talk to Olivier and
Gabri about the weather.

How was it his favorite place on earth was so close to
his least favorite?

'What's that?' Jean Guy Beauvoir laid a hand on his
arm. 'Can you hear it?'

Gamache listened. He heard birds. He heard a slight
breeze rustling the old leaves at his feet. And he heard
something else.

A rumble. No, more than that. A muffled roar. Had the
old Hadley house come to life behind them? Was it growling and growing?

Ripping his eyes from the tranquility of the village he
looked around slowly until his eyes finally fell on the house.

It stared back, cold, defiant.

'It's the river, sir,' said Beauvoir, smiling sheepishly.
'The Rivière Bella Bella. Spring run-off. Nothing more.'
He watched as the Chief Inspector stared at the house, then
Gamache blinked and turned to Beauvoir, smiling slightly.

'Are you sure it wasn't the house growling?'

'Pretty sure.'

'I believe you,' Gamache laughed. He placed his large
hand on the younger man's soft leather jacket then started
toward the old Hadley house.

As he approached he was surprised to see peeling paint
and jagged, broken windows. The 'For Sale' sign had fallen
over and tiles were missing from the roof and even some
bricks from the chimney. It was almost as though the house
was casting parts of itself away.

Stop that, he said to himself.

'Stop what?' Beauvoir asked, almost running to catch
up to the chief, the boss's long strides picking up speed as
they neared the house.

'I said that out loud, did I?' Gamache suddenly stopped.
'Jean Guy,' Gamache began, but he didn't know what he

wanted to say. While Beauvoir waited, his handsome face going from respectful attention to quizzical, Gamache thought.

What do I want to tell him? To be careful? To know things weren't as they appeared? Not the Hadley house, not this case, not even their own homicide team.

He wanted to pull this young man away from the house. Away from the investigation. Away from him. As far from him as possible.

Things were not as they seemed. The known world was shifting, reforming. Everything he'd taken as a given, a fact, as real and unquestioned, had fallen away.

But he was damned if he was going to fall with it. Or let anyone he loved go down.

'The house is falling apart,' said Gamache. 'Be careful.'

Beauvoir nodded. 'You too.'

Once inside Gamache was surprised by how mundane the place felt. Not evil at all. If anything it felt kind of pathetic.

'Up here, Chief,' Agent Isabelle Lacoste called, her brown hair hanging down as she looked over the dark wood banister. 'She died in this room.' Lacoste waved behind her and disappeared.

'*Joyeuses Pâques*,' she said a moment later when Gamache had climbed the stairs and walked into the room. Agent Lacoste was dressed in comfortable and stylish clothes, like most of the Québécoises. In her late twenties she'd already had two children and hadn't bothered to work off all the weight. Instead she dressed well and was perfectly happy with the results.

Gamache took in the sight. A luxurious four-poster bed stood against one wall. A fireplace with a heavy Victorian mantel sat across from it. On the wooden floor was a huge Indian rug in rich blues and burgundies. The walls held intricate William Morris wallpaper and the lamps, both floor and table, were festooned with tassels. A colorful scarf was artfully draped over a lamp on a vanity.

It was as though he'd stepped back a hundred years.

Except for the circle of chairs in the middle of the room. He counted them. Ten. Three had fallen over.

'Careful, we haven't quite finished,' Lacoste advised as Gamache took a step toward the chairs.

'What's that?' Beauvoir pointed to the rug and what looked like ice pellets.

'Salt, we think. At first we thought it might be crystal meth or cocaine, but it's just rock salt.'

'Why put salt on a carpet?' Beauvoir asked, not expecting an answer.

'To cleanse the space, I think,' was her unexpected reply. Lacoste seemed not to appreciate the oddity of her answer.

'I beg your pardon?' Gamache asked.

'There was a séance, right?'

'That's what we've heard,' agreed Gamache.

'I don't understand,' said Beauvoir. 'Salt?'

'All will be revealed.' Lacoste smiled. 'There're lots of ways of doing a séance but only one involves salt in a circle and four candles.'

She pointed to the candles on the rug inside the ring. Gamache hadn't noticed them. One had also fallen over and as he leaned closer he thought he could see melted wax on the carpet.

'They're at the compass points,' Lacoste continued. 'North, south, east and west.'

'I know what a compass point is,' said Beauvoir. He didn't like this at all.

'You said there's only one way to do a séance that involves candles and salt,' said Gamache, his voice calm and his eyes sharp.

'The Wicca way,' said Lacoste. 'Witchcraft.'

CHAPTER 12

Madeleine Favreau had been scared to death.

Killed by the old Hadley house, Clara knew with a certainty. And now Clara Morrow stood outside, accusing it. Lucy, on her leash, was swishing back and forth, anxious to leave this place. And so was Clara. But she felt she owed Madeleine this much. To face down the house. To let it know she knew.

Something had awoken last night. Something had found them huddled in their tight little circle, friends doing something foolish and silly and adolescent. Nothing more. No one should have died. And no one would have if they'd held the séance in any other place. No one had died at the bistro.

Something in this grotesque place had come to life, come down that hallway and into the cobwebbed old bedroom and taken Madeleine's life.

Clara would remember it for the rest of her own life. The shrieks. They seemed all around. Then a thud. A candle sputtering out. Chairs falling over as people either leaped to help or leaped to leave. And then the flashlights clicking on and bouncing maniacally over the room, then stopping. Illuminating one thing. That face. Even in the bright and warm sunshine of the day Clara felt the dread tighten, like a cloak she couldn't quite shrug off.

'Don't look,' Clara had heard Hazel call, presumably to Sophie.

'*Non*,' Monsieur Béliveau yelled.

Madeleine's eyes were wide and staring, as though the balls were straining to escape their sockets. Her mouth was open, lips tight, frozen in a scream. Her hands, when Clara grabbed them to offer comfort she knew was too late, were curled into talons. Clara looked up and saw a movement outside their circle. And heard something too.

Flapping.

'*Bonjour*,' Armand Gamache called as he left the house. Clara started and came back to the day. She recognized the large, elegant figure walking purposefully toward her.

'Are you all right?' he asked, seeing her distress.

'Not really.' She half smiled. 'Better for seeing you.'

But she didn't look better. In fact, tears started down her face and Gamache suspected they were far from the first. He stood quietly beside her, not trying to stop the tears, but allowing her her sorrow.

'You were here last night.' It was a statement, not a question. He'd read the report and seen her name. In fact, she was the first on his list to question. He valued her opinion and her eye for detail, for things visible and those not. He knew he should consider her a suspect, along with everyone else at the séance, but the truth was he didn't. He considered her a precious witness.

Clara wiped the sleeve of her cloth coat over her face and across her nose. Armand Gamache, seeing the results, brought a cotton handkerchief from his pocket and handed it to her. She'd hoped the worst of the tears were over, but they seemed in full flood, like the Bella Bella. A run-off of grief.

Peter had been wonderful last night. Racing to the hospital, never once saying 'I told you so,' though she'd said it often enough herself as she'd choked out the story to him.

Then driving Myrna, Gabri and her home. Offering rooms and comfort to a stricken, dumbfounded Hazel and a strangely relaxed Sophie. Was she numb with grief? Or was that giving Sophie the benefit of the doubt, as they'd always done?

The offer had been refused. Even now Clara couldn't begin to imagine how awful it must have been for Hazel to return home, alone. With Sophie, certainly, but in reality alone.

'Was she a friend?' They turned and walked away from the house, toward the village.

'Yes. She was a friend to everyone.'

Gamache, she noticed, was silent as he walked beside her, his hands clasped behind his back and his face thoughtful.

'What are you thinking?' she asked, then after a moment's silence answered her own question. 'You're thinking she was murdered, aren't you?'

They'd stopped again. Clara couldn't walk and process this staggering thought at the same time. She could barely stand and carry it. She turned and stared at Gamache. Was she always this slow, she wondered? Of course he'd think that. Why else would the head of homicide for the Sûreté du Québec be there, unless Madeleine was murdered?

Gamache gestured to the bench on the village green.

'Why all the picnic tables?' he asked as they sat down.

'We had an Easter egg hunt and picnic.' Was it only yesterday?

Gamache nodded. They'd hidden eggs for Florence and then had to find them all again themselves. Next year she'd be able to do it, he thought.

'Was Madeleine murdered?' Clara asked.

'We think so,' he said. After a moment to allow her to absorb the information he asked, 'Does that surprise you?'

'Yes.'

'No, wait. Please think about it. I know at first everyone's surprised by murder. But I want you to really think about the question. If Madeleine Favreau was murdered, would it surprise you?'

Clara turned to Gamache. His deep brown eyes were thoughtful, his moustache was trim and graying, the hair under his cap groomed and curling slightly. His face was strong with laugh lines radiating from the corners of his eyes. He spoke to her in English, as a courtesy, she knew. His English was perfect and, strangely, he had a British accent. She'd been meaning each time they'd met to ask him about that.

'Why do you speak with an English accent?'

His eyebrows rose and he turned a mildly surprised face to her.

'Is that the answer to my question?' he asked with a smile.

'No, professor. But it's something I've been meaning to ask and keep forgetting.'

'I went to Cambridge. Christ's College. Studied history.'

'And honed your English.'

'Learned my English.'

Now it was Clara's turn to be surprised.

'You didn't speak English before arriving in Cambridge?'

'Well, I could say two things.'

'And those were . . .'

' "Fire on the Klingons," and "My God, Admiral, it's horrible." '

Clara snorted.

'I watched American television when I could. Particularly two shows.'

'*Star Trek* and *Voyage to the Bottom of the Sea*,' said Clara.

'You'd be surprised how useless those phrases are in Cambridge. Though "My God, Admiral, it's horrible" could be used in a pinch.'

Clara laughed and imagined young Gamache in Cambridge. Who goes across the world to a foreign country to go to university without knowing the language?

'Well?' Gamache's face had turned serious.

'Madeleine was lovely, in every sense. She was easy to like and I suspect easy to love. I could see loving her, had we had more time. I can't believe someone killed her.'

'Because of who she was, or because of who someone wasn't?'

That was the question, thought Clara. Accepting murder

meant accepting there was a murderer. Among them. Close. Someone in that room, almost certainly. One of those smiling, laughing, familiar faces hid thoughts so vile they had to kill.

'How long has Madeleine lived here?'

'Well, she actually lives outside the village, off that way.' Clara pointed into the rolling hills. 'With Hazel Smyth.'

'Who was also there last night, with someone named Sophie Smyth.'

'Her daughter. Madeleine came to live with them about five years ago. They'd known each other for years.'

Just then Lucy gave a yank on her leash and Clara looked over to see Peter walking through their gate and across the dirt road, waving. She looked around for cars then unclipped Lucy. The elderly dog bounded across the green and right into Peter, who doubled over. Gamache winced.

Straightening up Peter limped over to their bench, two muddy pawprints on his crotch.

'Chief Inspector.' Peter put out his hand with more dignity than Gamache had thought possible. Gamache rose and shook hands warmly with Peter Morrow. 'Sad time,' said Peter.

'It is. I was just saying to Clara we think it's possible Madame Favreau didn't die naturally.'

'Why do you say that?'

'You weren't there, were you?' Gamache ignored Peter's question.

'No, we'd had people for dinner last night and I stayed to clean up.'

'Would you have gone if you could?'

Peter barely hesitated. 'No. I didn't approve.' Even to his own ears he sounded like a Victorian vicar.

'Peter tried to talk me out of going,' said Clara. All three were standing now and Clara took Peter's hand. 'He was right. We shouldn't have done it. Had we all stayed away from there,' Clara cocked her head toward the house on the hill, 'Madeleine would still be alive.'

It was probably true, thought Gamache. But for how long? There were some things you couldn't escape and death was one.

Inspector Jean Guy Beauvoir watched as the last of the Crime Scene team packed up then he backed out of the bedroom and closed the door. Ripping a length of tape from a yellow roll he stuck it across the door. He repeated that several times more than he normally would. Something in him felt the need to seal away whatever was in that room. He'd never admit it, of course, but Jean Guy Beauvoir had felt something growing. The longer he stayed the more it grew. Foreboding. No, not foreboding. Something else.

Emptiness. Jean Guy Beauvoir felt he was being hollowed out. And he suddenly knew that if he stayed there would be just a chasm and an echo where his insides had been.

He ached to get out. He'd looked over at Agent Lacoste, wondering whether she felt the same. She knew altogether too much about that witchcraft bullshit for his liking. Murmuring a Hail Mary as he sealed the room, he stepped back to admire his handiwork.

Had he known how the artist Christo had wrapped the Reichstag he might have seen a similarity. Yellow Crime Scene tape smothered the door.

Taking the stairs two at a time he was out into the sunshine in a flash. The world was so much brighter, the air so much fresher, for having come from that tomb. Even the roar of the Rivière Bella Bella was comforting. Natural.

'Great, you haven't left yet.'

Beauvoir turned and saw Agent Robert Lemieux striding toward him, a smile on his young and eager face. Lemieux hadn't been with them long, but he was already Beauvoir's favorite. He liked young agents who idolized him.

Still, Beauvoir was surprised.

'Did the Chief Inspector call you in?' Beauvoir knew Gamache's plan was to keep the investigation simple until they knew for sure it was murder.

'No. Heard about it from one of my cop friends down

here. I'm visiting my parents over in Ste-Catherine-de-Hovey. Thought I'd drop in.'

Beauvoir looked at his watch. One o'clock. Now that he was out of the damned house he wondered if the emptiness he'd felt was just hunger pangs. Yes, that must be it.

'Come with me. The chief's in the bistro, probably having the last croissant.' Even though he was kidding Beauvoir could feel his anxiety rising. Suppose it was true? He hurried to the car and the two men drove the hundred yards or so into Three Pines.

Armand Gamache sat in front of the open fireplace sipping a Cinzano and listening. Even in late April a warm fire was welcome. Olivier had greeted him with a hug and a licorice pipe.

'*Merci, patron,*' said Gamache, returning the hug and accepting the pipe.

'It's just too shocking to absorb,' said Olivier, beautifully dressed in corduroys and oversized cashmere sweater. Not a fine blond hair out of place, not a crease or smudge to mar the look. By contrast his partner had forgotten to put his dentures in and was unshaven. A thick black stubble had rubbed Gamache's cheek when he and Gabri embraced.

Peter, Clara and Gamache followed Gabri to the sun-faded sofa by the fire while Olivier got their drinks, and now Myrna joined them just as they settled in.

'I'm glad to see you.' She took a seat in a nearby wing chair.

Gamache looked at the large black woman with affection. She ran his favorite bookstore.

'Why are you here?' she asked, her intelligent eyes kind and trying to soften the bluntness of the question.

He felt a certain empathy for the telegraph man on his wobbly bicycle during the war. The bearer of catastrophic news. Viewed always with suspicion.

'He thinks she was murdered, of course,' said Gabri, though without his dentures it sounded as though Gamache was 'tinking.'

'Murdered?' said Myrna, with a snort. 'It was horrible, violent even, but not murder.'

'How was it violent?'

'I think we all felt assaulted,' said Clara and they nodded.

Beauvoir and Lemieux thrust open the bistro door just then, talking. Gamache caught their attention and raised his hand. They fell silent and walked over to the gathering by the fireplace.

The sun was streaming through the leaded glass windows and in the background other patrons could be heard murmuring. Everyone was subdued.

'Tell me what happened,' said Gamache quietly.

'The psychic had spread the salt and lit the candles,' said Myrna, her eyes open and seeing the scene. 'We were in a circle.'

'Holding hands,' Gabri remembered. His breathing had become fast and shallow and he looked as though he might pass out from the memory alone. Gamache thought he could almost hear the large man's heartbeat.

'I've never been so terrified,' said Clara. 'Not even driving through a snowstorm on the highway.'

Everyone nodded. They'd all felt the stunning certainty that this was how their lives would end. In a fiery crash, spinning out of control, invisible in the swirling, chaotic snow.

'But that was the whole point, wasn't it?' asked Peter, perching on the arm of Clara's wing chair. 'To scare yourselves?'

Was that why they'd done it? wondered Clara.

'We were there to cleanse the place of evil spirits,' said Myrna, but in the clear light of day it sounded ridiculous.

'And maybe to scare ourselves just a little,' admitted Gabri. 'Well, it's true,' he added, seeing their faces. And Clara had to admit, it was true. Could they have been so foolish? Were their lives so sedate, so boring, they had to seek and manufacture danger? No, not manufacture. It was always there. They'd courted it. And it had responded.

'Jeanne, the psychic,' Myrna explained to Gamache, 'said she could hear something coming. We were quiet for a moment and, well, I think I heard something too.'

'So did I,' said Gabri. 'By the bed. Someone was turning over on the bed.'

'No, it was from the corridor,' said Clara, tearing her eyes from the fire and looking at their faces. It was reminiscent of the night before, all their faces lit by the fire, all eyes lunar and their bodies taut, as though prepared to bolt. She was back in that dreadful room. Smelling spring flowers, like a funeral home, and hearing those steps shuffling up behind her. 'Steps. There were steps. Remember Jeanne said they were coming. The dead were coming.'

Beauvoir felt his heart contract and his hands grow numb. He wondered whether Lemieux would mind if he held his hand, but decided he'd rather die.

'They're coming, she said,' agreed Myrna. 'Then she said something else.'

'From the roof and somewhere else,' said Gabri, trying to recall the words.

'From the attic,' Myrna corrected.

'And the basement,' said Clara, looking straight at Armand Gamache. He felt the blood drain from his face. The basement of the old Hadley house still haunted him.

'And that was when it happened,' said Gabri.

'Not quite,' said Clara. 'She said one more thing.'

'They're all around us,' said Myrna quietly. 'Be here. Now!'

She clapped her hands and Beauvoir almost died.

CHAPTER 13

'And then she died,' said Gabri. Olivier came up behind and placed his hands on Gabri's shoulders. Gabri screamed.

'*Tabernacle*. Are you trying to kill me?'

The spell was broken. The room brightened again and Gamache noticed that a huge tray of sandwiches had appeared on the coffee table.

'What happened then?' Gamache asked, taking an open-faced melted goat cheese and arugula sandwich on a warm baguette.

'Monsieur Béliveau carried her downstairs while Gilles ran for his car,' said Myrna, helping herself to a grilled chicken and mango sandwich on a croissant.

'Gilles?' asked Gamache.

'Sandon. Works in the woods. He and his partner Odile were there too.'

Gamache remembered them from the list of witnesses in his pocket.

'Gilles drove. Hazel and Sophie went with them,' said Clara. 'The rest of us took Hazel's car.'

'God, Hazel,' said Myrna. 'Has anyone spoken to her today?'

'I called,' said Clara, looking at the platter, but not really hungry. 'Spoke to Sophie. Hazel was too upset to speak.'

'Hazel and Madeleine were close?' Gamache asked.

'Best friends,' said Olivier. 'Since high school. They lived together.'

'Not as lovers,' said Gabri. 'Well, not as far as I know.'

'Don't be absurd, of course they're not lovers,' said Myrna. 'Men. They think if two grown women live together and show affection they're lesbians.'

'It's true,' said Gabri, 'everyone makes that assumption about us.' He patted Olivier's knee. 'But we forgive you.'

'Was Madeleine Favreau ever heavy?'

Gamache's question was so unexpected he was met with blank stares, as though he'd spoken Russian.

'Fat, you mean?' Gabri asked. 'I don't think so.'

The others shook their heads.

'But she hadn't lived here all that long, you know,' said Peter. 'What would you say? Five years?'

'About that,' Clara agreed. 'But she fit in immediately. Joined the Anglican Church Women with Hazel—'

Gabri groaned. '*Merde.* She was supposed to take over this summer. Now what am I supposed to do?'

He was screwed, though not, he had to admit, quite as much as Madeleine herself.

'*Pauvre* Gabri,' said Olivier. 'A personal tragedy.'

'Well, you try running the ACW. Talk about murder,' he said to Gamache. 'Maybe Hazel'll do it? You think?'

'No I don't "tink,"' said Olivier. 'And you'd better not ask her now.'

'Is it possible someone else was in that house?' Gamache asked. 'Most of you heard sounds.'

Clara, Myrna and Gabri were quiet then, remembering the ungodly noises.

'What do you believe, Clara?' Gamache asked.

What do I believe? she asked herself. That the devil killed Madeleine? That evil lives in that house, possibly even put there by us? Perhaps the psychic was right and every unkind, every malevolent thought they'd ever had had been expelled from their idyllic village and eaten by that monstrosity. And it was ravenous. Maybe bitter thoughts were addictive. Once tasted you wanted more.

But had everyone really let go of all their bitter thoughts? Was it possible someone was holding on to theirs, hoarding them? Devouring them, swallowing them until they were bloated with bitterness and had become a walking, breathing version of the house on the hill?

Was there a human version of that wretched place, walking among them?

What do I believe? she asked herself again. She had no answer.

After a moment Gamache got up. 'Where can I find Madame Chauvet, the medium?' He reached into his pocket to pay for the sandwiches and drinks.

'She's staying at the B & B,' said Olivier. 'Should I get her?'

'No, we'll walk over. *Merci, patron.*'

'I didn't go,' Olivier whispered to Gamache as he handed him his change at the till on the long wooden bar, 'because I was too afraid.'

'I don't blame you. There's something about that house.'

'And that woman.'

'Madeleine Favreau?' Gamache found himself whispering now.

'No. Jeanne Chauvet, the psychic. Do you know what she said to Gabri as soon as she arrived?'

Gamache waited.

'She said, "You won't get laid here." '

Gamache absorbed the unlikely words.

'Are you sure? It seems a strange thing for a psychic to worry about. It's not—'

'True? Of course not. In fact—well, never mind.'

Gamache walked out the door into the splendid day with Olivier's last whispered warning in his ears.

'She's a witch, you know.'

The three Sûreté officers walked along the road that circled the village green.

'I'm confused,' Agent Lemieux said, running a little to keep up with Gamache's strides. 'Was it murder?'

'I'm confused too, young man,' said Gamache, stopping

to look at him. 'What are you doing here? I didn't call you out.'

Lemieux was taken aback by the question. He'd expected the Chief Inspector to be delighted, thanking him even. Instead Gamache was looking at him with patience and slight puzzlement.

'He's visiting his parents not far from here, for Easter,' said Beauvoir. 'A friend on the local Sûreté told him about the case.'

'I came on my own. I'm sorry, have I done something wrong?'

'No, nothing wrong. I just want to keep the investigation as discreet as possible, until we know whether it's murder.' Gamache smiled. His people needed to be self-starters, though perhaps not quite as eager as this one. But he'd grow out of it soon enough, and Gamache wasn't sure if that would be a good day.

'So we don't know for sure?' asked Lemieux, hurrying to catch up as Gamache resumed walking toward the large brick house on the corner.

'I don't want anyone to know yet, but she had ephedra in her blood,' explained Gamache. 'Heard of it?'

Lemieux shook his head.

'I'm surprised. You like sports, *n'est-ce pas?*'

The young agent nodded. It was one of the things that had bonded him to Beauvoir. Their love of the Montreal Canadiens hockey team. The Habs.

'Ever heard of Terry Harris?'

'The running back?'

'Or Seamus Regan?'

'The outfielder? Played for the Lions? They both died. I remember reading about it in *Allô Sport*.'

'They took ephedra. It's used in diet pills.'

'That's it. Harris collapsed during practice and Regan was actually playing. I was watching on TV. It was a hot day and everyone thought it was heat stroke. But it wasn't?'

'They were told by their coaches to lose weight fast, so they were taking diet pills.'

'That was a couple of years ago,' said Beauvoir. 'Ephedra's banned now, isn't it?'

'As far as I know, but I might be wrong. Can you check it out?' Gamache asked Lemieux.

'Absolutely.'

Gamache smiled as he walked to the attractive B & B. He liked Lemieux's enthusiasm. It was one of the reasons he'd asked the young man to join the team. Lemieux had been with the Cowansville detachment when Gamache was last down investigating a murder and had impressed him.

The victim in that case had lived in the old Hadley house.

They stepped onto the sweeping veranda of the B & B. The three-story brick building had once been a stop on the stagecoach route between Williamsburg and St-Rémy and sat on what was now called the Old Stage Road. Olivier had once told him that Gabri had made him buy it so he could tell friends he was 'on the stage.'

Stepping inside, he was met with wood floors, rich Indian rugs, and genteel faded fabrics. It felt like an old country house and invited relaxation.

But he wasn't there to relax. He was there to find out what had killed Madeleine Favreau. Was it a simple heart attack brought on by excitement or fear? Had she taken the ephedra herself? Or was something more sinister at work, hidden behind the pleasant facade of Three Pines?

Olivier said Jeanne Chauvet was in the small bedroom on the main floor.

'Stay here,' Gamache ordered Lemieux while he and Beauvoir walked down the short corridor.

'Think she might overpower us?' Beauvoir whispered with a smile.

'I think she might,' said Gamache, seriously, and knocked on the door.

CHAPTER 14

Silence.

Gamache and Beauvoir waited. Sunlight and fresh air wafted through the slightly open window at the end of the corridor, the simple white sheers moving slightly in the breeze.

Still they waited. Beauvoir was itching to knock again. Harder this time, as though insistence and impatience could conjure a person. Would that it were true. He was anxious to meet this woman who socialized with ghosts. Did she like them? Is that why she did it? Or perhaps no real person wanted to be with her? Maybe the only company she could find was the dead, who might not be as picky as the living. She had to be crazy, he knew. After all ghosts weren't real. They don't exist. Except maybe the Holy Ghost. But if— No. He wouldn't go down that road. He looked over at Gamache's patient profile, as though this was exactly how he wanted to spend his day. Standing in a corridor staring at a closed door.

'Madame Chauvet? This is Armand Gamache, of the Sûreté. I'd like to speak to you.'

Beauvoir smiled a little. It looked as though the Chief Inspector was addressing the door.

'I see that smile, monsieur. Perhaps you'd like to try?' Gamache stepped aside and Beauvoir stepped up to the door, pounding it with the heel of his hand.

'Sûreté, open up.'

'Brilliant, *mon ami*. Just what will appeal to a woman on her own.' Gamache turned and walked down the corridor, looking back at Beauvoir. 'I only let you do that because I know she's not in there.'

'And I only did it because I knew you'd be amused.'

'There's a key on the peg,' Lemieux pointed out when they returned. 'Couldn't we let ourselves in?'

'Not yet,' said Beauvoir. 'Not without a warrant and not until we know it's murder.' Still, he liked Lemieux's thinking. 'What now?' he asked Gamache.

'Search the place.'

While Beauvoir and Lemieux searched the dining room, gourmet kitchen, bathrooms and basement, Gamache walked into the living room and sat in the oversized leather chair.

He closed his eyes and cleared his mind. He was worried. Where was Jeanne Chauvet? What was she doing? What was she feeling? Guilt? Remorse? Satisfaction?

Was the séance a tragic failure or a spectacular success?

Agent Robert Lemieux stood on the threshold between the living and dining rooms watching the Chief Inspector.

At times young Agent Lemieux was racked with doubt. A kind of crisis of faith that his parents talked of suffering decades ago. But his church was the Sûreté, the place that had taken him in, given him purpose. While his parents eventually left their church, he'd never leave his. Never leave it, and never, ever betray it. His parents had raised him, fed him, disciplined and loved him. But the Sûreté had given him a home. He loved his parents and sisters, but only other officers knew what it was like to be in the Sûreté. To walk out of the door, all cocky and swaggering, but being careful to tell his cat he loved her, just in case.

Watching Chief Inspector Gamache, eyes closed, head tilted back exposing his throat, so trusting, Lemieux wondered just for an instant. Had what he'd been told about Gamache really been true? Once, not so long ago, Lemieux had worshipped Gamache. On his first visit to headquarters as a recruit he'd seen the famous man striding down the hall, junior officers in tow, decoding the most intricate and brutal of cases. And yet he'd had time to smile and nod a greeting. They'd studied his cases. They'd watched and cheered as Armand Gamache had brought down the dirty Superintendent Arnot. And saved the Sûreté.

But things weren't always as they seemed.

'Nothing.' Beauvoir brushed by Lemieux into the living room. Gamache opened his eyes and looked at the two men, his gaze resting on Lemieux. Their eyes held.

Then Gamache blinked and he rocked himself out of the chair.

'You've had enough rest. Time to work. Agent Lemieux, please stay here in case Jeanne Chauvet comes back. You and I,' he said to Beauvoir as they made for the door, 'are going to see Hazel Smyth.'

As he watched Gamache and Beauvoir walk to their car Lemieux hit the speed dial on his cell phone.

'Superintendent Brébeuf? It's Agent Lemieux.'

'Anything?' the confident voice came down the line.

'A couple of things I think might be helpful.'

'Good. Any sign of Agent Nichol?'

'Not yet. Should I ask?'

'Don't be a fool, of course you shouldn't. Tell me everything.'

There was a pause at the other end of the line. Brébeuf clenched his jaw. He was not a patient man, though he'd waited this long to get Gamache. They'd grown up together, joined up together, risen through the ranks together. They'd both gone after the Superintendent's job, Brébeuf remembered with satisfaction. It was the little gift he kept in the back of his mind and unwrapped in moments of stress. Now he did it again. Unfolding the layers of his smiling, nodding, forelock-tugging manner toward his best friend. And then he reached the great and unexpected gift. He'd prevailed. He'd won the promotion over the great Armand Gamache. And it had been enough, for a while. Until the Arnot case.

Quickly he replaced the wrapping and shoved the comforting thought to the back of his mind. He needed to focus, to be careful now.

'You know, son, why we're doing this.'

'Yes sir.'

'Don't be charmed by him, don't be fooled. Most are. Superintendent Arnot was, and look what happened to him. You need to focus, Lemieux.'

When Lemieux had related the events of the day Brébeuf paused, thinking.

'There's something I want you to do. It's a risk, but not, I think, a very big one.' He gave Lemieux his instructions. 'This will all be over soon,' he said kindly, 'and when it is, the officers with the courage to stand up for what they believe in will be rewarded. You're a brave young man and, believe me, I know how difficult this is.'

'Yes sir.'

Brébeuf hung up. As soon as this case was over he'd have to figure out what to do with Robert Lemieux. The young agent was really too impressionable.

Agent Lemieux hung up, a strange sensation in his chest. Not the tightening he'd had ever since Superintendent Brébeuf had appealed for his help, but a loosening, a euphoria.

Had Superintendent Brébeuf just offered him a promotion? Could he do what was best and benefit at the same time? How far up could he ride this? It might turn out all right after all.

Hazel Smyth was waiting for Madeleine to come home. Each footfall, each creak of the floorboards, each turn of a knob was her.

Then not. Every minute of the day Hazel lost Madeleine again. And now the door to the living room opened and Hazel looked up, expecting to see Mad's cheery face and a tea tray—it was tea time after all. But instead she saw her daughter's cheery face.

Sophie stepped in holding a huge glass of red wine for herself and made her way around the crowded room until she'd reached the sofa.

'So, what's for dinner?' she said, flopping into a chair and picking up a magazine.

Hazel stared at this stranger. It was as though she'd lost both of them last night. Madeleine dead and Sophie possessed. This wasn't the same girl. What had happened to morose, selfish Sophie?

The thing in front of her was radiant. It was as though the spirit of Madeleine had entered Sophie. Only without the heart. Without the soul. Whatever was radiating from Sophie wasn't joy or love or warmth.

But it was happiness. Madeleine was dead, horribly, grotesquely dead. And Sophie was happy.

It scared Hazel almost to death.

Beauvoir drove while Gamache navigated, trying to read the map while the car bounced along the heaved and holed road. He saw nothing of their progress except lurching squiggles and dots. It was fortunate he didn't get car sick.

'It's just beyond here.' Gamache folded the map and looked through the windshield. 'Watch out.'

Beauvoir yanked the steering wheel but they hit the pothole anyway.

'You know I was doing just fine before you looked up,' he said.

'You hit every hole between here and Three Pines. Watch out.'

The car rammed into another hole and Gamache wondered how long his tires would hold.

'We go through the village of Notre-Dame-de-Roof Trusses and out the other side. There's a turn off to the right. Chemin Erablerie.'

'Notre-Dame-de-Roof Trusses?' Beauvoir couldn't believe his ears.

'You expected maybe St-Roof Trusses?'

At least Three Pines made sense, thought Beauvoir. Williamsburg and St-Rémy made sense. Weren't Roof Trusses something to do with building?

Goddamned English. Trust them to choose a name like that. Like calling a village Royal Bank or Concrete Foundation. Always building, always bragging. And what was with this case? Didn't anyone die a normal death in Three Pines? And even their murders weren't normal. Couldn't they just haul off and stab each other, or use a gun or a bat? No. It was always something convoluted. Complicated.

Very unQuébécois. The Québécois were straightforward, clear. If they liked you, they hugged. When they murdered you, they just whacked you over the head. Boom, done. Convicted. Next.

None of this 'is it' or 'isn't it' shit.

Beauvoir was beginning to take this personally, though he was grateful the case had taken him away from the Easter egg hunt with his in-laws. There weren't actually any children. Just him and his wife, Enid. Her parents had expected them to spend the morning searching for chocolate eggs they'd hidden all over the house. They'd even kidded that it should be easy for him since he was an investigator, after all. He thought the easiest way would be to simply put his gun to his father-in-law's head and force him to say where the goddamned eggs were. But then the miraculous call had come. His calling.

He wondered how poor Enid was doing. Well, too bad. They were her crazy parents.

They were through the village of Notre-Dame-de-Roof Trusses in no time. Sure enough there was a huge faded sign in the yard of a small factory advertising 'Roof Trusses.' Beauvoir shook his head.

The old brick house overlooked the road, a few large maples on the front lawn and what Gamache suspected would be lush perennial beds full of flowers in a few weeks close to the house and along the drive. It was a tiny, tidy home that today spoke of potential. Leaves not yet out, flowers not yet up, grass not yet growing.

Gamache loved to see inside the homes of people involved in a case. To look at the choices they made for their most intimate space. The colors, the decorations. The aromas. Were there books? What sort?

How did it feel?

He'd been in shacks in the middle of nowhere, carpets worn, upholstery torn, wallpaper peeling off. But stepping in he'd also noticed the smell of fresh coffee and bread. Walls were taken up with immense smiling graduation photos and on rusty pocked TV trays stood modest chipped vases with cheery daffodils or pussy willows or some tiny wildflower picked by worn hands for eyes that would adore it.

And he'd been in mansions that felt like mausoleums.

He was anxious to see how Madeleine Favreau's home felt. From the outside it felt sad, but he knew most places felt just a little sad in spring, when the bright and playful snow had gone and the flowers and trees hadn't yet bloomed.

The first thing that struck him on entering the house was that it was almost impossible to move. Even in the narrow mudroom they'd somehow managed to stuff an armoire, a bookcase and a long wooden bench under which piles of muddy boots and shoes had been thrown.

'My name is Armand Gamache.' He bowed slightly to the middle-aged woman who opened the door.

She was neatly dressed in slacks and a sweater. Comfortable, conventional. She smiled a little as he brought out his warrant card.

'It's all right, Chief Inspector. I know who you are.' She stepped aside and let them in. Gamache's first impression was of a decent person trying to find her way in an indecent situation. She spoke French to them, though with a heavy English accent. She was courteous and contained. The only sign of something amiss were dark circles under her eyes, as though grief had physically struck her.

But Armand Gamache knew something else. Grief sometimes took time to tell. The first days for relatives or close friends of murder victims were blessedly numb. They almost always held together, going through the motions of a normal life, so that a casual observer would never know disaster had just rammed into them. Most people fell to pieces gradually, like the old Hadley house.

As he watched Gamache could almost see the inevitable horsemen on the hill, above Hazel, snorting and pounding the ground, straining to be released. They brought the end of everything Hazel knew, all that was familiar and predictable. This contained woman was courageously holding off the marauding army of grief, but soon it would break free and sweep down and over her, and nothing familiar would be left standing.

'Clara Morrow called to see how I was doing and offer some food. She told me you might be coming.'

'I could have brought the food. I'm sorry.' He was trying to get his coat off without whacking Beauvoir, who was crammed against the now closed door. A few books fell from the case and Gamache rapped his knuckles on the armoire, but eventually the coat came off.

'No need to be,' said Hazel, taking the coat and trying to open the armoire. 'Told her we have plenty. In fact I can't talk long. Poor old Madame Turcotte's had a stroke and I need to take her dinner.'

They followed Hazel deeper into her home.

The dining room was barely passable and when they finally broke through to the living room Gamache felt like an African explorer, having arrived in the Dark Continent. He hoped they could make camp here for a while. If they could clear enough space.

The small room held two sofas, including the largest one he'd ever seen, as well as an assortment of chairs and tables. The tiny brick house was stuffed, crammed, bloated and dark.

'It's a little cozy in here,' she said as the three of them sat, Gamache and Beauvoir on the massive sofa and Hazel in the worn wing chair opposite. A bag of mending sat at her feet. Her chair, Gamache knew. But it wasn't the best chair in the room. That one was empty and sat nearest the fireplace. A book was splayed open on the table under the lamp.

A book in French by a Québécois writer Gamache admired.

Madeleine Favreau's seat. The best in the room. Now how was that decided? Did she just take it? Did Hazel offer? Was Madeleine Favreau a bully? Was Hazel a professional victim?

Or perhaps they were just good friends who decided things naturally and amicably and took turns taking 'the best.'

'I can't believe she's gone,' said Hazel, sitting down as though her legs had given way. Loss was like that, Gamache knew. You didn't just lose a loved one. You lost your heart, your memories, your laughter, your brain and it even took your bones. Eventually it all came back, but different. Re-arranged.

'Had you known Madame Favreau long?'

'All my life, it seems. We met in high school. Had the same homeroom the first year and became friends. I was kind of shy but for some reason she took to me. Made my life easier.'

'Why was that?'

'Having a friend, Chief Inspector. All you need is one. Makes all the difference.'

'You must have had friends before, madame.'

'True, but not like Madeleine. When she was your friend, something magical happened. The world became a brighter place. Does that make sense?'

'It does,' Gamache nodded. 'A veil is lifted.'

She smiled at him gratefully. He did understand. But now, slowly, she could feel the veil lowering again. Madeleine was barely dead and already the dusk was approaching and with it that emptiness. It was spreading across her horizon.

One was dead and one was left behind. One. Again.

'But you haven't always lived together?'

'Good Lord, no.' Hazel actually laughed, surprising herself. Perhaps the dusk was just a threat. 'We went our separate ways after high school but met up again a few years ago. She's lived here almost five years now.'

'Was Madame Favreau ever overweight?'

He was getting used to seeing the baffled looks when he asked this question.

'Madeleine? Not that I know of. She'd put on a few pounds over the years since high school, but that was twenty-five years ago. It's natural. But she was never fat.'

'Though you hadn't seen her for a few years.'

'True,' Hazel admitted.

'Why did Madame Favreau move in?'

'Her marriage had failed. We were each living on our own so we decided to share. She was in Montreal at the time.'

'Was it hard making space?'

'Now I think you're being diplomatic, Chief Inspector,' and Hazel smiled. He realized he liked her. 'Had she brought a toothpick we'd have been in trouble. Happily she didn't. Madeleine brought herself, and that was enough.'

There it was. Simple, unforced, private. Love.

Across from him Hazel closed her eyes and smiled again, then her brows drew together.

The room suddenly ached. Gamache wanted to take her composed hands in his. Any other senior officer in the Sûreté would think this not only weakness, but folly. But Gamache knew it was the only way he could find a murderer. He listened to people, took notes, gathered evidence, like all his colleagues. But he did one more thing.

He gathered feelings. He collected emotions. Because murder was deeply human. It wasn't about what people did. No, it was about how they felt, because that's where it all started. Some feeling that had once been human and natural had twisted. Become grotesque. Had turned sour and corrosive until its very container had been eaten away. Until the human barely existed.

It took years for an emotion to reach that stage. Years of careful nurturing, protecting, justifying, tending and finally burying it. Alive.

Then one day it clawed its way out, something terrible.

Something that had only one goal. To take a life.

Armand Gamache found murderers by following the trail of rancid emotions.

Beside him Beauvoir squirmed. Not, Gamache thought, because he was impatient. Not yet anyway. But because the sofa seemed to have found a life of its own and was sending out tiny spikes.

Hazel opened her eyes and looked at him, smiling a little in thanks, he thought, for not interfering.

Upstairs they heard a thump.

'My daughter, Sophie. She's visiting from university.'

'She was at the séance last night, I believe,' said Gamache.

'It was stupid, stupid.' Hazel hit the arm of her chair with her fist. 'I knew better.'

'Then why did you go?'

'I didn't go to the first one, and tried to stop Madeleine—'

'The first one?' Beauvoir sat up and actually forgot that a million little pins were sticking into his bottom.

'Yes, didn't you know?'

Gamache was always amazed and a little disconcerted that people seemed to think they knew everything immediately.

'Tell us, please.'

'There was another séance on Friday night. Good Friday. At the bistro.'

'And Madame Favreau was at that?'

'Along with a bunch of other people. Nothing much happened though so they decided to try another. This time at that place.'

Gamache wondered whether Hazel Smyth deliberately didn't name the old Hadley house, like actors who call *Macbeth* 'the Scottish Play.'

'Do they do many séances in Three Pines?' Gamache asked.

'Never before as far as I know.'

'So why two in one weekend?'

'It was that woman's fault.' As she spoke a chunk fell from her facade and he glimpsed something inside. Not sorrow, not loss.

Rage.

'Who, madame?' Gamache asked, though he knew the answer.

The needles stuck deeper into Beauvoir's bottom and were heading forward.

'Why are you here?' Hazel asked. 'Was Madeleine murdered?'

'Who are you talking about? What woman?' Gamache repeated firmly.

'That witch. Jeanne Chauvet.'

All roads lead back to her, thought Gamache. But where was she?

CHAPTER 15

Armand Gamache opened the door to Madeleine Favreau's bedroom. He knew this was as close as he would ever come to meeting the woman.

'So, was Madeleine murdered?'

The words came along the upstairs hallway and met them at the bedroom door.

'You must be Sophie,' said Beauvoir, walking toward the young woman who'd spoken, her long dark hair moist from a recent shower. Even a few paces away he could smell the fruity, fresh fragrance of the shampoo.

'Good guess.' She smiled fully at Beauvoir and cocked her head to one side, extending her hand. Sophie Smyth was slim and dressed in a white terrycloth robe. Beauvoir wondered if the young woman knew the effect this had.

He smiled back and thought she probably did.

'Now, you were asking about murder.' Beauvoir looked thoughtful, as though he was seriously contemplating her question. 'Do you have many dangerous thoughts?'

She laughed as though he'd said something both riotous and clever and pushed him playfully.

Gamache slipped into Madeleine's room, leaving Jean Guy Beauvoir to work his dubious magic.

The bedroom smelled slightly of perfume, or more likely an eau de toilette. Something light and sophisticated. Not the fulsome, heady aroma of young women that he'd caught in the hallway.

He turned around, taking it in. The room was small and bright, even in the waning sun. Slight white curtains framed the window and were meant to obscure, not block, the light. The room was painted a clean, refreshing white and the bedspread was chenille, with its telltale bumps. The bed was a double—Gamache doubted larger would have fitted—and brass. It was a good antique and as he walked by it he allowed his large hand to drag along the cool metal. Lamps stood on the bedside tables, a stack of books and magazines on one, an alarm clock on the other. The digital clock said 4:19 p.m. He pulled a hanky from his pocket and pressed the alarm button. It flashed to 7 a.m.

In her closet hung rows of dresses and skirts and blouses. Most size 12, one a size 10. In the honey pine chest of drawers the top one contained items of underwear, clean but not folded. Next to those were bras and socks. In other drawers were some sweaters and a few T-shirts though it was clear she hadn't yet made the switch from winter to summer. And wouldn't now.

'So,' Beauvoir leaned against the hallway wall, 'tell me about last night.'

'What do you want to know?' Sophie leaned as well, about a foot from him. He felt uncomfortable, his personal space violated. Still, he knew he'd asked for it. And it was better than that sofa with its pricks.

'Well, why did you go to the séance?'

'Are you kidding? Three days here, in the middle of nowhere with two old women? Had they said we were going to swim in boiling oil I'd have gone.'

Beauvoir laughed.

'I'd actually been looking forward to coming home. You know, like, with laundry and stuff. And Mom always makes me my favorite food. But, God, after a few hours, enough already.'

'What was Madeleine like?'

'When, this weekend or always?'

'Was there a difference?'

'When she first came here she was nice, I guess. I was only here for about a year then went to university. Only saw them on holidays and in the summer after that. I liked her at first.'

'At first?'

'She changed.' Sophie turned from her side and leaned her back against the wall, her chest and hips thrust out, and stared at the blank wall opposite. Beauvoir was quiet. Waiting. He knew there was more and he suspected she wanted to tell him.

'Not as nice this time. I don't know.' She looked down, her hair falling in front of her face so that Beauvoir could no longer see her expression. She mumbled something.

'Pardon?'

'I'm not sorry she's dead,' Sophie said into her hands. 'She took things.'

'Like what? Jewelry, money?'

'No, not those things. Other things.'

Beauvoir stared at Sophie's hair then lowered his gaze to her hands. One clasped the other as though she needed to be held and no one else was offering.

Gamache picked up the books on Madeleine's bedside table. English and French. Biographies, a history of Europe after World War II, and a work of literary fiction by a well-known Canadian. An eclectic taste.

Then he shoved his long arm between box-spring and mattress, sweeping it up and down. In his experience, if people were going to have books, or magazines, that embarrassed them, this was where they were hidden.

The next hiding place was less for 'hiding' and more for simple privacy. The drawer in the bedside table. Opening it up he found a book there.

Now why didn't she keep it with the rest? Was it a secret? It looked harmless enough.

Picking it up he looked at the cover photo of a smiling

elderly woman in tweeds and long, exuberant necklaces. In one eloquent hand she held a cocktail. *Paul Hiebert's Sarah Binks*, the cover said. He flipped it open and read at random. Then he sat on the side of the bed and read more.

Five minutes later he was still reading and smiling. At times laughing out loud. He looked around guiltily, then closed the book and slipped it into his pocket.

After a few minutes he'd completed his search, ending up at the dresser by the door. Madeleine kept a few framed photographs there. He picked one up and saw Hazel with another woman. She was slim with very short dark hair and gleaming brown eyes. Doe eyes, made larger by the haircut. Her smile was full and without artifice or agenda. Hazel was also relaxed and smiling.

They looked natural together. Hazel calm and content and the other woman radiant.

At last Armand Gamache had met Madeleine Favreau.

'Sad house,' said Beauvoir, looking in the rearview mirror. 'Was it ever happy, do you think?'

'I think it was a very happy house once,' said Gamache.

Beauvoir told the chief about his conversation with Sophie. Gamache listened then looked out the window, seeing only the odd light in the distance. Night fell as they bumped back to Montreal.

'What was your impression?' Gamache asked.

'I think Madeleine Favreau squeezed Sophie out of her own home. Not on purpose, maybe, but I think there wasn't enough room for her. There's barely room in there to move and the addition of Madeleine was too much. Something had to give.'

'Something had to go,' said Gamache.

'Sophie.'

Gamache nodded into the darkness and thought about a love so all-consuming it ate up and spat out Hazel's own daughter. How would that daughter feel?

'What did you find?' Beauvoir asked.

Gamache described the room.

'But no ephedra?'

'None. Not in her room, not in the bathroom.'

'What do you think?'

Gamache picked up his cell phone and dialed. 'I think Madeleine didn't take the ephedra herself. She was given the dose.'

'Enough to kill.'

'Enough to murder.'

CHAPTER 16

'Hi, Dad.' Daniel's harried voice came through the phone. 'Where's her bunny? We can't sit on the plane for seven hours without the bunny. And the gar.'

'When're you heading to the airport?' Gamache asked, looking at the time on the Volvo console.

Five twenty.

'We should've left half an hour ago. Florence's gar is missing.'

This made perfect sense to the Chief Inspector. Florence's other grandfather, Papa Grégoire, had given her a yellow pacifier which she loved. Papa Grégoire had said in passing that Florence sucked on it the way he used to suck on cigars. Florence heard and it became her 'gar.' Her most precious possession. No gar, no flight.

Gamache wished he'd thought of hiding it.

'What, honey?' Daniel's voice, off the mouthpiece, called. 'Oh, great. Dad, we found them. Gotta go. Love you.'

'I love you too, Daniel.'

The line went dead.

'Want me to drive to the airport?' Beauvoir asked.

Gamache looked at the time again. Their flight to Paris was at seven thirty. Two hours.

'No, it's all right. Too late. *Merci.*'

Beauvoir was glad he asked, and even happier the chief had said no. A small blossom of satisfaction opened in his chest. Daniel was gone. The chief was all his again.

Despond not, though times be bale,
And baleful be,
Though winds blow stout—

Odile stared at the bags of organic cereal on the shelves, for inspiration. 'Though winds blow stout,' she repeated, stuck. She had to find something that rhymed with 'gale.'

'Pale? Pail? Shale? Though winds blow stout like a great big whale?' said Odile, hopefully. But no, it was close, but not quite right.

All day in the store that she and Gilles ran in St-Rémy she'd been inspired to write. It had flooded out of her so that now the counter was awash with her works, scribbled on the backs of receipts and empty brown paper bags. Most, she felt sure, were good enough to be published. She'd type them up and send them off to the *Hog Breeder's Digest*. They almost always accepted her poems, often without change. The muse wasn't always so generous, but today Odile found her heart lighter than it had been in months.

All day people had visited the shop, most wanting a small purchase and a lot of information, which Odile was happy to supply, after being prodded. Wouldn't do to appear too anxious. Or pleased.

'You were there, dear?'

'It must have been horrible.'

'Poor Monsieur Béliveau. He was quite in love with her. And his wife barely two years gone.'

'Was she really scared to death?'

That was the one memory Odile didn't want to revisit. Madeleine frozen in a scream, as though she'd seen something so horrible it had turned her to stone, like the whatever it was from those myths, the head with the snakes. It had never seemed that scary to Odile, whose monsters took human shape.

Yes, Madeleine had been scared to death and it served her right for all the terror she'd visited upon Odile in the last few months. But now the terror was gone, like a storm blown over.

A storm. Odile smiled and thanked her muse for coming through again.

> *Though winds blow stout, a hurricane,*
> *What's that, what's that to you and me.*

It was past five and time to lock up. A good day's work.

Chief Inspector Gamache called Agent Lemieux, still at the B & B.

'She's not back yet, Chief. But Gabri is.'

'Pass the phone to him, please.'

After a pause the familiar voice came on. '*Salut, patron.*'

'*Salut,* Gabri. Did Madame Chauvet arrive by car?'

'No, no she just materialized. Of course she arrived by car. How else does anyone get here?'

'Is her car still there?'

'Ah, good question.' Gamache could hear Gabri carrying the phone out the door and presumably onto the veranda. '*Oui, c'est ici.* A little green Echo.'

'So she couldn't have gone far,' said Gamache.

'Do you want me to open the door to her room? I can pretend I'm cleaning. I have the key with me now,' Gamache heard tinkling as the key was lifted from its peg, 'and I'm walking down the corridor.'

'Could you give it to Agent Lemieux, please? He should be the one to open the door.'

'Fine.' Gamache could feel Gabri's annoyance. A moment later Lemieux spoke.

'I've unlocked the door, Chief.' There was an agonizing pause while Agent Lemieux stepped into the room and put on the light. 'Nothing. Room's empty. So's the bathroom. Want me to search the drawers?'

'No, that's going too far. I just wanted to make sure she wasn't there.'

'Dead? I wondered too, but she isn't.'

Gamache asked to speak to Gabri again.

'*Patron,* we might need rooms for tomorrow night.'

'For how long?'

'Until the case is over.'

'Suppose you don't solve it? Will you stay forever?'

Gamache remembered the elegant inviting bedrooms with their soft pillows and crisp linens and beds so high they needed little step stools to reach. The bedside tables with books and magazines and water. The lovely bathrooms with old tiling and new plumbing.

'If you made eggs Florentine every morning, I would,' Gamache said.

'You're an unreasonable man,' said Gabri, 'but I like you. And don't worry about rooms, we have plenty.'

'Even over the Easter break? You're not full?'

'Full? No one knows about us, and I hope to keep it that way,' snorted Gabri.

Gamache hung up after asking Gabri to call when Jeanne Chauvet returned and telling Lemieux to go home for the night. Looking out the window at the other cars whizzing along the autoroute into Montreal, Gamache wondered.

Where was the psychic?

He always secretly hoped a voice would whisper some answers, though he didn't know what he'd do if he started hearing voices.

He gave it a moment and when no voice answered, he picked up the phone and made another call.

'*Bonjour*, Superintendent. Still at work?'

'Just leaving. What've you got, Armand?'

'This was murder.'

'Now, is that a feeling you're getting or is there an actual fact in the case?'

Gamache smiled. His old friend knew him well and like Beauvoir had a certain distrust of Gamache's 'feelings.'

'Actually, my spirit guide told me.'

There was a pause on the other end then Gamache laughed.

'That's a joke, Michel. *Une blague*. This time there's an actual fact. Ephedra.'

'As I remember I told you about the ephedra.'

'True, but there was no ephedra in her bedroom or bath-room or anywhere reasonable she might have put it. All the evidence says this was a woman who didn't feel she needed to lose weight. Had no eating disorder that would lead her to use a known dangerous drug. No obsession with weight and diets. No books or magazines on the subject. Nothing.'

'You think someone gave her the ephedra.'

'I do. I'm taking this on as a murder investigation.'

'I agree. I'm sorry to have taken you away from your holiday, though. Will you get back in time to see Daniel before he goes?'

'No, he's on his way to the airport now.'

'Armand, I'm sorry.'

'Not your fault,' said Gamache, though Brébeuf, who knew him so well, could hear the regret. 'Give my love to Catherine.'

'I will.'

Hanging up, Gamache felt relief. For a few months now, maybe longer, he'd sensed a change in his friend, as though a film had descended, come between them. Something had obscured the intimacy they'd always had. It was nothing obvious, and Gamache had even wondered if he was imag-ining it, had asked Reine-Marie about it after a dinner with the Brébeufs.

'It's nothing I can put my finger on,' he'd struggled to explain. 'Just a—'

'Feeling?' she'd smiled. She trusted his feelings.

'Perhaps slightly more than that. His tone is different, his eyes seem harder. And sometimes he says things that seem intentionally insulting.'

'Like that comment about Quebecers who move to Paris, thinking they're better than others.'

'You heard that too. He knows Daniel's moved there. Was that a dig?' If so, it was just one of many from Michel lately. Why?

He'd searched his memory and couldn't come up with any reason Michel might have for hurting him. He couldn't remember doing anything to bring this on.

'He loves you, Armand. Just give him space. Catherine says they're worried about their son's marriage. They've separated.'

'Michel didn't tell me,' said Gamache, surprised that that hurt. He thought they told each other everything. He wondered whether maybe he should be more circumspect himself, but caught that instinct. How easy it is, he thought, to retaliate. He'd give Michel as much space and time as he needed, and let him take out some of his frustration on him. It was natural to lash out at people close by.

Michel was worried about his son. Of course it would be something like that. It couldn't possibly be about him, about their friendship.

But now, hanging up the phone, Gamache smiled. Michel had sounded like his old self. His old buoyancy was back. Whatever had come between them was gone.

Michel Brébeuf hung up the phone and stared at the wall, smiling.

There it was. Brébeuf had the answer to the question that had tormented him for months. How? How was he supposed to bring down a contented man?

Now Michel Brébeuf knew.

CHAPTER 17

Agent Yvette Nichol woke up early the next morning, too excited to sleep. Finally, it was here. The day she'd longed for. When Gamache would finally see what she was made of.

She looked at herself in the mirror. Short, reddish hair, brown eyes, skin with purple marks where she'd picked at it. Though she was slim her face always seemed a little pudgy, like a balloon with hair.

She sucked in her cheeks, biting them between her molars. Better, though she couldn't go through life like that.

She'd gotten her father's features and her mother's personality. She'd always been told that, though she'd never much liked her mother and wondered whether her aunts and uncles said it to annoy her. Her mother had died suddenly, one day there and gone the next.

Her mother had always been an outsider. Tolerated by her father's extended family of babbling aunts and uncles, but never loved. Or respected. Or accepted. She'd tried, Nichol knew. Taking on the petty prejudices and opinions of the Nickolevs. But they'd only laughed at her, and changed their opinions.

She was pathetic. Always striving to fit in, to get the affection of people who'd never, ever give it, and despised her for trying.

'You're just like your mother.' The heavily accented words lay leaden in Yvette Nichol's head. It was, perhaps, the only French her aunts and uncles spoke. Memorized as one might memorize a swear word. Fuck. Shit. You're just like your mother. Hell.

No, it was her father she loved. And he loved her. And protected her from the swarm of accents and smells and insults in her own home.

'Don't put any make-up on.' His voice penetrated the bathroom door. She smiled. He clearly felt she was beautiful enough.

'You'll look younger without it. More vulnerable.'

'Dad, I'm a Sûreté officer. With homicide. I don't want to look vulnerable.'

He was forever trying to get her to use tricks so people would like her. But she knew tricks were useless. People wouldn't like her. They never did.

Her boss had called yesterday, interrupting Easter lunch with the relatives. All going on about how it was better in Romania or Yugoslavia or the Czech Republic. Speaking in their own languages then making a to-do when she didn't understand. But she did understand, enough to know they asked her father every year why she never painted eggs or baked the special bread. Always finding fault. No one had commented on her new haircut or new clothes or asked about her job. She was an agent with the Sûreté du Québec, for God's sake. The only successful one in the entire pathetic family. And could they ask about that? No. Had she been a goddamned painted egg they'd have shown more interest.

She'd run down the hallway with the phone and ducked into her bedroom, so her boss wouldn't hear the hilarity at her expense, the cackling that passed as laughter.

'Do you remember what we talked about a few months ago?'

'About the Arnot case?'

'Yes, but you must never mention that name again. Understand?'

'Yes sir.' He treated her like a child.

'A case has come up. It's not certain it's murder, but if it is you'll be on the team. I've made sure of it. It's time. Are you sure you can do it, Agent Nichol? If not, you need to tell me now. There's too much at stake.'

'I can do it.'

And she'd believed it when she'd said it. Yesterday. But suddenly it was today. It was murder. It was time.

And she was scared to death. In less than two hours she'd be in Three Pines with the team. But while they tried to find a murderer, she'd try to find a traitor to the Sûreté. No, not find. Bring to justice.

Agent Yvette Nichol liked secrets. She liked gathering other people's and she liked having her own. She put them all in her own secret garden, built a wall around them, kept them alive, thriving and growing.

She was good at keeping secrets. And she wondered whether maybe her boss had chosen her because of that. But she suspected the reason was more mundane. He'd chosen her because she was already despised.

'You can do this,' she said to the strange young woman in the mirror. Fear had suddenly made her ugly. 'You can do it,' she said with more conviction. 'You're brilliant, courageous, beautiful.'

She raised her lipstick to her lips with an unsteady hand. Lowering it for a moment she looked sternly at the girl in the mirror.

'Don't fuck this up.'

Clasping her wrist with her other hand she guided the bright red drug store hue over her lips, as though her head was an Easter egg and she was about to paint it. She'd make her relatives proud, after all.

Agent Isabelle Lacoste stood in the clear morning light on the road outside the old Hadley house staring at the buckled and heaved walk. It looked as though something was trying to tear itself from the earth.

Her courage had finally found its limits. After more than five years with Chief Inspector Gamache on homicide, facing deranged and demented murderers, she had finally been stopped by this house. Still, she forced herself to stand there a moment longer, then turned and walked away, her back to the house, feeling it watching her. She picked up speed until she was sprinting to her car.

She took a deep breath and turned to stare again at the house. She needed to go in. But how? Alone wasn't any good; she knew she'd never make it past the threshold alone. She needed company. Looking down into the village, to the smoke drifting from chimneys, to the lights in the homes, imagining people just sitting down for their first cup of coffee and warm toast and jam, she wondered whom she'd pick. It was a strangely powerful feeling, and she wondered if this was how judges had felt when Canada still had the death penalty.

Then her gaze fell on one home in particular. And she realized then that there had never been much doubt whom she'd pick.

'I'll get it,' Clara called from her studio. She'd risen early hoping in the fresh morning light she'd see what Peter had seen a few days ago. The flaw in the work. The colors that were off. The wrong shade of blue perhaps? Or green? Should it be viridian green instead of celadon? She'd deliberately stayed away from Marian Blue, but maybe that was the mistake.

She had just a week now to complete the painting before Denis Fortin arrived.

Time was running out. And something was wrong with the work and she didn't know what. She sat on the stool, sipping her strong morning coffee, eating a Montreal bagel, hoping the spring sun would tell her.

But it was silent.

Dear God, what am I going to do?

Just then someone knocked on the door. She wondered whether that was God, but thought he probably didn't knock.

'No, you're working,' called Peter from the kitchen, glancing at the clock. Just after seven. 'I'll get it.'

He'd felt horrible about what he'd said about Clara's work. He'd since tried to tell her he'd over-reacted. There was nothing wrong with it. Just the opposite. But she'd thought he'd been condescending then. It would never occur to her that he'd lied the first time. That her painting was brilliant. It was luminous and extraordinary and all the words he dreamed would be applied to his own works.

True, gallery owners and decorators loved his paintings. He took an object from life, a twig say, and got in so close it was unrecognizable, abstract. For some reason the idea of obscuring the truth appealed to him. Critics used words like complex and deep and riveting. And all that had been enough, until he'd seen Clara's painting. Now he longed for someone, just one person, to look at his works and call them 'luminous.'

Peter hoped Clara wouldn't change a thing in this painting. And he hoped she would.

Now he strolled to the door, opening it to reveal Agent Isabelle Lacoste.

'*Bonjour*,' she smiled.

'Is it God?' Clara called from her studio.

Peter looked at Lacoste who shook her head apologetically.

'No, not God, honey. Sorry.'

Clara appeared wiping her hands on a rag and smiled warmly. 'Hello, Agent Lacoste. Haven't seen you in a while. Would you like a coffee?'

Isabelle Lacoste really wanted a coffee. Their home smelled of fresh brew and toasted bagel and a warm fire on this chilly spring morning. She wanted to sit and talk to these welcoming people, warming her hands on a mug. And not go back to the house. And she could, she knew. No one on the homicide team knew she was there. Her purpose was deeply personal, a private little ritual.

'I need your help,' she said to Clara, who raised her eyebrows in surprise. And lowered them when she heard what Isabelle Lacoste wanted.

Myrna Landers was humming to herself and grinding coffee to press into her Bodum. Bacon was frying and two brown eggs sat on her wooden kitchen counter, ready to be broken into the frying pan. She didn't often have more than toast and coffee but every now and then she set her face for a full breakfast. She'd heard someone say once that all the English secretly crave is breakfast three times a day. And for herself she knew it to be true. She could live on a diet of bacon, eggs, croissants, sausages, pancakes and maple syrup, porridge and rich, brown sugar. Fresh-squeezed orange juice and strong coffee. Of course, she'd be dead in a month.

Dead.

Myrna's spatula hovered over the bacon she'd been prodding. It spat at her hand but she didn't react. She was back in that dreadful room on that dreadful night. Turning Madeleine over.

'God, that smells good,' came a familiar voice from the other end of the loft. Myrna brought herself back and turned to see Clara and another woman standing there, taking off their muddy boots. The other woman was looking around in amazement.

'*C'est magnifique*,' said Lacoste, wide-eyed. Now all she wanted was to sit at the long refectory table, eat bacon and eggs and never leave. She took in the whole room. Exposed wood beams, darkened with age, ran above their heads. The four walls were brick, almost a rose color, with bold, striking abstracts on the walls, broken only by bookcases stuffed full and large mullioned windows. Worn armchairs sat on either side of the wood stove in the center of the room, with a large sofa facing it. The floors were wide-plank honey pine. Two doors led, Lacoste suspected, into a bedroom and a bathroom.

She was at home. Lacoste suddenly wanted to take Clara's hand. Her home was here. In this loft. But it was also with these women.

'*Bonjour.*' The large, black woman in a caftan was walking toward her, arms outstretched and a smile on her lovely face. '*C'est Agent Lacoste, n'est-ce pas?*'

'*Oui.*' Lacoste gave and received kisses on each cheek.

Then Myrna turned and exchanged hugs and kisses with Clara.

'Come for breakfast? There's plenty. I can put on more. What is it?'

She could see the strain in Clara's face.

'Agent Lacoste needs our help.'

'What can I do?' Myrna looked at the young woman, simply and elegantly dressed, like most young Québécoises. Myrna felt like a house next to her. A comfortable and happy home.

Lacoste told her, feeling as though her very words were soiling this wonderful place. When she'd finished Myrna stood very still and closed her eyes, and when she opened them she spoke.

'Of course we'll help, child.'

Ten minutes later, the bacon off the element, the kettle un-plugged and Myrna fully dressed, the three women walked slowly through the gently stirring village. A slight mist hung over the pond and clung to the hills.

'I remember when your neighbor died,' Lacoste said to Clara, 'you did a ritual.'

Myrna nodded. She remembered walking through Three Pines with a stick of smoking sage and sweetgrass. It was meant to invite joy back into a place burned by the brutal act of murder. It had worked.

'An old pagan ritual from a time when pagan meant peasant and peasant meant worker and being a worker was a significant thing,' said Myrna.

Agent Isabelle Lacoste was silent. She hung her head, looking down at her rubber boots as they squelched into the muddy road. She loved it here. Nowhere else could she walk in the very middle of a road and trust no one would run her down. She could smell the earth and the sweet pine forest on either side of them.

'Was Madeleine murdered?' Clara asked. 'Is that why you want to do this?'

'Yes, she was.'

Myrna and Clara stopped.

'I don't believe it,' said Myrna.

'Poor Madeleine,' said Clara. 'Poor Hazel. She does so much for others and now this.'

If kind acts could protect us from tragedy, thought Lacoste, the world would be a kinder place. Enlightened self-interest, perhaps, but at least enlightened. Is that what I'm about now? Trying to buy favor? Trying to prove how kind I am to whatever power decides life and death and hands out rewards?

The three women looked once more at their destination, rising over the village. Goddamned Hadley house, thought Clara as they trudged forward. Taken another life.

She hoped it was satisfied, hoped it was full. She was glad she hadn't had breakfast yet and hoped she didn't smell of bacon and eggs.

'Why do you do this?' Myrna asked Lacoste, quietly.

'Because I think it's possible the . . .' She stopped and tried again. 'Because you never know . . .'

Myrna turned and took her hand. Agent Lacoste wasn't used to suspects and witnesses holding her hand, but she didn't pull back.

'It's all right, child. Look at us. We're two old crones, Clara and I. We lit a fucking great pole of sage and sweet-grass and fumigated the village for evil spirits. I think we might understand.'

Isabelle Lacoste laughed. All her adult life she'd been ashamed of her beliefs. She'd been raised a Catholic, but one cold, dreary morning while looking at a purple stain on the asphalt where a young man had died in a hit and run she'd closed her eyes and spoken to the dead man.

Told him he was not forgotten. Never forgotten. She'd find out who did this to him.

That had been her first. It had seemed innocent enough, but another sort of instinct had kicked in. It had told her to be careful. Not of the dead, but of the living. And when she was caught by a colleague her fears had proved well founded. She'd been mocked and ridiculed mercilessly. She'd been hounded through the halls of the Sûreté, laughed and sneered at for communicating with spirits.

Just as she was about to quit, when she actually had the letter in hand and was waiting outside her supervisor's office, the door opened and out came Chief Inspector Gamache. Everyone knew him, of course. Even without the notoriety of the Arnot case, he was famous.

He'd looked at her and smiled. Then he did the most extraordinary thing. He put out his large hand, introduced himself and said, 'I'd consider it a privilege, Agent Lacoste, if you'd come and work with me.'

She'd thought he was kidding. His eyes never left her.

'Please say yes.'

And she had.

She suspected Chief Inspector Gamache knew that at each and every homicide scene, when the activity subsided, the teams had gone home and the air had closed back in around the place, Isabelle Lacoste was still there.

Speaking to the dead. Reassuring them Chief Inspector Gamache and his team were on the case. They would not be forgotten.

Now, standing in the fresh, gentle light, holding Myrna's rough hands and looking into Clara's warm blue eyes, she let her guard down.

'I think Madeleine Favreau's spirit is still there.' She looked over to the desolate house on the hill. 'Waiting for us to free it. I want her to know we're trying and we won't forget her.'

'It's a sacred thing you do,' said Myrna, squeezing her hands. 'Thank you for asking us to help.'

Isabelle Lacoste wondered if they'd be thanking her in a few minutes. Finally the three women stood shoulder to shoulder in front of the old Hadley house.

'Come on,' said Clara. 'It's not going to get easier.'

She plunged down the uneven walkway to the front door and tried the knob.

'It's locked,' she said, images of returning to Myrna's

and feasting on maple-cured bacon and eggs over easy and warm toast and home-made marmalade rising in her mind. They'd tried, they'd done their best, no one could—

'I have the key,' said Lacoste.

Damn.

At that same moment Armand Gamache and Jean Guy Beauvoir were entering the Cowansville Hospital. A few people were lounging outside having cigarettes, one dragging an oxygen tank behind her. The two men gave her a wide berth.

'What took you so long?'

Agent Yvette Nichol stood in the doorway of the gift boutique, her ill-fitting blue pant suit dirty at the cuffs from mud, her hair cut in a pageboy, out of fashion since the 1600s, and wearing lipstick that looked as though someone had taken a potato peeler to her lips.

'Agent Nichol.' Beauvoir nodded. That sullen, sulky face turned his stomach. He knew, just knew, Gamache had made a horrible mistake inviting her on the team. He was damned if he knew why the chief had done it.

But he could guess. It was Gamache's personal mission to help every failing, falling, flawed creature. And not just help, like with a nice letter of recommendation, but actually put them on his team. He'd pick them up and put them on homicide, the most prestigious unit in the Sûreté, working for the most famous detective in Quebec.

Beauvoir himself had been the first.

He'd been so disliked at his detachment in Trois-Rivières, he'd been permanently assigned to the evidence cage. Literally a cage. The only reason he hadn't quit was because he knew his very presence pissed off the bosses. He was full of rage. A cage was probably where he belonged.

Then the Chief Inspector had found him, taken him onto homicide and a few years later promoted him to inspector and his second in command. But Jean Guy Beauvoir never totally left the cage. Instead it had moved inside and in it he kept the worst of his rage, where it couldn't cause damage. And beside that cage sat another, quieter cage. In it, curled up in a corner, was something that frightened him far more than his fury. Beauvoir lived in terror that one day the creature in there would escape.

In that cage he kept his love. And if it ever got out it would go straight to Armand Gamache.

Jean Guy Beauvoir looked over at Agent Nichol and wondered what she kept in her cage. Whatever it was, he hoped it was well locked. The stuff she allowed out was malevolent enough.

They descended to the lowest level of the hospital, into a room that held nothing natural. Not light, not air, which smelled of chemicals, not the furniture, which was aluminum. And not death.

A middle-aged technician matter-of-factly slid Madeleine Favreau from a drawer. He casually unzipped the bag then reeled back.

'Oh, shit,' he shrieked. 'What happened to her?'

Even though they were prepared it still took a moment for the hardened homicide investigators to climb back into their bodies. Gamache was the first to recover, and speak.

'What does it look like to you?'

The technician inched forward, craning his head to the limits of his neck, then peeked inside the bag again.

'Fuck me,' he exhaled. 'I don't know, but I sure don't want to go that way.' He turned to Gamache. 'Murder?'

'Scared to death,' said Nichol, entranced. She couldn't stop staring at that face.

Madeleine Favreau was stuck in a scream. Her eyes bulging, her lips stretched across her teeth, her mouth wide and silent. It was hideous.

What could cause that?

Gamache stared back. Then he took a deep breath.

'When will Dr Harris be in?' he asked. The technician consulted the work schedule.

'Ten,' he said, gruffly, trying to make up for his little shriek earlier.

'*Merci*,' Gamache said and walked out, the other two in his wake along with the stench of formaldehyde.

Myrna, Lacoste and Clara made straight for the stairs. Clara's short legs strained to keep up with Myrna who was hauling herself up two at a time. Clara tried to stay hidden behind Myrna hoping the fiends would find her friend first. Unless they were coming up behind. Clara looked behind and rammed into Myrna, who'd stopped dead in the corridor.

'Had my father seen that,' she said to Clara, 'he'd insist we get married.'

'Nice that there are still some old-fashioned men.'

Myrna had stopped because Agent Lacoste, in the lead, had stopped. Suddenly. Halfway down the corridor.

Clara looked around her protective Myrna and saw Lacoste standing very alert.

Oh, God, she thought. What now?

Slowly Lacoste edged forward. Myrna and Clara edged with her. Then Clara could see it. Yellow strips of tape, scattered on the floor. Yellow strips of tape dangling from the frame of the door.

The police tape had been violated, not simply removed, or even cut. It had been shredded. Something had wanted very badly to get in.

Or to get out.

Through the open doorway Clara could see the dim room. Lying in the center of their chairs, on the salt circle, was a tiny bird, a robin.

Dead.

CHAPTER 18

Agent Robert Lemieux shoved more wood into the massive black stove in the center of the old railway station. Around him technicians set up desks and chalk boards, computer terminals and printers. The space was almost unrecognizable as an old station abandoned by the Canadian National Railways. It was even hard to recognize as the current home of the Three Pines Volunteer Fire Department, except for the huge red fire truck. Technicians were carefully removing posters on fire safety and a few celebrating the Governor General's Award for Literature. There, glowering from one of them was their own fire chief, Ruth Zardo, on the occasion of receiving the GG. She looked as though someone had thrown excrement on her.

Inspector Beauvoir had called the night before and ordered him to get to Three Pines early to help set up the space. So far all he'd done was stay out of everyone's way and light the fire. He'd also stopped at the local Tim Horton's in Cowansville and picked up Double Double coffees and boxes of doughnuts.

'Good, you're here.' Inspector Beauvoir marched in, followed by Agent Nichol. Nichol and Lemieux glared at each other.

Try as he might he couldn't think what he'd done to create such hostility in her. He'd tried to be her friend. Those had been Superintendent Brébeuf's orders. To ingratiate himself with everyone. And he had. He was good at it. All his charmed life he'd made friends easily. Except her. And it bugged him. She bugged him, perhaps because she actually showed what she felt and this confused and upset him. She was like a dangerous new species.

He smiled at Nichol now and received a sneer in return.

'Where's the Chief Inspector?' Lemieux asked Beauvoir. Five desks were set in a circle with a conference table in the center. Each desk had its own computer now and the phones were just being hooked up.

'He's with Agent Lacoste. They'll be here soon. Here they are now.' Beauvoir nodded to the door. Chief Inspector Gamache, in his field coat and tweed cap, was walking across the room, Agent Lacoste behind him.

'We have a problem,' said Gamache after nodding to Lemieux and removing his cap. 'Sit down please.'

The team assembled around the conference table. The technicians, all familiar with Gamache, tried to keep their noise level down.

'Agent Lacoste?' Gamache hadn't bothered to take off his coat, and now Beauvoir was alert to something serious. Isabelle Lacoste, also still in her coat and rubber boots, took off her light gloves and spread her hands on the table in front of her.

'Someone's broken into the room at the old Hadley house.'

'The crime scene?' asked Beauvoir. This almost never happened. Few people were that stupid. Instinctively he looked toward Nichol but dismissed the idea.

'I had my kit with me so I took pictures and fingerprints. As soon as the technicians are ready I'll send these off to the lab, but here, you can see the pictures.'

She handed round her digital camera. It would be far clearer when the images were transferred to their computers, but still it was enough to hush them. Gamache, who'd already seen them, went and had a word with the technicians who changed their priority to the communications.

For a moment even Inspector Beauvoir was speechless.

'The tape wasn't just torn, it was shredded.' He hated

the way his body felt. All numb, and his head felt light as though something had detached itself and was floating above him. He wanted it back, and he clenched his fists harder and harder until his short nails were biting into his palms.

It worked.

'What's that,' said Nichol. 'Looks like someone shit.'

'Agent Nichol,' said Gamache. 'We need constructive, not childish, comments.'

'Well, it does,' said Nichol, looking at Lemieux and Lacoste, who weren't about to help her even if they agreed. And Beauvoir for one did. Sitting on the floor in the center of the chairs was a small dark mound. It looked like a small pile of shit. Was it bear poop? Was that what had shredded the tape? Had a brooding bear found shelter in the old Hadley house?

It made sense.

'It's a bird,' said Lacoste. 'A baby robin.'

Beauvoir was glad he'd kept his mouth shut. Bear. Baby bird. Whatever.

'Poor thing,' said Lemieux and received a withering look from Nichol and a small smile from Gamache.

'This one's ready to go, sir.' A technician signaled from one of the computers. The tech sat down and held out his hand. Lacoste handed him the camera and the fingerprint kit. Within moments the prints had been sent to Montreal and the photos were up on the screen. Soon, one by one, each computer came to life, each with the same disturbing scene, like a ghoulish screen saver. From the hallway a picture of the shredded police tape in the foreground and the tiny bird, dead in the middle of the circle of chairs.

What does that house want? Gamache wondered. Anything that went in alive came out either dead or different.

'*Alors*,' said Beauvoir when they were back around the conference table. 'As you all know, this is now a murder investigation. Let me bring you up to speed.' He reached forward and took one of the large cups, expertly pinning back the plastic lip to sip from, then opened a box of chocolate glaze doughnuts.

Succinctly Inspector Beauvoir related what they knew of the victim and the murder. As Beauvoir described the séance the noise level in the room dropped until there was silence. Gamache looked up and noticed another ring had formed around them, a ring of technicians who'd gravitated to the account as campers might huddle around a fire listening to a ghost story.

'Why did they have a séance?' asked Lemieux.

'A better question is, whose idea was it,' said Nichol, dismissing Lemieux.

'It seems to have been Gabri Dubeau's idea to do the first one at the bistro,' said Beauvoir. 'But we don't know who thought of the old Hadley house.'

'Why do you say it's important to know who first suggested it?' Gamache asked.

'Well, isn't it obvious? If you're going to scare someone to death you don't do it in Disneyland. You choose a place that's already got people scared. The old Hadley house.'

Nichol all but bleated 'duh' into the Chief Inspector's face. There was silence as everyone waited for his reaction. He paused for a moment then nodded.

'You might be right.'

'But she wasn't scared to death,' said Beauvoir, turning on Nichol. Angry for her insubordination and furious at Gamache for allowing it. What was wrong with him? What game was he playing, allowing her to even be on the team? Why did he cut her so much more slack than he would anyone else? Beyond all the other arguments, it just wasn't good for discipline. But seeing the look of disgust on their faces he knew no one else in the room was likely to use Agent Yvette Nichol as a role model. 'If you'd keep your mouth shut and listen you'd know she was poisoned. Right?'

'Ephedra,' said the Chief Inspector. 'The doctor first thought she'd died of a heart attack, but since she was so young he decided to do a blood test. Came back with massive levels of ephedra.'

Nichol crossed her arms over her chest and sat silent.

'I researched ephedra yesterday afternoon,' said Lemieux, taking out his notebook. 'It's not actually a chemical. It's a plant. An herb called *Ephedra dis-ta-chya*.' Lemieux sounded it out slowly and carefully, though no one was likely to correct him. 'It's grown all over the world.'

'Is it like marijuana?' asked Lacoste.

'No, it's not a hallucinogen or relaxant. Just the opposite. It used to be used in Chinese medicine shops as tea for relieving,' he consulted his notes again, 'colds and asthma, but then I guess someone—'

'Don't guess,' said Gamache, quietly.

'I'm sorry.' Lemieux put his head down and flipped rapidly through his notes, back and forth, while the whole team stared. He finally found the scribble. 'A pharmaceutical company named Saltzer realized it worked as a diet supplement. It increases the metabolism, and that burns fat. The market for that was huge, way bigger than as a decongestant or cold remedy. Everyone wants to lose weight.'

'But not everyone needs to,' said Lacoste. 'That's the problem. They created a demand where there shouldn't be one.'

'Are you familiar with ephedra?' Gamache asked.

'Heard of it, but that's all. But I am familiar with issues of body image. Most girls think they're fat, don't they?' She made the mistake of looking at Nichol who shrugged. After all, Lacoste hadn't supported her when she'd made the shit comment, so she was on her own.

'This isn't about body image,' said Beauvoir, trying to bring it back on track.

'Maybe it is,' said Gamache. 'Madeleine Favreau was forty-four, early middle age. A search of her room showed she had no problems with her body, no diet books or weight loss articles, not even any diet drinks or products in the fridge.'

Nichol smiled at Lacoste. Gamache hadn't agreed with her gross generalization.

'We have no reason to think she was taking ephedra to lose weight,' he said.

'Could she have been taking it for a cold?' Lacoste asked, undeterred by the maniacal Nichol.

'It's not sold as a cold remedy any more,' said Lemieux.

'And even if it was, there was none in her room or the bathroom. We'll do another search, but unless she hid it, and she didn't really have reason to, then someone else slipped it to her.'

'Which is why you declared this a murder,' said Beauvoir.

'Which is why I think this might have something to do with body image.'

They looked at him, perplexed, having lost the thread of what he was saying.

'Madeleine Favreau wasn't taking ephedra, but someone was. Someone had bought it, probably for themselves, and then used it on her.'

'But ephedra is banned in Canada. Health Canada pulled it years ago,' said Lemieux. 'It's also banned in the US and Britain.'

'Why?' asked Lacoste.

Agent Lemieux consulted his notes again. He didn't want to make a mistake here. 'There were 155 deaths in the US and more than a thousand incidents reported by doctors. Mostly heart and stroke. And not in the elderly. These were for the most part young and vigorous people. An investigation was launched and it was decided that ephedra certainly burned fat, but it also raised the heart rate and blood pressure.'

'Then a couple athletes died,' said Beauvoir.

'A baseball and a football player, that's right,' agreed Lemieux. 'That was when the baby robin really hit the fan.' Even Gamache smiled. Nichol did not. 'An investigation was launched and it was discovered that ephedra affects the heart, but mostly in people with a pre-existing condition.'

'So it'll raise the heart rate of anyone,' recapped Beauvoir. This was what he craved. Facts. 'But can actually kill people with already damaged hearts. Did Madame Favreau have a damaged heart?'

'No medication in her medicine cabinet,' said Gamache. 'We won't have the coroner's report until later today.'

'I wonder how many people have heard of ephedra?' said Beauvoir. 'I hadn't, but then I don't diet. Presumably most people who diet have heard of it, is that fair to say?' He turned to Lacoste, who thought about it. She dieted every now and then. Like most women she owned a funhouse mirror that one day showed her fat, the next slim.

'I think anyone who diets habitually would know about it,' she said, slowly, trying to figure it out. 'Dieters become obsessed with losing weight and any product that promises to do it without effort would be noticed.'

'So we're looking for a dieter?' asked Nichol, confused.

'But there's a problem,' said Lemieux. 'You can't buy it here. Or in the States.'

'That is a problem,' conceded Gamache.

'Except,' came a voice behind them. The technician who'd downloaded the information was sitting at one of their desks, looking out from behind a flat screen. 'You can order ephedra on-line.' He pointed to the screen in front of him. Getting up, they moved to his station.

There on the screen was a long list of Googled sites, all offering to ship perfectly safe ephedra to anyone desperate and stupid enough to want it.

'Still,' said Armand Gamache, straightening up. 'The ephedra alone wouldn't do it. Once the ephedra was in her body the potential was there, but the murderer needed one more thing. An accessory. The old Hadley house.' To everyone's amazement he turned to Nichol. 'You were right. She was scared to death.'

CHAPTER 19

Clara leaned back and reached for her mug. In front of her were the remains of breakfast. Crumbs. The plate looked so forlorn she popped a couple of slices of bread into the teepee toaster and closed the doors.

She and Myrna had stayed with Agent Lacoste at the old Hadley house while she did whatever she needed to do. Not nearly fast enough in their opinion. Most of the time Clara had stood just inside the room and stared at the little bird, curled on its side, legs up to its chest, not unlike Madeleine, though smaller. And with feathers. Well, maybe not so much like Madeleine. Still, there was a similarity. They were both dead.

But while Clara felt terrible about Madeleine, she carried no guilt. Unlike this little creature. She knew she'd helped kill it. They'd all known there was a bird. In fact, that was why they'd decided to use this particular room, in hopes of maybe saving it.

Had she even tried? No. Instead she'd been terrified the bird would attack out of the shadows. Far from trying to save the bird Clara had hated it. Wanted it to die, or at least go away, or failing that attack someone else.

And now it was here. Dead. A baby. A tiny, frightened robin, which probably fell down the chimney from its nest and only wanted to find its mother and its home again.

Finally Agent Lacoste had been ready. The three women had held hands and stared at the salt circle. And each sent silent thoughts out to Madeleine. While Agent Lacoste had seen only the grotesque shell, Clara and Myrna remembered her alive. It was liberating, seeing Madeleine smiling and laughing. Glowing. Listening and taking everything in with those interested eyes. The living Madeleine became more real. As it should be.

Then Clara thought of the bird, and apologized to it, and promised to do better next time.

It was the most peaceful few moments in the old Hadley house Clara had ever spent. Still, none of them protested when it was time to leave.

Chief Inspector Gamache had been driving by just as they'd left and Agent Lacoste flagged him down. Myrna and Clara said hello then walked back to the loft. While Myrna put the bacon back on, Clara called Peter to tell him where she was.

'Have you seen the paper?' he asked.

'No, we were too busy doing an exorcism.'

'You're at Myrna's? Wait there. I'll be right over.'

Myrna put on more bacon and ground some coffee while Clara set the table and cut the bread for the teepee toaster. By the time Peter arrived breakfast was ready.

'From Sarah's.' He held a paper bag. Clara kissed him and took it.

Croissants.

Twenty minutes later Peter licked his finger and wiped a bit of butter from Clara's cheek. Not even close to her mouth. How does she do it, he marveled. It was like a superpower without purpose.

'I dropped by Monsieur Béliveau's store too,' he said, pouring coffees.

'Is he open?' Myrna asked. 'I didn't notice.'

'As always. He came over for dinner last night, you know,' said Peter, opening some jam jars. One still had the wax on top and he needed to dig it out with a knife. 'Hardly ate anything.'

'Not surprised,' said Myrna. 'I think he loved her.'

The other two nodded. Poor man. To lose two women he

loved within a few years. He'd been so sweet over dinner the night before. Even bringing a pie from Sarah's Boulangerie. But his energy had flagged and within half an hour he just sat there, moving food about on his plate. Peter kept filling his wine glass, and Clara prattled on about getting the garden ready. That was the beauty of friends, she knew. Nothing was expected of Monsieur Béliveau, and he knew it. Sometimes it's just nice not to be alone. He'd left early, right after supper. And he'd seemed a little livelier. Clara and Peter had taken Lucy and walked with Monsieur Béliveau across the village green to his home. On the veranda Clara and Peter had hugged him but offered no easy words of comfort. To do that would be to simply comfort themselves. What Monsieur Béliveau needed was to feel bad. And then he'd feel better.

Now, over breakfast Clara and Myrna told Peter about their morning so far. He listened, amazed by their courage to go back into that house and astonished by their stupidity. Did they really believe Madeleine's spirit was hovering around the room and could hear them? Never mind the supposed spirit of a dead bird. And, even more disconcerting, did an officer with the Sûreté believe it? But that reminded him. He reached for the paper he'd brought and opened it.

'Listen to this.'

'Golf scores?' Myrna asked, pouring more coffee and offering some to Clara. Peter was hidden behind *La Journée*, the Montreal paper.

'This is in the city column.' Peter poked his head round the paper to find Myrna pouring cream into her coffee and Clara opening the doors of the toaster to gingerly remove the bread. Giving one piece to Myrna, Clara reached for the marmalade and started speading it thick upon her toast. They were paying absolutely no attention. He ducked back behind the paper with a smile. That would soon change, he knew. He started to read out loud.

'It is a matter of some concern that a senior officer in the Sûreté du Québec is living way beyond his means. According to my sources a man in his position should be making no more than ninety-five thousand dollars. Even that, in my opinion, is far too much. Still, even on that overly generous salary his lifestyle exceeds his apparent income. Wearing high-end clothing, mostly from England. Taking vacations in France. Living in style in Outremont. And, just recently, buying a Volvo.'

Peter slowly lowered the paper to see a tableau. Myrna and Clara were staring at him, their eyes almost as wide as their mouths. Toast arrested halfway up.

He lifted the paper again, to read the last line. The knife thrust. The twist as it struck home.

'And all this since the sad case of Superintendent Pierre Arnot. What did he have to do to earn this money?'

Gabri watched as his guest sipped the last of her herbal tea and replaced the cup. He was peeking from the kitchen side of the swinging door, and through the crack he could see her getting up.

Jeanne Chauvet had returned to the B & B after dinner the night before. Gabri had smiled, given her the key to her room and discreetly called Gamache at home.

'She's back,' he'd whispered.

'*Pardon?*'

'She's back,' he'd said, with more vigor.

'Who is this?'

'Oh, for Christ's sake, the witch is back,' Gabri yelled into the phone.

'Gabri?'

'No, Glinda. Of course it's me. She came back five minutes ago. What should I do?'

'Nothing, *patron*. Not tonight, but make sure she doesn't leave until I get there tomorrow. *Merci.*'

'When will you be here? How do I stop her? *Allô? Gamache, allô?*'

He'd stared at the ceiling all night, trying to figure out how to contain the little woman downstairs. And now the moment had come. She was rising from the table.

Was this mousy little woman a murderer? He thought she probably was. She was certainly responsible for that séance, and that séance had killed Madeleine. Had almost killed him, come to that. Was that her intention? Was this awful woman trying to kill him? Was he the real target? But who'd want him dead?

Suddenly a very long list appeared, from the little girl he'd tormented in grade two to the friends whose recipes he'd stolen, to the deliberately hurtful remarks he'd made about people behind their backs but within earshot. So clever and cutting. People had laughed and Gabri had eaten it up and had tried not to notice the look of pain, of confusion and hurt, on the faces of people who'd considered him a friend.

Wasn't that why he and Olivier had decided to move here? Partly to get away from the mountain of crap they'd created in their old lives, but mostly to live in a place where kindness trumped cleverness.

He'd begun again here, but had his old life found him? Had one of those old fags found him and hired this witch to get him?

Yes, it was the only reasonable explanation. If she didn't kill him now, and she might not what with Gamache here, she would at the very least curse him. Make something wither and fall off. He hoped it wasn't his hair.

Jeanne looked around the dining room then slowly walked down the corridor to her room.

Is she climbing out the window at the far end? Gabri wondered. Just the sort of tricky thing she was likely to do. He opened the door a little wider and poked his head out. The cat escaped and walked nonchalantly into the dining room.

'Looking for your mistress, you little shit?' whispered Gabri, now convinced Olivier's damned cat had become Jeanne's familiar. Whatever that was. But Gabri knew it wasn't good. Craning his neck to look through the crack in the door he saw the coast was clear. He squeezed his bulk through the narrowest possible opening in the door, which was actually wide open by the time he was halfway through, then tiptoeing along he peeked down the corridor. The window was open, but the screen was still in place.

Gabri decided the most strategic position would be the front desk. After about thirty seconds of intense vigilance, he decided maybe he should play free cell on the computer while he waited for either Gamache to arrive or the witch to kill him. No need to be bored. As he moved the mouse a picture popped up on the screen.

Ephedra, it said. Gabri read, considered placing an order, then decided to call Olivier instead.

'I wonder if he's seen it,' Clara said, lowering her toast. She was finally full, if not fed up.

'He looked perfectly relaxed when we ran into him this morning,' said Myrna.

'He'd hardly show it, would he?' said Peter, taking Clara's toast.

'What is it with that Arnot case? That was years ago,' said Myrna.

'Five at least,' agreed Peter. He sat up and put his hands on the table in a studied, relaxed manner. He'd once been snapped at by Ruth for being pompous and pedantic. Both unfair, he knew, but still it had stung. Since then he'd been careful not to appear too formal or superior when telling people things they might not know. Like how to cut a tomato properly or hold a newspaper, or giving them information, like the Arnot case.

Peter had read about it at the time. It was all over the news, the cause célèbre for months.

'I remember now.' Myrna turned to Peter. 'You became obsessed with it.'

'I did not become obsessed. It was an important case.'

'It was interesting,' agreed Clara. 'Of course, we didn't know Gamache yet, but everyone had heard of him.'

'He was one of the stars of the Sûreté,' said Myrna.

'Until the Arnot case,' said Peter. 'The defense made Gamache out to be a self-serving hypocrite. Happy to take the honors that went with power but fundamentally weak. Driven by jealousy and pride.'

'That's right,' agreed Myrna, remembering more as she cast her mind back. 'Didn't the defense imply he'd set Arnot up?'

Peter nodded. 'Arnot was a superintendent in the serious crimes squad. At the trial it came out that Arnot had ignored some violent crimes, even murder. Just let it happen.'

'Especially when it involved natives,' said Myrna, nodding.

'I was just about to say that. Eventually, Pierre Arnot had ordered his most trusted officers to actually kill.'

'Why?' Clara asked, trying to remember back that far.

Peter shrugged. 'The notion put forward by papers like this,' he held up his copy of *La Journée*, 'was that Arnot was just allowing the criminals to kill each other instead of innocent people. A community service.'

There was silence in Myrna's loft as the three remembered the shocking revelations. All the more shocking since the Québécois, French and English, had respect, even affection for the Sûreté. Until this. The trial had ended all that.

Peter remembered watching the news. Watching the senior Sûreté officers arriving grim-faced every day. The microphones and cameras thrust into their faces. At first they'd arrived together, a show of unity. But in the end two were cut out of the herd.

Gamache and his immediate superior. A Superintendent someone. The Superintendent had been the only one to publicly stand beside Gamache. It was almost touching to watch the two men growing wearier and more drawn as the revelations and accusations and bitterness increased.

But still Gamache had smiled when asked the same stupid, leading, insulting questions by reporters. He'd been calm, old-fashioned in his courtesy. Even when he'd been accused of disloyalty. Even when, finally, he'd been accused of being an accomplice. Of knowing about the murders and giving his tacit approval. After all, Arnot had implied, how could the head of homicide not have known?

'It was awful,' said Clara. 'Like watching the Hinden-burg crash over and over in slow motion. Something noble had been wrecked.'

Peter wondered whether Clara was thinking of Gamache or the Sûreté itself.

'The papers were sure torn,' he said. 'Most supported Gamache, but some called for his resignation.'

'That paper,' Myrna jutted her head toward *La Journée*, folded next to Peter, 'ran editorials saying Gamache should be in the same cell as Arnot. Let the two kill each other.'

'What happened to Arnot and the others?' Clara asked.

'In some penitentiary somewhere. It's a wonder they haven't been killed by the inmates yet.'

'I bet that asshole Arnot is running the place,' said Myrna. She balled up her napkin and threw it with as much force as a paper napkin could achieve onto the table. The other two stared at her, surprised by her sudden anger.

'What is it?' asked Clara.

'Don't you get it? We've just talked about that case as though it was some episode on a TV drama. It was real. That man Arnot killed people. Killed the very people he was supposed to help. Why? Because they were natives, full of despair and sniff. And the one man who put a stop to it, who had the balls to stand up to Arnot and the entire Sûreté hierarchy, they tried to destroy too. Arnot's psychotic, and I don't say that lightly. I know the signs. I've diagnosed and worked with psychotic people for years. Don't you get it?'

She looked at Peter and Clara then leaned over and picked up Peter's paper, slapping it back down on the table, as though punishing it.

'It's not over. The Arnot case is still going on.'

The phone rang and Clara picked it up.

'It's Olivier,' she said, covering the mouthpiece. 'Wow, thanks. I'll pass it along.' Clara hung up and turned to the others. 'Have you ever heard of ephedra?'

CHAPTER 20

Jean Guy Beauvoir handed out the assignments.

Agent Isabelle Lacoste was to look into the life of Madeleine Favreau, Agent Nichol was to go through the list of suppliers of ephedra and find out if any shipped recently to the area, and Robert Lemieux would accompany Inspector Beauvoir and Chief Inspector Gamache.

'But that's not right,' said Nichol, stunned by Beauvoir's mistake in judgment. 'He started looking into epilepsy, or whatever it is.'

'Ephedra,' said Beauvoir. 'Weren't you even listening?'

'Look, it's on the computer, isn't it?'

Beauvoir swung around and glared at Gamache, making sure the boss understood how ridiculous this woman was.

'The point is,' continued Nichol, apparently oblivious of the impression she made, 'he started it, he should finish it.'

'What? Is that a new rule?' asked Beauvoir. 'This isn't a school yard and this isn't a debate. You'll do as you're ordered.'

'Fine. Sir.' Nichol stomped back to her desk, not acknowledging Lemieux's attempt to catch her eye and smile an apology.

After they'd gone and the technicians were busy in another part of the room, Nichol brought out her cell phone. It'd been vibrating all through the meeting and it was all she could do not to answer. But that would have been a disaster.

'*Oui, allô*,' she said and wasn't at all surprised to hear the familiar voice.

'Tell me what's happening,' he said. She did and there was a pause on the other end. 'I don't like this. You should be with Gamache. Did you do something wrong? Did you upset him?'

'Of course not. I even came up with the cause of death. Everyone was saying it was that drug stuff and I said she was scared to death. The chief even agreed and said it.'

'Wait a minute, are you saying you showed him up in front of his entire team?'

'It's not hard.'

'What have I told you? What have I taught you? Don't antagonize him.'

'What? So, I'm supposed to just agree?'

'There's more at stake here than a single case. You know that. Don't fuck up.'

'Stop saying that.'

'Stop fucking up.'

The line went dead.

Armand Gamache nodded to two people sitting at a small round table outside Olivier's Bistro, taking advantage of the fresh spring sun. Given a chance Quebecers stayed out on *terrasses* late into the fall and got back as soon as they could in the spring. Wearing turtleneck sweaters and coats, hats and gloves, they sought the sunshine.

These two were dipping biscotti into their cappuccinos and talking animatedly. The part of the conversation Gamache picked up sounded very much like the tendril of words he'd caught in the wind as they'd walked by the people standing on the village green with their dogs.

The village seemed to have one song today, with a single lyric.

Ephedra.

Gamache stopped and stared hard at Agent Lemieux who had a smile on his face and seemed to be enjoying the pleasant spring day.

'Did you hear that?' Gamache asked. Lemieux cocked his head to one side, listening.

'Is it a robin?'

Inspector Beauvoir shook his head.

'Listen more closely, please,' said Gamache.

Lemieux became very quiet and listened, closing his eyes. He heard the river marauding past. He heard birds, though perhaps not robins. He heard people talking. He heard the word 'ephedra.'

He opened his eyes and stared at Gamache.

'Those two sitting at the bistro table must have something to do with the murder,' he whispered. Then he heard 'ephedra' again. This time from the direction of Monsieur Béliveau's general store.

'Agent, perhaps you can tell me how you did your research yesterday.' Gamache was looking at him quite sternly.

'Well, I was waiting for the psychic to return and noticed a computer on the desk, so I looked it up.'

'Using Gabri's computer.'

'Yes.'

'And did you close the sites you looked at?' Inspector Beauvoir asked.

'I'm sure I did.'

'I'd never use ephedra, far too dangerous,' a villager was saying to her companion as they walked by the men, pausing to smile at Gamache, who raised his hat to them. 'But I hear Gabri used to use it, or was it Olivier? And frankly, Myrna could use a pill or two.'

Gamache replaced his cap and stared at Lemieux. It was one of the most disconcerting looks he'd ever had. Part demanding and part searching.

'Maybe I didn't erase it. I'm sorry. What a fool.' Robert Lemieux dropped his head and shook it. He all but stomped his foot. 'I'm sorry, sir.'

'You do know what this means,' said Beauvoir.

'Yes sir. It means everyone in the village, probably in the county, now knows we're interested in ephedra. They're smart enough to figure out why.'

'It means the murderer knows we know and will certainly dispose of the pills if he hadn't already,' said Gamache. 'This is probably the only ephedra-free community in Quebec now.'

Lemieux lifted his head and let it flop back so that his nose was pointing to the blue sky. 'I'm sorry. You're right. I didn't even think.'

'How could you not think? Well, think now. What do you think we're about?' Beauvoir hissed, trying not to raise his voice for the villagers to hear. 'Someone here is a murderer. Someone here isn't afraid to kill. Do you know what stops most people from killing? Fear. Fear of getting caught. We're dealing with someone who's fearless. Very scary person, Lemieux. And you just handed them a huge advantage.'

Gamache listened with interest, though without agreement. Fear might stop some people from committing murder, but he knew for certain fear was what drove most people to kill. It was what nested below all the other emotions. It was what twisted and turned the other emotions into something sick. It was an alchemist and could turn daylight into night, joy into despair. Fear, once taken root, blocked the sun. And Gamache knew what grew in that darkness. He searched for it every day.

'You're right, you're absolutely right,' said Lemieux. 'I'm sorry.'

He looked squarely at Gamache, who stared back sternly. Then Lemieux saw the slightest softening. Lemieux relaxed. Brébeuf was right. Intentionally leak the ephedra information, get them angry at you, apologize like hell.

Everyone loves a sinner, but none more than Gamache. And why not? After all the sinning he himself had done. After setting up Arnot and almost destroying the Sûreté, of course the great Gamache would love sinners.

Lemieux wondered what it would be like when he himself was head of homicide. Not right away, of course. But Brébeuf would have to reward him. And he'd move up quickly. And when this was over there'd be promotions to be had.

'Be careful,' Gamache said softly and for a terrible instant Lemieux wondered whether Gamache's searching look could actually penetrate the skin. Did he know?

'What do you mean?' he asked.

'You must pay better attention,' said Gamache, still staring at him.

I won't be weak, like him, thought Lemieux. And I won't stop at Chief Inspector.

'We're going to have to cover more ground more quickly,' said Gamache. 'Inspector, I'd like you and Agent Lemieux to split up and interview everyone who witnessed the murder.'

'You?' asked Beauvoir.

'I'll be with Jeanne Chauvet.'

Beauvoir took his chief by the elbow and led him a step or two away from Lemieux.

'I should come along,' said Beauvoir.

'To interview the psychic, Jean Guy? Why?'

'Well.' Beauvoir looked up at the old Hadley house then away. 'It just might be better. That wasn't simply a regular tarot card reading or Ouija board my mother and her friends used to do. Jeanne Chauvet's a witch.'

'And you think she'll conjure evil spirits against me?'

Gamache wasn't smiling, wasn't mocking Beauvoir. He seemed to be genuinely interested to know.

'I don't believe in ghosts,' said Beauvoir. 'I think they're manufactured to serve a purpose.'

'What purpose?'

'My wife talks about angels. She wants to believe in guardian angels, because it makes her feel less afraid, less alone.'

'And evil spirits, are they manufactured too?'

'I think so. By parents and the church, so that we'll be afraid and do as we're told.'

'So evil spirits create fear and angels calm it,' said Gamache, thinking about it.

'I think it's all in our minds,' said Beauvoir. 'I think it's what we want to believe. Madeleine Favreau believed in ghosts and it killed her. If she hadn't she wouldn't have been so afraid and that ephedra wouldn't have stopped her heart. You said as much yourself. She was scared to death. She was killed by her beliefs. By someone taking advantage of them. You believe in things I don't. I'm afraid she'll take advantage of that. Get inside your head.'

'The psychic? You think she'll crawl inside my head and use my beliefs against me?'

Beauvoir nodded and refused to drop his gaze, though he longed to. This was territory he hated. Things he literally couldn't quite grasp.

'I know you're saying this because you care.' Gamache held his gaze. 'But my beliefs comfort, they don't kill. They're who I am, Jean Guy. They can't be used against me because they are me.'

'You believe in spirits.' Beauvoir wasn't going to let it go. 'I know you don't go to church, but you still believe in God. Suppose she said she'd conjure evil spirits, then where'd you be?'

'I guess I'd have to call on the angels,' Gamache smiled. 'Look, Jean Guy, at some point in all our lives we're going to be faced with exactly that question. What do you believe? At least I have my answer, and if it kills me, it kills me. But I won't run away.'

'I'm not asking you to run away, just to accept help. Let me come.'

Gamache wavered. 'There's too much to be done. You have your assignment.'

Beauvoir held Gamache's gaze, then dropped it. He knew then what would kill Gamache. Not an evil spirit, not a ghoul or a ghost. But his own pride.

CHAPTER 21

'So, I hear you're a witch.'

'I prefer Wiccan. I expect you're a Catholic.'

Gamache raised his brows. The woman in front of him was probably in her early forties though it was hard to tell. Gamache suspected she'd looked middle-aged since kindergarten. She wore a sensible skirt and flat shoes. Her sweater was of good quality, though out of date as well. He wondered where she got it. From her mother? From a second-hand shop? All she needed was a pinafore and she'd look like something from the Beatrix Potter books he'd bought Florence. Her features were small and pointy and her eyes gray. He had the impression he was interviewing a woodland creature. One with a very sharp brain.

'Lapsed,' said Gamache. Was Beauvoir right? Was this woman trying to get into his head? Strangely enough that's where Beauvoir seemed to think he kept his beliefs. They were actually nowhere near his head.

'Wiccan?' he asked.

'Practicing,' she nodded and gave him a small, but warm, smile.

The two were sitting in the living room of the B & B, a fire in the hearth. It was going to be a mild day but a fire was still welcome. The room was elegant and simple, a surprise to anyone who met Gabri before meeting his living space. Gamache wondered which was genuine, the flamboyant man or his dignified and comfortable home.

'We were looking for you yesterday. Do you mind telling me where you went?'

'Not at all. But I have a question for you first. Was Madame Favreau murdered?'

'Didn't Gabri tell you?'

'Well, yes he did. But he also told me he'd written *The Producers* only to have it stolen by Mel Brooks, and that Ruth is his father.'

Gamache laughed.

'He must allow himself one truth a day, and I'm afraid his news about Madeleine Favreau was it. She was murdered.'

Jeanne closed her eyes for a moment and sighed. 'Ephedra?'

Damn Lemieux, he thought. 'Two truths,' he said.

'What is ephedra?'

She asked it so naturally he wondered whether she was curious or cunning. If she really didn't know then she was innocent of the crime.

'My question first, please. Where did you go yesterday afternoon?'

'I was just up the hill.'

'At the old Hadley house?'

The revulsion in her face was instant, as though a curtain had suddenly been raised and he had a glimpse of what was back there.

'No, not that place. I hope never again to go there.' She looked hard at him, strip-mining his face for any indication he was going to ask her to do just that. Gamache thought it was a look dentists would recognize. Frightened patients pleading with just their eyes, 'Don't hurt me.'

Then the moment was gone. 'I was at the other extreme. The little church.'

'St Thomas's?'

'Yes. It's beautiful. I felt the need for quiet, for a peaceful place to pray.'

She saw his confusion.

'What? Witches don't pray? Or we only pray to the fallen angels not the ones who hang around St Thomas's?'

'I know nothing about the Wiccan,' said Gamache. 'I'd like to hear.'

'Will you come with me?'

'Where to?'

'Are you afraid?' She wasn't laughing at him.

He paused for a moment to think about that. He tried not to lie to suspects. Not because he was a moral or ethical man, but because he knew if found out it weakened his position. And Chief Inspector Gamache would never do that. Not for something as foolish as a lie.

'I'm always a little afraid of the unknown,' he admitted. 'But I'm not afraid of you.'

'You trust me?'

'No.' He smiled. 'I trust myself. Besides, I have a gun and you probably don't.'

'Not my weapon of choice, it's true. It's such a lovely day it's a shame to be inside. I'm only suggesting a walk. Perhaps we can go back to the chapel.'

They stood on the wide veranda for a moment, beside the rocking chairs and wicker tables, then descended the sweeping stairs and fell into step. They walked in silence for a minute or two. It was a golden day with every shade of green imaginable just appearing. The dirt road was finally dry and the air smelled of fresh grass and buds. Purple and yellow crocuses dotted the lawns and the village green. Great fields of early daffodils bobbed, having spread and naturalized all over Three Pines, their bright yellow trumpets catching the sun. After a minute Gamache took off his field coat and draped it over his arm.

'It's very peaceful,' said Jeanne. Gamache didn't answer. He walked and waited. 'It's like a mystical village that only appears for people who need it.'

'Did you?'

'I needed a rest, yes. I'd heard about the B & B and decided to book in at the last minute.'

'How'd you hear about it?'

'A brochure. Gabri must have advertised.'

Gamache nodded. The sun was warm on his face, though not hot.

'Nothing like that has ever happened to me before. No one has ever died at one of my rituals. And no one has ever been hurt. Not in the physical sense.'

Gamache longed to ask, but decided to stay quiet.

'People often hear things that upset them emotionally,' said Jeanne. 'Spirits don't seem to care much for people's feelings. But for the most part contacting the dead is a very gentle, even tender experience.'

She stopped and looked at him. 'You said you know nothing about the Wicca. I assume that means you know nothing about our rituals as well.'

'That's true.'

'Séances aren't about hauntings or ghosts or demons. They aren't about exorcisms even. Not really. They're not even about death, though we do contact the spirits of the dead.'

'What are they about?'

'Life. And healing. When people ask for a séance chances are they need healing. On the surface it might appear to be about titillation or a game to pass the time and scare each other, but someone there needs something resolved, in order to get on with their lives. They need to let something or someone go. That's what I do. That's my job.'

'You're a healer?'

Jeanne stopped and looked directly into Gamache's deep brown eyes. 'I am. All Wicca are. We're the crones, the midwives, the medicine women. We use herbs and ritual, we use the power of the Earth and the power of the mind and soul. And we use the energy of the universe and we use spirits. We do whatever we can to help wounded souls heal.'

'There are a lot of wounded souls.'

'Which is why I came here.'

'To find more or to rest from your labors?'

Jeanne was about to answer when her face suddenly

changed. It went from earnest and concentrated to perplexed. She stared off at something behind him.

He turned round then he too suddenly looked perplexed. Ruth Zardo was limping slowly down her walkway, quacking.

Jean Guy Beauvoir found La Maison Biologique without difficulty. The organic store was on rue Principale in St-Rémy, right across from the *dépanneur* where people bought their cigarettes, beer and Loto-Québec tickets. The two stores enjoyed more cross-fertilization than might have been expected, since both shops dealt with hope. Hope the lottery would go their way, hope it wasn't too late to reverse global warming. Hope that organic foods would counter the effects of nicotine. Odile Montmagny herself liked a puff every now and then, generally after a glass, or bottle, of cheap wine bought at the *dépanneur*.

As Inspector Beauvoir entered the empty shop he noticed a strange unnatural smell. It was a musky, dark aroma as though the various herbs and dried flowers, incense and powders were locked in battle.

In short, it stank.

A pretty, pudgy woman in her late thirties or early forties was standing behind the counter, her hand flat on a closed exercise book. Cheaply cut and dyed hair sat limply around her face. She looked pleasant and unremarkable. For the briefest moment she also looked annoyed, as though he'd entered her private space. Then she smiled. It was the practiced smile of someone used to pleasing.

'*Oui? Est-ce que je peux vous aider?*'

'Are you . . .' He brought out the piece of paper the Chief Inspector had given him with the names of everyone who was at the séance. He looked down at it, drawing the performance out slightly. He wanted her full attention. He knew perfectly well what her name was, of course. He just wanted to mess with her mind. Get her off balance. Now he looked up only to see her looking down at the red notebook under her hand. She'd escaped in the moment he'd taken to pause. Her mind, far from being messed with, had actually wandered back to her own business.

'Are you Odile Montmagny?' he asked loudly.

'Yes.' She smiled pleasantly, almost vacuously.

'My name is Inspector Beauvoir. I'm with the Sûreté du Québec. Homicide.'

'Not Gilles?' She was transformed. Her body went rigid, her face focused and frightened. Her hand moved from the notebook to the wooden counter and her fingers tried to dig into the surface.

'Gilles?' he repeated. He knew immediately what she was thinking and didn't yet want to ease her mind.

'What's happened?' she pleaded.

Odile thought she was going to pass out. Her head had gone numb and her heart was throwing itself against her ribcage as though desperate to break out, to find Gilles.

'I'm here about Madeleine Favreau.'

He watched her closely. Her flaccid, empty face had come alive. Her eyes shone, her brain was focused. She looked brilliant. And terrified. And gorgeous. Then it all dissolved. Her head, thrust forward toward him in desperation, sagged. All the muscles collapsed. In a blink the old Odile had returned. Pretty, dull, eager. But he'd seen what was under there. He'd seen what he suspected few knew existed, perhaps even Odile herself. He'd seen the brilliant, gorgeous, dynamic woman who lived trapped beneath the safe layer of dullness and smiles, of dye and sensible goals.

'Madeleine was murdered? But she had a heart attack, I'm sure of it.'

'*Oui, c'est vrai.* But her heart attack was helped. She was given a drug that caused it.'

'A drug?'

Had no one called Odile from Three Pines? Everyone had converged on Olivier's Bistro to get the latest news. It was their broadcast center, with Gabri as the anchor. Beauvoir had found himself interviewing the only person in the area no one thought to call. Beauvoir felt suddenly very sorry for this woman and her eager, searching face. He felt sorry for her and slightly repulsed. Losers always repulsed him which was one of the reasons he'd never liked Agent Nichol. From the moment he'd met her a few years earlier he'd known she wasn't just trouble, but worse than that. She was a loser. And in Beauvoir's experience losers were the most dangerous people. Because eventually they got to the stage where they had nothing more to lose.

'It's called ephedra,' he said.

She seemed to consider the word. 'And it stopped her heart? Why would someone kill her that way?'

Not 'why would someone kill her?' but 'why do it that way?' It was the way, not the woman, that seemed to surprise Odile.

'How well did you know Madame Favreau?'

'She was a customer. Used to buy her fruit and vegetables here. There were some vitamins she'd pick up too.'

'A good customer?'

'Regular. She'd come about once a week.'

'Did you see each other socially?'

'Never. Why?' Did she seem defensive?

'Well, you had dinner together Sunday night.'

'That's true, but it wasn't our idea. Clara invited us over before the séance. We didn't even know Madeleine would be there.'

'Would you have gone had you known?' Beauvoir knew he was on to something. Could feel it. Could see the defensiveness in her face, could hear it in her tone.

Odile hesitated. 'Probably. I didn't have anything against Madeleine. As I said, she was a customer.'

'But you didn't like her.'

'I didn't know her.'

Beauvoir let the silence stretch. Then he looked around the shop more closely. It was a jumble of items. Food and produce seemed to be on one side and clothing and furniture on the other. On the food side he could see clay pots with wooden lids and scoops hanging from them. He could see coarse sacks and on the wooden shelves climbing the walls were hundreds of glass jars filled with what looked like grass. Could they be dope? He walked closer, noticing Odile staring at him, and peered at the jars. They had names like 'Bee Balm' and 'Ma Huang' and 'Beggar's Button' and his favorite, 'Cardinal Monkeyflower'. He took it down and opening the lid he sniffed tentatively. It smelled sweet. He couldn't believe the Pope had ordained a Cardinal Monkeyflower. He wondered if there was a village named after him near Notre-Dame-de-Roof Trusses.

A bookcase held volumes on how to run a small organic farm, how to build an off-grid home, how to do your own weaving. Why would anyone want to do that?

Jean Guy Beauvoir wasn't completely insensitive to the environmentalist movement, and had even contributed to a few fundraisers on the ozone layer or global warming or something. But to choose to live a primitive life, thinking that would save the world, was ridiculous. However, one thing did attract him. A simple wooden chair. Its wood was burled and polished and smooth to the touch. Beauvoir caressed it and didn't want to lift his hand. He looked at it for a long while.

'Try it,' said Odile, still stationed behind the counter.

Beauvoir looked back at the chair. It was deep and inviting, like an armchair, only wood.

'It'll hold you, don't worry.'

He wished she'd stop talking. Just let him enjoy looking at this marvelous piece of furniture. It was like a work of art he actually understood.

'Gilles made it.' She interrupted his thoughts again.

'Gilles Sandon? From here?'

She smiled cheerily. 'Yes. My Gilles. That's what he does.'

'I thought he worked in the woods.'

'Finding trees to make furniture.'

'He finds his own trees?'

'Actually, he says they find him. He goes for walks in the woods and listens. When a tree calls him he goes to it.'

Beauvoir stared at her. She'd said this as though that's what Ikea did too. As though it was perfectly natural and normal to hear trees, never mind listen to them. He looked back at the chair.

Are they all nuts? wondered Beauvoir. The chair no longer spoke to him.

CHAPTER 22

Agent Robert Lemieux waited his turn at Monsieur Béliveau's general store. At first he thought he'd find a *dépanneur*, filled with junk food, cigarettes, cheap beer and wine, odds and ends people suddenly found they needed, like envelopes and candles for cake. But instead he found a real grocery store. One his *grand-mère* would have recognized. The dark wood shelves held neatly displayed cans of vegetables and preserves, cereals and pastas and jams and jellies, soups and crackers. All good quality, all neat and orderly. No overcrowding, no gluttony. The floors were scuffed but clean linoleum and a fan moved slowly round on the tongue-in-groove ceiling.

Behind the counter a tall, older man stooped to listen while an even older woman counted out change on the counter to pay for her groceries, talking nonstop. She told him about her hips. She told him about her son. She told him about the time she'd visited South Africa and how much she'd loved it there. And finally, in a soft and kindly voice, she told him she was sorry for his loss. And she reached one spotted hand out, the veins bulging and blue, and laid it on his long, thin, very white fingers. And held it there. He didn't flinch. Didn't withdraw his hand. Instead he looked into her violet eyes and smiled.

'*Merci, Madame Ferland.*'

Lemieux watched her leave, grateful she'd finally stopped talking, then took her place.

'Nice lady.' He smiled at Monsieur Béliveau, who was watching Madame Ferland swing open the door to the store, stand on the veranda, look both ways as though lost, then walk very slowly away.

'*Oui.*'

The whole village knew that Madame Ferland had lost her son the year before, though she chose not to talk about it. Until today. When she talked about him to Monsieur Béliveau, who recognized the gift of sorrow shared.

Now he turned back to the fresh young man in front of him. His dark hair was conservatively cut, his face clean-shaven and likeable. He looked nice.

'My name is Robert Lemieux. I'm with the Sûreté.'

'*Oui, monsieur.* I gathered that. You're here about Madame Favreau.'

'I understand you had a special relationship with her.'

'I did.' Monsieur Béliveau saw no reason to deny it now, though he wasn't sure exactly what his relationship had been with Madeleine, at least not her side. He was certain only about how he'd felt.

'And what was that relationship?' Agent Lemieux asked. He wondered whether he was being too blunt, but he also knew he might not have this man's attention for long. Another customer would walk in at any moment.

'I loved her.'

And there the words sat in the space between them, where Madame Ferland's loose change had warmed a spot.

Agent Lemieux was ready for this response. It's what the chief had told him was probably the case. Or at least that their relationship was more than casual. Still, looking at the gaunt, gray, solemn old man in front of him he couldn't figure it out. This man must be over sixty and Madeleine Favreau had been in her early forties. But age wasn't the difference that surprised him. From the pictures he'd seen of the victim she'd been beautiful. All of them had her smiling or laughing, enjoying herself. Full of life and delight. Lemieux suspected she could have had anyone she wanted. So why had she chosen this caved-in man, this elderly, stooped, quiet man?

Perhaps she hadn't. Perhaps he'd loved her and she'd felt differently. Perhaps she broke his heart, and he'd attacked hers.

Had this one who smelled of crackers and looked like a dried-up washcloth killed Madeleine Favreau? For love?

Young Agent Lemieux couldn't believe it.

'Were you lovers?' The very thought disgusted him, but he put on his sympathetic face and hoped he'd remind Monsieur Béliveau of a son.

'No. We had not made love.' Monsieur Béliveau said it simply, without embarrassment. He was beyond caring about things like that.

'Do you have a family, monsieur?'

'No children. I had a wife. Ginette. She died two and a half years ago. October twenty-second.'

Chief Inspector Gamache had sat Robert Lemieux down when he'd first joined homicide, and given him a crash course in catching killers.

'You must listen. As long as you're talking you're not learning, and this job is about learning. And not just the facts. The most important things you learn in a homicide investigation you can't see or touch. It's how people feel. Because,' and here the Chief Inspector had leaned forward and Agent Lemieux had had the impression this senior officer was about to take his hands. But he didn't. Instead he looked squarely into Lemieux's eyes. 'Because, we're looking for someone not quite right. We're looking for someone who appears healthy, who functions well. But who is very sick. We find those people not by simply collecting facts, but by collecting impressions.'

'And I do that by listening.' Agent Lemieux knew how to tell people what they wanted to hear.

'There are four statements that lead to wisdom. I want you to remember them and follow them. Are you ready?'

Agent Lemieux had taken out his notebook and, pen poised, he'd listened.

'You need to learn to say: I don't know. I'm sorry. I need help and I was wrong.'

Agent Lemieux had written them all down. An hour later he was in Superintendent Brébeuf's office, showing him the list. Instead of the laughter he'd expected the Superintendent's lips had grown thin and white as he clenched his jaws.

'I'd forgotten,' said Brébeuf. 'Our own chief told us those things when we first joined. That was thirty years ago. He said them once and never again. I'd forgotten.'

'Well, they're hardly worth remembering,' said Lemieux, judging that was what the Superintendent wanted to hear. He was wrong.

'You're a fool, Lemieux. Do you have any idea who you're dealing with? Why the hell did I think you could do anything against Gamache?'

'You know,' Lemieux said, as though he hadn't heard the reproach, 'it almost seems as though Chief Inspector Gamache believes those things.'

As I did once, said Brébeuf to himself. Once, when I loved Armand. When we trusted each other and pledged to protect each other. Once, when I could still admit I was wrong, I needed help, I didn't know. When I could still say, I'm sorry.

But that was long ago now.

'I'm not such a fool, you know,' said Agent Lemieux softly.

Brébeuf waited for the inevitable whining, the doubts, the need for reassurance, yes we're doing the right thing, yes Gamache betrayed the Sûreté, you're a clever young man, I know you see through his deceit. Brébeuf had needed to repeat these things so often to the beleaguered Lemieux he almost believed them himself.

He stared at the agent and waited. But Brébeuf saw a poised, self-contained officer.

Good. Good.

But a tiny, cool breeze enveloped Brébeuf's heart.

'One other thing he told me,' said Lemieux at the door now, smiling disarmingly. 'Matthew 10:36.'

Brébeuf watched, stone-faced, as Agent Lemieux closed

the door softly behind him. Then he began breathing again, shallow, fast breaths, almost gasps. Looking down he saw he'd made a fist of his hand, and filling that fist, crumpled and balled, was the paper with the four simple statements.

And filling his head, like a fist, were Lemieux's last words.

Matthew 10:36.

He'd forgotten that too. But what he knew he'd remember for a very long time was the look on Lemieux's face. What he'd seen there wasn't the familiar squirrely, needy, pleading look of a man who wanted to be convinced. Instead, he'd seen the look of a man who no longer cared. It wasn't cleverness he'd surprised there, but cunning.

Now Agent Lemieux listened and waited for Monsieur Béliveau to tell him more, but the old grocer seemed content to also wait.

'How did your wife die?'

'Stroke. High blood pressure. She didn't die immediately. I was able to bring her home and care for her for a few months. But she had another one and that took her. She's buried up behind St Thomas's church in the old cemetery there, with her parents and mine.'

Agent Lemieux thought there would be nothing worse than to be buried here. He planned to be buried in Montreal or Quebec City, or Paris, the retired and revered President of Quebec. Up until recently the Sûreté had provided him with a home, a purpose. But Superintendent Brébeuf had unwittingly given him something else. Something missing from his life. A plan.

Robert Lemieux's plan didn't include being with the Sûreté long. Just long enough to rise through the ranks, make a name for himself, then run for public office. Anything was possible. Or would be, once he brought down Gamache. He'd be a hero. And heroes were rewarded.

'*Bonjour, Monsieur Béliveau.*' Myrna Landers came in, filling the store with sunshine and smiles. 'Am I interrupting?'

'No, not at all.' Agent Lemieux closed his notebook. 'We were just having a small talk. How are you?'

'Not too bad.' She turned to Monsieur Béliveau. 'How are you doing? I hear you had dinner with Clara and Peter last night.'

'I did. It was a comfort. I'm doing exactly as you might expect.'

'It's a sad time,' said Myrna, deciding not to try to jolly Monsieur Béliveau out of his rightful sorrow. 'I've come for a paper. *La Journée*, please.'

'There's quite a call for that paper today.'

'There's a strange article in it.' She wondered whether she should keep it quiet but decided that horse had bolted. She paid for the paper and flipped through the pages until she found the city column.

All three leaned over it then all three rose, like devotees after ancient prayers. Two were upset. One was ecstatic.

Just then a quacking sound took them to the swinging screen door and out onto the veranda.

CHAPTER 23

'Monsieur Sandon,' Inspector Beauvoir called for the gazillionth time. He was getting a little worried. He was deep in the woods outside St-Rémy. Odile had told him where to find Gilles's truck and his trail through the woods. The truck had been easy. Beauvoir had only gotten lost twice on the way to this cul-de-sac, but finding the man was proving more difficult. The trees were just beginning to bud so his view wasn't obscured by the leaves, but it was heavy going what with downed trees, swamps, and rocks. It wasn't his natural habitat. He scrambled over slimy stones and stumbled through mud puddles, hidden under a layer of decaying autumn leaves. His fine leather shoes, not sensible he knew but he couldn't yet lower himself to rubber, were filled with water, mud and sticks.

Odile, as he'd stepped into the fresh air from the cloying aromas of the organic store, had shouted a phrase that still resonated in his ears.

'Watch out for bears,' she'd sung cheerily after him.

He'd picked up a stick when he'd entered the woods. To knock the bear on the nose. Or was that sharks? Well, he was ready either way. The bear could always use the stick as a toothpick after eating him.

He had a gun but he'd been so thoroughly trained by Gamache not to ever take it out unless he was certain to use it, it remained holstered.

Beauvoir had watched enough news reports about bear

attacks to know that black bears weren't generally dangerous, unless you got between mother and child. He also knew they were dangerous if startled. So screaming 'Monsieur Sandon' had taken on a dual purpose.

'Monsieur Saaaandonnnn.'

'I'm here,' came the sudden response. Beauvoir stopped and looked around.

'Where?' he yelled.

'Over here. I'll find you.'

Now Beauvoir heard footsteps through the autumn leaves, and the cracking of twigs. But he saw no man. The sound grew louder and still no man. It was like the approach of a ghost.

Damn, shouldn't have thought that, thought Beauvoir, feeling his anxiety rise. I don't believe in ghosts. I don't believe in ghosts.

'Who are you?'

Beauvoir turned round and on the top of a slight rise stood a massive man. Broad-chested, powerful and tall. He wore a shaggy knitted hat and his red beard stuck out in all directions. He was covered in mud and bark.

Yeti. Big Foot. There was some old creature his grandmother had told him about. The Green Man. Half man, half tree. This was him.

Beauvoir gripped his stick.

'Inspector Beauvoir, Sûreté du Québec.'

It had never sounded more feeble. Then the Green Man laughed. Not a malicious, 'I'm going to tear you limb from limb' laugh. But a laugh of genuine amusement. He came down the small hill, winding gracefully between old growth trees and saplings.

'Thought you were a tree talking to me just now.' He put out his massive, filthy hand and Beauvoir took it. He too laughed. It was hard not to feel cheerful in this man's company. 'Though they're generally a little less obvious when they speak.'

'The trees?'

'Oh, yes. But you're probably not here to talk about them.

Or to them.' Sandon reached out and put his hand squarely on a massive trunk beside him. Not leaning against it, but as a sort of touchstone. Even without Odile's obscure comments Beauvoir could tell this man had a singular relationship with the woods. If Darwin had concluded man evolved from trees, Gilles Sandon would be the missing link.

'That's true. I'm investigating the murder of Madeleine Favreau. I believe—' Beauvoir stopped. The large man in front of him had taken a step back as though Beauvoir had physically pushed him.

'Her murder? What are you saying?'

'I'm sorry, I assumed you knew. You do know she's dead.'

'I was there. I took her to the hospital.'

'I'm afraid the coroner's report says her death wasn't natural.'

'Well of course it wasn't natural. There was nothing natural about that night. Should never have invited those spirits into the room. It was that psychic.'

'She's a witch,' said Beauvoir and couldn't believe he'd let that out. Still, it was the truth. He thought.

'Not surprised,' said Sandon, recovering himself a little. 'Should have known better. All of us, but especially her. There are strange things done in this world, son. And strange things done in the next. But I'll tell you something.' He stepped closer to Beauvoir and leaned down. Beauvoir braced himself for the stench of hard work and little soap. Instead this man smelled of fresh air and pine. 'The strangest is what happens between the worlds. That's where those spirits live, trapped. Not natural.'

'And listening to trees is?'

Sandon's face, so stern and troubled for a moment, smiled once again. 'One day you'll hear them. In the quiet, some whisper you'd mistaken for the wind all your life. But it'll be the trees. Nature is talking to us all the time, it's just hearing that's the problem. Now I can't hear water or flowers or rocks. Well, actually, I can but just a little. But trees? Their voices are clear to me.'

'And what do they say?' Beauvoir couldn't quite believe

he'd asked the question and certainly couldn't believe he actually wanted to know the answer.

Gilles looked at Beauvoir for a moment. 'One day I'll tell you, but not just now. I don't think you'll believe me so it'd be a waste of your time and mine. But one day, if I think you won't mock or hurt their feelings, I'll tell you what the trees are saying.'

Inspector Beauvoir was surprised to find his own feelings were hurt. He wanted this man to trust him. And he wanted to know. But he also knew Sandon was right. He thought it was bullshit. Maybe.

'Can you tell me about Madeleine Favreau?'

Sandon stooped and picked up a stick. Beauvoir expected him to break it and worry it in his leather hands, but instead he just held it as one might hold a small hand.

'She was beautiful. I'm not good with words, Inspector. She was like that.' He pointed the stick into the woods. Beauvoir looked over and saw sunlight glowing on light green buds and falling on the golden autumn leaves. There was no need for words.

'She was new to this area,' said Beauvoir.

'Only came a few years ago. Lived with Hazel Smyth.'

'Were they lovers, do you think?'

'Hazel and Madeleine?' This seemed to be a new, though not revolting, idea for Sandon. He frowned and considered it. 'Might have been. Madeleine was full of love. People like that sometimes don't need to distinguish between men and women. I know they loved each other, if that's what you mean, but I think you mean something else.'

'I do. And you're saying it wouldn't surprise you?'

'No, but only because I think Madeleine loved a lot of people.'

'Including Monsieur Béliveau?'

'I think if she felt anything for that man it was pity. His wife died a few years ago, you know. And now Madeleine dies.'

The rage boiled up and out of the man so quickly Beauvoir wasn't prepared for it. Sandon looked as if he wanted to hit something, or someone. He glared around savagely, his fists clenched, tears running from his eyes. Beauvoir could see the calculation in his mind. Tree or man, tree or man. Which one would he smash?

Tree, tree, tree, Beauvoir pleaded. But the rage passed and now Sandon was leaning against the huge oak for support. Hugging it, Beauvoir saw, and felt absolutely no inclination to mock.

Turning back to Beauvoir Sandon dragged his checkered sleeve across his face, rubbing away the tears and other stuff.

'I'm sorry. I thought I'd gotten it all out, but I guess not.' Now the huge man smiled sheepishly at Beauvoir over the gigantic sleeve he held to his face. Then he lowered it. 'Came here yesterday. It's where I feel most at home. I walked over to the creek and just screamed. All day. Poor trees. But they didn't seem to mind. They scream too, sometimes, when there's clear cutting going on. They can feel the terror of the other trees, you know. Through their roots. They scream and then they weep. Yesterday I screamed. Today I wept. I thought it was over. I'm sorry.'

'Did you love Madeleine?'

'I did. I challenge you to find someone who didn't.'

'Someone didn't. Someone killed her.'

'Still can't quite take that in. Are you sure?' When Beauvoir was silent the big man nodded, but still seemed numb to the idea.

'There's a drug called ephedra. Ever heard of it?'

'Ephedra?' Gilles Sandon thought about it. 'Can't say I have, but I don't go in much for pharmaceuticals. I have an organic shop in St-Rémy.'

'La Maison Biologique. I know. I was there earlier talking to Odile. Does she know?'

'What?'

'That you loved Madeleine?'

'Probably, but she'd know it wasn't the same sort of love. Madeleine was the sort you adore from a distance, but I couldn't imagine approaching her. I mean, look at me.'

Beauvoir did and knew what Sandon meant. Huge, filthy,

at home in the woods. Not many women would fall for this. But Odile had and Beauvoir knew enough about women, and certainly enough about murder, to recognize a motive.

Ruth Zardo walked very slowly down the path from her tiny clapboard home to the opening in the dry stone wall that led onto the Commons. Gamache and Jeanne watched. Across the village green Robert Lemieux, Myrna and Monsieur Béliveau watched. A few people were interrupted mid-errand to stare.

All eyes were on the elderly woman limping and quacking.

Ruth, her head uncovered and her short-cropped white hair ruffling slightly in the breeze, looked behind her at the ground and stopped. Then she did something Gamache had never seen before. She smiled. A simple, easy smile. Then she continued walking.

Out the opening she came, inching along. And behind her came the quacking. Two tiny, fluffy birds.

'There's a crone,' said Jeanne.

'Ruth Zardo,' said Gamache, laughing and thinking she wouldn't get much argument in this village.

Jeanne turned to him, stunned.

'Ruth Zardo? The poet? She's Ruth Zardo? Who wrote,

> *I didn't feel the aimed word hit*
> *And go in like a soft bullet.*
> *I didn't feel the smashed flesh*
> *Closing over it like water*
> *Over a thrown stone.*

'That Ruth Zardo?'

Gamache smiled and nodded. Jeanne had quoted from one of his favorite poems by Ruth, 'Half-Hanged Mary.'

'Oh, wow.' Jeanne was almost trembling. 'I thought she was dead.'

'Only parts of her,' said Gamache. 'She seems to be doing it in stages.'

'She's a legend in my circles.'

'Witches' circles?'

'Ruth Zardo. That poem, "Half-Hanged Mary"? It's about a real woman, Mary Webster. They thought she was a witch so they strung her up from a tree. This was back in the witch-hunt days. Late sixteen hundreds.'

'Here?' Gamache asked. He was a student of Quebec history and while he'd come across many odd and brutal events, none would match the witch-hunts.

'No, Massachusetts.' She was still staring at Ruth, though so was everyone else. Ruth had progressed about a foot along the Commons, the baby birds behind her flapping their tiny wings, like vestiges, and going up on their little webbed feet. 'Amazing woman,' said Jeanne, almost in a dream.

'Ruth or Mary?'

'Both, really. Have you read her poems?'

Gamache nodded.

> *I was hanged for living alone,*
> *For having blue eyes and a sunburned skin,*
> *Tattered skirts, few buttons,*
> *A weedy farm in my own name,*
> *And a surefire cure for warts.*

'That's it,' said Jeanne, following Ruth with her eyes as a morning glory follows the sun.

> *Up I go like a windfall in reverse,*
> *A blackened apple stuck back into the tree.*

'Unbelievable. And yet,' Jeanne finally broke contact with Ruth and turned a slow but full circle, 'I can believe it of this village. Where else would people go to be safe? To get away from the burning times.'

'Is that why you came here?'

'I came because I was tired, burned out. Now there's something. A burned-out witch.' She laughed and they both turned back toward the small white clapboard chapel on the side of the hill, and walked toward it.

'And yet you agreed to do a séance.'

'It's the training. Hard to say no.'

'The training or the woman? You don't have to be a healer to find it hard to say no.'

'I've always found it difficult, it's true,' she said. They'd reached St Thomas's and climbed the half-dozen wooden steps to the small veranda. Gamache opened the large wooden door but Jeanne was standing with her back to him. Looking at Ruth, then shifting her gaze to the three great pine trees on the village green.

'Is that just a coincidence? A village called Three Pines with three pines on the green?'

'No. This village was created by the United Empire Loyalists fleeing across the border from the States in the war with Britain. It was just woods then. Still is, I guess.' Gamache had joined her and now the two of them stood side by side looking over the village, and the dense forests beyond.

'It was impossible for the Loyalists to know when they were safe. So a code was devised. Three pine trees in a clearing meant they could stop running.'

'They were safe,' said Jeanne, and seemed to sag. 'Oh, dear Lord, thank you,' she whispered.

Gamache stood in the gentle, golden sun and waited until Jeanne was ready to go inside.

'We were in a circle and that witch put salt down,' said Gilles. The two men were sitting on stones by the creek in full flight. Beauvoir was listening and tossing pebbles into the water. Sandon was staring at the creek, its surface covered in dancing silver flecks where the sun caught movement. 'I should have left then, but I don't know, we all got caught up. It was a sort of hysteria, I think. I could hear things in the dark. It was scary.'

Beauvoir stole a quick glance at Sandon, but the man didn't seem embarrassed by his admission.

'Then she started calling the spirits, and saying she could hear them, and I could too. It was terrible. She'd lit candles and somehow that made the darkness even deeper. And then there was the shuffling. There was something there, I know it. That witch brought something back from the dead. Even I know that's a mistake.'

'What happened then?'

Sandon was breathing heavily, back in that wicked room, surrounded by darkness and terror and something else.

'She could hear something coming. Then she clapped her hands. I thought I'd die. There were two screams, maybe more. Horrible sounds. Then a thump. I was almost blind with fear but I saw Madeleine drop. I was too scared to move at first, but Clara got there and so did Myrna. By the time I could move a few people were gathered around Madeleine.'

'Including Monsieur Béliveau?'

'No, he wasn't there. I got there before him. I thought she'd just fainted. Honestly I was grateful it was her and not me. And then we turned her over.'

'I couldn't believe it,' said Jeanne, remembering back to that face she'd spent the last two days running from. 'We tried to find a pulse, tried to do CPR, but she was so rigid it was impossible. It was as though she was frozen in place, as though the life had been ripped right out of her. You say a drug called . . .' she seemed to struggle for the name. Gamache let her, wondering whether this was an act. 'I've forgotten the name, but some drug did that?'

'Ephedra. It's actually an herb, a natural substance. It's used by people who want to diet, but it's been banned. Too dangerous. What was your impression of the group?'

'This was actually the second séance. The first was Friday night at the bistro.'

'Good Friday,' said Gamache.

'There were tensions I could feel, mostly from two of the men. Not Gabri. The other two. The tall, sad man and the huge bearded one. But men are often like that at séances. They either don't believe and are full of negative energy, or they do believe and are embarrassed by their fear. Again, negative energy. But I actually had the impression they weren't just upset about being there. I think they didn't like each other. The big man was more obvious about it, but that grocer man—'

'Monsieur Béliveau,' said Gamache.

'There's something dark about him.'

Gamache looked at her with surprise. What little he knew of the man he liked. He seemed courtly and almost timid.

'He's hiding something,' said Jeanne.

'We all are,' said Gamache.

'You come here every day?' Beauvoir asked after Sandon had finished his story. It sounded like a pickup line and Beauvoir tried not to blush.

'Uh huh. To find the wood for my furniture.'

'I saw some of your stuff at the store. It's fantastic.'

'The trees let me do it.'

'They let you cut them down?' asked Beauvoir, surprised.

'Of course not, what do you think I am?'

A murderer? Beauvoir completed his thought. Did he think that?

'I walk the woods and wait for inspiration. I only use dead trees. I guess we have a lot in common, you and me.'

For some reason this pleased Beauvoir, though he couldn't think what they had in common.

'We both deal in death, profit by it you might even say. Without dead trees I'd have no furniture, without dead people you'd have no job. Course, you people sometimes hurry it along.'

'What do you mean?'

'Come on, did you read the paper today?' Sandon reached behind him and pulled a folded and crushed tabloid from his back pocket. He handed it to Beauvoir, pointing with one filthy finger.

'See. I thought they'd put all the rotten ones in jail, but I guess there's one still out there. Or out here, really. You seem like a decent sort. Must be tough having a dirty boss.'

Beauvoir barely heard the comments. He felt as though

he'd tumbled into the paper and was trapped by the words. One word.

Arnot.

Jeanne was quiet for a moment, taking in the small wooden chapel. Simple white and green lily of the valley filled it with fragrance so that the place smelled of old wood, lemon Pledge, books and flowers. And it looked like a jewel. Sunlight was made green and blue and red as it passed through the stained glass windows, the most prominent of which wasn't the risen Christ behind the altar, but the one on the side of the chapel. With the three young men in uniform. The sun passed through them and spilled their colors onto Gamache and Jeanne, so that they were sitting in the warmth, the essence, of the boys.

'Be careful.' She turned away from Gamache and looked at a patch of red light at his feet.

'What do you mean?'

'All around you, I can see it. Be careful. Something's coming.'

CHAPTER 24

Jean Guy Beauvoir found Gamache sitting in St Thomas's. The chief and the witch were side by side, staring ahead. He might, he knew, be interrupting the interrogation, but he didn't care. In his hand he held the newspaper, full of filth. Gamache turned and seeing Beauvoir he smiled and rose. Beauvoir hesitated then shoved the paper into his breast pocket.

'Inspector Beauvoir, this is Jeanne Chauvet.'

'Madame.' Beauvoir took her hand and tried not to flinch. Had he known when he'd woken that morning he'd be shaking hands with a witch, well. Well, he wasn't sure what he'd have done differently. It was, he had to admit, one of the things he loved about his job. It was unpredictable.

'I was just leaving,' said the witch, but for some reason she was holding on to Beauvoir's hand. 'Do you believe in spirits, Inspector?'

Beauvoir almost rolled his eyes. He could just imagine the interrogation dissolving into the chief and the witch discussing spirits and God.

'No, madame, I don't. I think it's a hoax, a way to prey on weak minds and take advantage of grieving people. I think it's worse than a hoax.' He yanked his hand from her grip. He was getting himself worked up. His rage was rattling the cage and he knew it was in danger of breaking out. Not normal, healthy anger, but rage that rips and claws indiscriminately. Blind and powerful and without conscience or control.

In his coat pocket, folded next to his chest, sat the words that would at the very least wound Gamache. Maybe more. And he was the one who had to deliver the blow. Beauvoir spewed his rage on this tiny, gray, unnatural woman in front of him.

'I think you prey on sad and lonely people. It's disgusting. If I had my way I'd put you all in jail.'

'Or string us up to an apple tree?'

'Doesn't have to be apple.'

'Inspector Beauvoir!' Armand Gamache rarely raised his voice, but he did now. And Beauvoir knew he'd crossed a line, crossed it and then some.

'I'm sorry, madame,' Beauvoir sneered, barely containing his anger. But the little woman in front of him, so insubstantial in many ways, hadn't moved. She was calm and thoughtful in the face of Beauvoir's onslaught.

'It's all right, Inspector.' She walked toward the door. Opening it she turned back. Now she was a black outline against the golden day.

'I was born with a caul,' she said to Beauvoir. 'And I think you were too.'

The door closed and the two men were left alone in the small chapel.

'She meant you,' said Beauvoir.

'Your powers of observation are as keen as ever, Jean Guy.' Gamache smiled. 'What is it? Did you want to make certain she hadn't messed with my mind?'

Now Beauvoir felt uneasy. The truth was, it looked as though the witch had behaved perfectly civilly. It was he who was about to mess with Gamache's mind. Silently he took the newspaper from his breast pocket and handed it to Gamache. The Chief Inspector looked amused then meeting Beauvoir's eyes his smile faded. He took the paper, put on his half-moon reading glasses and in the silence of St Thomas's read.

Gamache grew very still. It was as though the world

around him had dipped into slow motion. Everything became more intense. He could see a gray hair in Beauvoir's dark head. He had the impression he could walk forward, pluck it and return to his place without Beauvoir's even noticing.

Armand Gamache could suddenly see things he'd been blind to.

'What does it mean?' asked Beauvoir.

Gamache looked at the banner. *La Journée*. A rag from Montreal. One of the tabloids that had pilloried him during the Arnot case.

'Old news, Jean Guy.' Gamache folded the paper and laid it on his field coat.

'But why bring up the Arnot case?' asked Beauvoir, trying to keep his voice as calm and reasonable as the chief's.

'Quiet news day. Nothing to report. The paper's a joke, *une blague*. Where did you get it?'

'Gilles Sandon gave it to me.'

'You found him? Good. Tell me what he said.'

Gamache picked up his coat and paper and Beauvoir reported on his morning's interviews with Sandon and Odile as they walked into the sun and back to the old railway station. Beauvoir grateful for the normalcy of it. Grateful the chief had just shrugged off the comments in the paper. Now he too could pretend it meant nothing.

The two men walked in sync, heads down. To an observer they'd look like father and son, out for a casual walk this fine spring day and deep in conversation. But something had just changed.

> *I didn't feel the aimed word hit*
> *And go in like a soft bullet.*

The smashed flesh closed over the aimed word and Armand Gamache continued to walk and listen and give his full attention to Inspector Beauvoir.

Hazel Smyth had been off to the funeral home in Cowansville. Sophie had volunteered to go but in a voice so sulky

Hazel decided she was better on her own. True, a number of her friends had said they'd go, but Hazel didn't like to bother them.

It was like being kidnapped and taken into a world of hushed words and sympathy for something she couldn't yet believe had happened. Instead of the Knitters Guide meeting she was looking at caskets. Instead of taking poor Aimée to her chemotherapy session or having tea with Susan and hearing about her screwed-up kids, she was trying to word the obituary announcements.

How to describe herself? Dear friend? Dear companion? Much missed by . . . Why were there no words that felt? Words that when you touched them you'd feel what was intended? The chasm left by the loss of Madeleine? The lump in the throat that fizzed and ached. The terror of falling asleep knowing that on waking she'd relive the loss, like Prometheus bound and tormented each day. Everything had changed. Even her grammar. Suddenly she lived in the past tense. And the singular.

'Mom,' Sophie called from the kitchen. 'Mom, are you there? I need your help.'

Hazel came back from a great distance and made her way to her daughter, slowly at first then with increased speed as the words penetrated.

I need your help.

In the kitchen she found Sophie leaning against the counter, her foot raised and a pained expression on her face.

'What is it? What happened?' Hazel bent to touch the foot but Sophie pulled it away.

'Don't. It hurts.'

'Here, sit down. Let me see it.'

She managed to coax Sophie over to the kitchen table and into a chair. Hazel put a cushion on another chair and tenderly lifted her daughter's leg so that it was resting on the chair and cushion.

'I twisted it in a pothole on the driveway. How many times have I told you to get those holes filled?'

'I know, I'm sorry.'

'I was getting your mail, and this happens.'

'Let me just see.' Hazel bent and with gentle practiced fingers began to explore the ankle.

Ten minutes later she had Sophie propped on the sofa in the living room, the television wand in her hand, a ham and cheese sandwich on a plate and a diet soda on a tray. She'd bound Sophie's sprained ankle in a tenser bandage and found a pair of old crutches from the last time her daughter had hurt herself.

Strangely enough the light-headedness, the distraction and befuddlement had lifted. Now she concentrated on her daughter, who needed her.

Olivier delivered the sandwich platter to the back room of his bistro. He'd also put a pot of mushroom and coriander soup and an assortment of beers and soft drinks on the sideboard. As the Sûreté team arrived for lunch Olivier took Gamache by the elbow and led him aside.

'Did you see today's paper?' Olivier asked.

'*La Journée*?'

Olivier nodded. 'They mean you, don't they?'

'I think they do.'

'But why?' Olivier was whispering.

'I don't know.'

'Do they do this sort of thing often?'

'Not often but it happens.' He said it so casually Olivier relaxed.

'If you need anything, let me know.'

Olivier hurried off to his lunch hour rush and Gamache got himself a bowl of soup, a grilled vegetable and goat cheese sandwich on panini and sat down.

His team sat around him, sipping soup, eating sandwiches and darting looks in his direction. Except for Nichol, who kept her head down. Somehow, though they were sitting in a circle, she managed to look as though she was at a separate table in a different room entirely.

Had he made a mistake bringing her here?

He'd worked with her for a couple of years now and

nothing seemed to have changed. That was the most worrisome. Agent Nichol seemed to collect resentments, collect and even manufacture. She was a perfect little producer of slights and sores and irritations. Her factory went night and day, churning out anger. She turned good intentions into attacks, gifts into insults, other people's happiness into a personal attack. Smiles and even laughter seemed to physically hurt her. She held on to every resentment. She let nothing go, except her sanity.

And yet Agent Yvette Nichol had shown an aptitude for finding murderers. She was a sort of idiot savant, who had that one ability, perhaps sensing a like mind.

But there was a reason she was on this case now. A reason he had to keep to himself.

He watched as Yvette Nichol leaned so close to her soup her hair dipped into it. It hung down and created an almost impenetrable curtain. But between the clumps he could just see her spoon sputter and spill its contents as it shook its way to her mouth.

'You've probably all seen this.' He held up a copy of *La Journée*.

They nodded.

'They're referring to me, of course, but it means nothing. It's just a slow news day after a long weekend and they decided to resurrect the Arnot case. That's all. I don't want this interfering with your work. *D'accord?*'

He looked around. Agent Lemieux was nodding agreement, Agent Nichol was soaking soup from the ends of her hair with a paper napkin and appeared not to have heard. Inspector Beauvoir was looking at him intently, then nodded curtly and picked up a huge roast beef and horseradish sandwich on a croissant.

'Agent Lacoste?'

Isabelle Lacoste was staring at him, unmoving. Not eating, not nodding, not speaking. Just staring.

'Tell me,' said Gamache, folding his hands in his lap, away from his food, giving her his full attention.

'I think it's something, sir. You always say everything happens for a reason. I think there's a reason that was put into the paper.'

'And what would that be?'

'You know, sir, what that reason is. It's what it's always been. They want to get rid of you.'

'Who are "they"?'

'The people in the Sûreté still loyal to Arnot.' She didn't even hesitate, didn't have to think about that. It helped, of course, that she'd spent all morning thinking about it and coming to that conclusion.

She watched as he absorbed her words.

Armand Gamache looked across the table and straight into her eyes. His own brown eyes were steady and thoughtful and calm. Through all the chaos, through all the threats and stress, through all the attacks, verbal and physical, they'd endured in trying to find murderers, this was what she always remembered. Chief Inspector Gamache, calm and strong and in charge. He was their leader for a reason. He never flinched. And he didn't flinch now.

'Their reasons are their own,' he finally said. 'I don't have to care.' He looked around at the others. Even Agent Nichol was looking at him, her mouth slightly open.

'What about others?' asked Lacoste. 'The people here? Or other agents in the Sûreté? People will believe it.'

'So?'

'Well, it could hurt us.'

'What would you have me do? Take out an ad saying it's not true? There are two things I can do. I can get upset and worry about it, or I can let it go. Guess which one I choose?'

He smiled now. The tension left the room for the first time and they were able to get on with their lunch and their reports. By the time Olivier cleared their plates and brought in the cheese course Beauvoir and Gamache had brought them up to speed. Robert Lemieux had reported on his interview with Monsieur Béliveau.

'What do we know of his wife?' Beauvoir asked. 'Ginette was her name?'

'Nothing yet,' said Lemieux, 'except that she died a few years ago. Is it important?'

'Could be. Gilles Sandon seemed to be hinting it was no coincidence that two women Monsieur Béliveau was involved with should die.'

'Yeah, a tree probably told him that,' mumbled Nichol.

'What was that, Agent?' Beauvoir turned on her.

'Nothing,' she said. Soup had dripped from her hair onto the padded shoulders of her cheap suit and crumbs clung to her chest. 'It's just that I don't think we can take seriously anything Sandon says. He's obviously nuts. He talks to trees, for God's sake. The same with that witch woman. She spreads salt, lights candles and talks to the dead. And you're paying attention to anything she says?' She directed this at Armand Gamache.

'Come with me, Agent Nichol.' Gamache carefully put his napkin on the table and rose. Without another word he opened the French doors to the flagstone patio at the back of the bistro, overlooking the river.

Beauvoir had a brief fantasy of the chief tossing her in, his last sight of Nichol flailing hands disappearing into the white foam, to be dumped into the poor Atlantic Ocean a week from now.

Instead the team watched Nichol gesturing wildly and actually stomping her feet while Gamache listened, face stern and serious. They could hear nothing over the roar of the river. Once he lifted his hand and she quieted down, grew very still. Then he spoke. She nodded, turned and walked away.

Gamache came back into the room, looking worried.

'Is she gone?' Beauvoir asked.

'Back to the Incident Room.'

'And then?'

'And then she'll come with me to the old Hadley house. I'd like you to come too,' Gamache said to Agent Lacoste.

Jean Guy Beauvoir managed to keep silent and even listened to Isabelle Lacoste's report, though his mind was squirreling. Why was Agent Nichol there? Why? If everything happened for a reason, what was the reason for her? There was one, he knew.

'Madeleine Favreau was forty-four years old,' reported Lacoste in her clear, precise voice. 'Born Madeleine Marie Gagnon in Montreal and raised in the Notre-Dame-de-Grâce *quartier*. On Harvard Street. Middle class, anglo upbringing.'

'Anglo?' asked Lemieux. 'With a name like that?'

'Well, semi-anglo,' admitted Lacoste. 'French father and English mother. Name was French but upbringing was mostly English. Went to public and high school in NDG. The school secretary actually remembered her. Said there are a few pictures of Madeleine in the main corridor. She was Athlete of the Year and president of the student council. One of those kids who simply excelled. She was also a cheerleader.'

Gamache was grateful Nichol wasn't there. He could just imagine what she'd do with this litany of success.

'Her grades?' he asked.

'The secretary's checking them for me. Should have the answer by the time we get back to the Incident Room. After high school—'

'Just a moment,' Gamache interrupted. 'What about Hazel Smyth? Did you ask about her? They went to school together.'

'Actually I did. Hazel Lang. Also forty-four. Lived on Melrose Avenue in NDG.'

Gamache knew the area. Old and settled homes. Trees and modest gardens.

'The secretary's looking her up too.'

'But didn't remember her immediately?'

'No, but then she wasn't likely to after all these years. After high school Madeleine went to university, studied engineering at Queens and got a job at Bell Canada. She left four and a half years ago.'

Beauvoir stared at Gamache. He couldn't get the con-
frontation with Nichol out of his head. Had any one of
them spoken to him like that in a meeting they'd be out in a
flash, and rightly so. And, frankly, none of them would
ever consider speaking to Armand Gamache like that. Not
out of some instinct for survival, but because they respected
him too much.

Why did Nichol treat the boss like that, and why did
Gamache allow it?

'The woman I spoke to worked in another department
and was at a lower level,' Lacoste continued her report,
'but she said Madame Favreau was a fair boss and very
smart. People liked her. I also spoke briefly with her
boss. Paul Marchand.' Lacoste consulted her notes. 'He's
Vice President of Research and Development. Madeleine
Favreau was a department head. Product development.
She also worked closely with their marketing department.'

'So when new products like a phone or something came
out,' said Lemieux, 'she'd work on it?'

'Her expertise was information technology. Very hot
field, IT. According to her boss she got that dossier not
long before leaving.'

Gamache waited. Isabelle Lacoste was as good an agent
as he'd ever worked with and should Inspector Beauvoir
leave for any reason she'd be his natural choice for second
in command. Her reports were thorough, clear and without
ambiguity.

'She was married to François Favreau but it didn't
work. They divorced a few years ago. But her boss doesn't
think that was the reason she left. He asked her why, but
she was vague on the reason but definite about her decision
and he respected that.'

'Did he have a theory?' Gamache asked.

'He did.' Lacoste smiled. 'Six years ago Madeleine
Favreau was diagnosed with breast cancer. Monsieur
Marchand thinks that, perhaps combined with the divorce,

was the reason. He was sorry about it. I could hear it in his voice, he liked her.'

'Loved her?' asked Gamache.

'I don't know. But there was affection there, I think, that went beyond simple respect. He was sorry she left.'

'And then she came here,' said Gamache, leaning back in his chair. Olivier knocked and brought in coffees and a tray of desserts. He took slightly more time than Gamache would have thought necessary then finally left, having to satisfy himself with baguette crumbs but not a single crumb of information.

'No children?' asked Lemieux.

Lacoste shook her head and reached for a chocolate mousse, whipped high above the cut-glass dish, and decorated with real cream and a raspberry. She dragged a dark, rich coffee toward her, satisfied with her report, and her lunch.

Beauvoir noticed there was just one mousse left. Lemieux had taken a fruit salad, which Beauvoir was relieved to see but viewed with some suspicion. Who would choose fruit over chocolate mousse? But now he himself was left with a terrible dilemma, a culinary Sophie's Choice. One mousse. Should he take it for himself or leave it for Gamache?

He stared at the mousse then lifting his eyes he saw Gamache also looking. Not at the dessert. At him. He had a very small smile on his face and something else. Something Beauvoir had rarely seen there.

Sadness.

Then Beauvoir knew. Knew everything. Knew why Nichol was still on the team. Knew why Gamache was even taking her with him that afternoon.

If officers loyal to Arnot wanted ammunition to bring down Gamache how best to do it? Plant someone on his team. Armand Gamache would know that. And instead of firing her, he decided to play a dangerous game. He kept her on. And more than that. He kept her close. So he could watch her. So he could also keep her away from the rest of them. Armand Gamache was throwing himself onto the grenade that was Yvette Nichol. For them.

Jean Guy Beauvoir reached out and, picking up the dessert, he placed the chocolate mousse in front of Armand Gamache.

CHAPTER 25

Clara Morrow dragged her hands through her hair and stared at the work on the easel. How had it gone from brilliant to crap so quickly? She picked up her brush again, then put it down. She needed a finer one. Finding it she dabbed it in the green oil paint, gave it just a touch of yellow and approached the painting.

But she couldn't. She no longer knew what she wanted to do.

Clara's hair stood out at the sides of her head with streaks of blue and yellow paint in it. She could have made a living as Clara the Clown. Even her face was streaked with color, though her eyes would scare any child who came close.

Haunted, fearful eyes. Less than a week now before Denis Fortin showed up. He'd called that morning and said he'd like to bring some colleagues with him. Colleagues was a word that always excited and intrigued Clara. Painters didn't have colleagues. Most barely had friends. But now she hated the word. Hated the phone. And hated the thing on the easel that was supposed to lift her from obscurity and make the art world finally take notice.

Clara backed away from the easel, afraid of her work.

'Look at this.' Peter's head appeared at her door. She'd have to consider closing it, she thought. No more interruptions. She never interrupted him when he was working so why did he think it was OK to not only speak to her, but expect her to leave the studio to look at what? A piece of bread with a hole in it that looked like the Queen? Lucy lying with her head under the carpet? A cardinal at their bird feeder?

Anything, as long as it was insignificant, was reason enough for Peter to interrupt her work. But she knew she was being unfair. If she knew one thing it was that Peter, while not necessarily understanding her work, was her biggest supporter.

'Come on, quick.' He gestured to her excitedly and disappeared.

Clara took off her pinafore, smearing oil paint on her shirt as she did, and left the studio, trying to ignore the relief she felt as she turned off the light.

'Look.' Peter practically dragged her over to the window.

There was Ruth on the village green, talking to someone. Only she was alone. There was nothing odd about that. It actually would have been strange had there been someone willing to listen to her.

'Wait for it.' Peter could sense her impatience. 'Look,' he said triumphantly.

Ruth said one last thing then turned and walked very slowly back across the green toward her home, carrying a canvas bag of groceries. As she walked two rocks seemed to move with her. Clara looked more closely. They were fuzzy sort of rocks. Birds. Probably the ubiquitous chickadees. Then the one in front flapped its wings and lifted up a little.

'Ducks,' said Clara, smiling, the tension disappearing as she watched Ruth and her two ducklings walk in line back to the small home on the other side of the green.

'I didn't see her go across to Monsieur Béliveau's for groceries, but Gabri did. He called and told me to look. Apparently the little guys waited outside the store for her, then followed her to the green.'

'I wonder what she was saying to them.'

'Probably teaching them to swear. Can you imagine?

Our own little tourist destination, the village with ducks that speak.'

'And what would they say?' Clara looked at Peter with amusement.

'Fuck!' they both said at once.

'Only a poet would have a duck that said fuck,' said Clara, laughing.

Then she noticed the Sûreté officers leaving the bistro and heading to the old railway station. She was considering going over to say hello, and maybe picking up some information, when she saw Inspector Beauvoir take Chief Inspector Gamache aside. From what Clara could see the younger man was talking and gesturing and the Chief Inspector was listening.

'Is that what you're doing?' Beauvoir tried to keep his voice down. He reached into Gamache's jacket and took the folded newspaper from where it protruded from his pocket. 'This isn't nothing. It's something, isn't it?'

'I don't know,' Gamache admitted.

'It's Arnot, isn't it? It's always fucking Arnot.' Beauvoir's voice was getting louder.

'You need to trust me with this, Jean Guy. This Arnot thing has been around far too long. Time to stop it.'

'But you're not doing anything. He's brought the fight to you, with this.' Beauvoir waved the paper.

From their window Peter and Clara saw the newspaper waved like a baton. Clara knew if they were watching so were others. Gamache and Beauvoir could not have chosen a more public place for their argument.

'You've known for months, years, that it wasn't over,' continued Beauvoir. 'But still you stayed silent. You're no longer consulted on major decisions—'

'But that's different. The senior officers aren't doing that because they agree with Arnot. They're punishing me for going against their decision. You know that. It's different.'

'But it's not right.'

'You think not? Do you really think when I arrested

Arnot I didn't expect this to happen?' Now Beauvoir's arm
stopped flapping and he grew very still. Gamache seemed
to envelop him in a sort of bubble. His brown eyes were so
intense, his voice so deep and forceful. He held Beauvoir
there, riveted. 'I knew that it would happen. The senior
council couldn't allow me to disobey orders and get away
with it. This is their punishment. And it's right. Just as what
I did was right. Don't confuse the two, Jean Guy. The fact
that I'll never get another promotion, the fact I'm not involved in deciding the direction of the Sûreté any more, is
not important. I saw that coming.'

Gamache reached out and took the newspaper from
Beauvoir and held it gently in his large hands. He lowered
his voice almost to a whisper. Nothing in Three Pines moved.
It was as though the squirrels and chipmunks and even the
birds were straining to hear. And he knew perfectly well
the people were.

'This is different.' He held the paper up. 'This is the
work of Pierre Arnot and the people still loyal to him. This
is revenge, not censure. This isn't Sûreté policy.'

Let's hope not, thought Beauvoir.

'I didn't see this coming,' admitted Gamache, looking at
the newspaper. 'Not years after the arrest and trial. Not after the Arnot murders were made public. I'd been warned
the Arnot case isn't over, but I failed to appreciate the loyalty he still commands. I'm surprised.'

He steered Beauvoir toward the stone bridge and over
the Bella Bella. Once across he stopped and for a moment
watched the frothing waters rush by, leaves and clumps of
mud caught up in the force of the normally gentle river.

'He's caught you off guard, sir,' said Beauvoir.

'Not completely,' said Gamache. 'Though I must admit I
was surprised by this.' He patted his pocket where the article sat again. 'I knew he'd try something, but I didn't know
what or when. I thought the attack would be more direct.
This shows a subtlety and a patience I didn't know he had.'

'But Arnot's not doing it. Not directly. He must have
people inside the Sûreté. Do you know who they are?'

'I can guess.'

'Superintendent Francoeur?'

'I don't know, Jean Guy. I can't talk about it. It's just suspicion on my part.'

'But Nichol used to work with Francoeur in narcotics. Francoeur and Arnot were best friends. He just missed being arrested himself for being an accessory to the murders. At the very least he probably knew what Arnot was doing.'

'We don't know,' repeated Gamache.

'And Nichol worked with him. He was the one who had her transferred back to homicide. I remember you argued with him about that.'

Gamache remembered that too. That cloying, reasonable voice moving like syrup down the telephone line. Gamache had known then. Known that there was a reason Nichol was sent back to him after he'd fired her once.

'She's working for Francoeur, isn't she,' said Beauvoir, a statement not a question. 'She's here to spy on you.'

Gamache stared at Beauvoir, taut and tight.

'Do you know what a caul is?'

'A what?'

'Jeanne Chauvet said she'd been born with one and she thought you had too. Do you know what it is?'

'Not a clue and I don't care. She's a witch. Are you really going to listen to her?'

'I listen to everybody. Be careful, Jean Guy. These are dangerous times and dangerous people. We need all the help we can get.'

'Including witches?'

'And maybe the trees,' said Gamache, smiling and raising his brows in a mock-arch expression. Then he pointed to the rushing water, whose noise had prevented others from hearing their conversation. 'The water's our ally. Now if we can just find some talking rocks we'll be undefeatable.'

Gamache looked around on the ground. Beauvoir found himself looking too. He picked up a rock, warm from the sun, but by then the chief was walking slowly toward the

Incident Room, his hands held comfortably behind his back, his face tilted up. Beauvoir could just see the small smile on it. He was about to chuck the rock into the river but hesitated. He didn't want to drown it. Fuck, he thought, tossing the rock up and down in his hand as he too walked to the Incident Room, once the seed is planted it really screws up your life. How was he supposed to chop down trees or even mow the grass if he was afraid of drowning a rock?

Goddamned witch.

Goddamned Gamache.

CHAPTER 26

Hazel Smyth backed away from the door, wiping her hands on her gingham apron.

'Come in,' she smiled politely, but no more.

Beauvoir and Nichol followed her into the kitchen. Every pot was out, either in use or in the sink. On the stove stood a brown earthenware jar with handles on either side. Beans baked in molasses and brown sugar and pork rinds. A classic Québécois dish. The room was filled with the rich, sweet aroma.

Baked beans were a lot of work, but it looked as though Hazel's drug of choice today was hard work. Casseroles lined the counter, like a battalion of tanks. And Beauvoir suddenly knew which battle they were fighting. The war against grief. The heroic and desperate effort to stop the enemy at the gates. But it was futile. For Hazel Smyth the Visigoths were on the hill and were about to sweep down, burning and destroying everything. Unrelenting, without mercy. She might delay grief, but she wouldn't stop it. She might even make it worse by running away.

Jean Guy Beauvoir looked at Hazel and knew she was about to be overcome, overwhelmed, violated. Her own heart would finally betray her, and open the gates to grief. Sorrow, loss, despair were snorting and trampling, rearing and gathering for the final charge. Would this woman survive, Beauvoir wondered? Some didn't. Most at the very least were changed forever. Some grew more sensitive, more compassionate. But many grew hard and bitter. Closed off. Never again risking this loss.

'Cookie?'

'*Oui, merci.*' Beauvoir took one and Nichol took two. Hazel's hands flew toward the kettle, the tap, the plug, the teapot. And she talked. Putting out a covering fire of words. Sophie had twisted her ankle. Poor Mrs Burton needed a drive to her chemo later this afternoon. Tom Chartrand was poorly and of course his own children would never come down from Montreal to help. On and on she went until Beauvoir didn't know about grief, but he himself was about to surrender.

The tea was placed on the table. Hazel had made up a tray and was carrying it to the stairs.

'Is that for your daughter?' Beauvoir asked.

'She's in her room, poor one. Can't move very easily.'

'Here, let me.' He took the tray and mounted the narrow stairs, lined with old floral wallpaper. At the top he walked along to a closed door and knocked with his foot. He heard two heavy steps and the door opened.

Sophie was standing there, a bored look on her face, until she saw him. Then she smiled, cocked her head to one side slightly and slowly, slowly lifted her hurt foot.

'My hero,' she said, limping backward and motioning him to put the tray on a dresser.

He looked at her for a moment. She was attractive, there was no denying that. Slim, her skin clear and her hair shiny and full. Beauvoir found her revolting. Sitting in her bedroom faking an injury and expecting her grieving mother to wait on her. And Hazel did. It was insane. What sort of person, what sort of daughter, did this? Granted Hazel was difficult to be around just now, what with the maniacal cooking and rapid-fire talking, but couldn't Sophie at least be with her? She didn't have to help necessarily, but she sure didn't have to add to her mother's burden.

'May I ask you a few questions?'

'Depends.' She tried to make the word seductive. She was, Beauvoir decided, the artless sort who tried to make every word seductive, and failed.

'Did you know Madeleine had had breast cancer?' He placed the tray on the dresser, shoving a make-up bag to the edge.

'Yeah, but, I mean, she'd gotten over it, right? She was fine.'

'Really? I thought it took five years before people were given the all clear, and it hasn't been that long, has it?'

'Almost. She seemed fine. Told us she was.'

'And that was enough for you.' Were all twenty-one-year-olds this self-absorbed? This callous? She really didn't seem to care that a woman who'd shared her home and her life had had cancer and had just been brutally murdered, right in front of her.

'What was it like living here after Madeleine arrived?'

'I dunno. I went away to university, didn't I? At first Madeleine made a big deal when I came back, but after a while she and Mom didn't care.'

'I can't imagine that's true.'

'Well, it is. I wasn't even going to go to Queens. I'd been accepted at McGill. Mom wanted me to go there. But Madeleine had been to Queens and she'd talked so much about it. The beautiful campus, the old buildings, the lake. She made it sound so romantic. Anyway, I applied without telling anyone and got accepted. So I decided to go to Queens.'

'Because of Madeleine?'

Sophie looked at him, her eyes hard, her lips white. It was as though her face was changing to stone. And he knew then. While her mother was desperately fighting to keep grief at a distance, Sophie had another battle. To keep grief in.

'Did you love her?'

'She didn't care for me, not at all. She just pretended. I did everything for her, everything. Even changed my fucking school. Went all the way to Kingston. Do you even know where that is? It's eight fucking hours' drive away.'

Beauvoir knew Kingston wasn't eight hours away. Maybe five or six.

'Takes a day to get home.' Sophie seemed to be losing control, the rock turning to lava. 'At McGill I could've come home every weekend. I finally understood. God, I was so stupid.' Sophie turned now and slapped the side of her head so hard it hurt even Beauvoir. 'She didn't care for me. She only wanted me out of the way. Far away. It wasn't me she loved. I finally got that.' Now Sophie balled up her fists and pounded them into her thigh. Beauvoir stepped forward and held her hands. He wondered how many bruises she carried, out of sight.

Armand Gamache stood at the bedroom door and looked in. Beside him the two agents stood, uneasily.

Mid-afternoon sunlight seeped in through the windows of the old Hadley house and seemed to stall part way. Instead of making the place bright and even cheerful, the shafts of light were thick with dust. Months, years, of neglect and decay swirled in the light, twisting as though alive. As the three officers had progressed further into the house the decay and dust grew thicker, kicked up by their steps, until the light itself dimmed.

'I'd like you to look around and tell me if anything's changed.'

The three officers stood at the door, the yellow police tape torn and hanging from the door frame. Gamache reached out and picked up a strand. It had been ripped and stretched. Not cut cleanly. Someone had clawed at it.

Beside him he could hear Agent Isabelle Lacoste breathing heavily, as though trying to catch her breath. On his other side Agent Robert Lemieux shifted from foot to foot.

Framed by the door was the murder scene. The heavy Victorian furniture, the fireplace with its dark mantelpiece, the four-poster bed that looked recently slept in though Gamache knew no resident had been in it in years. All those things were oppressive, but natural. Then his eyes shifted to the unnatural.

The circle of chairs. The salt. The four candles. And the addition. The tiny bird, fallen on its side, its small wings spread slightly as though struck down in flight. Its legs up around its reddish chest, its tiny eyes wide and staring. Had it stood on the chimney with its brothers and sisters, staring at the whole wide world in front of them, prepared to fly? Had the others, teetering on the edge, finally taken off? But what had happened to this little one? Instead of flying, had it fallen? Does one always fail, always fall?

It was a baby robin. A symbol of spring, of rebirth. Dead.

Had it too been scared to death? Gamache suspected it had. Did everything that entered this room die?

Armand Gamache stepped in.

Yvette Nichol began wandering around the kitchen. She couldn't stand the talking any more. On and on the woman went. At first Hazel had sat with her at the Formica table but eventually she got up to check the cookies and put the cool ones into a cookie tin.

'For Madame Bremmer.' As though Nichol cared. While Hazel talked and worked Nichol wandered the room, looking at the cookbooks, the collection of blue and white dishes. She moved to the photo-laden fridge, covered with pictures, mainly of two women. Hazel and another. Madeleine, Nichol decided, though the smiling, attractive woman and the shrieking thing in the morgue looked not at all alike. Picture after picture. In front of the Christmas tree, at a lake, cross-country skiing, gardening in the summer, hiking. In each one Madeleine Favreau was smiling.

Yvette Nichol knew something then, something she knew no one else would see. Madeleine Favreau was a fake, a fiction, an act. Because Nichol knew no one could possibly be that happy.

She stared at one showing a birthday celebration. Hazel Smyth was fixated on something outside the frame and wearing a funny baby blue hat with sparklers; Madeleine Favreau was in profile, listening, her head resting on one hand. She was looking at Hazel with unmasked adoration. A fat young woman sat beside Madeleine, stuffing cake into her face.

Nichol's cell phone vibrated and thrusting the photograph into her pocket she walked into the stuffed living room, kicking a sofa leg as she went.

'*Merde. Oui, allô?*'

'Did you just swear at me?'

'No.' She reacted rapidly, habitually, to the rebuke.

'Can you talk?'

'A little. We're at a suspect's house.'

'How's the investigation going?'

'Slowly. You know Gamache. He plods along.'

'But you're back with him now. That's good. Don't lose track of him. There's too much at stake.'

Nichol hated these calls, hated herself for answering the phone. Hated even more the excitement she felt when the phone rang. And then the inevitable letdown. Treated like a child yet again. There was no way she could admit she was really with Beauvoir. She was supposed to be with the Chief Inspector, then at the last minute the two had gone into the tiny office off the Incident Room, and when they'd come out Beauvoir had stridden to the door calling for her to join him.

And so she found herself alone in the oppressive living room. It felt like the homes of so many aunts and uncles, stuffed with belongings. From the Old Country, they'd said, but who could smuggle a matching living room/dining room set out of Romania or Poland or Czechoslovakia? Where would you hide the plush pink carpets and heavy curtains and garish pictures as you stole across the border? But somehow their infinitesimal homes were crammed full of things that had become family heirlooms. Chairs and tables and sofas were scattered about like litter, dropped on the floor as another person might drop a Kleenex. Each time Nichol visited her aunts and uncles more heirlooms had appeared until there seemed little room for people. And perhaps that was the point.

She had the same impression here. Things. Too many things. But one thing caught her eye. A yearbook, sitting on the sofa. Open.

A shriek tore through the stillness of the room. Lacoste froze. Beside her Chief Inspector Gamache turned to face whatever caused it.

'Sorry.' Lemieux stood sheepishly at the door with a length of yellow tape in his hand, after ripping it from the wood. 'I'll try to do it more quietly.'

Isabelle Lacoste shook her head and could feel her heart subsiding to its normal beat.

'Has the room changed?' Gamache asked her.

Lacoste looked around. 'Looks the same to me, *patron*.'

'Someone broke in. I can't imagine they came into this place without a purpose. But what was it?'

Armand Gamache looked slowly around the room, now familiar though far from comfortable. Was anything missing? Why would someone break the police tape to get in? To take something? Or to replace something?

Was there another reason?

The only thing obviously different about the room was the bird. Had it been killed on purpose? Was this a ritual sacrifice? But why a little bird? Weren't sacrifices larger? Cattle or dogs or cats? He realized he was just making that up. He actually had no idea about sacrifices. The whole thing seemed macabre.

He knelt down, his feet crunching the coarse salt on the carpet as he tilted his head to get a better look at the bird.

'Should I bag it?' Lacoste asked.

'Eventually, yes. Do you have any thoughts?'

Gamache knew Lacoste had been there that morning not to check on the scene, but to do her own private ritual.

'The bird looks terrified, but that might be just my imagination.'

'We have a bird feeder on our balcony,' said Gamache, straightening up. 'We have our morning coffee out there in good weather. Every bird who comes to it looks terrified.'

'Well, you and Madame Gamache are very frightening people,' said Lacoste.

'I know she is.' He smiled. 'Petrifies me.'

'Poor man.'

'Unfortunately, I don't think we can read too much into the facial expression of the dead bird,' said Gamache.

'Good thing we still have tea leaves and entrails,' said Lacoste.

'That's what Madame Gamache always says.'

His smile faded as he looked down at the bird curled at his feet, a dark stain on the white salt, its eye staring black, blank. He wondered what it had last seen.

Hazel Smyth closed the yearbook and smoothed its faux leather cover, hugging it to her chest, as though that might staunch the wound, stop whatever it was that was flowing out of her. Hazel could feel it. Could feel herself weakening. The solid, angular book bit into her soft breasts as she pressed harder and harder, no longer hugging but gripping it now, thrusting the yearbook with all their young dreams deeper and deeper into her chest. Relieved by the physical pain, she wished the edges sharper so they'd actually cut instead of simply bruise. This was pain she could understand. The other was terrifying. It was black and empty and hollow and stretched on forever.

How long could she live without Madeleine?

The full horror of her loss was just coming into view.

With Mad she'd found a life full of kindness and thoughtfulness. She was a different person with Mad. Carefree, relaxed, lighthearted. She actually voiced her opinions. Actually had opinions. And Madeleine had listened. Hadn't always agreed, but had always listened. From the outside theirs must have been an unremarkable, even dull life. But from the inside it was a kaleidoscope.

And slowly Hazel had fallen in love with Madeleine. Not in a physical way. She had no desire to sleep with Mad, or even kiss her. Though sometimes when Mad sat on the sofa at night with her book and Hazel was in her wing chair with her knitting, Hazel could see herself getting up, walking to the sofa and putting Madeleine's head on her breast. Just where the yearbook was now. Hazel stroked the book and imagined the lovely head lying there instead.

'Madame Smyth.' Inspector Beauvoir interrupted Hazel's daydream. The head on her chest became cold and hard. Became a book. And home became cold and empty. Once again Hazel lost Madeleine. 'May I see the book?'

Beauvoir held out his hand tentatively.

Agent Nichol had found the yearbook sitting open in the living room and had brought it into the kitchen with her, not expecting Hazel's reaction. It was a reaction no one could have expected.

'That's mine. Give it to me,' Hazel had growled, approaching Nichol with such venom the young agent handed it over without hesitation. Hazel took it and sitting down she hugged it to her. For the first time since they'd arrived the room was silent.

'May I?' Beauvoir reached for it. Hazel seemed not to understand. She looked as though he wanted her to detach her arm. Finally she let go of the book.

'It's from our graduating year.' Hazel leaned across him and flipped the pages to the graduation pictures. 'Here's Madeleine.'

She pointed to a smiling, happy girl. Below her picture was typed, *Madeleine Gagnon. Most likely to end up in Tanguay.*

'It was a joke,' said Hazel. Tanguay was the women's prison in Quebec. 'Everyone knew Mad would be a success. They were poking fun at her.'

Jean Guy Beauvoir was willing to accept that Hazel believed it, but he knew most jokes had some basis in truth. Did some of Madeleine's high school friends see something else in her?

'Do you mind if we take this with us? You'll get it back.'

Hazel very obviously minded, but shook her head.

The book reminded Beauvoir of something else. Something Gamache had asked him to ask Hazel.

'What do you know about Sarah Binks?'

He could see by Hazel's face the question sounded like nonsense. Blahdity-blah, blah-binks.

'The Chief Inspector found a book called *Sarah Binks* in Madeleine's bedside drawer.'

'Really? That's odd. No, I've never heard of it before. Was it a—'

'A dirty book? I don't think so. The Chief Inspector's been reading it and laughing.'

'Sorry, I can't help.' It was said politely but Beauvoir could see something else at work. Hazel was disconcerted. By the book or the fact her best friend had kept something secret?

'You've told us about the night Madeleine died, but there was another séance, a few days earlier.'

'On Friday night at the bistro. I wasn't there.'

'But Madame Favreau was. Why?'

'Didn't I tell you this before? With the Chief Inspector?' It was all a bit of a blur to Hazel.

'You did, but sometimes people's minds are a little cloudy when we first talk to them. It's good to hear the story again.'

Hazel wondered if that was true. Her mind, far from clearing, was becoming more and more befuddled.

'I don't really know why Mad went. Gabri had put up a notice in the church and the bistro telling everyone that the great psychic Madame Blavatsky was staying at his place and had agreed to bring back the dead. For one night only.' Hazel smiled. 'I don't think anyone took it seriously, Inspector. Certainly not Madeleine. I think it was just a fun evening. Something different.'

'But you didn't approve?'

'I think there're some things best not toyed with. At best it would be a waste of time.'

'And at worst?'

Hazel didn't answer right away. Instead her eyes flitted around the kitchen as though seeking some place safe to land. But finding nothing she returned to his face.

'It was Good Friday, Inspector. *Le Vendredi saint.*'

'So?'

'Think about it. Why is Easter the most important Christian holy day?'

'Because that's when Christ was crucified.'

'No. Because that's when Christ rose.'

CHAPTER 27

As Lacoste snapped pictures in the bedroom of the old Hadley house and Lemieux bagged the tape, Gamache opened and closed drawers in the cabinets, bedside table and vanity. Then he walked over to the bookcase.

What had someone wanted in here so much they'd been desperate enough to break the Sûreté cordon?

Gamache smiled as he saw *Parkman's Works*, that odious history of Canada, taught in schoolhouses more than a century ago to kids willing to believe natives were shifty savages and Europeans actually brought civilization to these shores.

Gamache opened one of the volumes at random.

In the form of beasts or other shapes abominable and unutterably hideous, the brood of hell, howling in baffled fury, tore at the branches of the sylvan dwelling.

Gamache closed the book and looked again at the cover, astonished. Was this really *Parkman's Works*? Parched and dry and guaranteed to kill of ennui? The brood of hell? It was *Parkman's Works*, he confirmed. And the section he'd opened was about Quebec.

'Agent Lacoste, could you come here?'

When she did he handed her the book. 'Could you open it, please?'

'Just open it?'

'*S'il vous plaît.*'

Isabelle Lacoste held the cracked leather volume between

her hands then slowly splayed the cover. The frail pages fanned then after a stunned moment they fell, until the book was open. Gamache leaned over and read, *In the form of beasts or other shapes abominable and unutterably hideous . . .*

The book opened itself to that page.

Gamache stared then finally replaced it on the bookcase and took down the one next to it. A Bible. He wondered if it was coincidence, or whether the hand that placed the books together knew the one needed the other. But which needed which? He glanced at the Bible and slipped it into his pocket. He knew what he still needed to do, and every little bit helped. The dark slit in the bookcase, where the Bible had sat, revealed the cover of the next book. A book that was blank on its spine.

Lacoste was back at work and didn't see Gamache slip the second book into his pocket too. But Lemieux did.

Gamache knew he was wasting time. The sun would soon set and he sure didn't want to do it in the twilight.

'I'm going to search the house. Are you all right here?'

Lacoste and Lemieux looked at him as his children Daniel and Annie had when he'd told them it was time they tried to swim across the bay without life jackets.

'You're strong enough swimmers.'

But still they couldn't believe he'd ask this of them.

'And I'll be right beside you in the rowboat.'

He could still see the hesitation in Daniel's eyes. But Annie dived right in. There was no way Daniel was going to be left behind so in he went too.

Daniel, sturdy and athletic, had swum the bay easily. Annie had barely made it. She was small and scrawny, as Reine-Marie had been at her age. But unlike Daniel, she lost no energy to fear. Still, she was so young and the bay so wide, she'd barely made it, sputtering the last few meters, her father encouraging her and practically dragging her to shore with his words, like ropes attached to the beloved little body. Twice he'd almost reached in and plucked her from the waters, but had waited and she'd found the strength to carry on.

Sun-warmed towels were wrapped around small excited bodies and Armand Gamache, holding and rubbing his children in his big, strong arms, had wondered if he'd made a mistake, having Annie try at the same time as Daniel. Not because Annie almost didn't make it, but because she had. In his arms he could feel Daniel pull away at first, then finally subside and agree to be held and comforted and congratulated.

Daniel, for all his bulk and strength, was the fragile one. The needy one. And still was.

Looking at Lacoste and Lemieux, he had the same impression. But which was strong and which was needy? And did it matter? As with his children, he believed in them both.

'Would you like some help?' Lacoste asked, resolved to the terrible task, if he wished it.

'You have enough to do, thank you. When you're finished go back to the Incident Room. I'm hoping the coroner will have something.'

Isabelle Lacoste watched him disappear into the darkness as though swallowed by the house.

He was gone and she was alone. With Lemieux. She liked Robert Lemieux. He was young and enthusiastic. There was never any struggle for power with him. Unlike Nichol, he was a pleasure to work with. Nichol was a complete disaster. Smug, sullen, self-absorbed. What disturbed Lacoste was why Chief Inspector Gamache kept her around. He'd fired her once, but when Nichol had been reassigned to homicide he'd simply given in. Without a fight.

And here she was again. Gamache could have assigned Nichol to cases in far-flung regions. He could have given her administrative jobs at Sûreté headquarters. But instead he assigned her to the most difficult field cases. With him.

Everything happens for a reason, Gamache said. Everything. And Lacoste knew there was a reason for this. She just wished she knew what it was.

'How're you doing?' Lemieux asked.

'Almost finished. You?'

'A couple more things I need to do. Why don't you head back?'

'No, I'll wait.' Lacoste didn't want to abandon Lemieux in this terrible place.

Lemieux's phone had been vibrating for five minutes now. All he wanted to do was answer it. Why wouldn't she leave? 'Why?'

'Can't you feel it?'

He knew he should at least pretend to be uncomfortable but the truth was the old Hadley house did nothing to him. But he could see the others, even Gamache, perhaps especially Gamache, react to it.

'It's like there's something here with us,' said Lacoste. 'As though something's watching us.'

They stood still, Lacoste hyper-vigilant, paying attention to every creak, every cranny, Lemieux riveted on the phone vibrating in his pocket.

'Careful,' he said. 'You'll scare yourself to death.'

'The murderer chose well. This place would scare the devil himself.'

'Look, you have a ton of work back at the Incident Room. I'm fine. Really.'

'Really?' she asked, desperate to believe it.

Leave, he wanted to scream.

'Really. I'm too stupid to be afraid.' He smiled. 'I don't think the devil takes stupid people.'

'I think he only takes stupid people,' said Lacoste, and wished they weren't standing in the old Hadley house talking about the devil. 'Okay, I'll see you later. You have your cell in case—'

'In case?' he smiled, teasing, and trying to get her to the door. 'I do.'

Isabelle Lacoste stepped into the dark hallway with its worn carpet and smell of mold and decay. As soon as his back was turned she ran down the hallway, down the stairs almost tripping over her feet, and out the door, as though spewed from some gloomy womb into the world.

'You knew Madeleine Favreau had breast cancer?' Inspector Beauvoir asked.

'Of course I knew,' Hazel said, surprised.

'But you didn't tell us.'

'I suppose I forgot. I never thought of her as a woman who'd had breast cancer and she didn't either. Hardly ever spoke of it any more. Just got on with her life.'

'It must have been a shock when she first discovered it. She'd have been in her early forties.'

'True. Women are getting it younger and younger it seems. But I didn't know her when she was first diagnosed. She looked me up when she was already in treatment. I think that happens a lot. Old friends become more important. We hadn't kept in touch after high school but she suddenly called and came down. It was as though no time had passed. She was weak from the chemo but as lovely as ever. She looked like her eighteen-year-old self, only bald and that only made her more beautiful. It was strange. I sometimes wonder whether chemotherapy doesn't take people almost to another world. So many seem so peaceful. Their faces become smooth, their eyes shine. Madeleine almost glowed.'

'Sure she wasn't having radiation?' Nichol asked.

'Agent Nichol,' Beauvoir barked. He could feel the stone he'd found by the Bella Bella and put in his pocket yearning to fly. To smash bone, to grind into that head until it hit her tiny, atrophied brain. And replace it. And who would know the difference? 'That was uncalled for.'

'It was only a joke.'

'It was cruel, Agent Nichol, and you know the difference. Apologize.'

Nichol turned to Hazel, her eyes hard. 'I'm sorry.'

'That's all right.'

Nichol knew she'd gone too far. But she'd been told to. To aggravate, to upset, to unsettle the team, that was her job.

For the sake of the Sûreté she was willing to do this. For her boss, whom she adored and loathed, she'd do this. Looking at Inspector Beauvoir's handsome face, engorged and enraged, she knew she'd succeeded.

'Madeleine went back to Montreal and finished her chemo,' continued Hazel after an awkward silence. 'But she came out every weekend after that. She wasn't happy in her marriage. There weren't any children, you know.'

'Why was she unhappy?'

'She said they just grew apart. She also thought it possible he couldn't deal with a successful wife. She excelled at everything she did, you know. Always had. That was just Madeleine.' Hazel looked to Beauvoir like a proud mother. He thought she'd be a good mother. Kind and caring. Supportive. And yet she'd raised that spoiled child upstairs. Some kids, he knew, were just ungrateful.

'It must be hard,' said Hazel.

'What must be?' Beauvoir had become lost in his own thoughts.

'Being around someone who was always successful. Especially if you're insecure. I think Mad's husband must have been insecure, don't you?'

'Do you know how we can find him?'

'He's still in Montreal. François Favreau's his name. Nice man. I've met him a few times. I have his address and phone number if you like.'

Hazel got up from the kitchen table and went over to a chest of drawers. Opening the top drawer she rummaged through it, her back to him.

'Why did you go to the second séance, Madame Smyth?'

'Madeleine asked me to,' Hazel said, moving papers around in the drawer.

'She asked you to the first and you didn't go. Why the second?'

'Found it.' Hazel turned round and handed an address book to Beauvoir who handed it to Nichol. 'What did you ask, Inspector?'

'The second séance, madame.'

'Oh, yes. Well it was a combination of things, as I remember. Madeleine actually seemed to have a good time at the first. Said it was silly, but in an amusement park kind of way. You know, the way we used to scare ourselves with the roller coaster and the haunted house? It sounded like fun and I kind of regretted missing the first.'

'And Sophie?'

'Well that was a given from the start. A bit of excitement in this burg, as she calls it. Sophie was excited about it all day.'

Hazel's animated face fell, slowly. Beauvoir could chart the memory of that night as it made its way across Hazel's face until the memory of Madeleine alive became the memory of Madeleine dead.

'Who would want to kill her?' Beauvoir asked.

'No one.'

'Someone did.' He tried to make it soft and gentle, as Gamache would, but even to his own ears the words sounded like an accusation.

'Madeleine was,' Hazel moved her hands gracefully in front of her, as though conducting or gently mining the air for words, 'she was sunshine. Every life she came into she brightened. Not because she tried. I try.' Hazel's hand now pointed to the casserole regiment. 'I run around trying to help people, without even being asked. And I know that can be annoying. Madeleine made people feel better just by spending time with them. It's hard to explain.'

And yet, thought Beauvoir, you're alive and she's dead.

'We think the ephedra was given to Madeleine at dinner. Did she complain about any of the food?'

Hazel thought then shook her head.

'Did she complain about anything that night?'

'Nothing. She seemed happy.'

'I understand she was seeing Monsieur Béliveau. What do you think of him?'

'Oh, I like him. His wife and I were friends, you know. She died almost three years ago. Madeleine and I sort of adopted him after that. Ginette's death tore him up.'

'He seems to have recovered well.'

'Yes, yes he does,' she said with perhaps a bit too much effort to appear blasé.

He wondered what was going on behind that placid, somewhat sad face. What did Hazel Smyth really think of Monsieur Béliveau?

CHAPTER 28

Gamache hummed a little as he walked through the kitchen of the old Hadley house. The hum was neither loud enough to scare a ghost, nor tuneful enough to be comforting. But it was human and natural and company.

Then Gamache ran out of kitchen and comfort. He faced another closed door. As a homicide officer he'd grown wary of closed doors, both literal and figurative, though he knew answers lived behind closed doors.

But sometimes something else lurked there. Something old and rotted and twisted by time and necessity.

Gamache knew people were like homes. Some were cheerful and bright, some gloomy. Some could look good on the outside but feel wretched on the interior. And some of the least attractive homes, from the outside, were kindly and warm inside.

He also knew the first few rooms were for public consumption. It was only in going deeper that he'd find the reality. And finally, inevitably, there was the last room, the one we keep locked, and bolted and barred, even from ourselves. Especially from ourselves.

It was that room Gamache hunted in every murder investigation. There the secrets were kept. There the monsters waited.

'What took you so long?' Michel Brébeuf spoke into his phone, frustrated and angry. He didn't like being kept waiting. And he sure as hell didn't like it when junior officers ignored his calls. 'You must have known it was me.'

'I did, but I couldn't answer. There're other things happening.'

Robert Lemieux's tone had stopped being obsequious. Since that last interview in Brébeuf's office something had changed. The power had somehow shifted and Brébeuf couldn't figure out how. Or why. Or what to do about it.

'Don't let it happen again.'

Brébeuf had meant it to be a warning, but instead it had come out petulant and whiny. Lemieux solidified his position by ignoring the comment.

'Where are you now?' Brébeuf asked.

'In the old Hadley house. Gamache is searching the rest of the house and I'm in the room where the murder happened.'

'Is he close to solving the case?'

'Are you kidding? A few minutes ago he was communing with a dead bird. The Chief Inspector's a long way from figuring this out.'

'Have you?'

'Have I what?'

'Figured out who murdered the woman.'

'That's not my job, remember?'

Superintendent Brébeuf noticed there was no longer any pretense about who was in charge. Even the 'sir's had disappeared. The likeable, malleable, ambitious but slightly stupid young officer had turned into something else.

'How's Agent Nichol doing?'

'She's a disaster. I don't know why you wanted her here.'

'She serves a purpose.' Brébeuf felt his shoulders drop from where they'd crept up around his ears. He had one secret from Lemieux anyway. Yvette Nichol.

'Look, you need to tell me why she's here,' said Lemieux, then after a pause, 'Sir.'

Now Brébeuf was smiling. God bless Agent Nichol. Wretched, lost Agent Nichol.

'Has the Chief Inspector seen the newspaper?'

There was a pause as Lemieux struggled with letting the Nichol thing go. 'Yes. He talked about it at lunch.'

'And?'

'Didn't seem to bother him. Even laughed.'

Gamache laughed, thought Brébeuf. He'd been clearly and personally attacked, and he'd laughed.

'That's all right. What I expected, actually.'

And it was. But he'd hoped for something else. In his daydreams he'd seen that familiar face stunned and hurt. Had even imagined Gamache phoning his best friend for support and advice. And what advice had Michel Brébeuf prepared and practiced?

'Don't let them win, Armand. Focus on the investigation and leave the rest to me.'

And Armand Gamache would relax, knowing his friend would protect him. He'd turn his attention fully to finding the killer, and not see what was creeping up behind him. Out of the long, dark shadow he himself created.

So far Gamache had peered into the attic, shining his light and scaring a few bats, and himself. He'd glanced around all the bedrooms and bathrooms and closets. He'd stridden purposefully through the cobwebbed living room with its heavy mantelpiece and moldings and into the dining room.

A strange thing happened in there. He could suddenly smell the appetizing aroma of a well-prepared dinner. It smelled of a Sunday roast, with warm gravy and potatoes and sweet parsnips. He could smell the caramelized onions and fresh, steaming bread, and even the red wine.

And he could hear laughter and conversation. He stood, mesmerized, in the dark dining room. Was the house trying to seduce him, he wondered? Make him lower his guard? Dangerous house that knew food would do that to him. But still the strange impression remained, of a dinner served long ago to people long dead and buried. People who'd been happy here, once. It was his imagination, he knew. Just imagination.

Gamache had left the dining room. If there was some-one, or something, hiding in this house he knew where he'd find it.

The basement.

He reached out for the doorknob. It was ceramic and cold to the touch. The door creaked open.

'You're back.' Agent Lacoste greeted Beauvoir with a wave, ignoring Nichol. 'How'd it go?'

'Brought this back.' He tossed the yearbook onto the conference table then told Lacoste about his interviews with Hazel and Sophie.

'What'd you think?' Lacoste asked after reflecting on what she'd heard. 'Did Sophie love Madeleine or hate her?'

'Don't know. It seems confused. Might be either.'

Lacoste nodded. 'Lots of girls get crushes on older women. Teachers, writers, athletes. I had a crush on Helen Keller.'

Beauvoir had never heard of Helen Keller, but the idea of Lacoste in a steamy relationship with this Helen gave him pause as he took off his coat. He could see their glis-tening bodies, intertwined –

'She was blind and deaf,' said Lacoste, knowing him enough to guess his reaction. 'And dead.'

That certainly changed the image in his mind. He blinked to blank it out.

'What a catch.'

'She was also brilliant.'

'But dead.'

'True. It crippled the relationship, I'm afraid. But I still adore her. Amazing woman. She said, "Everything has its wonders, even darkness and silence."' Lacoste remem-bered herself. 'What were we talking about?'

'Crushes,' said Nichol and could have kicked herself. She wanted them to forget she was there.

Beauvoir and Lacoste turned to look at her, surprised she was there and surprised she'd said something helpful.

'So you really had a crush on Helen Keller?' said Nichol. 'She was nuts, you know. I saw the movie.'

Lacoste shot her a look of complete dismissal. Not even disdain. She made Nichol disappear.

Darkness and silence, thought Nichol. It's not always wonderful.

She watched as Inspector Beauvoir and Agent Lacoste turned their backs to her and walked away.

'You say it's natural for a girl Sophie's age to be confused?' Beauvoir asked Lacoste.

'Lots are. Emotions are all over the place. It'd be normal for her to love Madeleine Favreau and then hate her. Then adore her again. Look at the relationships most girls have with their mothers. I called the lab,' said Lacoste. 'The report from the break-in won't be ready until the morning but the coroner emailed her preliminary report and said she'd drop by on her way home. Wants to meet the chief in the bistro in about an hour.'

'Where is he?' Beauvoir asked.

'Still at the old Hadley house.'

'Alone?'

'No. Lemieux's there too. I need to talk to you about something.' She shot a look at Nichol, now sitting at her desk, staring at her screen. Playing free cell, Lacoste guessed.

'Why don't we walk? Get some air before the storm,' said Beauvoir.

'What storm?'

She'd followed him to the door. He opened it and nodded.

Lacoste could only see blue sky and the odd cloud. It was a beautiful day. She looked at him in profile, staring at the sky as well, his face grim. Lacoste looked more closely. And there, just above the dark pine forest on the ridge of the hill, behind the old Hadley house, she saw it.

A black slash rising, as though the sky was a dome, cheerful and bright, and artificial. And someone was opening that dome.

'What is that?'

'Just a storm. They look more dramatic in the country. In the city with the buildings we can't see all that.' He waved casually toward the slash as though all storms looked like something wicked approaching.

Beauvoir put his coat back on, and once out the door turned to walk over the stone bridge into Three Pines but Lacoste hesitated.

'Do you mind if we walk this way?' She pointed in the opposite direction, away from the village. He looked and saw an attractive dirt road winding into the woods. The mature trees arched overhead, almost touching. In the summer it would be gently shaded but now, in early spring, the branches held only buds, like tiny green flares, and the sun shot through easily. They walked in silence into a world of sweet aromas and birdsong. Beauvoir remembered Gilles Sandon's claim. That trees spoke. And maybe, sometimes, they sang.

Finally Lacoste was certain no one, especially Nichol, could overhear.

'Tell me about the Arnot case.'

Gamache looked into the darkness and silence. He'd been in the basement once before. He'd opened this same door in the middle of a fierce storm, in the dark, desperate to find a kidnapped woman. And he'd stepped into a void. It was like every nightmare coming true. He'd crossed a threshold into nothingness. No light, no stairs.

And he'd fallen. As had the others with him. Into a wounded and bloody heap on the floor below.

The old Hadley house protected itself. It seemed to tolerate, with ill grace, minor intrusions. But it grew more and more malevolent the deeper you went. Instinctively his hand went into his pants pocket, then came out again, empty.

But he remembered the Bible in his jacket and felt a little better. Though he didn't himself go to church, he knew the power of belief. And symbols. But then he thought about the other book he'd found and brought with him from the murder scene and whatever comfort he'd felt evaporated, seemed to be pulled from him and disappear into the void in front of him.

He shone the flashlight down the stairs. At least this time there were stairs. Putting his large foot tentatively on the first rung he felt it take his weight. Then he took a deep breath, and started down.

'I'm sorry?' said Beauvoir.

'I need to know about the Arnot case,' said Lacoste.

'Why?' He stopped in the middle of the country road and turned to look at her. She faced him squarely.

'I'm no fool. Something's going on and I want to know.'

'You must have followed it on TV or in the papers,' said Beauvoir.

'I did. And in police college it was all anyone was talking about.'

Beauvoir's mind went back to that dark time, when the Sûreté was rent. When the loyal and cohesive organization started making war on itself. It put its wagons in a circle and shot inwards. It was horrible. Every officer knew the strength of the Sûreté lay in loyalty. Their very lives depended on it. But the Arnot case changed everything.

On one side stood Superintendent Arnot and his two co-defendants, charged with murder. And on the other, Chief Inspector Gamache. To say the Sûreté was split in half would be wrong. Every officer Beauvoir knew was appalled by Arnot, absolutely sickened. But many were also appalled by what Gamache did.

'So you know it all,' said Beauvoir.

'I don't know it all, and you know that. What's wrong? Why are you freezing me out of this? I know there's something going on. The Arnot case isn't dead, is it?'

Beauvoir turned and walked slowly down the road, further into the woods.

'What?' Lacoste called after him. But Beauvoir was silent. He brought his hands behind his back and held them, walking slowly and thinking it through.

Should he tell Lacoste everything? How would Gamache feel about that? Did it matter? The chief wasn't always right.

Beauvoir stopped and looked behind him to Isabelle Lacoste standing firmly in the middle of the road. He gestured her to him and as she approached he said, 'Tell me what you know.'

The simple phrase surprised him. It was what Gamache always said to him.

'I know Pierre Arnot was a superintendent in the Sûreté.'

'He was the senior superintendent. He'd come up through narcotics and into serious crime.'

'Something happened to him,' said Lacoste. 'He became hardened, cynical. Happens a lot, I know. But with Arnot there was something else.'

'You want the inside story?'

Lacoste nodded.

'Arnot was charismatic. People liked him, loved him even. I met the man a few times and felt the same way. He was tall, rugged. Looked like he could take down a bear with his hands. And smart. Whip smart.'

'What every man wants to see in the mirror.'

'Exactly. And he made the agents under him feel powerful and special. Very potent.'

'Were you drawn to him?'

'I applied to his division but was turned down.' It was the first time he'd told anyone that, except Gamache. 'I was working in the Trois-Rivières detachment at the time. Anyway, as you've probably heard, Arnot commanded a near mythic loyalty among his people.'

'But?'

'He was a bully. Demanded absolute conformity. Eventually the really good agents dropped out of his division. Leaving him with the dregs.'

'Bullies themselves or agents too scared to stand up to a bully,' said Lacoste.

'Thought you said you didn't know the inside story.'

'I don't, but I know school yards. Same everywhere.'

'This was no school yard. It started quietly at first. Violence on native reserves unchecked. Murders unreported. Arnot had decided if the natives wanted to kill themselves and each other then it should be considered an internal issue and not interfered with.'

'But it was his jurisdiction,' said Lacoste.

'That's right. He ordered his officers on the reserves to do nothing.'

Isabelle Lacoste knew what that meant. Kids and sniff. Glue and gasoline-soaked rags inhaled until their young brains froze. Numb to the violence, abuse, despair. They didn't care any more. About anything, or anyone. Boys shot each other and themselves. Girls were raped and beaten to death. Perhaps calling the Sûreté post desperate for help and getting no answer. And the officers, almost always a kid on his or her first assignment, were they staring at the phone with a smile knowing they'd satisfied their boss? One less savage. Or were they scared to death themselves? Knowing that more than a young native was being killed. They too were dying.

'What happened then?'

CHAPTER 29

Everything creaks when you're afraid. Armand Gamache
remembered the words of Erasmus and wondered whether
the creak he'd just heard was real or just his fear. He swung
his flashlight to the stairs behind him. Nothing.

He could see the floor was dirt, hardpacked from years
of weight. It smelled of spiders and wood rot and mold. It
smelled of all the crypts he'd ever been in, exhuming bodies of people taken before their time.

What lay buried down here? He knew something was.
He could feel it. The house seemed to claw at him, to cloy
and smother, as though it had a secret, something wicked
and malicious and cruel it was dying to say.

There it was again. A creak.

Gamache spun around and the puny circle of light from
his flashlight threw itself against the rough stone walls, the
beams and posts, the open wooden doors.

His cell phone began vibrating.

Taking it out he recognized the number.

'*Allô.*'

'*C'est moi,*' said Reine-Marie, smiling at her colleague
and walking into one of the aisles of books at the Bibliothèque Nationale. 'I'm at work. Where are you?'

'The old Hadley house.'

'Alone?'

'Hope so.' He laughed.

'Armand, did you see the newspaper?'

'I did.'

'I'm so sorry. But we've known it was coming. It's almost a relief.'

Armand Gamache was never more glad he'd married this woman, who made his battles theirs. She stood steadfast beside him, even when he tried to step in front. Especially then.

'I've tried to get Daniel but there's been no answer. Left a message though.'

Gamache had never questioned Reine-Marie's judgment. It made for a very relaxing relationship. But he wasn't sure why she'd call their son in Paris about some scurrilous article.

'Annie called just now. She saw it too and said to pass on her love. She also said if there's anyone you'd like her to kill, she'll do it.'

'How sweet.'

'What are you going to do about it?' she asked.

'*Franchement*, I thought I'd ignore it. Not give it any legitimacy.'

There was a pause.

'I wonder if maybe you should speak to Michel.'

'Brébeuf? Why?'

'Well, after the first one, I felt the same way, but I wonder whether it's gone too far.'

'The first? What do you mean?' His flashlight flickered. He jostled it and the light burned bright again.

'Tonight's paper. The early edition of *Le Journal de Nous*. Armand, haven't you seen it?'

His flashlight flickered off, then after a long moment came back on, but the light was dim and frail. Once again he heard the creak. This time behind him. He spun round and pointed the dull light toward the stairway, but it was empty.

'Armand?'

'I'm here. Tell me what the paper says, please.'

As he listened the sorrow of the old Hadley house

closed in. It crept toward him and ate the last of his light, until finally he was standing in the bowels of the old Hadley house in complete darkness.

'Natives killing each other wasn't enough for Arnot,' said Beauvoir. He and Lacoste walked side by side through the late afternoon sun as it dappled the dirt road at their feet. 'Arnot ordered his two top officers into the reserves to stir up trouble. *Agents provocateurs*.'

'And then?' It was almost unbearable, but she had to know. She listened to the terrible words as they walked through the tranquil forest.

'And then Pierre Arnot ordered his officers to kill.'

Beauvoir found it hard to say. He stopped and looked into the forest, and after a moment or two the roar between his ears settled and he could make out the singing again. A robin? A blue jay? A pine? Was that what made Three Pines remarkable? Did the three giant trees on the village green sometimes sing together? Was Gilles Sandon right?

'How many died?'

'Arnot's men never kept track. There's a team from the Sûreté still trying to find all the remains. The murderers killed so many they couldn't remember where they put all the bodies.'

'How did they get away with it? Didn't the families complain?'

'To whom?'

Lacoste dropped her head and looked at the ground between her feet. The betrayal was complete.

'The Sûreté,' she said, in a small voice.

'One mother from the Cree nation kept trying. For three months she held bake sales and sold hats and mitts she'd knitted and finally raised enough money for a plane ticket. One way. To Quebec City. She'd made a sign and went to the provincial government to protest. She spent all day in front of the National Assembly but no one stopped. No one paid attention. Eventually some men kicked her off the property, but she went back. Every day for a month she'd show up, sleeping on a park bench every night. And every day she was told to leave.'

'The National Assembly? But they can't do that. That's public property.'

'She wasn't at the National Assembly. She thought she was, but she was actually picketing in front of the Château Frontenac Hôtel. No one told her. No one helped her. All they did was laugh.'

Lacoste knew Quebec City well, and could see the turreted, majestic hotel rising from the cliffs overlooking the St Lawrence river. She could see how someone unfamiliar with the city could make that mistake, but surely there was a sign. Surely she'd ask directions. Unless.

'She spoke no French?'

'And no English. Only Cree,' Beauvoir confirmed. In the silence Lacoste saw the formidable hotel, and Beauvoir saw the tiny, etched old woman with the shining eyes. A mother desperate to know what happened to her son, without the words to ask.

'What happened?' asked Lacoste.

'Can't you guess?' asked Beauvoir. They'd stopped again and Beauvoir was looking at Lacoste, her face troubled. Then her expression cleared.

'Chief Inspector Gamache found her.'

'He was staying at the Château Frontenac,' said Beauvoir. 'He'd seen the woman when he'd gone out in the morning, and noticed she was still there when he returned. He spoke to her.'

Isabelle Lacoste could see the whole scene. The chief, solid and courtly, approaching the solitary native woman. Lacoste could see the fear in her dark eyes as yet another official approached and wanted to move her along, out of sight of decent people. And she wouldn't understand Chief Inspector Gamache. He'd try French then English and she'd just stare up at him, wizened and worried. But one thing she would understand. He was kind.

'Her placard was in Cree, of course,' Beauvoir continued. 'The chief left her and brought back tea and sand-wiches and an interpreter from the Aboriginal Center. It was early fall and they sat on the side of the fountain in front of the hotel. You know it?'

'In the park? Under the old maple trees? I know it well. I sit there too whenever I visit Vieux Québec. The street performers are just down the hill in front of the cafés.'

'They sat there,' Beauvoir nodded, 'drinking tea and eating sandwiches. The chief said the elderly woman said a little prayer before eating, blessing their food. She was obviously starving, but she paused for prayer.'

Beauvoir and Lacoste were no longer looking at each other. They were facing each other on the dirt road, in the sunshine, but staring in opposite directions. Off into the woods, each in their own thoughts, playing out in their heads the scene in Old Quebec.

'She told him her son was missing. She told him he wasn't the only one. She told him about her village on the shores of James Bay, which until a year earlier had been dry. No alcohol, by decision of the band council. But the chief had been killed, the elders intimidated, the council of women disbanded. And then the alcohol had arrived, flown in by float plane. Within months their peaceful village was in ruins. But that wasn't the worst.'

'She told him about the murders,' said Lacoste. 'Did he believe her?'

Beauvoir nodded. Not for the first time he wondered what he'd do in the same situation. And not for the first time the ugly little answer came. He'd have been one of the ones snickering at her. And assuming he'd had the decency to approach, would he have believed her tale of intimidation and betrayal and murder?

Probably not. Or worse, he might have, but would have turned his back on her anyway. Pretended he hadn't heard. Hadn't understood.

He hoped that was no longer true, but he didn't know. All he knew for sure was that the elderly Cree woman's luck had turned.

At first Gamache had told no one about this encounter, not even Beauvoir.

He'd spent weeks flying from reserve to reserve across Northern Quebec. The snow was beginning to fall by the time he had his answers.

From the moment he'd looked into her eyes, sitting in that park in Old Quebec, he'd believed her. He was sickened and appalled, but he was in no doubt she was telling the truth.

Policemen had done this. She'd watched as these men had led the boys into the woods. The men had returned but the boys hadn't. Her son, Michael, was one of them. Named for the Archangel, he'd fallen in the woods and she'd searched and searched but couldn't find him.

Instead she'd found Armand Gamache.

'Who's there?' Gamache stood stock-still. His eyes had adjusted and his ears were attuned.

The creaking increased and grew closer. He tried not to think about what Reine-Marie had just told him, but to focus on the sound which seemed to be all around him.

Finally, something slightly darker appeared from behind one of the basement doors. The black toe of a black shoe. Then a leg swung slowly into view. He saw with complete clarity the leg, the hand, the gun.

Gamache didn't move. He stood in the very middle of the room and waited.

Now they were facing each other.

'Agent Lemieux,' said Gamache softly. He'd known as soon as he'd seen the revolver. But that hadn't eased the danger. He knew once a gun was drawn the gunman was committed to a course of action. A sudden fright could make him jerk his hand.

But Agent Lemieux's hand wavered not at all. He stood square in the rectangle of the room, the gun at waist level, pointing at the Chief Inspector.

Then, slowly, the muzzle lowered.

'Is that you, sir? You gave me a fright.'

'Didn't you hear me calling?'

'Was that you? I couldn't make out the words. It just sounded like a moan. I think this house is getting to me.'

'Do you have a flashlight? Mine's gone out,' said Gamache, walking toward Lemieux.

A beam of light appeared at Gamache's feet.

'Is your gun in your holster now?'

'Yes sir. Wait until people hear I drew on you.' Lemieux gave a strained little laugh. Gamache didn't. Instead he continued to stare at Lemieux. Then he finally spoke, his voice stern.

'What you just did is grounds for dismissal. You must never, ever draw your gun unless you're going to use it. You know that and yet you chose to ignore your training. Why?'

Lemieux had intended to spy on Gamache. But the chief's hearing was too good. Surprise was lost, but something else might be gained. Since Gamache was rattled by the house, why not rattle him a little more? He wondered how Brébeuf would react if he got rid of the Gamache problem by giving him a fatal heart attack. He'd tossed small stones and seen Gamache spin round. He'd moved a piece of rope so that something appeared to slither, and seen Gamache step back. And finally, he'd drawn his gun.

But Gamache had called his name, almost as though he'd known it was him. And the advantage had been lost. Worse than that, Chief Inspector Gamache seemed to have expanded. He stood absolutely unwavering in front of Lemieux, radiating not rage nor even fear, but power. Authority.

'I asked you a question, Agent Lemieux. Why did you draw your gun?'

'I'm sorry,' Lemieux stammered, falling back on the time-tested recipe of contrition and confession. 'I got scared, being here all alone.'

'You knew I was here.'

Gamache wasn't crumbling before this wretched display.

'And I was looking for you, sir. I heard something. Voices, and I knew you wouldn't be talking to anyone so I thought maybe there was someone else. Maybe the person who broke the police tape. Maybe you needed help. But,' Lemieux hung his head and shook it, 'there's no excuse. I could have killed you. Do you want my gun?'

'I want the truth. Don't lie to me, son.'

'I'm not lying, sir, really. I know it sounds pathetic, but I just got scared.'

And still Gamache was silent. Was this not going to work? Lemieux wondered.

'Oh, God. I'm a total screw-up. First the ephedra thing and now this.'

'It was a mistake,' said Gamache, his voice still hard but not as hard as before.

He'd won. What had Brébeuf said? 'Everyone loves a sinner, but none more than Gamache. He believes he can save the drowning. Your job is to drown.'

And so he had. He'd purposely left the ephedra clue up on Gabri's computer, to be caught and forgiven, and now he'd been caught again. Drawing his gun had been stupid, but he'd managed to turn a mistake into an advantage. And Gamache, pathetic, weak Gamache, was actually forgiving him for drawing his gun. That was Gamache's drug of choice, his weakness. He loved to forgive.

'Did you find anything, sir?'

'Nothing. This house isn't ready to give up its secrets.'

'Secrets? The house has secrets?'

'Houses are like people, Agent Lemieux. They have secrets. I'll tell you something I've learned.'

Armand Gamache dropped his voice so that Agent Lemieux had to strain to hear.

'Do you know what makes us sick, Agent Lemieux?'

Lemieux shook his head. Then out of the darkness and stillness he heard the answer.

'It's our secrets that make us sick.'

Behind him, a small creak broke the silence.

CHAPTER 30

'What happened then?' asked Lacoste. They were on their way back to the Incident Room. Once out of the canopy of trees they could see the storm cloud rising. It now blocked a quarter of the sky. Its progress was slow, but determined.

'*Pardon?*' Beauvoir asked, distracted by the sight of the cloud.

'The Chief Inspector? He had the evidence against Arnot and the others, what'd he do with it?'

'I don't know.'

'Oh, come on. You must know. He told you all the other stuff. The story about the Cree woman never came out in court.'

'No. They decided to keep that quiet, in case she became a target. You can't tell anyone.'

Lacoste was about to protest that anyone who might care was locked up, but then she remembered the morning's newspaper article. Someone still cared.

'I won't.'

Beauvoir nodded curtly and continued walking.

'There's more,' Lacoste said, running to catch up. 'What is it?'

'Agent Nichol.'

'What about her?'

Beauvoir knew he'd gone too far. Cautioned himself to stop. But still the words escaped, eager to find an accomplice, to find sympathetic company.

'She was sent by Superintendent Francoeur to spy on the Chief Inspector.'

The words themselves seemed to stink.

'*Merde*,' said Lacoste.

'*Merde*,' agreed Beauvoir.

'No, really. Shit.' Lacoste pointed to the ground. Sure enough, a huge pile of shit steamed by the side of the road. Beauvoir tried to twist out of the way but still managed to step in the side of it.

'God, it's disgusting.' He lifted his foot, all soft Italian leather and softer, stinking shit. 'Aren't people supposed to pick up after their dogs?'

He scraped the side of his shoe on the road, covering the leather with dirt as well as the shit.

'It isn't dog poop,' said an authoritative voice.

Beauvoir and Lacoste looked around but saw no one. Beauvoir peered into the forest. Had one of the trees stopped singing and actually spoken? Was it possible the very first words he heard from a tree were 'It isn't dog poop'? He turned to see Peter and Clara Morrow walking toward them. Guess not, thought Beauvoir, and wondered how long they'd been there and what they'd heard.

Peter bent and examined the pile. Only country people, thought Beauvoir, were endlessly fascinated by shit. Country people and parents.

'Bear,' Peter said, straightening up.

'We just walked by here minutes ago. You mean a bear was behind us?'

Were they kidding, Beauvoir wondered? But the couple was straight-faced and as serious as he'd ever seen them. Peter Morrow held a tightly rolled newspaper.

'Is the Chief Inspector around?'

'No, sorry. Can I help?'

'He's bound to see it eventually,' said Clara to Peter.

Peter nodded and handed Beauvoir the paper.

'We saw it this morning.' Beauvoir offered it back.

'Look again,' said Peter. Beauvoir sighed and opened it up. The banner said *Le Journal de Nous*. Not *La Journée*, as he'd expected. And there in the very center was a large picture of the Chief Inspector and his son Daniel. They were in some sort of stone building. It looked like a crypt. And Gamache was pushing an envelope on Daniel. The caption read, *Armand Gamache handing envelope to unknown man.*

Beauvoir scanned the story then had to go back and try to read more slowly. He was so upset he could barely take it in. The words blurred and bobbed and drowned in a gush of anger. Finally, gasping for air, he lowered the paper and as he did he saw Armand Gamache crossing the bridge, accompanied by Robert Lemieux. Their eyes met and Gamache smiled warmly, but when he saw the paper and the look on his young inspector's face the smile faded.

'*Bonjour.*' Gamache shook hands with Peter and bowed slightly to Clara. 'I see you've seen the latest.' He nodded to the paper in Beauvoir's hand.

'Have you?' Beauvoir asked.

'No, but Reine-Marie read it to me.'

'What're you going to do?' Beauvoir asked. It was as though the others had disappeared and all that existed for Beauvoir was the Chief Inspector, and the remarkable storm cloud rising behind him.

'I'll sit with it for a while.' Gamache nodded to the others, turned and walked to the Incident Room.

'Wait.' Beauvoir ran to catch up. He stepped in front of Gamache just before he reached the door. 'You can't just let them say these things. It's libel at the very least. My God, did Madame Gamache read it all to you? Listen to this.' Beauvoir snapped the paper open and began reading. 'At the very least the Sûreté du Québec owes Quebecers an explanation. How can a corrupt officer remain on the force? And in a position of great influence? It was clear during the Arnot investigation that Chief Inspector Gamache was himself involved and had a personal vendetta against his superior. But now he seems to have gone into business for himself. Who is the man he's slipping the envelope to, what's in the envelope, and what is the man being hired to do?'

Beauvoir crunched the paper in his hands and looked

Gamache straight in the face. 'This is your son. You're hand-ing an envelope to Daniel. There's no reason for any of this shit. Come on. All you have to do is pick up the phone and call the editors. Explain what you're doing.'

'Why?' Gamache's voice was calm, his gaze clear and without anger. 'So they can make up more lies? So they can know they've hurt me? No, Jean Guy. Just because I can an-swer an accusation doesn't mean I must. Trust me.'

'You're always saying that as though you need to remind me to trust you.' Now Beauvoir didn't care who heard. 'How many times do I have to prove it before you stop say-ing "trust me"?'

'I'm sorry.' And Gamache looked stricken for the first time. 'You're right. I don't doubt you, Jean Guy. Never have. I trust you.'

'And I trust you,' said Beauvoir, his voice calm now, his agitation lifted and caught in the gusts and taken from him. For a moment he imagined the word 'trust' replaced by an-other, but he knew 'trust' was enough. He looked at the big man and knew Gamache hadn't put a foot wrong yet. Cer-tainly Gamache wasn't the one with shit all over his Italian leather boots.

'Do what you must,' he said. 'I'll support you.'

'Thank you, Jean Guy. Right now I must call Daniel. It's getting late in Paris.'

'And Chief,' Lacoste now felt it safe to approach, 'the coroner wants a word. She said she'd meet you in the bistro at five.'

Gamache looked at his watch. 'Did you find anything in the room to explain the break-in?'

'Nothing,' said Lacoste. 'Did you find anything?'

What should he say? He'd found sorrow and terror and truth? We're only as sick as our secrets, he'd told Lemieux. Gamache had emerged from that cursed basement with a secret of his own.

Gilles Sandon hugged a leg to him and began caressing it. Up and down his rough hand went, agonizingly slowly.

With each pass his hand crept further up until finally he'd run out of leg.

'You're so smooth,' he said, blowing on the leg and picking minute particles from it. 'Wait until I oil you. Rich tung oil.'

'Who're you talking to?'

Odile slumped against the doorway. The contents of her glass and Gilles's workroom both swirled. Normally she turned her anger into wine and swallowed it, but lately it hadn't worked so well.

Gilles looked up, startled, as though caught in a humiliating and private act. The worn piece of fine sandpaper fluttered to the floor. He could smell the wine. Five o'clock. Maybe it wasn't that bad. Most people have a drink or two at five. After all, there was the fine Québécois tradition of the *'cinq à sept.'*

'I was talking to the leg,' he said, and for the first time the words sounded ridiculous.

'Isn't that sort of a silly thing to do?'

He looked at the leg, destined to be part of a fine table. It had honestly never before occurred to him it was silly. He wasn't a stupid man and knew most people didn't talk to trees but he figured that was their problem.

'I've been working on another poem. Wanna hear it?'

Without waiting for an answer Odile rolled off the door jamb and walked slowly and with great care to the front counter of their store. She returned with her notebook.

'Listen.

> *How prone is piebald man to mourn,*
> *And make ado of nothing much,*
> *To strew his rosy path with thorn,*
> *And rusty nails, yea, plenty such.*

'Wait.' She fell against the doorway as he turned his back. 'There's more. And you can drop that fucking thing.'

He looked down and realized he was strangling the leg, his fingers tight and white as though the blood had leached from him into the wood. After a moment's hesitation, he placed it carefully on the floor, making sure to put it on a bed of woodchips.

> *'Tis not for he the sparrow pipes,*
> *Nor blows the bullfrog in the rill,*
> *Ah, not for he the heron wipes,*
> *His stately nose upon his quill.*

Odile lowered her book and gave Gilles a knowing look. Nodding a few times she closed her book and walked with great concentration back into the store. Gilles watched and wondered what she was trying to tell him. How was it he understood trees but not Odile?

He suddenly felt uneasy as though ants were crawling inside his skin. Bringing the wooden leg to his face he inhaled deeply and was transported to the forest. The tender, watchful forest. Safe. But even there his thoughts ran him to earth.

What did Odile know? Wasn't a quill a type of pen? Was she planning to write something less abstruse about him? Was she warning him? If so, she had to be stopped.

He tapped his palm rhythmically with the exquisite wooden leg as he thought.

At his desk Armand Gamache smoothed the crumpled newspaper. Up until that moment he'd only had people read it to him and that had been shocking enough. But his heart gave a contraction as he looked at the picture. Daniel's hand on the envelope he'd forced on him just yesterday morning. Daniel, beautiful Daniel, a big bear of a man. Couldn't everyone see they were father and son? Were the editors deliberately blind? But Gamache knew the answer to that. Someone was blocking out their reason.

He reached for the phone and dialed Daniel.

Dr Sharon Harris pulled her car up to the kerb and was about to go into the bistro. Through its mullioned window she could see the Morrows and a few others she knew slightly. She could see the fire jumping in the grate and Gabri holding a tray of drinks and telling a story to an amused group of villagers. As she watched, Olivier expertly took the tray from Gabri and delivered the drinks to another group. Gabri sat down, crossed his massive legs and continued the story. She thought she saw him take a sip from someone's whiskey, but she wasn't sure. She turned and looked at the village. Lights were beginning to appear and the sweet scent of log fires was in the air. The three massive pines on the village green threw long evening shadows now. She looked into the sky. More than night was closing in. She'd listened to the forecast in the car and even Environment Canada was surprised that such a mammoth system had suddenly appeared. But what did it contain? The forecasters didn't know. Could be rain or sleet or even snow at this time of year.

Since she didn't see Chief Inspector Gamache in the bistro Dr Harris decided to sit on the bench on the green and get some air. As she bent to sit down something beneath the bench caught her eye. She picked it up, examined it, and smiled.

Across the road Ruth Zardo's door opened and the elderly woman came out. She stood there for a moment and Harris had the impression Ruth was talking to some invisible person. Then she clumped down the steps and at the bottom said a few more words into the air.

Finally lost it, thought Dr Harris. Fried her brain with verse and worse.

Ruth turned and did something that horrified Dr Harris, who knew the misanthrope slightly. She smiled and waved at the young doctor. Dr Harris waved back and wondered what malevolent scheme Ruth had hatched to make her so happy. Then she saw it.

As Ruth limped across the road two tiny birds formed a very small tail behind her. One was spreading its wings and flapping, the other was limping a little and falling behind. Ruth stopped and waited, then started again, more slowly.

'Quite a family,' said Gamache, landing in the seat beside Dr Harris.

'Look what I found.'

Dr Harris opened her fist and there in the cradle of her palm sat a tiny egg. A robin's egg blue, but not actually a robin's egg. It was also green and pink in a pattern so intricate and delicate Gamache had to put on his half-moon glasses to appreciate it.

'Where on earth did you find that?'

'Right here, under the bench. Can you believe it? It's wood, I think.' She handed it to him. He brought it up to his face and stared at it until his eyes crossed.

'Beautiful. I wonder where it came from.'

Dr Harris was shaking her head. 'This place. How do you explain a village like Three Pines where poets take ducks for walks and art seems to fall from the skies?'

On the mention of skies both of them looked at the storm cloud, now almost halfway up the sky.

'I wouldn't expect many Rembrandts from that,' said Gamache.

'No. More abstract than classic, I think.'

Gamache laughed. He liked Dr Harris.

'Poor Ruth. You know she smiled at me just now.'

'Smiled? Do you think she's dying?'

'No, but I think the little one is.'

Dr Harris pointed to the smaller of the ducks, struggling across the grass to the pond. The two sat on their bench and watched. Ruth went over to the straggler and walked very slowly beside it, the two limping along like mother and child.

'What killed Madeleine Favreau, doctor?'

'Ephedra. She had five or six times the recommended level of ephedra in her system.'

Gamache nodded. 'That's what the toxicology said, of course. Could it have been given to her over dinner?'

'Had to have been. It works fairly quickly. I don't think it'd be a problem slipping it into any of the food.'

'But there's more, isn't there,' said Gamache. 'Not everyone who dies from ephedra has a look of horror on their faces.'

'True. You want to know what really killed her?'

Gamache nodded.

Sharon Harris looked up from his strong, calm face and nodded to the hillside.

'That killed her. The old Hadley house.'

'Come along, doctor. Houses don't kill.' Gamache tried to sound convincing.

'Perhaps not, but fear does. Do you believe in ghosts, Chief Inspector?' When he was silent she went on. 'I'm a doctor, a scientist, but I've been in homes that scare the hell out of me. I've been invited to parties in perfectly fine places. New houses even, and felt a dread. Felt a presence.'

She'd debated with herself all the way over. Should she tell him everything? Should she admit this? But she knew she had to. To find a killer, she had to expose herself. But she knew she'd never admit these things to any other Sûreté officer.

'Do you believe in haunted houses?' Gamache asked.

Dr Harris was suddenly eleven and creeping through the pine forest toward the Tremblay place. It was buried in the woods, abandoned, dark, brooding.

'Someone was killed there once,' her friend had hissed into her ear. 'A kid. Strangled and stabbed.'

She'd heard he'd been beaten to death by his uncle, but someone else had said he'd died of starvation.

However he went, he was still there. Waiting. Waiting to possess the body of some other kid. To come alive again, and avenge his death.

They'd crept to within yards of the Tremblay place. It was night and the dark woods closed in and all things familiar and comforting during the day became unfamiliar. Branches cracked and footsteps approached and something creaked and little Sharon Harris had fled, running, tumbling through the forest, trees reaching out and scraping flesh from her face and behind her she heard panting. Was it her friend, abandoned by her? Or the dead boy, reaching out? She could feel his freezing hands on her shoulders, desperate to take a life.

The faster she ran the more terrified she became until she finally broke through the trees sobbing and petrified, and alone.

Even today, as she leaned in to the mirror, she could see the tiny scars made by the trees and her own terror. And she remembered that night she'd left her best friend to be taken instead of her. Of course, the friend had burst through the trees a moment later, also sobbing. And they both knew that dead boy had indeed stolen something. He'd stolen the trust between friends.

Sharon Harris believed houses could be haunted, but she knew for sure people were.

'Do I believe in haunted houses, Chief Inspector? Are you really asking me that? A doctor and a scientist?'

'I am,' he smiled.

'Do you believe it?'

'Now, you know me, doctor. I believe everything.'

She hesitated for a moment, then decided, what the hell.

'That place is haunted.' She didn't have to look, they both knew what she meant. 'By what, I don't know. Madeleine Favreau knows, but she had to die to find out. Me? I don't want to know that badly.'

The two sat quietly on the bench in the very center of the peaceful village. Around them, as they talked about ghosts and demons and death, people walked their dogs and chatted and gardened. Gamache waited for Dr Harris to continue, and watched as Ruth tried to coax the tiny balls of fluff into the pond.

'I did a bit of research this afternoon on ephedra. It's from the'—she pulled a notepad from her pocket—'gymnosperm shrub.'

'It's an herb, isn't it?' said Gamache.

'You knew?'

'Agent Lemieux told me.'

'It grows all over the place. It's an old-fashioned cold remedy and antihistamine. The Chinese knew about it centuries ago. Called it Ma Huang. Then the pharmaceuticals got hold of it and started making Ephedrine.'

'You say it grows all over the place—'

'You're wondering whether it grows here? It does. There's one over there.' She pointed to a huge tree on a front lawn. Gamache got up and walked over to it, bending down to pick up a leathery, brown leaf, fallen in the autumn.

'It's a ginkgo tree,' said Dr Harris, joining him and picking up a leaf of her own. It was an unusual shape, more of a fan than a classic leaf, with thick veins, like sinews. 'It's part of the gymnosperm family.'

'Could someone extract ephedra from this?' Gamache showed her his leaf.

'I don't know whether it comes from the leaf or the bark or something else. What I do know is that being from the same family doesn't necessarily mean it has ephedra in it. But as I said before, the combination of ephedra and a scare wasn't enough.'

They turned and walked back to the bench, Gamache rubbing the leaf between his fingers, feeling its skeleton in his hand.

'Something else had to happen?' he asked.

'Something else had to exist,' Dr Harris nodded.

'What?' Gamache asked, hoping she wasn't going to say a ghost.

'Madeleine Favreau had to have had a heart condition.'

'Did she?'

'She did,' said Dr Harris. 'According to my autopsy, she had fairly severe heart damage, almost certainly from her breast cancer.'

'Breast cancer damages the heart?'

'Not the cancer, but the treatment. The chemo. Breast cancer in younger women can be extremely aggressive so doctors give high doses of chemo to fight it. The women are normally consulted before it's done, but the equation is simple. Feel wretched for months, lose your hair, risk a heart problem or almost certainly die of breast cancer.'

'Jesus wept,' whispered Gamache.

'I think so.'

'You're looking very serious.' Ruth Zardo had walked up to their bench. 'Fucking up the Favreau case?'

'Probably.' Gamache rose and bowed to the old poet. 'Do you know Dr Harris?'

'Never met.' They shook hands. This was about the tenth time Sharon Harris had been introduced to Ruth.

'We've been admiring your family.' Gamache nodded toward the pond.

'Do they have names?' Dr Harris asked.

'The big one's Rosa and the little one's Lilium. They were found among the flowers by the pond.'

'Beautiful,' said Dr Harris, watching Rosa plop into the pond. Lilium took a step and stumbled. Ruth, her back to the birds, somehow sensed something was wrong and limped rapidly to the pond, lifting the little one out, soaking but alive.

'That was close,' said Ruth, dabbing gently at the duckling's face with her sleeve. Sharon Harris wondered if she should say something. Surely Ruth had noticed how frail Lilium was?

'Storm's almost here.' Dr Harris looked to the sky. 'I really don't want to be on the road in that. But I have one more piece of information you need.'

'What is it?' Gamache accompanied her to her car as Ruth walked home, Rosa quacking behind and Lilium in the palm of her hand.

'I don't think this contributed to her death, not directly anyway, but it is puzzling. Madeleine Favreau's breast cancer had returned. And badly. There were lesions on her liver. Not large, but I'd say she wouldn't have seen Christmas.'

Gamache paused to digest this information.

'Would she have known?'

'I don't know. It's possible she didn't, but honestly? The women I know who've had breast cancer get so in tune with their bodies, it's almost psychic. It's a powerful connection. Descartes was wrong, you know. There is no division between mind and body. These women know. Not the initial diagnosis, but if it comes back? They know.'

Sharon Harris got in her car and drove off just as the first huge drops of rain fell and the winds picked up and the sky over the tiny village grew purple and impenetrable. Armand Gamache made it to the bistro before the heavens opened. Settling into a wing chair he ordered a Scotch and a licorice pipe and gazing out the window as the storm closed in around Three Pines he wondered who would want to kill a dying woman.

CHAPTER 31

'Good book?'

Myrna leaned over Gamache's shoulder. He'd been so absorbed in his book he hadn't even seen her coming.

'I don't know,' he admitted, and handed it to her. He'd emptied his pockets of the books he'd gathered. He felt like a mobile library. Where other investigators gathered fingerprints and evidence, he gathered books. Not everyone would agree it was a move in the right direction.

'Terrible storm.' Myrna flopped into the large chair opposite and ordered a red wine. 'Thank heaven I don't have to go outside. In fact, if I wanted I'd never have to go outside again. Everything I need is here.'

She opened her arms happily, her colorful caftan draping over the arms of her chair.

'Food from Sarah and Monsieur Béliveau, company and coffee here—'

'Your red wine, your highness,' said Gabri, lowering the bulbous glass to the dark wood table.

'You may go now.' Myrna inclined her head in a surprisingly regal gesture. 'I have wine and Scotch and all the books I could want to read.'

She lifted her glass and Gamache lifted his.

'*Santé*.' They smiled at each other, sipped, and stared at the torrential rain streaming down the leaded glass windows.

'Now, what have we here?' Myrna put on her reading glasses and examined the small leather volume Gamache had given her. 'Where'd you find this?' she finally asked, letting her glasses drop on their rope to land on the plateau of her bosom.

'The room where Madeleine died. It was in the book-case.'

Myrna immediately put the book down, as though wickedness was communicable. It sat between them, its cover simple and striking. A small hand outlined in red. It looked like blood, but Gamache had satisfied himself it was ink.

'It's a book on magic,' said Myrna. 'Couldn't see a pub-lisher or ISBN number. Probably vanity printed in small numbers.'

'Any idea how old it is?'

Myrna leaned over, but didn't touch it again.

'Leather's cracking a bit at the spine and some pages look loose. Glue must have dried. I'd say it was made be-fore the First World War. Is there an inscription?'

Gamache shook his head.

'Ever seen anything like it in your store?' he asked.

Myrna pretended to think but knew the answer. She'd remember something that macabre. She loved books. All books. She had some on the occult and some on magic. But if anything came in like the one sitting between them she'd give it away quick. To someone she didn't like.

'Nope, never.'

'How about this one?' Gamache reached into his inside pocket and brought out the book he'd recently read from cover to cover, and was loath to give up.

He'd expected a polite, curious look. Perhaps even amuse-ment and recognition. He hadn't expected horror.

'Where'd you find that?' She grabbed it out of his hand and shoved it down the side of the chair.

'What is it?' Gamache asked, astonished by her reac-tion.

But Myrna wasn't listening. Instead her eyes scanned the room, resting on Monsieur Béliveau standing at the door, befuddled. Then he moved away.

Reaching down she brought out the book and placed it on the table. Now a small stack of books sat there. The strange leather-bound volume with the red hand, a Bible, and this new one with the comic cover that had created such turmoil.

'Who is Sarah Binks?' He tapped the top book.

'She's the Sweet Songstress of Saskatoon,' said Myrna, as though that explained everything. Gamache had already searched the Internet for Sarah Binks, and knew about the book, a supposed tribute to the worst poet ever born. It was big-hearted, warm and funny, and it had been hidden by Madeleine.

'I found it in the back of a drawer in Madeleine's bedroom.'

'Madeleine had it?'

'You expected someone else?'

'I can never keep track of books. People lend them all over the place. Bane of a bookseller's life. Instead of buying they borrow.'

And she did look put out, but not, he suspected, by rogue books. She was scanning the room, suddenly jumpy and ill at ease.

'What's the matter?' he asked, then had his answer. Myrna's eyes had stopped their travels and had settled back on the gaunt man at the bar. Monsieur Béliveau was looking sad and lost.

'He's always like that.' She took a handful of nuts, spilling a bunch of cashews onto the table. Gamache absently picked them up and popped them into his mouth.

'Meaning?'

Myrna hesitated for a moment. 'I know he's had reason. His wife was sick for a long time before she died. And now Madeleine's death. And yet he's able to go to work, open the store and function just fine.'

'Maybe he's used to grief. Maybe for him it's become normal.'

'Maybe. If you lost your wife would you go to work the next day?'

'Madeleine wasn't his wife,' said Gamache, hurrying to drown out the image of Reine-Marie dead.

'Ginette was and he opened his store the next day. Is he brave, or are we seeing the near enemy?'

'The what?'

'The near enemy. It's a psychological concept. Two emotions that look the same but are actually opposites. The one parades as the other, is mistaken for the other, but one is healthy and the other's sick, twisted.'

Gamache put his glass down. The condensation made his fingers slightly wet. Or was it the sweat that had suddenly appeared on his palms? The noises of the storm, the rain and hail pounding frantically on the window, the conversation and laughter inside the bistro receded.

He leaned forward and spoke, his voice low. 'Can you give me an example?'

'There are three couplings,' said Myrna, herself leaning forward now, and whispering though she didn't know why. 'Attachment masquerades as Love, Pity as Compassion and Indifference as Equanimity.'

Armand Gamache was quiet for a moment, looking into Myrna's eyes, trying to divine from them the deeper meaning of what she'd just said. There was a deeper meaning, he knew it. Something important had just been said.

But he hadn't understood it fully. His eyes drifted to the fireplace while Myrna leaned back in her overstuffed chair and swirled her red wine in its bulbous glass.

'I don't understand,' Gamache said finally, bringing his eyes back to Myrna. 'Can you explain?'

Myrna nodded. 'Pity and compassion are the easiest to understand. Compassion involves empathy. You see the stricken person as an equal. Pity doesn't. If you pity someone you feel superior.'

'But it's hard to tell one from the other,' Gamache nodded.

'Exactly. Even for the person feeling it. Almost everyone would claim to be full of compassion. It's one of the noble emotions. But really, it's pity they feel.'

'So pity is the near enemy of compassion,' said Gamache slowly, mulling it over.

'That's right. It looks like compassion, acts like compassion, but is actually the opposite of it. And as long as pity's in place there's not room for compassion. It destroys, squeezes out, the nobler emotion.'

'Because we fool ourselves into believing we're feeling one, when we're actually feeling the other.'

'Fool ourselves, and fool others,' said Myrna.

'And love and attachment?' asked Gamache.

'Mothers and children are classic examples. Some mothers see their job as preparing their kids to live in the big old world. To be independent, to marry and have children of their own. To live wherever they choose and do what makes them happy. That's love. Others, and we all see them, cling to their children. Move to the same city, the same neighborhood. Live through them. Stifle them. Manipulate, use guilt-trips, cripple them.'

'Cripple them? How?'

'By not teaching them to be independent.'

'But it's not just mothers and children,' said Gamache.

'No. It's friendships, marriages. Any intimate relationship. Love wants the best for others. Attachment takes hostages.'

Gamache nodded. He'd seen his share of those. Hostages weren't allowed to escape, and when they tried tragedy followed.

'And the last?' He leaned forward again. 'What was it?'

'Equanimity and indifference. I think that's the worst of the near enemies, the most corrosive. Equanimity is balance. When something overwhelming happens in our lives we feel it strongly but we also have an ability to overcome it. You must have seen it. People who somehow survive the loss of a child or a spouse. As a psychologist I saw it all the time. Unbelievable grief and sorrow. But deep down inside people find a core. That's called equanimity. An ability to accept things and move on.'

Gamache nodded. He'd been deeply affected by families who'd risen above the murder of a loved one. Some had even been able to forgive.

'How's that like indifference?' he asked, not seeing the connection.

'Think about it. All those stoic people. Stiff upper lip. Calm in the face of tragedy. And some really are that brave. But some,' she lowered her voice even more, 'are psychotic. They just don't feel pain. And you know why?'

Gamache was silent. Beside him the storm threw itself against the leaded glass as though desperate to interrupt their conversation. Hail hammered the glass and snow plastered itself there, blotting out the village beyond until it felt as though he and Myrna were in a world all their own.

'They don't care about others. They don't feel like the rest of us. They're like the Invisible Man, wrapped in the trappings of humanity, but beneath there's emptiness.'

Gamache felt his own skin grow cold and he knew goose bumps had sprung up on his arms under his jacket.

'The problem is telling one from another,' Myrna whispered, straining to keep an eye on the grocer. 'People with equanimity are unbelievably brave. They absorb the pain, feel it fully, and let it go. And you know what?'

'What?' Gamache whispered.

'They look exactly like people who don't care at all, who are indifferent. Cool, calm and collected. We revere it. But who's brave, and who's the near enemy?'

Gamache leaned back in his seat, warmed by the fire. The enemy, he knew then, was near.

Agents Lacoste and Lemieux had left for the day and Inspector Beauvoir was alone in the Incident Room. Except for Nichol. She was hunched over her computer, her pasty face looking like something dead.

The clock said six. Time to go. He picked up his leather coat and opened the door. Then closed it quickly.

'Holy shit.'

'What?' Nichol wandered over. Beauvoir stepped back and invited her to open the door. She looked at him with suspicion then quickly did so.

A blast of ice-cold rain hit her, and something else. As she leaped further back she noticed something bouncing. Hail. Fucking hail? The door was banging now in the wind and as she reached to shut it she noticed snow swirling in the light as well.

Fucking snow?

Rain, hail and snow? Where're the frogs?

Just then a phone rang. It was the tinny tune of a cell phone. A familiar tune, but not one Beauvoir could place. It certainly wasn't his. He looked at Nichol who finally had some blood in her face. She looked made up by a vindictive mortician, great red splotches on her cheeks and forehead. The rest remained waxy.

'I believe your phone is ringing.'

'Not mine. Lacoste must have left hers.'

'It's yours.' Beauvoir stepped toward her. He had a pretty good idea who would be on the other end of the line. 'Answer it.'

'It's a wrong number.'

'If you won't, I will.' He advanced on her and she backed up.

'No. I'll get it.' She opened it slowly, obviously hoping the ringing would stop before she had to hit the button. But the phone kept ringing. Beauvoir advanced. Nichol jumped back but wasn't quick enough. In a flash Beauvoir had grabbed the phone.

'*Bonjour?*' he said.

The line was dead.

The bistro was nearly empty. The fire crackled softly in the grate, sending amber and crimson light spilling into the room. It was warm and comfortable, and quiet, except for the occasional thud as the storm produced a particularly violent blast.

Beauvoir brought a book from his satchel.

'Wonderful,' said Gamache, reaching for the yearbook. He leaned back in his chair, put on his glasses, reached for his red wine and disappeared. Beauvoir didn't think he ever saw the chief as happy as when he had a book in his hands.

Beauvoir took a slice of crisp baguette, smeared it thickly with pâté and ate. Outside the wind howled. Inside all was calm and relaxed.

A few minutes later the door opened and Jeanne Chauvet blew in, her hair and a look of shock plastered to her face. Gamache rose from his seat and bowed to her slightly. She chose a table well away from them.

'What do you want to bet Nichol chased her out of the B & B and into the storm? Only she could scare a woman who raises the dead for a living.'

Their starters arrived. Gabri put a lobster bisque in front of Gamache and a French onion soup before Beauvoir.

The two men ate and continued their conversation. This was Beauvoir's favorite part of any investigation. Putting his head together with the Chief Inspector. Tossing around thoughts, ideas. Nothing formal, no notes taken. Just thinking out loud. With food and drink.

'What struck you?' asked Gamache, tapping the yearbook. His soup was smooth with a rich taste of lobster and lightly flavored with cognac.

'I thought her grad photo caption might be significant.'

'That Tanguay prison remark. Yes, I caught that too.'

Gamache turned once more to the grad photos, this time looking at Hazel. She'd obviously just been to the beauty shop before the picture. Her hair was puffy, her eyes black with too much liner and bulging. Her inscription read, *Hazel enjoyed sports and the drama club. She never got mad.*

She never got mad, thought Gamache and wondered whether that was an example of equanimity or indifference. Who never got mad?

He turned to the Drama Society page. And there was Hazel, smiling, her arm round a heavily made-up actress. Underneath the picture was written, *Madeleine Gagnon as Rosalind in* As You Like It. A description of the school play, a singular success, was written by its producer. Hazel Lang.

'Wonder how Madeleine had time for it all. Sports, school play,' said Beauvoir. 'She was even a cheerleader.' He flipped through the book until he found the page. 'Here, see? There she is.'

Sure enough, there was Madeleine, full smile, hair gleaming even in the black and white photo. All wore short kilts. Tight little sweaters. Fresh and cheerful faces. All young, all lovely. Gamache read the names of the squad. Monique, Joan, Madeleine, Georgette. And one missing. A girl named Jeanne. Jeanne Potvin.

'Did you notice the name of the missing cheerleader?' Gamache asked. 'Jeanne.'

He turned the book around for Beauvoir then looked over at the solitary woman at her table.

'You don't really think . . .' Beauvoir jerked his head in that direction.

'Stranger things have happened.'

'Like séances and ghosts? You think maybe she magically transformed herself from a beautiful cheerleader into that?'

Both men looked at the mousy woman dressed in a drab sweater and slacks.

'*I have seen flowers come in stony places, And kind things done by men with ugly faces,*' Gamache said, watching Jeanne Chauvet.

Just then Olivier appeared with their dinner. Beauvoir was doubly pleased. Not only did he get his food, but it stopped the chief from reciting more poetry. Beauvoir was growing tired of pretending to understand stuff that totally went over his head. Gamache's *coq au vin* filled the table with a rich, earthy aroma and an unexpected hint of maple. Delicate young beans and glazed baby carrots sat in their own white serving dish. A massive charbroiled steak smothered in panfried onions was placed in front of Beauvoir. A mound of *frites* sat in his serving dish.

Beauvoir could have died happily right there and then, but he'd have missed the *crème brûlée* for dessert.

'Who do you think did it?' Beauvoir asked, chomping on *frites*.

'For a woman so loved we seem to have no end of suspects,' said Gamache. 'She was murdered by someone who had access to ephedra and who knew about the séance. But the murderer probably knew one other thing.'

'What?'

'That Madeleine Favreau had a heart condition.'

Gamache told Beauvoir about the coroner's report.

'But no one we've talked to has mentioned it,' said Beauvoir, sipping his beer. 'Is it possible the murderer didn't know? He thought giving her ephedra and taking her to the old Hadley house would be enough.'

Gamache wiped up gravy with soft, warm bread. 'It's possible.'

'But if Madeleine had a heart condition, why keep it secret?'

And what other secrets might Madeleine have had, and tried to take with her screaming into the grave?

'Maybe the murderer just got lucky,' said Beauvoir. But both men knew although this was a murder that had relied on many things, luck wasn't one of them.

CHAPTER 32

Jeanne Chauvet sat with her back to the room and tried to pretend she liked being alone. Tried to pretend she was mesmerized by the warm and lively fire. Tried to pretend she didn't feel bruised and buffeted by the cold stares of the villagers, almost as violent as the storm outside. Tried to pretend she belonged. In Three Pines.

She'd felt immediately comfortable the moment her little car had glided down du Moulin a few short days ago, the village bathed in bright sun, the trees covered in chartreuse buds, the people smiling and nodding gently to each other. Some even bowed to each other as Gamache had just now in a courtly, courteous way that seemed only to exist in this magical valley.

Jeanne Chauvet had seen enough of the world, this and the others, to know a magical place. And Three Pines was one. She felt as though she'd been swimming all her life, but an island had risen. That night she'd lain in bed in the B & B, snuggled into the crisp clean linen, and been sung to sleep by the frogs in the pond. Years of tired started to slip away. Not exhaustion, but a weariness as though her very bones had been fossilized, turned to stone, and were dragging her to the weedy bottom.

But that night in bed she knew Three Pines had saved her. From the moment she'd received the brochure through the mail she'd dared to hope.

But then she'd seen Madeleine that Friday night at the

séance and her island had sunk, like Atlantis. She was once again in over her head.

She took a sip of Olivier's strong, rich coffee, made a warm caramel color by the cream, and pretended the villagers, so friendly when she'd first arrived, hadn't themselves turned to stone, cold and hard and unforgiving. She could almost see them marching toward her, with torches in the hands and terror in their eyes.

All because of Madeleine. Some things never changed. All Jeanne had ever wanted was to belong, and all Madeleine had ever done was take that from her.

'May we join you?'

Jeanne started and looked up. Armand Gamache and Jean Guy Beauvoir were looking down at her, Gamache with a warm smile on his face, his eyes thoughtful and kind. The other looked grumpy.

He doesn't want to be here with me, thought Jeanne, though she knew she didn't have to be a psychic to figure that one out.

'Please.' She indicated the soft chairs on either side of the hearth, their faded fabrics warmed by the fire.

'Are you planning to move anywhere else?' Gabri huffed.

'The night is young, *patron*,' Gamache smiled. 'May I offer you something?' he asked Jeanne.

'I have my coffee, thank you.'

'We were about to order some liqueurs. It feels a night for one.' He looked briefly at the mullioned window, reflecting the warm interior of the bistro. The old panes quivered in another blast, and a slight tinkling told them the hail wasn't finished.

'God,' sighed Gabri, 'how can we live in a country that does this to us?'

'I'll have an espresso and a brandy and Benedictine,' said Beauvoir.

Gamache turned to Jeanne. For some reason she felt in the company of her father, or perhaps her grandfather, even though the Chief Inspector couldn't be more than ten years her elder. There was something old world about him, as though he was from another age, another era. She wondered if he found it hard in this world. But she thought not.

'Yes, please. I'd like a . . .' She thought for a moment then turned to look at the row of liqueur bottles on a shelf at the back of the bar. Tia Maria, crème de menthe, cognac. She turned back to Gabri, 'I'll have a Cointreau, *s'il vous plaît.*'

Gamache ordered his own then the three of them discussed the weather, the Eastern Townships, and the conditions of the roads until their drinks arrived.

'Have you always been psychic, Madame Chauvet?' asked Gamache once Gabri had reluctantly left.

'I think so, but it wasn't until I was about ten that I realized not everyone saw the world as I did.' She brought the tiny glass to her nose and sniffed. Orange and sweet and somehow warm. Her eyes started watering just from the smell. She brought the Cointreau to her lips and wetted them with the syrupy liquid. Then she lowered the glass and licked her lips. She wanted this to last. The tastes, smells, sights. The company.

'How'd you find out?'

She didn't normally talk about these things, but then people didn't normally ask. She hesitated and looked at Gamache for a long moment. Then she spoke.

'At a friend's birthday party. I looked at all the wrapped presents and knew exactly what was in them.'

'Well, as long as you didn't say anything,' said Gamache, then looked at her more closely. 'But you did, didn't you?'

Beauvoir was a little miffed by this psychic turn by the chief. After all, he was the one who was supposed to have been born with a caul. He'd spent the late afternoon, after Nichol had hightailed it back to the B & B, surfing the web for information on cauls. Took him a while to figure out how to spell it. Cowels. Kowls. Calls. Then he remembered that Batman supposedly wore one. So he Googled Batman, and everything fell into place. Every day held its surprises.

At first he thought she meant he'd been born with a silly mask and pointy black ears. But then something even more macabre appeared on his screen.

'Yes,' Jeanne was saying. 'I was about halfway through the pile, telling everyone what each parcel held, when the birthday girl burst into tears. I remember to this day looking around the room. All the little girls, my friends, were staring at me. Angry and upset. And behind them their mothers. Afraid.

'It was never the same after that. I think I'd always seen things but I assumed everyone did. Heard voices, saw spirits. Knew what would happen next. Not for everything. It was selective. But enough.'

Her voice was cheery, but Gamache knew it couldn't have been easy. He looked over her shoulder to the villagers at their tables, having a relaxing and quiet dinner. But not one had approached Jeanne. The weirdo, the psychic. The witch. They were kind people, he knew. But even kind people can be afraid.

'It must have been hard,' said the chief.

'Others have it harder. Believe me, I know. I'm no one's victim, Chief Inspector. Besides, I never, ever lose my keys. Can you say that?'

She was looking at Gamache as she said it, but the wide smile on her face faded a little as she turned to look directly at Jean Guy Beauvoir. Her face was so full of understanding, of caring, he almost admitted that he too had never, ever lost his keys.

He'd been born with a caul. He'd called his mother and asked and after a hesitation she'd admitted it.

'*Mais, Maman*, why not tell me?'

'I was too embarrassed. It was a shameful thing at the time, Jean Guy. Even the nuns at the hospital were upset.'

'But why?'

'A baby born with a caul is either cursed or blessed. It means you see things, know things.'

'And did I?' He felt a fool asking. After all, he should be the one to know.

'I don't know. Every time you said something odd we ignored you. After a while you stopped. I'm sorry, Jean Guy. Maybe we were wrong, but I didn't want you to be cursed.'

Me, or you? he almost asked.

'But maybe I'd be blessed, Maman.'

'That's a curse too, *mon beau*.'

He'd been delivered of his mother with a veil over his entire head. Something between himself and this world. A membrane that should have stayed with his mother but somehow ended up coming with him. It was rare and upsetting and even today, according to his research, people believed those born with cauls were fated to lead unusual lives. Lives filled with spirits, with the dead and dying. And the ability to divine the future.

Was that why he was in homicide? Was that why he chose to spend all day with the newly dead, and hunt people who created ghosts? For more than ten years he'd mocked and ribbed and criticized the chief for relying so heavily on intuition. And the chief had just smiled and continued while he himself had bowed before the perfection of facts, of things you could touch and see and feel and hear. Now he wasn't so sure.

'What brought you here?' Gamache was asking Jeanne Chauvet.

'I got a brochure through the mail. It looked wonderful and I needed a rest. I think I told you this before.'

'Being a psychic's tiring?' asked Beauvoir, suddenly interested.

'Being a receptionist at a car dealership's tiring. I needed a rest and this just seemed perfect.'

Should she tell them the rest? The writing across the top of the brochure? She'd seen the same one in the vestibule of the B & B, and there was no writing. Had someone really taken the time to write that strange statement on her brochure just to lure her to Three Pines? Or was she paranoid?

'Where're you from?' Gamache asked.

'Montreal. Born and raised.'

Gamache handed her the yearbook. 'Look familiar?'

'It's a yearbook. I have one too from my school. Haven't looked at it in years. Probably lost it by now.'

'I thought you said you never lose things,' said Beauvoir.

'Nothing I don't want to lose,' she smiled, handing Gamache back the book.

'What high school did you go to?' Gamache asked.

'Gareth James High School, in Verdun. Why?'

'Just trying to make connections.' Armand Gamache swirled his cognac lazily in his glass. 'People rarely murder people they don't know. There's something about this case.'

He let it hang there, not feeling any need to explain. After a moment Jeanne spoke.

'There's an intimacy about it,' she said quietly. 'No, there's more. It feels crowded.'

Gamache nodded, still looking into his amber liqueur. 'The past caught up with Madeleine Favreau on Easter Sunday, in the old Hadley house. You brought something to life.'

'That's not fair. I was invited to do the séance. It wasn't my idea.'

'You could have said no,' he said. 'You've just said you know things, sense things, see things. Couldn't you see something coming?'

Outside the wind howled as Jeanne Chauvet thought back to that night in this very bistro. Someone had suggested another séance. Someone had suggested the old Hadley house. And something had changed. She'd felt it. A dread had crept into their happy, laughing circle.

She'd stolen a look at Madeleine, lovely, laughing Madeleine, looking weary and nervous. Madeleine hadn't even recognized her.

Jeanne had seen then the thinly masked revulsion Mad felt at the very idea of a séance at the old Hadley house.

And that had been enough. A truck could have been bearing down upon them and all Jeanne would see was a way to hurt Madeleine.

It had never occurred to her to decline the second séance.

CHAPTER 33

'Shouldn't you be in the studio?' Peter asked, pouring himself another coffee and walking to the long pine table in their kitchen. He'd promised himself he'd say nothing. And certainly not remind Clara time was slipping away. The last thing she needed to hear was that Denis Fortin would be there in just a few days. To see her still unfinished work.

'He'll be here in less than a week,' he heard himself saying. It was as though something had possessed him.

Clara was staring at the morning paper. The front page talked about the terrible storm that downed trees, cut off roads, caused power failures across Quebec, and then disappeared.

The day had dawned overcast and a little drizzly. A normal day in April. The snow and hail had melted by morning and the only signs of the storm were twigs blown down and flowers flattened.

'I know you can do it.' Peter sat beside her. Clara looked exhausted. 'But maybe you need a little break. Take your mind off the painting.'

'Are you nuts?' She looked up. Her deep blue eyes were bloodshot and he wondered if she'd been crying. 'This is my big chance. I don't have any time left.'

'But if you go into your studio now you might mess it up even more.'

'Even more?'

'I didn't mean that. I'm sorry.'

'God, what'm I going to do?' She wiped her tired eyes with her hand. She'd been awake most of the night, at first lying in bed trying to get back to sleep. When that hadn't worked she'd obsessed about the painting. She no longer knew what she was doing with it.

Was she so upset by Madeleine's death she couldn't clear her mind enough to create? It was a convenient and comforting thought.

Peter took her small hands and noticed they were stained with blue oils. Had she not cleaned them from yesterday or had she been in the studio already this morning? Instinctively he brought his thumb over to the oil and smeared it. It was from this morning.

. 'Look, why don't we have a little dinner party? We could invite Gamache and a few others. Bet he's ready for a home-cooked meal.'

As the words came out he was stunned by the cruelty of each and every one of them. That was exactly the last thing Clara should be doing. She shouldn't be distracted, she needed to work through this fear, needed to be undisturbed in her studio. A dinner party, right now, would be disastrous.

Was he nuts, Clara wondered? The painting was a mess and Peter was suggesting she hold a party? But while she seemed to have lost her talent, her muse, her inspiration, her courage, one thing she hadn't lost was her certainty that Peter wanted the best for her.

'Good idea.' She tried to smile. Panic, she was discovering, was exhausting. She looked at the clock on the stove. Seven thirty. Picking up her coffee and calling to Lucy their golden retriever she put on a coat, rubber boots and a hat and went out.

The air smelled fresh and clean or if not clean, at least natural. Dirt. It smelled of fresh leaves and wood and dirt. And water. And wood smoke. The day smelled wonderful but looked like a slaughter. All the young tulips and daffodils had been flattened by the storm. Bending down she lifted one, hoping it would get the idea, but it flopped back as soon as she let go.

Clara had never really taken to gardening. All her creative energies went into her art. Happily, Myrna loved gardening, and even more happily she had no garden herself.

In exchange for meals and movies Myrna had turned Clara and Peter's modest garden into lovely perennial beds of roses and peony, delphiniums and foxglove. But in late April only the spring bulbs dared to bloom, and look what happened to them.

Armand Gamache had awoken to a slight knocking on his door. His bedside clock said 6:10. A dull light was coming into his comfortable room. He listened and there again was the tapping. Creeping out of bed he slipped on his dressing gown and opened the door. There was Gabri, his thick dark hair standing up on one side like Gumby. He was unshaven and wore a shabby dressing gown and fluffy slippers. It seemed the more elegant and sophisticated Olivier became the more disheveled Gabri grew. The universe in balance.

Olivier must be particularly splendid today, thought Gamache.

'*Désolé*,' whispered Gabri. He lifted his hand and Gamache saw a newspaper. His heart dropped.

'This just arrived. I thought you'd like to see it before anyone else.'

'Anyone?'

'Well, I saw it. And Olivier. But no one else.'

'You're very kind, Gabri. *Merci.*'

'I'll make coffee. Come down when you're ready. At least the storm's over.'

'You think?' said Gamache and smiled. He shut the door, put the paper on the bed then showered and shaved. Refreshed, he stared down at the paper, a splotch of black and grey against the white sheets. He quickly turned the pages before his courage flagged.

And there it was. Worse than he'd expected.

His jaw clamped shut, his back teeth clenching and unclenching. He could feel himself breathing heavily as he stared at the photograph. His daughter Annie. Annie and a man. Kissing.

'Anne Marie Gamache with her lover, Maître Paul Miron of the public prosecutor's office.'

Gamache closed his eyes. When he opened them the photograph was still there.

He read the piece, twice. Forcing himself to go slowly. To chew, swallow and digest the repugnant words. Then he sat quietly and thought.

Minutes later he called Reine-Marie, waking her up.

'*Bonjour, Armand*. What time is it?'

'Almost seven. Sleep well?'

'Not really. I did a bit of tossing. You?'

'Same,' he admitted.

'I have some bad news. Henri ate your favorite slippers, well one anyway.'

'You're kidding. He's never done it before. I wonder why he'd suddenly do that.'

'He misses you, as do I. He loves not wisely but too well.'

'You didn't eat my other slipper, did you?'

'Just a little nibble round the edges. Barely noticeable.'

There was a pause then Reine-Marie said, 'What is it?'

'Another article.'

He could see her in their wooden bed with its simple duvet and feather pillows and clean white sheets. She'd have two pillows behind her back and the sheets up around her chest, covering her naked body. Not out of shame or bashfulness, but to keep warm.

'Is it very bad?'

'Bad enough. It's about Annie.' He thought he heard a sharp intake. 'It shows her kissing a man they identify as Maître Paul Miron. A Crown Prosecutor. Married.'

'As is she,' said Reine-Marie. 'Oh, poor David. Poor Annie. It's not true, of course. Annie would never do that to David. To anyone. Never.'

'I agree. The gist is that I got out of being charged with

murder along with Arnot because I had Annie sleep with the prosecutor.'

'*Armand! Mais, c'est épouvantable.* How can they? I don't understand how anyone can do this.'

Gamache closed his eyes and felt a hole open in his chest, where Reine-Marie should be. He wished with all his heart he was with her. Could hold her to him, could wrap his strong arms around her. And she could hold him.

'Armand, what're we going to do?'

'Nothing. We stand firm. I'll call Annie and talk to her. I spoke to Daniel last night. He seems all right.'

'What do these people want?'

'They want me to resign.'

'Why?'

'Revenge for Arnot. I've become a symbol of the shame that was brought on the Sûreté.'

'No, that's not it, Armand. I think you've become too powerful.'

After he hung up he called his daughter and woke her up too. She slipped off into another room to talk, then heard David stirring.

'Dad, I have to talk to David. I'll call you later.'

'Annie, I'm sorry.'

'It's not your fault. God, he's heading downstairs to the paper. Gotta go.'

For a moment Armand Gamache imagined the scene in their home in the Plateau Mont-Royal *quartier* of Montreal. David rumpled and bewildered. So in love with Annie. Annie impetuous, ambitious, full of life. And so in love with David.

He made one more call. To his friend and superior, Michel Brébeuf.

'*Oui, allô,*' came the familiar voice.

'Am I disturbing you?'

'Not at all, Armand.' The voice was pleasant and warm. 'I was going to call you this morning. I saw the papers yesterday.'

'Have you seen this morning's?'

There was a pause then Gamache heard Michel call, 'Catherine, has the paper arrived? *Oui?* Could you bring it here? Just a moment, Armand.'

Gamache heard the rustle as Brébeuf turned the leaves of the paper. Then it stopped.

'*Mon Dieu. Armand, c'est terrible. C'est trop.* Have you talked to Annie?'

She was Michel's goddaughter and a particular favorite.

'Just now. She hadn't seen it. She's talking to David right now. It isn't true, of course.'

'You're kidding, because I believe it,' said Brébeuf. 'Of course it's lies. We know Annie would never have an affair. Armand, this is getting dangerous. Someone's going to believe this crap. Perhaps you should explain.'

'To you?'

'No, not to me, but to the reporters. That first picture was of you talking to Daniel. Why don't you just call the editor and straighten him out? And I'm sure you have an explanation for the envelope. What was in it anyway?'

'The one I gave to Daniel? Nothing significant.'

There was a pause. Finally Brébeuf spoke, seriously. 'Armand, was it a *crêpe*?'

Gamache laughed. 'How'd you guess, Michel? That's exactly what it was. An old family *crêpe* my *grand-mère* made.'

Brébeuf laughed then grew silent. 'If you don't stop these insinuations they'll just grow. Hold a news conference, tell everyone Daniel's your son. Tell them what was in the envelope. Tell them about Annie. What's the harm?'

What was the harm?

'The lies will never end, Michel. You know that. It's a monster with an endless supply of heads. Lop off one head and more appear, stronger and more vicious. If we respond they'll know they have us. I won't do it. And I won't resign.'

'You sound like a child.'

'Children can be wise.'

'Children are willful and selfish,' Brébeuf snapped. There was silence. Michel Brébeuf forced himself to pause. To count to five. To give the impression of massive thought. Then he spoke.

'You win, Armand. But will you let me work behind the scenes? I have some contacts at the papers.'

'Thank you, Michel. I'd appreciate it.'

'Good. Go to work, concentrate on the investigation. Keep your focus and don't worry about this. I'll take care of it.'

Armand Gamache dressed and headed downstairs, plunging deeper and deeper into the aroma of strong coffee. For a few minutes he sipped his coffee, ate a flaky croissant, and talked to Gabri. The disheveled man had toyed with the handle of his mug and told Gamache about coming out, about telling his family, about telling his co-workers at the investment house. And as he spoke Gamache realized Gabri knew how he was feeling. Naked, exposed, being made to feel shame for something not shameful. And in his oddly quiet way Gabri was saying he wasn't alone. Thanking Gabri, Gamache put on his rubber boots and waxed Barbour field coat and went for a walk. He had a lot to ponder and he knew that everything is solved by walking.

It was drizzling slightly, and all the joyous spring flowers were lying down, like young soldiers slaughtered on a battlefield. For twenty minutes he walked, his hands clasping each other behind his back. Round and round the quiet little village he went and watched as it came alive, as lights appeared at the windows, dogs were put out, fires were lit in grates. It was peaceful and calm.

'Hello there,' called Clara Morrow. She stood in her garden, a mug in her hand and a raincoat over her nightgown. 'Just surveying the damage. Are you free for dinner tonight? We thought we might invite a few people over.'

'Sounds wonderful, thank you. Would you join me?' Gamache indicated his circular walk round the Commons.

'Sure.'

'How's your art? I hear Denis Fortin's coming to visit soon.' Seeing her face he knew he'd stepped in something sticky and stinky. 'Or shouldn't I have said anything?'

'No, no. It's just that I'm struggling a little. Things that were so clear a few days ago are suddenly muddy and confused. You know?'

'I know,' he said ruefully.

She looked at him. She often felt foolish, ill constructed, next to others. Beside Gamache she only ever felt whole.

'What did you think of Madeleine Favreau?'

Clara paused to collect her thoughts. 'I liked her. A lot. Didn't really know her all that well. She'd just joined the ACW. Lucky Hazel.'

'How so?'

'Hazel was supposed to take over from Gabri this September as president, but then Madeleine said she'd do it.'

'Didn't that upset Hazel?'

'You've clearly never been an Anglican Church Woman.'

'I'm not Anglican.'

'It's great fun. We hold church socials and teas and twice a year we have a sale of goods. But it's hell to organize.'

'So that's hell,' smiled Gamache. 'Only mortal sinners run ACWs?'

'Absolutely. Our punishment is to spend eternity begging for volunteers.'

'So Hazel was happy to get out of it?'

'Thrilled, I should think. Probably why she brought Madeleine into it in the first place. They were a good team, though quite different.'

'How so?'

'Well, Madeleine always made you feel good about yourself. She laughed a lot and listened well. She was a lot of fun. But if you were sick or in need, it was Hazel who'd show up.'

'Was Madeleine superficial, do you think?'

Clara hesitated. 'I think Madeleine was used to getting what she wanted. Not because she was greedy but just because it always happened.'

'Did you know she had cancer?'

'I did. Breast cancer.'

'Do you know whether she was healthy?'

'Madeleine?' Clara laughed. 'Healthier than you or me. She was in great shape.'

'Had she changed at all in the last few weeks or months?'

'Changed? I don't think so. Seemed the same to me.'

Gamache nodded then continued. 'We think the substance that killed her was slipped into her food at dinner. Did you see or hear anything at all strange?'

'In that group? Anything normal would set off alarms. But you're saying that someone at our dinner killed her? Gave her the ephedra?'

Gamache nodded.

Clara thought about it, replaying the dinner in her mind. The food arriving, being warmed up, prepared, set out. People sitting down. Passing round the various dishes.

No, it all seemed natural and normal. It was a terrible thought that one of them around that table had poisoned Madeleine, but not, it must be said, a surprise. If it was murder, one of them did it.

'We all ate out of the same dishes, helping ourselves. Could the poison have been meant for someone else?'

'No,' said Gamache. 'We've had the leftovers tested and there's no ephedra in any of the dishes. Besides, you all helped yourselves, right? To have any control over who got the ephedra the murderer had to have slipped it to Madeleine directly. Shoved it into the food on her plate.'

Clara nodded. She could see the hand, see the action, but not the person. She thought of the people at her dinner. Monsieur Béliveau? Hazel and Sophie? Odile and Gilles? True, Odile murdered verse, but surely nothing else.

Ruth?

Peter always said Ruth was the only person he knew capable of murder. Had she done it? But she hadn't even been at the séance. But, maybe she didn't have to be.

'Did the séance have anything to do with it?' she asked.

'We think it was one ingredient. As was the ephedra.'

Clara sipped her now cool coffee as they walked.

'What I don't understand is why the murderer decided to kill Madeleine that night.'

'What d'you mean?' asked Gamache.

'Why give her ephedra in the middle of a dinner party? If the murderer needed a séance why not do it Friday night?'

It was a question that hounded Gamache. Why wait until Sunday? Why not kill her Friday night?

'Maybe he tried,' he said. 'Did anything odd happen that Friday night?'

'More odd than contacting dead people? Not that I remember.'

'Who did Madeleine have dinner with?'

'Hazel, I guess. No, wait, Madeleine didn't go home for dinner. She stayed here.'

'Had dinner at the bistro?'

'No, with Monsieur Béliveau.' She looked over at his home, a large rambling clapboard house facing the green. 'I like him. Most people do.'

'Most, but not all?'

'Don't you let anything pass?' she laughed.

'When I miss things or let them pass they gather in a heap then rise up and take a life. So, I try not to.' He smiled.

'I guess not. The only person I've ever seen actually cut Monsieur Béliveau was Gilles Sandon. But then Gilles's quite a character. Do you know him?'

'He works in the woods, doesn't he?'

'Makes amazing furniture, but I think there's a reason he works with trees and not people.'

'How does Monsieur Béliveau feel about him?'

'Oh, I don't think he even notices the slights. He's such a gentle man and kind. He only went to the séance to keep Mad company, you know. I could tell he didn't like it at all. Probably because of his dead wife.'

'Afraid she'd come back?'

'Maybe,' Clara laughed. 'They were very close.'

'Do you think he expected her to show up?'

'Ginette, his dead wife? None of us expected anything. Not that first night at the bistro, anyway. It was a lark. But still, I think it upset him. He didn't sleep well that night, he said.'

'The next séance was different,' said Gamache.

'We were crazy to go there.' She had her back to the old Hadley house, but she could feel it staring at her.

Gamache turned, feeling a chill born from the inside and growing to meet the cold damp air on his skin. It was the menace on the hill, poised, waiting for the right moment to swoop down on them. But no, Gamache thought. The old Hadley house wouldn't swoop. It would creep. Slowly. Almost unnoticed until you woke up one morning swallowed by its despair and sorrow.

'As we were walking up the hill that night,' said Clara, 'something kind of strange happened. We started off all bunched up, talking, but as we got closer we stopped talking and drifted apart. I think that house creates isolation. I was almost the last. Madeleine was walking behind me.'

'Monsieur Béliveau wasn't with her?'

'No, strange that. He was talking with Hazel and Sophie. He hadn't seen Sophie in a while. I think they must be friends because Sophie made sure to sit next to him at dinner. As I walked I passed Odile standing on the road. Then I heard Odile and Madeleine talking behind me.'

'Was that unusual?'

'Not unheard of, but I didn't think they had much in common. I can't remember exactly what was said, but I have the impression Odile was sucking up. Telling Mad how lovely she was and popular. Something like that, but the funny thing is it seemed to upset Madeleine. I'm afraid I tried to hear more but couldn't.'

'What do you think of Odile?'

Clara laughed then stopped herself. 'I'm sorry, that wasn't very nice. But every time I think of Odile I think of her poetry. I can't imagine why she writes it. Do you think she thinks it's good?'

'It must be difficult to know,' said Gamache, and Clara felt fear snake around her heart and into her head again. Fear that she was as delusional as Odile. Suppose Fortin shows up and laughs? He'd seen a few of her works but maybe he was drunk or not in his right mind. Maybe he'd seen Peter's and thought they were Clara's. That must be it. There's no way the great Denis Fortin could really like her work. And what work? That wretched half-finished accusation in her studio?

'Have Odile and Gilles been together long?' asked Gamache.

'A few years. They've known each other forever but only got together after his divorce.'

Clara was silent, thinking.

'What is it?' asked Gamache.

'I was thinking of Odile. It must be difficult.'

'What?'

'I get the feeling she's trying so hard. Like a rock climber, you know? But not a very good one. Just clinging on for dear life and trying not to show how scared she is.'

'Clinging on to what?'

'To Gilles. She only started writing poetry when they got together. I think she wants to be part of his world. The creative world.'

'What world does she belong in?'

'I think she belongs in the rational world. With facts and figures. She's wonderful at running the store. Turned it around for him. But she won't hear a compliment about that. She only wants to hear that she's a great poet.'

'It's interesting she'd choose poetry when one of the greatest poets in Canada is a neighbor,' said Gamache, watching as Ruth walked down the steps of her veranda. She paused, turned back, bent down, then straightened up.

'I married one of the greatest artists in Canada,' said Clara.

'Do you see yourself in Odile?' he asked, astonished.

Clara was silent.

'Clara, I've seen your work.' He stopped and looked at

her directly and for an instant the snake retreated, her heart expanded, her head cleared, as she looked into his deep brown eyes. 'It's brilliant. Passionate, exposed. Full of hope, belief, doubt. And fear.'

'I've got plenty of that for sale. Want some?'

'I'm rather flush right now myself, thank you. But you know what?' He smiled. 'All will be as it should, if we just do our best.'

Ruth was standing on her front lawn, staring down. As they approached they saw the two baby birds.

'Morning.' Clara waved. Ruth looked up and grunted.

'How're the babies?' Clara asked then she saw. Little Rosa was squawking around preening and parading herself. Lilium was standing still, staring ahead. She looked afraid, like that tiny bird in the old Hadley house. Gamache wondered whether maybe she'd been born with a caul.

'They're perfect,' snapped Ruth, daring them to contradict her.

'We're having people over for dinner. Want to come?'

'I was planning to anyway. I'm out of Scotch. You be there?' she asked Gamache, who nodded.

'Good. You're like a Greek tragedy. I can take notes and write a poem. Your life will have meaning after all.'

'You have relieved me, madame,' said Gamache and gave her a small bow.

'There's someone else I'd like you to invite,' he said as they resumed their walk. 'Jeanne Chauvet.'

Clara kept walking, staring straight ahead.

'What is it?' he asked.

'She scares me. I don't like her.'

It was one of the few times Gamache had ever heard Clara say that. Above him the old Hadley house seemed to grow.

CHAPTER 34

Agent Isabelle Lacoste was tired of hanging around the lab. The report on the fingerprints was ready, she was assured. They just couldn't find it.

She'd already been off to interview François Favreau, Madeleine's husband. He was gorgeous. Like a *GQ* model in midlife. Tall and handsome and bright. Bright enough to give her straight answers to her questions.

'I heard about her death, of course. But we hadn't been in touch for a while and I didn't really want to bother Hazel.'

'Not even with sympathy?'

François moved his coffee cup a half-inch to the left. She noticed that his cuticles were ragged. Worry always finds its way to the surface.

'I just hate that sort of thing. I never know what to say. Here, look at this.' He took some papers from a nearby desk and handed them to her. On them he'd scrawled, *I'm so sorry for your loss, it must leave a big –*

Hazel, I wish –

Madeleine was such a lovely person, it must have been –

On and on, for three pages. Half-finished sentences, half-baked sentiments.

'Why don't you just tell her how you feel?'

He stared at her with a look she knew. It was the same one her husband used. Annoyance. It was obviously so easy for her to feel and to express it. And impossible for him.

'What went through your mind when you heard she was

murdered?' Lacoste had learned that when people couldn't talk of feelings they could at least talk about their thoughts, and often the two collided. And colluded.

'I wondered who'd done it. Who could hate her that much.'

'How do you feel about her now?' She kept her voice soft, reasonable. Cajoling.

'I don't know.'

'Is that true?'

The silence stretched on. She could see him teetering on the verge of an emotion, trying not to fall in, trying to cling to the rational rock of his brain. But eventually that rock betrayed him, and both fell together.

'I love her. Loved her.' He put his head softly in his hands, as though cradling himself, his long, slim fingers poking out of his dark hair.

'Why did you divorce?'

He rubbed his face and looked at her, suddenly bleary.

'It was her idea, but I think I pushed her to it. I was too chicken shit to do it myself.'

'Why did you want to?'

'I couldn't take it any more. At first it was wonderful. She was so gorgeous and warm and loving. And successful. Everything she did she was good at. She just glowed. It was like living too close to the sun.'

'It blinds and burns,' said Lacoste.

'Yes.' Favreau seemed relieved to have words. 'It hurt being that close to Madeleine.'

'Do you really wonder who killed her?'

'I do, but . . .'

Lacoste waited. Armand Gamache had taught her patience.

'But I'm not sure I was surprised. She didn't mean to hurt people, but she did. And when you get hurt enough . . .'

There was no need to finish the sentence.

Robert Lemieux had stopped at the Tim Horton's in Cowansville on his way to Three Pines and now a stack of Double Double coffees stood in the middle of the conference table along with cheerful cardboard boxes of doughnuts.

'My man,' exclaimed Beauvoir when he saw them, clapping Lemieux on the back. Lemieux had further ingratiated himself by starting the ancient cast-iron woodstove in the middle of the room.

The place smelled of cardboard and coffee, of sweet doughnuts and sweet wood smoke.

Inspector Beauvoir called the morning meeting to order just as Agent Nichol arrived, late and disheveled as always. They gave their reports, and Chief Inspector Gamache ended by telling them about the coroner's report.

'So Madeleine Favreau had a bad heart,' said Agent Lemieux. 'The murderer had to have known that.'

'Probably. According to the coroner three things had to come together.' Beauvoir was standing next to an easel which held sheaves of large white paper. He wielded a magic marker like a baton and wrote as he spoke. 'One: mega-dose of ephedra. Two: scare at the séance and three: bad heart.'

'So why wasn't she killed at the Friday night séance?' asked Nichol. 'All three elements were in place, or at least two of the three.'

'That's what I've been trying to figure out,' said Gamache. He'd been listening and sipping his coffee. His fingers were a little sticky from a chocolate glazed doughnut. He wiped them with the tiny paper napkin and leaned forward. 'Was the Good Friday séance a dress rehearsal? Was it a prelude? Did Madeleine say or do something that led to her murder two days later? Are the two séances connected?'

'It seems too much of a coincidence that they're not,' said Lemieux.

'Oh please,' said Nichol. 'Don't try to suck up to him,' and she flicked her hand toward Gamache.

Lemieux was silent. He'd been instructed to suck up. It was what he did best and did it, he thought, with great subtlety, but now this bitch actually called him on it in the middle of the morning meeting. His facade of reason and long-suffering was cracking under the mocking of Nichol. He despised her, and if he didn't have a larger purpose, he'd turn his attention to her.

'Look,' continued Nichol, dismissing Lemieux. 'It's so obvious. The question isn't how they're connected, but how they're not. What was different about the two séances?'

She sat back, triumphant.

Oddly, no one jumped to congratulate her. The silence stretched on. Then Chief Inspector Gamache slowly got up and walked over to Beauvoir.

'May I?' He reached for the marker then turned and began writing on a clean sheet of paper, *How are the two séances different?*

Nichol smirked and Lemieux nodded, but beneath the table his hands clenched.

Isabelle Lacoste had gone from François Favreau directly to the high school in Notre-Dame-de-Grâce. It was a large red-brick building with an 1867 date stone. The building looked and felt nothing like her own high school. Hers had been modern, sprawling, French. Yet as soon as she stepped into the old building she was immediately back in the crowded halls of her school. Trying to remember her combination, trying to get her hair to stay down, or up or whatever the trend was. Always trying, like a kayaker shooting the rapids and feeling one stroke behind.

The sounds were familiar, voices bouncing off metal and concrete, shoes screeching on hard floors, but it was the smells that had transported her. Of books and cleaner, of lunches languishing and rotting behind hundreds of lockers. And fear. High school smelled of that more than anything else, even more than sweaty feet, cheap perfume and rotten bananas.

'I put together a dossier for you,' said Mrs Plant, the school secretary. 'I wasn't here when Madeleine Gagnon went to school. In fact, none of the teachers or staff is still here. That was thirty years ago. But all our archives are on computer now so I printed out her report cards and found some other things you might be interested in. Including these.'

She put her hand on a stack of yearbooks, the secular school's Bible.

'That's very kind, but I think the report cards will be enough.'

'But I spent half of yesterday in the storeroom finding these.'

'Thank you. I'm sure they'll be great.' Agent Lacoste hoisted them into her arms, balancing the file on top precariously as they left the office.

'We have some pictures of her on the wall, you know.' Mrs Plant walked ahead. The halls were beginning to fill and the place echoed with unintelligible shouts as kids hailed and assailed each other.

'Down here. All sorts of pictures. I have to get back to the office. Will you be all right?'

'You've been very helpful. I'll be fine.'

For the next few minutes Lacoste moved slowly down the long, concrete corridor, looking at old photographs framed and hung, of victorious school teams and school government. And there was young Madeleine Favreau, *née* Gagnon. Smiling, healthy, with every expectation of a long and exciting life. Jostled by the kids now crowding into the halls Agent Lacoste wondered what high school must have been like for Madeleine. Did she also smell of fear? She didn't look it, but then the most fearful people often didn't.

Gamache took his seat again and reached for his coffee. They all looked at the new list. Under the heading *How are the two séances different?* he'd written,

> Hazel
> Sophie
> Dinner party
> Old Hadley house
> Jeanne Chauvet more serious

He explained that on being interviewed the psychic had said she wasn't prepared for the first, it had been Gabri's little surprise, and so she hadn't taken it seriously. She'd judged they were really just a bored group of villagers looking for titillation. So she'd given them the cheap, Hollywood version. Silly melodrama. But when someone later told her about the old Hadley house and somehow the idea of contacting the dead there had come up, she'd taken it seriously.

'Why?' asked Lemieux.

'You're not really that thick,' snapped Nichol. 'The old Hadley house is supposedly haunted. She contacts ghosts for a living. Hello?'

Beauvoir, ignoring Nichol, got up and wrote,

        Candles
        Salt

'Anything else?' he asked. He liked writing things on the board. Always had. He liked the smell of magic marker. The squeak it made. And the order it created from random ideas.

'Her incantations,' said Gamache. 'They're important.'

'Right,' said Nichol, rolling her eyes.

'For setting atmosphere,' said Gamache. 'That was a major difference. From what I understand the Good Friday séance was frightening, but the Sunday night one was terrifying. Maybe the murderer tried to kill Madeleine Friday night but it just wasn't scary enough.'

'So who suggested the old Hadley house?' asked Lemieux and shot Nichol a look, daring her to mock him again. She just sneered and shook her head. He could feel the rage rising from his chest, boiling there and bubbling to his throat. It was bad enough to be mocked, to be insulted, to be accused of sucking up. But to be dismissed as pathetic was the worst.

'I don't know,' said Gamache. 'We've asked and no one can remember.'

'But if you think the move to the old Hadley house was key then that lets out Hazel and Sophie,' said Beauvoir.

'Why?' asked Lemieux.

'They weren't there to suggest it.'

There was a pause.

'But Sophie's the only person who's different from the first to the second séance,' said Nichol. 'I don't think the first had anything to do with murder. I think it only occurred to someone later. And that's because that someone wasn't at the first séance.'

'But Sophie isn't the only new person,' said Lemieux. 'Her mother was only at the second séance as well.'

'But she could have been at the first. She was invited. If she'd wanted to kill Madeleine, then she would have been there.'

'And maybe that was why she went to the second,' said Gamache. 'The first didn't work, so she had to make sure the second did.'

'And bring along her own daughter? Come on.' Nichol opened her notebook and brought out the photo she'd taken off the fridge door at the Smyth place.

'Look at this.' She flicked it onto the table. Beauvoir handed it down the table to Gamache who stared at it. The photo showed three women. Madeleine in the middle in profile looking with great and open affection at Hazel, who was wearing a silly hat and smiling. Happy and delighted, a look of great affection on her face too. She was also in profile, looking off camera. At the other end of the picture sat a plump young woman, a piece of cake about to go into her mouth. In the foreground sat a birthday cake.

'Where'd you get this?'

'The Smyth place, from the fridge.'

'Why'd you take it? What interests you about it?' Gamache was leaning forward, watching Nichol intently.

'It's the face. It says it all.'

Nichol waited to see whether the others would get it. Would they see that Madeleine Favreau, so pretty and smiling and attentive, was a fake? No one was really that happy. She had to be pretending.

'You're right,' said Gamache, turning to Beauvoir. 'Do you see? Her?' Gamache put his large finger close to the photo.

Beauvoir leaned in and studied the picture then his eyes opened wide.

'That's Sophie. That girl taking a bite of cake. It's Sophie.'

'Heavier,' Gamache nodded.

He turned the photograph over. Across the back was written the date the picture was taken. Two years ago.

In only two years Sophie Smyth had dropped twenty, thirty pounds?

Gamache's phone rang just as the meeting was breaking up.

'Chief, it's me,' said Agent Lacoste. 'I finally have the report on the fingerprints. We know who broke into the room at the old Hadley house.'

Hazel Smyth seemed to have trouble functioning now. Like a toy whose connections were faulty, she lurched from full speed to stop, then top speed again.

'We have some questions, Madame Smyth,' said Beauvoir. 'And we'll need to do a thorough search. A few officers from the Cowansville detachment will be here soon. We have a warrant.'

He reached into his pocket but she whizzed off, saying, 'No need, Inspector. Sophie! Sooophieee.'

'What is it?' came the petulant reply.

'Visitors. It's the police again.' She seemed to sing-song it.

Sophie appeared, clunking down the stairs with her crutches, her leg wrapped tightly now in a tenser bandage. The injury seemed to be getting worse, judging by her winces. Beauvoir wondered whether maybe she wasn't injured after all.

He took out the picture and showed it to both women.

'That's from the fridge,' said Hazel, looking toward the appliance. Her energy had ebbed again and now she seemed barely able to speak. Her head was bowed as though too heavy and when she breathed, it lifted slightly then drooped again.

'When was it taken?' Beauvoir asked.

'Oh, ages ago,' said Sophie, reaching for it. He moved it away from her. 'Five or six years at least.'

'Couldn't have been, dear,' said Hazel as though each word cost her an effort. 'Madeleine's hair is long. All grown back. It was just a couple of years ago.'

'Is this you?' He pointed to the pudgy girl.

'I don't think so,' said Sophie.

'Let me see,' said Hazel.

'No, Ma, no need. My ankle hurts really badly. I think I knocked it on the stairs coming down.'

'Poor one.' Hazel's energy bopped back up. She rushed to a cupboard in the kitchen. Beauvoir could see a variety of medicine bottles. He followed her there and watched as she shoved past the first rank of pills, digging deeper. Then he stopped her hand.

'May I?'

'But Sophie needs an aspirin.'

He took a bottle off the shelf. Low dose aspirin. He glanced at Hazel who was looking at him anxiously. She knows, he thought. She knows her daughter fakes her injuries and she bought the low dose on purpose. He handed a tablet to Hazel then put on his gloves, thin like membranes. Something told him there was more than aspirin in this jumble of pills. He'd decided if he was born with a caul he needed to start trusting his instincts.

Ten minutes later he was surrounded by pill bottles. Pills for headaches, pills for backaches, pills for menstrual cramps, pills for yeast infections. Vitamins. And even a bottle of jelly beans.

'Pills for visiting kids,' Hazel explained.

Just about the only pill ever manufactured that was not in the cupboard was ephedra.

The team from the local office of the Sûreté had shown up and were well into the search of the Smyth place. Unfortunately it would probably take ten times their number to do the dump justice. It was worse than Beauvoir had thought, and he was an expert at thinking the worst.

Two hours had gone by and the only significant thing to happen was they seemed to have lost two of their men. They were discovered wandering in the basement. Beauvoir took a break and sat on a sofa in the dining room, jammed against a breakfront which was jammed against another sofa. As soon as he landed on it the sofa threw him back. It expulsed him. He tried again, landing with less force. Now he felt the hard coils and had the impression they were recoiling, to toss him out again. He'd become a circus act.

An agent called him upstairs and when he arrived he saw the officer holding a medicine bottle.

'Where'd you find it?' Beauvoir asked.

'In the make-up case.'

The agent pointed to Sophie's room. Behind him he heard Sophie clunking quickly up the stairs, then the clunking stopped and he heard nimble feet taking the stairs two at a time.

'What is it?' came Hazel's voice from the other direction.

Beauvoir showed the bottle to the two women.

'Ephedra,' Hazel read on the label. 'Sophie, you promised.'

'Shut up, Mom. That's not mine.'

'It was found in your case,' said Beauvoir.

'I don't know where it came from. It's not mine.'

She was scared, he could tell. But was she telling the truth?

As Gamache walked into the house he smelled toast and coffee. It felt very still and comfortable. The wide-plank wood floors were a deep amber. There was no fire in the grate, but Gamache saw ashes and a mostly consumed log.

The room was cheerful and bright, even in the dull day, with large windows and French doors leading to a back garden. The furniture was old and comfortable and on the walls were landscapes from the area and a few portraits. Where there were no pictures there were bookshelves.

Gamache would have loved to spend time in this room, under other circumstances.

'The room where Madeleine was killed was broken into two nights ago,' said Gamache. 'We know you did it.'

'You're right. It was me.'

'Why?'

'I wanted the house to take me too,' said Monsieur Béliveau.

He told his story clearly, his dry hands rubbing each other as though needing human contact.

'It was the day after Madeleine died. I don't know if you've ever lost someone you love, Chief Inspector, but it's as though everything familiar has changed. Food tastes different, home isn't home any more, even friends have changed. Much as they might want to, they can't follow you down that road. Everything seemed so far away, muffled. I couldn't even understand what people were saying.' He smiled unexpectedly. 'Poor Peter and Clara. They had me over for dinner. I think they were worried about me and I don't think I did anything to ease their minds. They wanted me to know I wasn't alone, but I was.'

His hands stopped their rubbing and now one hand held the other.

'About halfway through dinner I knew I had to die. It hurt too much. As Peter and Clara talked about gardening and cooking and the day's events I cataloged ways to kill myself. Then it came to me. I would go back up there and sit in that room by myself and wait.'

Nothing stirred. Even the mariner's clock on the mantelpiece seemed silent, as though time was standing still.

'I knew if I waited in the dark long enough whatever is in that house would find me. And it did.'

'What happened?' Gamache asked.

'The thing that killed Madeleine arrived.' He said this without apology, without embarrassment. Just a fact. Something from another world arrived in his, and had come to drag him away. 'It came down the hall. I could hear it, clawing and scraping. It was pitch black and I had my back to the door, but I knew it was there. Then it screamed, as it did that night. Shrieked right in my ear. I reached up to fight it off.'

He waved his thin arms in their gray wool sweater about his head, as though he imagined himself back in that room.

'And then I ran away. I ran screaming from that room.'

'You chose life,' said Gamache.

'No I didn't. I was just too scared to die. Not like that anyway.' He leaned forward, his eyes intense, staring at Gamache. 'There's something in that house. Something that attacked me.'

'Not any more, monsieur. You killed it.'

'I did?' He leaned back as though shoved by this unexpected thought.

'It was a baby robin. Probably as scared as you.'

It took Monsieur Béliveau a moment to understand.

'I was right, then. The thing that brings death was in that room,' he said. 'It was me.'

CHAPTER 35

'Love what you've done with the place,' said Olivier as he set out the napkins and bowls at the old railway station. Putting the soup tureen on the filing cabinet under the list of murder suspects, he was happy to see his name wasn't there, and happier still to see Gabri's was. Wait until he told him. Freak him out completely.

A steaming chicken stew with dumplings was placed in the middle of the conference table.

The Chief Inspector had stopped by the bistro to ask Olivier to bring them lunch.

'How's Monsieur Béliveau?' Olivier had asked. He'd seen Gamache walk along the Common from his home.

'He's been better, I imagine,' Gamache had said.

'And worse. I remember how sad he was after Ginette died. Thank God for Hazel and Madeleine. Brought him out of himself. Invited him to everything, especially important days like Christmas. Saved his life.'

As he'd walked back to the Incident Room Gamache wondered whether Béliveau would thank them for that. He also thought of Hazel, alone now herself, and wondered whether eventually the two would gravitate together.

Once back at the old railway station Gamache was met by Beauvoir, just back from searching Hazel's home. Within minutes Agent Lacoste arrived from Montreal and they gathered around the conference table. The meeting was in full swing when Olivier came with lunch.

He took his time, but still they didn't say a word. Inspector Beauvoir ushered him to the door and closed it firmly behind him. Olivier leaned in to the cold metal for a moment but heard nothing.

There was, in fact, nothing to be heard, except serving spoons on porcelain as red lentil and curried apple soup and rich, chunky stew were served up. Soft drinks were popped open and Beauvoir had a beer.

'Reports,' said Gamache.

'We found the ephedra,' said Beauvoir, putting the medicine bottle on the table. 'We took fingerprints and transmitted them to Montreal.' He'd already reported to Gamache, but now the rest of the team heard about the search and the discovery.

'Sophie Smyth denies the stuff's hers,' said Beauvoir, 'but she would. She's admitted strong, maybe obsessive feelings for Madeleine. And she's a liar. I wasn't sure about her injured leg, but when she had to she sure ran on that ankle fast enough. You should have seen her mother's face.'

'Angry about the faked ankle?' asked Lemieux.

'You can't really be that stupid,' said Nichol and Lemieux shot her a look of unmistakable loathing.

'Agent Nichol, I'm warning you,' said Gamache.

'No really,' said Nichol. 'How are you possible?' she asked Lemieux, who was gripping the table. 'Hazel Smyth was stunned to see the ephedra bottle in her daughter's possession,' Nichol said very slowly into Lemieux's face. 'This is a murder investigation. Not a doctor's office. Who the fuck cares about her ankle, except a moron.'

'That's it. Come with me.' Gamache walked across the room to the door, taking the medicine bottle with him. Nichol caught Lemieux's eyes and jerked her head in Gamache's direction.

'He means you, asshole.'

Lemieux made to get up.

'Agent Nichol,' Gamache called, his voice cold and carrying.

Nichol smirked at Lemieux and shook her head as she got up, mumbling 'Fucking loser' as she walked by.

'What's wrong, sir?' she asked at the door. Her cockiness had vanished with her audience. It was just the two of them now.

'You're going too far. You have to leave.'

'You're firing me?'

'Not yet. I'm sending you to Kingston, to ask questions about Sophie Smyth at Queens University.'

'Kingston? But that's half a day away. I won't get there 'til dark.'

'Later than that. You need to drop this at the lab on your way through Montreal. I want the results tomorrow morning.'

Nichol stared at him then finally spoke, her voice low. 'I think you're making a mistake, sir.'

Gamache met her eyes. His voice when he spoke was calm, steady, but still Nichol stepped back a half-pace from his intensity. 'I know what I'm doing. You need to leave. Now.'

From the door he watched her go. Never full of grace, Agent Nichol slouched across the bridge, kicking a stone as she went.

Gamache returned to the meeting. The place seemed lighter without Agent Nichol. Gamache was happy to see Lemieux looking more relaxed.

Olivier had also brought a platter of brownies and date squares for dessert. Over coffee and dessert they heard about Monsieur Béliveau.

'He went there to die?' said Agent Lacoste, putting her brownie down. 'That's so sad.'

Sad. There was that word again, thought Gamache. Poor, sad Monsieur Béliveau. But unexpectedly what came to mind wasn't the tired old grocer but the baby bird. Its shriek magnified by fear. Killed because it wanted company.

Then it was Lacoste's turn to report on her trip to Montreal.

'The school secretary gave me these.' She put two dossiers on the conference table. 'Madeleine and Hazel's school records. I haven't gone through them yet. Madeleine seems to have been a bit of a legend in that school.'

Beauvoir reached for the dossiers while Lacoste ducked under the table again and came up holding a stack of year-books.

'I tried to get out of it, but she also gave me these.' She put the yearbooks on the table and reached for her brownie again. It was rich and homemade and instead of icing on the top it had a thick layer of fluffy marshmallow, grilled under the broiler.

'You spoke to Madeleine's former husband?' Gamache asked.

'François Favreau wasn't much help. Madeleine was the one who asked for the divorce but he admits he forced her into it by behaving badly. He also admits he still loves her, but he said living with her was like living too close to the sun. It was glorious, but painful.'

They sat in silence, eating and thinking. Lacoste thought about a woman killed for being brilliant, Lemieux about murdering Nichol, Beauvoir about Sophie who probably killed the woman she loved; and Armand Gamache thought about Icarus.

Jean Guy Beauvoir drove while Armand Gamache looked out the window and tried not to notice the potholes and ruts and chasms in the road. Entire towns could be thriving in some of them.

He brought his mind back to the case.

Sophie Smyth had the ephedra. She'd been at the second séance but not the first, which would explain why the murder had happened then. And she admitted to intense feelings for Madeleine. And there was one more thing. Something Clara had told him that morning that Gamache hadn't paid attention to, but that further condemned Sophie. A question that nagged him was how the murderer put the ephedra in Madeleine's food. Clara said Sophie had hurried to take the seat right next to Monsieur Béliveau. But that would also put her next to Madeleine. Sophie had deliberately seated herself between them.

Why?

Two possible reasons. She was so jealous of their relationship she wanted to come between them, literally. Or, she wanted to be able to give Madeleine the ephedra.

Or both.

She had motive and opportunity.

After lunch Gamache had ordered a patrol car to watch the Smyth house, but he wouldn't act until he had proof the bottle belonged to Sophie. In the morning they'd make an arrest.

In the meantime there were answers to other questions he needed.

He looked at his watch.

'The first editions of the paper will be out in an hour,' said Beauvoir. 'Monsieur Béliveau will keep one for us.'

'*Merci.*'

'I'm glad you sent Nichol away. Things will be easier.'

When Gamache didn't answer Beauvoir continued. 'You've never told me what happened when you realized what Arnot was doing. Some came out in court, of course. But I know there's more.'

Gamache saw the countryside going by. The trees just coming alive. It was like witnessing the moment life began.

'An emergency meeting of the senior council was called,' said Gamache, his eyes no longer seeing the miracle of new life but seeing the cold conference room at Sûreté headquarters. The officers arriving. No one except Brébeuf and himself aware of why the meeting was called. Pierre Arnot smiling urbanely and laughing with Superintendent Francoeur as the two took swiveling chairs side by side.

'I dimmed the lights and projected pictures on the wall. Pictures of boys from the school yearbooks. Then pictures of them dead. One after another. Then I read the witness reports, and the lab reports. Everyone was confused. Trying to figure out what I was getting at. Then one by one they grew quiet. Except Francoeur. And Arnot.'

He could see the blue eyes, cold like marbles. And he could sense the brain, active, rushing from fact to fact, desperate to refute them. At first Arnot had been relaxed, confident in his superiority, sure no one could ever get the better of him. But as the meeting progressed he grew restive, furtive.

Gamache had done his homework. Had worked on the case for almost a year, quietly, in his spare time and on holidays. Until every single escape route Arnot might try was locked and barred and blocked, and locked again.

Gamache knew he had only one shot, and that was this meeting. If Arnot walked free, Gamache and many others, Brébeuf included, were doomed.

He'd marshaled his facts but he knew there was one potent weapon Arnot would use. Loyalty. Officers of the force would rather die than be disloyal, to each other and to the Sûreté. Arnot commanded great loyalty.

And Arnot had won.

Faced with the facts he'd admitted the crimes of incitement to murder and actual murder. But he'd prevailed upon the council, in recognition of his position and his years of service, to allow him and the two officers implicated with him to not be arrested. Not yet. They'd put their affairs in order, make things right for their families, say their goodbyes, and then go to Arnot's hunting camp in the Abitibi region. And kill themselves.

Avoid the shame of a trial. Spare the Sûreté the public humiliation.

Gamache had argued ferociously against such folly. But he'd been defeated by a council afraid of Arnot and afraid of the public.

To Gamache's astonishment Pierre Arnot had walked free. At least for a while. But a man like that can create a lot of grief in very little time.

'And that's when we took the case in Mutton Bay?' asked Beauvoir.

'As far from Montreal as we could get, yes,' admitted Gamache. He'd sent Reine-Marie away and asked his friend Marc Brault with the Montreal police to assign officers to protect his children. Then he himself had taken a ski plane to Quebec City, then on to Baie Comeau, then Natashquan, Harrington Harbour and finally the tiny fishing village of Mutton Bay. And there he'd looked for a murderer and found himself. In a dingy diner on the rocky shore of the village. It smelled of fish, both fresh and fried, and a ragged, craggy fisherman, as though made from the rocks themselves, sitting alone in a booth had looked over and given Gamache a smile of such unexpected radiance Gamache had immediately known what he had to do.

'That's when you left,' said Beauvoir. 'You headed back to Montreal. Next thing I knew Pierre Arnot and the two others were all over the newspapers.'

Ironic really, thought Gamache, and tried not to look at his watch again.

Gamache had driven to the Abitibi and stopped the suicide. All the way back the other two officers, drunk and hysterical with relief, wept. But not Arnot. He sat bolt upright between them and stared into the rearview mirror, at Gamache. Gamache had known as soon as he'd entered the cabin that Arnot had had no intention of committing suicide. The others, yes. But not Arnot. For four hours through a snowstorm, Gamache endured the stare.

The media had hailed him a hero but Armand Gamache knew he was no hero. A hero wouldn't have hesitated. A hero wouldn't have run away.

'What was the reaction when you showed up with Arnot and the others?' Beauvoir asked.

'As cordial as you'd expect,' said Gamache, smiling. 'The council was in a rage. I'd gone against their wishes. They accused me of being disloyal, and I was.'

'Depends what you need to be loyal to. Why'd you do it?'

'Stop the suicides? The mothers deserved more than silence,' said Gamache after a moment. 'The Cree woman I met and the others deserved a public apology, an explanation, a pledge it won't happen again. Someone had to step forward and accept blame for what happened to their children.'

Like most officers in the Sûreté Beauvoir had been sickened and ashamed when he'd heard what Arnot had done. But Armand Gamache had redeemed them, proved not all Sûreté officers were vile. The vast majority of officers of all ranks had aligned themselves firmly and without question behind him. As had most newspapers.

But not all.

Some accused Gamache of collusion, of having a vendetta against Arnot. They even insinuated that he was one of the murderers and was framing the popular Arnot.

And now that accusation was back.

'How many Arnot supporters are left in the Sûreté?' Beauvoir asked, his voice businesslike. This wasn't idle chit-chat. He was gathering tactical information.

'I don't want you involved.'

'Well, fuck you.'

Jean Guy Beauvoir had never spoken to the chief like that and they were both stunned by the words and the force behind them.

Beauvoir pulled the car to the side of the road. 'How dare you. I'm so tired of this, of being treated like a child. I know you outrank me. I know you're older and wiser. There, happy? But it's time you let me stand next to you. Stop shoving me behind you. Stop it.'

He whacked his palms on the steering wheel with such force he almost broke it, and could feel the bruising at the bone. To his horror tears sprang to his eyes. It's the palms, only the palms, he told himself.

But the cage deep down was empty. He hadn't buried it well enough or deep enough. His love for Gamache tore through him and threatened to rip him apart.

'Get out,' Gamache said. Beauvoir fumbled with the seatbelt release then finally managed to tumble onto the dirt road. It was deserted. The rain had stopped and the sun was struggling out, much as Beauvoir had.

Gamache was standing solid beside him.

'Fuck you,' Beauvoir screamed with all his might. All he wanted to do was howl. To ball up his fists and hit something or someone and howl. Instead he sobbed. And flailed around, blind to the world. He didn't know how long it took, but eventually his senses came back. First he saw some light, then heard some birds, then smelled the forest after the rain. Slowly he came to himself, as though coming into the world again. And standing there was Gamache. He hadn't left. Hadn't tried to contain him, stop him. Soothe him. He'd just let Beauvoir howl and sob and lash out.

'I just want . . .' Beauvoir's voice trailed off.

'What do you want?' Gamache asked quietly. The sun was behind him and all Beauvoir could see was his outline.

'I want you to trust me.'

'I think there's more.'

Beauvoir was wrung out, weak and exhausted. The two men stared at each other. The sun caught the drops of water clinging to the branches of the trees and they shone.

Gamache very slowly walked to Beauvoir and put out his hand. Jean Guy stared at it, large and powerful. And as though watching someone else he saw his own hand rise up and softly land. His hand was slender, almost delicate inside the chief's.

'From the moment I saw you angry and bitter, assigned to that evidence room at the Trois-Rivières detachment, I knew,' said Gamache. 'Why do you think I took you on when no one else wanted you? Why do you think I made you my second in command? Yes, you're a gifted investigator. You have a knack for finding murderers. But there was more. We have a connection, you and I. A connection I feel with all members of the team but you most strongly. You're my successor, Jean Guy. The next in line. I love you like a son. And I need you.'

Beauvoir's nose and eyes burned and a sob escaped, rushing to join the others already caught in the wind as though the emotion was as natural as the trees.

The two men embraced and Beauvoir whispered into Gamache's ear, 'I love you too.'

Then they parted. Without embarrassment. They were father and son. And all Beauvoir's envy of Daniel had departed, been let go.

'You need to tell me everything.'

Gamache still hesitated.

'Ignorance won't protect me.'

Then Armand Gamache told him everything. Told him about Arnot, told him about Francoeur, told him about Nichol. Beauvoir listened, stunned.

CHAPTER 36

Odile Montmagny was busy with a customer wondering about the difference between firm and soft tofu. While she tended to business Gamache and Beauvoir wandered around the shop, looking at the rows of organic food and bins of teas and herbs. At the back of the shop, they found Sandon's furniture. Gamache had a love of antiques, especially Quebec pine. Modern design often left him baffled. But looking at Gilles's tables and chairs and stools, his bowls and walking sticks, Gamache had the feeling he was looking at a remarkable fusion of old and new. The wood seemed destined to form these shapes, as though it had grown for hundreds of years in the forests of Quebec, waiting to be found by this man and put to this use. And yet the designs were anything but traditional. They were modern and bold.

'Want one?' Odile asked. Gamache could smell the sour wine, imperfectly masked under a breath mint. It was a repulsive combination and it was all he could do not to lean away.

'I'd love one, but perhaps not today,' he said. 'We have a few more questions, I'm afraid.'

'No problem. We're quiet today. Quiet most days.'

'Gives you a chance to write your poetry, I suppose.'

She perked up. 'You've heard of my poetry?'

'I have, madame.'

'Would you like to hear one?'

Beauvoir tried to catch the chief's eye, but Gamache seemed oblivious to Beauvoir's ocular gymnastics.

'I would consider it an honor, if it's not too much trouble.'

'Here, sit here.' She practically shoved Gamache into one of Gilles's chairs. He expected to hear a great cracking sound, breaking both the chair and his bank balance in one go. But nothing happened. The chair, the wood and his savings were solid.

Odile returned with her worn notebook, the one Beauvoir had seen her slam shut on his previous visit.

She cleared her throat and adjusted her shoulders, as a fighter might before the foe.

> Over the moor at dusk there fled
> The dismal clouds, and we,
> Facing the rain, with might and main,
> Me and my love and me.
>
> The seagull screamed, the reeds were bent,
> But hand in hand the three,
> We hurried on—going against the wind,
> Me and my love and me.

'I call it "Me and My Love and Me."'

Gamache was too stunned to speak but Beauvoir found his voice.

'That was wonderful. I could see the whole thing.'

And he meant it. He was used to hearing Gamache's obscure quotes, mostly of Ruth Zardo's unintelligible stuff that didn't even rhyme. This at least made sense. He could see the bird, hear it screaming, see the rain.

'Would you like another one?'

'I'm afraid I do have to ask some questions.' Gamache patted the stool next to him. 'Lovely thought as that is.'

Odile sat and wavered a little, trying to stay upright.

'What did you think of Madeleine Favreau?'

'She was all right. Came in here sometimes, but I didn't know her well. I'm sorry she's dead. Any idea who did it?'

'Do you?'

Odile thought.

'I think it was that friend of hers. Hazel. Always so nice. Too nice. Drive you nuts. Definitely a suspect. Though, actually, maybe she's more likely to be murdered. Are you sure the right person was killed?'

'You had words with Madeleine as you all walked to the old Hadley house.'

'Did I?' Odile's skills as a liar rivaled her skills as a poet.

'You did. You were overheard.'

'Oh, we talked about this and that.'

'You argued, madame,' said Gamache, firmly but quietly. He could see Odile in profile, her jawline weak and soft.

'No, we didn't argue,' she said. Gamache knew all he needed to do was wait, and hope another customer didn't come in.

'She was trying to take Gilles,' said Odile in a fetid explosion, her sour breath hitting Gamache as though the words had been trapped inside too long. 'I know that's what she wanted. Always smiling at him, always touching him.' She mimicked Madeleine's actions by pawing Gamache's arm. 'She just wanted him to pay attention to her, and he wouldn't.'

'Is that true?' Gamache asked.

'Of course it's true. He loves me.' The last word was almost inaudible. Her mouth hung open, some long spittle drooling out. Her nose ran and tears had sprung to her eyes. Her face had dissolved as though in acid.

Did Madeleine try to take Gilles from Odile? Gamache wondered. If so, there were two motives for murder. Odile to kill her rival. And Monsieur Béliveau out of jealousy. What had Clara said? Madeleine always got what she wanted. But what had she wanted? Whom had she wanted? Gilles or Monsieur Béliveau? Or neither?

'What did you argue about that night?' Gamache pressed.

'I asked her to stop. All right? Satisfied? I begged her to stay away from Gilles. She could have any man. She was gorgeous and smart. Everyone wanted to be with her. Who wouldn't? But me? I know what people think of me. I'm stupid and dull and can only do figures. I've loved Gilles all my life and he finally chose me. Me. And no one was going to take him away. I begged her to let me have him.'

'And what did she say?'

'She denied the whole thing. Let me make a fool of myself, humiliate myself, then didn't even have the courage to admit what a slut she was.'

As they left Gamache shook her hand, feeling it wet and slimy. But that was how grief often felt. Beauvoir managed to get away without the handshake.

They found Gilles Sandon deep in the woods. They'd followed the chopping sound and cresting a small hill and climbing over a dead and decayed log they'd seen the huge man with his axe working on a downed tree. They watched for a moment the powerful and graceful movements as his massive arms raised the ancient tool and brought it down on the wood. Then he stopped, paused and turned round to look directly at them. All three stared at each other, then Sandon waved.

'You're back,' he called to Beauvoir.

'And brought the boss.'

Sandon strode over to them, his feet crackling twigs underfoot.

'No bosses out here,' he said to Beauvoir, then turned to size Gamache up. 'You're the one in the papers.'

'I am,' said Gamache, with ease.

'You don't look like a murderer.'

'I'm not.'

'And I'm supposed to believe that?'

'You'll believe what you choose. I don't care.'

Sandon grunted then finally indicated a stump as though it was a silk-upholstered chair.

'You were a lumberjack once, I believe,' said Gamache, sitting on the stump.

'In the dark days, yes. I'm not ashamed of it any more. I didn't know any better.'

But he looked ashamed.

'What didn't you know?' asked Beauvoir.

'I told you. That trees are alive. I mean, we all know they're living, but don't really think of them as alive, you know? But they are. You can't kill something that's alive. It's not right.'

'How did you find out?' Gamache asked.

Sandon reached into his pocket and brought out a dirty hanky. He rubbed the blade of his axe and cleaned it as he spoke.

'I was working as a logger for one of the mills around here. Went into the forest every day with my team. Cut down trees, hooked them to tractors and dragged them to the logging road to be picked up. Back-breaking work, but I liked it. Outside, fresh air. No bosses.'

He looked suspiciously at Gamache, his weathered face covered by a red and graying beard, his eyes keen but distant.

'One day I walked into the woods with my axe and I heard a whimpering. Sounded like a baby. It was this time of year. Best time for cutting trees. But it's also the time when animals have babies. The crew was just arriving and the whimpering grew louder. Then I heard a scream. I shouted to the guys to stop, to be quiet and listen. The whimpering had turned into a cry. It was all around. And I could feel it too. I'd always felt at home in the forest, but suddenly I was afraid.

'"Don't hear nothin'," said one of the guys and hit the tree again. And again there was a scream. You can figure the rest. Something had changed overnight. I'd changed. I could hear the trees. I think I could always hear their happiness. I think that's why I felt so happy myself in the forest. But now I could hear their terror too.'

'What did you do?'

'What could I do? What would you do? I had to stop it. Had to stop the killing. Can you imagine cutting down a forest that was screaming at you?'

Beauvoir could, especially if the screaming went on all day.

'But mostly trees are quiet. Just want to be left alone,' Gilles continued. 'Funny how I learned freedom from creatures that are rooted in place.'

Gamache thought that made perfect sense.

'I was fired, but I would've quit anyway. I'd walked into the forest that day a logger and I walked out something else entirely. The world was never the same. Couldn't be. My wife tried to understand but couldn't. She finally left with the kids. Went back to Charlevoix. Don't blame her. Relief really. She kept trying to tell me trees don't talk and they don't sing and they sure as hell don't scream. But they do. We lived in different worlds.'

'Does Odile live in your world?' Beauvoir asked.

'No,' Gilles admitted. 'I actually haven't met anyone who does. But she accepts it. Doesn't try to change me or convince me I'm wrong. She takes me as I am.'

'And Madeleine?'

'She was like something beautiful and exotic. Like walking through the forest here and coming across a palm tree. It takes your attention.'

'Did you have an affair with her?' Beauvoir asked, more bluntly than Gamache would have liked, but it was his style.

'I did not. It was enough to admire from afar. I might talk to trees, but I'm not crazy. She wasn't interested in me. And I wasn't interested in her, not really. Fantasy, maybe, but not in the real world.'

Beauvoir wondered what exactly Sandon considered the 'real' world.

'Why don't you like Monsieur Béliveau?' asked Gamache. It took Sandon a moment to tear his mind away from Madeleine and focus on the austere grocer. He looked down at his massive hands and picked at a callus.

'There was a magnificent oak on his land. It'd been hit by lightning and a huge limb was hanging loose. I could hear it crying so I asked if I could remove the limb, help the tree. He refused.'

'Why?' asked Beauvoir.

Gilles looked at them. 'Said I'd kill the whole tree by taking off the branch. That was a risk, I admitted, but told him the tree was in pain and it would be more merciful for it to either live healthy or die quickly.'

'But he didn't believe you?'

He shook his head. 'Took four years for that tree to die. I could hear it crying for help. I begged Béliveau but he wouldn't hear of it. Thought the tree was getting better.'

'He didn't know,' said Gamache. 'He was afraid.'

Gilles shrugged, dismissive.

'And the fact he was seeing Madeleine wasn't part of it?' asked Gamache.

'He should have protected her. He should have protected the tree. He looks so gentle but he's a bad one.'

What had Monsieur Béliveau called himself? Gamache tried to remember. The thing that brings death. That was it. First his wife, then Madeleine, then the bird. And the tree. Things died around Monsieur Béliveau.

The men were silent, inhaling the sweet, musty aroma of moist pines and autumn leaves and new buds.

'Now I come out here and find trees already dead and turn them into furniture.'

'Give them new life,' said Gamache.

Sandon looked at him. 'I don't suppose you hear the trees?'

Gamache cocked his head, listening, then shook it. Sandon nodded.

'Are there any ginkgo trees around?' Gamache asked.

'Ginkgo? A few, not many. They're mostly from Asia, I think. Very old trees.'

'You mean they live a long time?' asked Beauvoir.

'That too, though not as long as sequoias. Some of them are thousands of years old, can you believe it? Love to have a conversation with one of them. No, a ginkgo doesn't last that long, but it's the oldest tree known. Prehistoric. Considered a living fossil. Imagine that.'

Gamache was impressed. Sandon knew a lot about the ginkgo tree. The ancient ginkgo family that produced ephedra.

A newspaper was folded neatly at his desk when they arrived back at the Incident Room. It was five o'clock and Robert Lemieux was working on his computer. He looked up and waved as they came in, his eyes falling on the newspaper as though commiserating with Gamache.

Jean Guy Beauvoir stood beside the chief as he reached for the paper. Gamache was reminded of a nature show he once saw about gorillas. When threatened they ran forward, focusing on the attacker, screaming and pounding their chests. But every now and then they'd reach out to touch the gorilla next to them. To make sure they weren't alone.

Beauvoir was the gorilla next to him.

There, on the front page, was a picture of Gamache looking foolish, his eyes half-closed, his mouth in a strange grimace.

SOÛL! insisted the type underneath, in capital letters. *Drunk!*

'I see you're a drunken, blackmailing, pimping murderer,' said Beauvoir.

'A Renaissance man,' said Gamache, shaking his head. But he was relieved. He first skimmed the article looking for Daniel, Annie. Reine-Marie. But all he found was his own name and Arnot's. Always linked, as though one didn't exist without the other.

He called his family and spent the next half-hour catching up with them, making sure all was as well as could be.

It was a strange world, he realized as he and Beauvoir made their way back to the B & B with their dossiers and yearbooks, when a good day was one where he was only accused of drunken incompetence.

CHAPTER 37

For the first time in twenty-five years Clara Morrow closed the door to her studio. Olivier and Gabri were arriving. Armand Gamache and his inspector, Jean Guy Beauvoir, had just walked in. Myrna had arrived earlier with shepherd's pie and a massive arrangement of flowers, branches in bud and what looked like a bonnet.

'There's a gift in there for you,' she said to Gamache.

'Really?' He hoped she didn't mean the bonnet.

Clara showed Jeanne Chauvet into the living room where everyone was massed. Gamache caught Clara's eye and smiled his thanks. She smiled back but he thought she looked tired.

'Are you all right?' He took the tray of drinks from her and placed it on its normal spot on the piano.

'Just a little stressed. Tried to paint this afternoon but Peter was right. Best not to try too hard if the muse isn't there. Fortunately I had the dinner to concentrate on.'

Clara looked as though she'd rather gnaw off her foot than be at this dinner party.

Olivier took the ceramic bowl of home-made pâté from Gabri, who was supposed to circulate with it but had decided to stand by the fire and talk to Jeanne instead.

'Pâté?' he asked Beauvoir, who took a large slice of baguette and smeared it thickly.

'So, I hear you're a witch,' Gabri said to Jeanne, and the room fell silent.

'I prefer Wicca, but yes,' said Jeanne matter-of-factly.

'Pâté?' asked Olivier, grateful to have the appetizers to hide behind. Would that they'd brought a horse.

'Thank you,' said Jeanne.

Ruth arrived, stomping into the cheery living room. Beauvoir took the distraction as a chance to speak to Jeanne privately.

'Agent Lemieux looked up your high school,' he said, guiding her into a quiet corner.

'Really? That's interesting,' though she didn't look interested.

'It was actually. There was no school.'

'I'm sorry?'

'No Gareth James High in Montreal.'

'But that's impossible. I went to it.' She seemed agitated, just the way Beauvoir wanted his suspects. He didn't like this woman, this witch.

'The school burned down twenty years ago. Convenient, don't you think?' He got up before she could respond.

'Where's my drink?' Ruth limped over to the piano. 'Wanted to get here earlier before you drank it all,' she said to Gamache. Olivier was deeply grateful someone more maladroit than Gabri was finally in the room.

'I've hidden bottles all over the house and if you're nice to me, Madame Zardo,' said Gamache, bowing slightly, 'I might tell you where some are.'

Ruth considered then seemed to conclude it was too much trouble. She grabbed what was a tumbler for water and handed it to Peter.

'Scotch.'

'How can you be a poet?' Peter asked.

'I'll tell you how, I don't waste good words on the likes of you.' She took the tumbler and swallowed a gulp.

'So why do you drink?' she asked Gamache.

'*Voyons*,' said Beauvoir. 'That newspaper article was a lie. He doesn't drink.'

'What newspaper article?' asked Ruth. 'And what's that?' She pointed to the Scotch in Gamache's hand.

'I drink to relax,' said Gamache. 'Why do you?'

Ruth stared at him but what she saw were the two baby birds, tucked into their little beds in her oven, snug in warmed towels and water bottles she'd bought at Canadian Tire. She'd fed Rosa and tried to feed Lilium, but she hadn't taken very much.

Ruth had kissed them softly on their little fluffy heads, getting a slight film of dander on her thin, old lips. It'd been a while since she'd kissed anything. They smelled fresh and felt warm. Lilium had bent down and pecked at her hand slightly, as though kissing back. Ruth had meant to leave for Peter and Clara's earlier, but had waited until Rosa and Lilium were asleep. She grabbed her kitchen timer and put two and a half hours on it, then slipped it into her moth-eaten cardigan.

She took a deep sip of her Scotch, and thought about it. Why did she drink?

'I drink so I don't get mad,' she said finally.

'Get mad or go mad?' mumbled Myrna. 'Either way, it isn't working.'

Over at the sofa Gabri had corralled Jeanne again. 'So what do witches do?'

'Gabri, shouldn't you be passing this round?' Olivier tried to hand him the pâté again, but Gabri just took a scoop himself and left Olivier holding it.

'We heal people.'

'I thought you did, well, the opposite. Aren't there wicked witches?'

'Please, dear Lord, don't let him welcome us to munchkin land,' Olivier murmured to Peter. Both men moved away.

'Some, but not as many as you might think,' Jeanne smiled. 'Witches are simply people with heightened intuition.'

'So it's not magic,' said Beauvoir, listening despite himself.

'We're not conjuring anything that isn't already there. We just see things others don't.'

'Like dead people?' asked Gabri.

'Oh, that's nothing,' said Ruth, shoving Myrna aside as she squeezed onto the sofa, bony elbows out. 'I see them all the time.'

'You do?' asked Myrna.

'I see them now,' said Ruth and the room grew silent. Even Peter and Olivier drifted back.

'Here?' asked Clara. 'In our house?'

'Especially here,' said Ruth.

'Now?'

'Right there,' said Ruth and she raised one certain finger and pointed. At Gamache.

There was an intake of breath and Gamache looked over at Beauvoir.

'Dead? He's dead?' whispered Clara.

'Dead? I thought you said dull. Never mind,' said Ruth.

'How can she be a poet?' Peter asked Olivier and the two walked away again to examine Peter's latest jigsaw puzzle.

'So who did it? Do you know yet who killed Madeleine?' asked Ruth. 'Or have you been too busy paying people off and drinking to actually do any work?'

Beauvoir opened his mouth and Gamache held up his hand, reassuring him it was a joke.

'We don't know, but we're getting close.'

This was a surprise to Beauvoir, who tried not to show it.

'Did you all know she'd had cancer?' Gamache asked. Everyone looked at each other and nodded.

'But that was a while ago,' said Myrna.

Gamache waited for more then decided he had to ask his question clearly.

'Was she still in remission, as far as you know?'

They looked perplexed and again searched out each other, passing glances in the sort of telepathy good friends have.

'Never heard otherwise,' said Peter. No one disagreed. Gamache and Beauvoir exchanged looks. Conversation started up again and Peter ducked into the kitchen to check on dinner.

Gamache followed him and found Peter stirring the lamb stew. Gamache picked up a baguette and a bread knife and gestured to Peter, who smiled his thanks.

The two worked quietly together, listening to the conversation in the next room.

'Hear tomorrow's supposed to be nice, finally,' said Peter. 'Sunny and warm.'

'April's like that, isn't it?' said Gamache, cutting the bread and putting it onto a tea towel nestled in a wooden bowl. Gamache lifted the towel and saw the signature burling of the wood. One of Sandon's bowls.

'Unpredictable, you mean?' said Peter. 'Difficult month.'

'Sunny and warm one day, then snow the next,' agreed Gamache. 'Shakespeare called it "the uncertain glory" of an April day.'

'I prefer T. S. Eliot. "The cruellest month." '

'Why do you say that?'

'All those spring flowers slaughtered. Happens almost every year. They're tricked into blooming, into coming out. Opening up. And not just the spring bulbs, but the buds on the trees. The rose bushes, everything. All out and happy. And then boom, a freak snowstorm kills them all.'

Gamache had the feeling they weren't talking about flowers any more.

'But what would you have happen?' he asked Peter. 'They have to bloom, even if it's for a short time. And they'll be back next year.'

'But not all.' Peter turned to look at Gamache, the wooden spoon in the air dripping thick gravy. 'Some never recover. We had the most beautiful rose bush just budding, and a hard frost killed it a few years back.'

' "A killing frost," ' quoted Gamache. ' "It nips his root. And then he falls, as I do." '

Peter was trembling.

'Who's falling, Peter? Is it Clara?'

'No one's falling. I won't allow it.'

'Strange in Canada, we talk all the time about the one thing we can't control. The weather. We can't stop a killing frost and we can't stop the flowers from doing what they're meant to do. Better to bloom even for an instant, if that's your nature, than live forever in hiding.'

'I don't agree.' Peter turned his back on his guest and practically puréed the stew.

'I'm sorry. I didn't mean to offend you.'

'You didn't,' said Peter to the wall.

Gamache took the bread to the long pine table, set for dinner, then returned to the living room. He reflected on T. S. Eliot and thought the poet had called April the cruellest month not because it killed flowers and buds on the trees, but because sometimes it didn't. How difficult it was for those who didn't bloom when all about was new life and hope.

'So let me get this straight,' said Olivier.

'He almost never says that,' Gabri assured Clara then turned back to the platter of shrimp Olivier was trying to get him to pass round. Gabri took one.

'Easter isn't a Christian holiday?' said Olivier.

'Well, it is,' said Jeanne. The little, nondescript woman had somehow managed to dominate the room full of strong personalities. She sat bunched into a corner of the sofa, squeezed between the arm and Myrna, and all eyes were on her. 'But the early church didn't know for sure when Christ was crucified so it chose a date, one that would fit into the pagan calendar of rituals as well.'

'Why would they want to do that?' asked Clara.

'The early church needed converts to survive. It was a dangerous and fragile time. In order to win over the pagans it adopted some of their feasts and rituals.'

'Church incense is like the smudging we do,' agreed Myrna. 'When we light dried herbs to cleanse a place.' She turned to Clara, who nodded. But it was a comforting ritual full of joy, not the somber swinging of the church censer, glum and vaguely threatening. She'd never seen the two as similar and wondered how the priests would feel about the comparison. Or the witches.

'That's right,' said Jeanne. 'Same with the festivals. We sometimes call Christmas Yuletide.'

'In some of the carols anyway,' said Gabri.

'And we have the Yule log,' Olivier pointed out.

'Yule is the ancient word for the winter solstice. The longest night of the year. Around December twenty-first. It's a pagan festival. So that's where the early Christian church decided to put Christmas.'

'So that a bunch of witches would celebrate? Come on,' said Ruth with a snort. 'Aren't you making yourselves out to be more important than you are?'

'Now, absolutely. The church hasn't been interested in us for hundreds of years, except maybe as firewood, as you know.'

'What do you mean? As I know?'

'You've written about the old beliefs. Many times. It runs through your poems.'

'You're reading too much into them, Joan of Arc,' said Ruth.

> *I was hanged for living alone,*
> *For having blue eyes and a sunburned skin,*
> *And breasts.*
> *Whenever there's talk of demons*
> *These come in handy.*

Jeanne quoted the poem, searching Ruth's face.

'Are you saying Ruth's a witch?' asked Gabri.

Jeanne tore her attention from the wizened old woman sitting bolt upright.

'In the Wiccan beliefs most old women are the keepers of wisdom, of the medicines, of the stories. They're the crones.'

'Well, she does practice bitchcraft. Does that count?' Gabri asked to roars of laughter and even Jeanne smiled.

'There was a time when most people were pagans and celebrated the old ways. Yule and Eostar. The spring equinox. Easter. You do rituals?' Jeanne asked Myrna.

'Some. We celebrate the solstice and do some smudging. It's a kind of hodgepodge of native and pagan beliefs.'

'It's a mess,' said Ruth. 'I went to a couple. Ended up stinking of sage smoke for two days. People in the pharmacy thought I'd smoked up.'

'Sometimes the magic works,' said Myrna to Clara with a laugh.

'Dinner,' Peter called from the kitchen. When they arrived he'd put the casseroles and stews and vegetables on the island along with plates. Clara and Beauvoir went around lighting the candles scattered throughout the kitchen so that by the time they'd taken their places it was like sitting in a darkened planetarium, filled with points of light.

Their plates piled high with lamb stew and shepherd's pie and fresh bread and smooth, fluffy mashed potatoes and baby beans, they tucked in, talking about gardens and the storm, about the Anglican Church Women and the condition of the roads.

'I called Hazel to see if they could come tonight, but she said no,' said Clara.

'She almost always says no,' said Myrna.

'Is that true?' asked Olivier. 'I never noticed that.'

'Neither had I,' said Clara, helping herself to another spoonful of potatoes. 'But now that I think of it, we wanted to take over dinners after Madeleine died but she wouldn't hear of it.'

'Some people are like that,' said Myrna. 'Always happy to help others, but they have difficulty accepting it. Too bad really. She must be having a horrible time. Can't imagine the pain she's in.'

'What excuse did she give for not coming tonight?' Olivier asked.

'Said Sophie'd sprained her ankle,' said Clara with a scowl. There were guffaws around the table. She turned to Gamache to explain. 'Sophie's always sick or injured in some way, at least as long as I've known her.'

Gamache turned to Myrna. 'What's your thinking about that?'

'Sophie? Easy. Attention-seeking. Jealous of Mom and Madeleine—' She stopped, realizing what she was saying.

'Don't worry,' said Gamache. 'We'd already figured that one out. Sophie's also lost weight recently.'

'Tons,' said Gabri. 'But she bobs up and down. Lost weight a few years ago too but put it all back.'

'Does it run in the family?' asked Gamache. 'Does Hazel's weight change?'

Again they looked at each other, except Ruth who stole a piece of bread from Olivier's plate.

'Hazel's been the same as long as I remember,' said Clara.

Gamache nodded and sipped his wine. 'Marvelous dinner, Peter. Thank you.' He raised his glass to Peter, who acknowledged the compliment.

'I thought for sure we'd be having game hens,' said Olivier to Peter. 'Isn't that your party dish this year?'

'But you aren't guests,' said Peter. 'We only do that for real people.'

'I think you've been hanging around Ruth,' said Olivier.

'Actually, we were going to make Rock Cornish game hens but we thought with your babies, you might not want to eat them,' Peter said to Ruth.

'What do you mean?' Ruth seemed genuinely perplexed and Gamache wondered whether she'd forgotten her ducklings weren't human, weren't her actual babies.

'So you wouldn't mind if we ate poultry?' Peter asked. 'Or even Brume Lake duck? We were going to barbecue some *confit du canard*.'

'Rosa and Lilium aren't chickens and they aren't ducks,' said Ruth.

'They aren't?' said Clara. 'What are they?'

'I think they're flying monkeys,' said Gabri to Olivier, who snorted.

'They're Canada geese.'

'Are you sure? They look pretty small, especially that Lilium,' said Peter.

Everyone was hushed and if Clara had been closer she

would have kicked him. Instead she kicked Beauvoir. Another example, he thought, of suppressed anglo rage. Can't trust them, can't kick them out, or back.

'So? She's always been small,' said Ruth. 'When they hatched she almost didn't make it out of her shell. Rosa was already out and squawking, but I could see Lilium thrashing back and forth, her wings trying to crack the shell.'

'What did you do?' asked Jeanne.

Her face, like all of theirs, was lit by candlelight, but while it made the others more attractive, it gave her a demonic expression, her eyes sunken and dark, the shadows strong.

'What do you think I did? I cracked the egg for her. Opened it up enough for her to get out.'

'You saved her life,' said Peter.

'Perhaps,' said Jeanne, sitting back and almost disappearing into the shadows.

'What'd you mean, perhaps?' demanded Ruth.

'The emperor moth.'

It wasn't Jeanne who spoke, but Gabri.

'Tell me you didn't just say "the emperor moth," ' said Clara.

'I did, and for a reason.' He paused, to make sure his audience was with him. He needn't have worried.

'It takes years for the moth to evolve from an egg into an adult,' he said. 'In its final stage the caterpillar spins a cocoon and then it dissolves completely until it's just liquid, then it transforms. It becomes something else entirely. A huge emperor moth. But it's not that easy. Before it can live as a moth it has to fight its way out of the cocoon. Not all make it.'

'They would if I was there,' said Ruth, taking another gulp.

Gabri was uncharacteristically silent.

'What? What is it?' demanded Ruth.

'They need to fight their way out of the cocoon. It builds their wings and muscles. It's the struggle that saves them. Without it they're crippled. If you help an emperor moth, you kill it.'

Ruth's glass stopped at her lips. For the first time since

any of them had known her, she didn't drink. Then she thumped the glass so hard on the table it shot a plume of Scotch into the air.

'Bullshit. What do you know about the natural world?'

There was silence then.

After a long minute Armand Gamache turned to Myrna.

'This is a beautiful flower arrangement, and I think you said there was something in it for me.'

'There is,' she said, relieved. 'But you have to dig for it.'

Gamache got up and delicately moved the branches aside. There, in the forest, was a book. He brought it out and sat back down.

'*The Dictionary of Magical Places*,' he read from the cover.

'Latest edition.'

'They found more magical places?' asked Olivier.

'Guess so. I saw what you were reading in the bistro yesterday and thought you might be interested in this too,' Myrna said to Gamache.

'What were you reading?' asked Clara.

Gamache went into the mudroom and returning with the books he'd been carrying, he placed them one on top of the other on the table. Staring up at them was a small hand outlined in red on the black leather cover. No one moved to touch it.

'Where'd you find that?' Jeanne asked. She looked upset.

'The old Hadley house. Do you know the book?'

Did she hesitate? he wondered. She reached out and he handed it to her. After examining it for a moment she put it down.

'It's a Hamsa hand. An ancient symbol to ward off the envious and the evil eye. It's also called the Hand of Miriam. Or Mary.'

'Mary?' said Clara, sitting slowly back in her chair. 'As in the Madonna?'

Jeanne nodded.

'It's all bullshit,' said Ruth, who'd wiped up the droplets of spilled Scotch with her finger and was sucking it.

'You don't believe in magic?' Jeanne asked.

'I don't believe in magic, I don't believe in God. There's no such thing as angels and there're no fairies at the end of the garden. Nothing. The only magic is this.' She raised her glass and took a gulp.

'Is it working?' asked Gamache.

'Fuck off,' said Ruth.

'Eloquent as ever,' said Gabri. 'I used to believe in God, but I gave it up for Lent.'

'Har-dee-har-har,' said Olivier.

'You want to know what I believe?' said Ruth. 'Here, give me that.'

Without waiting she leaned over and snatched the second book from the table. The cracked and worn Bible Gamache had taken from the old Hadley house. She squinted and brought it close to a candle as she tried to find the right page. The room was silent, the only sound the slight sizzling of a candle wick.

'*Behold I show you a mystery,*' read Ruth, her voice as worn as the Bible she held. '*We shall not all sleep, but we shall all be changed, In a moment, in the twinkling of an eye, at the last trump: for the trumpet shall sound, and the dead shall be raised incorruptible, and we shall be changed.*'

Into the silence they stared.

The dead shall be raised.

And then Ruth's alarm went off.

CHAPTER 38

Gamache couldn't sleep. His bedside clock said 2:22. He'd been lying awake watching the bright red numbers change since the clock had said 1:11. He'd been woken up not by a bad dream, not by anxiety or a full bladder. He'd been woken up by frogs. Peepers. An army of invisible frogs at the pond spent most of the night singing a mating call. He would have thought they'd be exhausted by now, but apparently not. At dusk it was joyful, after dinner it was atmospheric. At 2 a.m. it was simply annoying. Anyone who said the country was peaceful hadn't spent time there. Especially in the spring.

He got up, put on his dressing gown and slippers, took a stack of books from the dresser and headed downstairs.

He relit the fireplace and made himself a pot of tea, then settled in staring at the fire and thinking of the dinner party.

Ruth had left as soon as her alarm went off, scaring the pants off everyone. She'd just read that extraordinary passage. St Paul's letter to the Corinthians. Quite a letter, thought Gamache. Thank God they kept it.

'Good night,' Peter had called from the door. 'Sleep tight.'

'Always do,' Ruth snapped.

The rest of the dinner had been peaceful and tasty. A pear and cranberry *tarte* was produced by Peter, from Sarah's Boulangerie. Jeanne had bought handmade chocolates from Marielle's Maison du Chocolat in St-Rémy and Clara put out a platter of cheese and bowls of fruit. Rich, aromatic coffee made the perfect end to the evening.

Over tea now, in the quietude of the B & B, Gamache thought about what he'd heard. Then he picked up one of the yearbooks. It was from the first year Madeleine had been at the high school and she didn't figure in many pictures. Hazel was in a few, on some of the junior teams. But as the years went by Madeleine seemed to bloom. Became captain of the basketball and volleyball teams. Beside her in all the shots was Hazel. Her natural place.

Gamache put down the books and thought a bit, then he picked one up again and looked for the missing cheerleader. Jeanne Potvin. Was it possible? Was it that easy?

'Fucking frogs,' said Beauvoir a few minutes later, shuffling into the living room. 'We just get rid of Nichol and now the frogs start acting up. Still, they're better-looking and less slimy. What're you reading?'

'Those yearbooks Agent Lacoste brought back. Tea?'

Beauvoir nodded and wiped a hand across his eyes. 'Don't suppose she brought back any *Sports Illustrated*?'

'Sorry, old son. But I did find something in this one. Our missing cheerleader. You'll never guess.'

'Jeanne?' Beauvoir got up and took the book from Gamache. He scanned the page until he found a picture of Jeanne Potvin. Then he looked at Gamache, taking a sip of tea and watching him over the rim of the mug.

'I'm glad it was your hunch and not mine. Not exactly caul-worthy.'

Jeanne Potvin, the missing cheerleader, was black.

'Well, it was worth a try,' said Beauvoir, not trying very hard to hide his amusement. Picking up *The Dictionary of Magical Places* he started flipping through it.

'There's an interesting section on caves in France in there.'

'Oh boy.' Beauvoir looked at the pictures for a while. Stone circles, old houses, mountains. There was even a magical tree. A ginkgo. 'Do you believe in this stuff?'

Gamache looked at Beauvoir over his half-moon glasses.

The younger man's hair was disheveled and he had a small shadow of beard. He brought his hand up to his own face and felt it rough. He then brought his hand to his head and felt the telltale ends there. What little hair he had was standing on end. They must look a fright.

'Frogs get you too?' Jeanne Chauvet wandered into the room in her dressing gown. 'Is there more?' She nodded to the tea.

'Always more,' Gamache smiled and poured the rest for her. She took the tea and was amazed to discover that even at almost three in the morning he smelled just a little of sandalwood and rosewater. It felt peaceful.

'We were just talking about magic,' said Gamache, sitting down once Jeanne had taken a seat.

'I asked if he believed in these things.' Beauvoir tapped the book Myrna had given them.

'You don't?' asked Jeanne.

'Not a bit.'

He looked over at the chief who'd snorted.

'Sorry,' Gamache apologized. 'It got away from me.'

Beauvoir, who knew nothing got away from the chief unless he wanted it to, scowled.

'Well, really.' Gamache sat forward. 'Who has his lucky belt? And his lucky coin? And his lucky meal before each hockey game?' Gamache turned to Jeanne. 'He'll only eat Italian *poutine* with his left hand.'

'We beat the Montreal Metro police drug squad in hockey. I scored a hat trick, and that night I'd eaten Italian *poutine* with my left hand.'

'Makes sense to me,' said Jeanne.

'Every time we get on a plane you have to sit in seat 5A. And you have to listen to the safety announcements all the way through. If I interrupt you, you pay no attention.'

'That's not magic, that's common sense.'

'Seat 5A?'

'It's a comfortable seat. OK, it's my favorite. If I sit there the plane won't crash.'

'Do the pilots know? Maybe they should sit there,' said

Jeanne. 'If it'll make you feel better, everyone has their superstitions. It's called magical thinking. If I do this, that will happen, even if the two aren't connected. If I step on a crack it'll break my mother's back. Or walk under a ladder, or break a mirror. We're taught early to believe in magic then spend the rest of our lives being punished for it. Did you know most astronauts take some sort of talisman with them into space to keep them safe? These are scientists.'

Beauvoir got up. 'I'm going to try to get some sleep. Want the book?' He offered it to Gamache who shook his head.

'I've already looked at it. Quite interesting.'

Beauvoir clumped up the stairs and when he was gone Jeanne turned to Gamache. 'You asked why I came here and I said it was for a rest, and that was true, but not the whole truth. I'd been sent a brochure but it wasn't until yesterday when I saw the others Gabri had that I realized mine was different. Here.'

She pulled two shiny brochures for the B & B out of her dressing gown pocket and handed them to Gamache. He stared at them. On the front were photographs of the B & B and Three Pines. The brochures were identical. Except for one thing. Across the top of the one mailed to Jeanne Chauvet was typed, *Where lay lines meet—Easter Special.*

'I've heard of lay lines, but what are they?'

'Whoever wrote this didn't know much either. They misspelled it. It's l-e-y, not l-a-y,' said Jeanne. 'They were first described in the 1920s—'

'As recently as that? I thought they were supposed to be ancient. Stonehenge, that sort of thing.'

'They are, but no one noticed until about ninety years ago. Some fellow in England, I've forgotten his name, looked at stone circles and standing stones and even the oldest cathedrals and noticed that they all line up. They're built miles and miles apart, but if you connect the dots they're in straight lines. He came to the conclusion there was a reason for this.'

'And it was?'

'Energy. The earth seems to give off more energy along these ley lines. Some people', she leaned forward and darted her eyes to make sure no one else was listening, 'don't believe this.'

'No,' he whispered back. Then he picked up her brochure. 'Someone knew you well enough to know how to get you here.'

And someone needed the psychic here at Easter. To contact, and create, the dead.

Ruth Zardo was also up, though she hadn't actually gone to bed. Instead she'd been sitting at the preformed white resin garden furniture she called her kitchen set, staring into the oven. It was on the lowest setting. Just enough to keep Rosa and Lilium warm.

It wasn't true what Gabri said. There was no way simply cracking the shell had hurt Lilium. She hadn't done much, just a little crack, just enough to give Lilium the idea, really.

Ruth got up, her hip and knees fighting her, and limped over to the oven, instinctively putting her shrunken and veined hand in to make sure the element was still on, but not too hot.

Then she bent over the little ones, watching for breath.

Lilium looked fine. She actually looked as though she'd grown. Ruth was sure she saw the little chest rise and fall. Then she slowly made her way back to the white resin chair. She stared a little longer at the pan in the oven then pulled a notebook toward her.

> *When they came to harvest my corpse*
> *(Open your mouth, close your eyes)*
> *Cut my body from the rope,*
> *Surprise, surprise:*
> *I was still alive.*

She could see the pink scalp and yellow beak poking through the shell. She was sure the little one had looked at her, and squealed. Called for help. She'd heard that geese bond with the first thing they see. What she hadn't heard was that it goes both ways. She'd reached out then, not capable of just watching the little one struggle. She'd cracked the shell. Freed little Lilium.

How could that be wrong?

Ruth laid down her pen and put her head in her hands, her knotty fingers clutching at the short white hair. Trying to contain the thoughts, trying to stop them from becoming feelings. But it was too late. She knew.

She knew that kindness kills. All her life she'd suspected this and so she'd only ever been cold and cruel. She'd faced kindness with cutting remarks. She'd curled her lips at smiling faces. She'd twisted every thoughtful, considerate act into an assault. Everyone who was nice to her, who was compassionate and loving, she rebuffed.

Because she'd loved them. Loved them with all her heart, and wouldn't see them hurt. Because she'd known all her life that the surest way to hurt someone, to maim and cripple them, was to be kind. If people were exposed, they die. Best to teach them to be armored, even if it meant she herself was forever alone. Sealed off from human touch.

But, of course, her feelings had to come out somehow, and so in her sixties the string of words she'd coiled inside came out. In poetry.

Jeanne was right, of course, thought Ruth. I do believe. In God, in Nature, in magic. In people. She was the most credulous person she knew. She believed in everything. She looked down at what she'd written.

> *Having been hanged for something*
> *I never said,*
> *I can now say anything I can say.*

Ruth Zardo picked up the little bird, no longer needing her warm, new towel. Lilium's head fell to one side, her eyes staring at her mother. Ruth lifted the tiny wings, hoping, maybe, she'd see a flutter.

But Lilium was gone. Killed by kindness.

Before, I was not a witch.
Now I am one.

Clara had been in her studio since midnight. Painting. A feeling had crept over her since the party. Not yet an idea, not even a thought. But a feeling. Something significant had happened. It wasn't what was said, not totally. It was more. A look, a sense.

She'd sneaked out of bed and practically run to her canvas. She'd stood back from it, staring for many minutes, seeing it as it was and as it could be.

Then she'd picked up her brush.

God bless Peter for suggesting the party. Without it she was sure she'd still be blocked.

CHAPTER 39

The next morning was splendid, a green and golden day. The early and young sun hit the village and everything shone, made fresh and clean by the rain of the day before. Despite being up for a couple of hours in the middle of the night Gamache rose early and went for his morning walk, tiptoeing between the worms on the road, another sign of spring. They at least were silent. After twenty minutes he was joined by Jean Guy Beauvoir, who jogged across the green to join him on his walk.

'We should wrap it up today,' said Beauvoir, watching Gamache appear to sneak along the road.

'Think so?'

'We'll get the report on the ephedra, then question Sophie again. She'll tell us everything.'

'She'll confess? Do you think she did it?'

'Nothing's changed, so yes, I think she did it. I take it you don't?'

'I think she had motive, opportunity and probably has the anger.'

'So what's the problem?'

Gamache stopped tiptoeing and turned to look at Beauvoir. It felt as though the day belonged to them. No one else was stirring yet in the pretty village. For a moment Gamache indulged in a fantasy. Of giving the Arnot people what they wanted. It would be so easy to drive into Montreal today and hand in his resignation. Then he'd pick up Reine-Marie from her job at the Bibliothèque Nationale and drive down here. They'd have lunch on the *terrasse* of the bistro over-looking the Rivière Bella Bella, then go house-hunting. They'd find a place in the village, and he'd buy one of San-don's lyrical rocking chairs and he'd sit in it reading his pa-per each morning and sipping his coffee and villagers would come to him when they had little problems. A sock missing from the clothes line. A family recipe mysteriously made by a neighbor for a party. Reine-Marie would join Arts Williamsburg and finally sign up for those courses she was longing to take.

No more murder. No more Arnot.

It was so tempting.

'Did you look at *The Dictionary of Magical Places*?'

'I did. You so subtly told me to look at the stuff on France.'

'I'm very clever,' agreed Gamache. 'And did you?'

'All I saw were caves they discovered about fifteen years ago. Had all these weird drawings of animals. Appar-ently cave men drew them thousands of years ago. I read for a while but frankly didn't see why it was so important. There're other caves with drawings. It's not as if that was the first they found.'

'True.'

Gamache could still see the images. Elegant, plump bi-son, horses, not one at a time but a lively herd, flowing across the rock face. Archeologists had been astonished by the images when they were first discovered, less than twenty years ago, by hikers in the woods of France. So detailed, so alive were the drawings archeologists first thought they must be the very pinnacle of the cave man's art. The last stage be-fore man evolved further.

And then came the astonishing discovery. The drawings were actually twenty thousand years older than anything they'd found before. It wasn't the last, it was the first.

Who were these people who managed what their

descendants couldn't? To shade, to make three-dimensional images, to so gracefully depict power and movement? And then the final, staggering discovery.

Deep inside one of the caves they found a hand, outlined in red. Never before in all the other cave drawings was there an image of the artist, or the people. But the person who created these had a sense of self. Of the individual.

In the book last night, *The Dictionary of Magical Places*, Armand Gamache had stared at that one image. Of the hand, outlined in red. As though the artist was declaring himself alive, after thirty-five thousand years.

And Gamache had thought of another image, not quite so old, on a book he'd found in a damned and decaying house.

'What makes them different is that they seem to be art for the pleasure of it. And magic. Scientists think the drawings were meant to conjure the actual beasts.'

'But how do they know?' asked Beauvoir. 'Don't we always say something's magic when we don't understand?'

'We do. That's what the witch-hunts were about.'

'What was it Madame Zardo called it? The burning times?'

'I'm not so sure they're over,' said Gamache, looking up at the old Hadley house then dragging his eyes back to the lovely and peaceful village. 'What interested me most, though, about those cave drawings was the name of the cave itself. Do you remember it?'

Beauvoir thought. But he knew no answer would be coming.

The chief turned back to his walk, and continued to tiptoe between the squiggling worms. Beauvoir watched him for a moment, the tall, elegant, powerful man, avoiding the worms. Then he too started walking, tiptoeing, so that from any of the mullioned windows around the village green they looked like two grown men in an awkward, though familiar, ballet.

'Do you remember the name?' Beauvoir asked when he caught up with the chief.

'Chauvet. They're the caves at Chauvet.'

* * *

When they got back to the B & B, they were met by the aroma of fresh-brewed *café au lait*, maple-cured back bacon and eggs.

'Eggs Benedict,' announced Gabri, rushing to greet them and take their coats. 'Yummy.'

He pushed them along through the living room and into the dining room where their table was set up. Gamache and Beauvoir sat down and Gabri placed two steaming, frothy *bols* of coffee in front of them.

'*Patron*, did you see a stack of books in the living room when you came down?' Gamache asked, taking a sip of the rich brew.

'Books? No.'

Gamache put his *bol* down and walked into the living room. Through the archway Beauvoir watched as he walked round and finally returned, replacing his white linen napkin on his lap.

'They're gone,' he said, though he didn't look upset.

'The yearbooks?'

Gamache nodded and smiled. He hadn't planned it, but this was good. Someone was rattled. Rattled enough to sneak into the B & B, which everyone knew was never locked, and take the yearbooks from twenty-five years ago.

'Yummy, yummy,' said Gabri, placing the platters in front of his guests. Each held two eggs on a thick slice of Canadian back bacon which in turn rested on a golden toasted English muffin. Hollandaise sauce was drizzled over the eggs and fruit salad garnished the edges of each plate.

'*Mangez*,' said Gabri. Gamache reached out his hand and took Gabri's wrist lightly. He looked up at the large, disheveled man. Gabri stood stock-still, staring. Then he lowered his eyes.

'What is it? What's happened?' Gamache asked.

'Eat. Please.'

'Tell me.'

Beauvoir's fork with a massive mound of egg, dripping

hollandaise, stopped almost at his mouth. He stared at the two men.

'There's more. It's the papers, isn't it?' said Beauvoir, suddenly knowing.

Both men followed Gabri into the living room. He pulled a newspaper out from where he'd stuffed it behind a cushion on the sofa. Handing it to Gamache he walked over to the television and turned it on. Then he walked to the stereo and turned the radio on.

Within seconds the room was full of accusations. Blaring from the stereo, from the morning news programs, from the newspaper headlines.

Daniel Gamache under investigation. Criminal record.

Annie Gamache on leave, her lawyer's license suspended.

Armand Gamache suspected of everything from murder to running a puppy mill.

The picture on the front page this time wasn't of Gamache, but of his son, in Paris, Roslyn behind him carrying Florence. All being jostled by reporters. Daniel looking angry and furtive.

Gamache could feel his heart pounding against his chest. He took a huge, ragged breath, realizing he'd been holding it. On the television was a live picture of a young woman leaving an apartment building, her briefcase up to her face.

Annie.

'Oh, God,' whispered Gamache.

Then she lowered the case and stood still. This seemed to stun the reporters who preferred their prey on the run. She smiled at them.

'No, don't,' whispered Beauvoir.

Annie raised her arm and gave them the finger.

'Annie,' Gamache mouthed, but no sound came out. 'I need to go.'

He rushed upstairs and grabbed his cell phone. He was surprised to see his finger shaking, barely able to connect with the speed dial. It was answered on the first ring.

'Oh, Armand, have you seen?'

'Just now.'

'I just got off the phone with Roslyn. They've taken Daniel into custody in Paris. He's suspected of drug-dealing.'

'All right,' said Gamache, some calm returning. 'All right. Let me think.'

'They won't find anything,' said Reine-Marie.

'They might.'

'But that was years ago, Armand. He was a kid, experimenting.'

'It's possible someone's planted something on him,' said Gamache. 'How was Roslyn?'

'Stressed.'

Reine-Marie didn't say it, would never want to add to his burden, but Gamache knew she was worried for the unborn baby. Women can miscarry after a blow like this.

There was silence.

This was so much more than Gamache had dreamed would happen. What was Brébeuf doing? Was this his idea of trying to stop it? With an effort he stopped raging against Brébeuf. He knew that was just a convenient target. He knew his friend was doing his best but that their adversaries were far more vicious than Gamache had expected and than Brébeuf could hope to control.

Someone had done their homework. Knew his family, knew Daniel's conviction years ago on drug possession. Knew Daniel was in Paris and perhaps even knew of the pregnancy.

'This has gone too far,' said Gamache, finally.

'What're you going to do?'

'I'm going to stop it.'

After a moment Reine-Marie asked, 'How?'

'I'll resign if necessary. They win. I can't endanger the family.'

'I'm afraid they'll no longer be satisfied with your resignation, Armand.'

He'd thought of that too.

Gamache called Michel Brébeuf and asked him to call a meeting of the senior Sûreté council for that afternoon.

'Don't be a fool, Armand,' Brébeuf had said. 'It's what they want.'

'I'm not a fool, Michel. I know what I'm doing.'

Both men hung up, Gamache grateful his friend would help, and Brébeuf knowing Gamache was indeed a fool.

The morning meeting was brief and tense.

Agent Lacoste reported on her conversation with Madeleine's doctor. She'd had an appointment two weeks before she was killed. The doctor confirmed that Madeleine's cancer had returned and spread to her liver. She'd told Madame Favreau. She'd arranged for palliative treatments, but those hadn't started by the time she was killed.

She'd come to the appointment alone. And yes, the doctor had the impression that while the diagnosis was devastating it wasn't a complete surprise.

Agent Nichol hadn't returned from Kingston yet and there wasn't a report from the lab on the contents of the ephedra bottle, though there was one on fingerprints. Sophie's and only Sophie's.

'Well, that seems to cinch it,' said Lemieux. 'She killed Madeleine Favreau out of jealousy. Came home, saw the opportunity with the séance, slipped her a few pills over dinner, and waited for the Hadley house to do the rest.'

Everyone was nodding. Through the window of the old railway station Gamache could see Ruth and Gabri walking slowly across the Commons and onto the village green. It was early, with the first freshness of day still holding the village. Behind Ruth came a bouncy little ball, spreading its wings. Alone.

'Sir?'

'I'm sorry, I beg your pardon.'

Everyone stared at Gamache. This was the most unsettling thing to happen yet. In all the years Beauvoir had known him Gamache had never, ever looked away from a conversation or meeting. He held their eyes and made them feel they were the only people on earth. He made his team feel precious and protected.

But today his attention wandered.

'What were you saying?' Gamache asked, turning back to the group.

'It seems clear Sophie Smyth is the murderer. Should we bring her in?'

'You can't.'

The voice came from behind them. There, next to the immense red fire engine, stood a very small woman. Hazel. Though barely recognizable. Grief had finally caught her. Now she looked shrunken, her eyes large and desperate.

'Please. Please don't.'

Gamache went to her, nodding to Beauvoir, and together they led Hazel into the tiny back room used for storage by the Three Pines volunteer fire department.

'Do you know something, Hazel, that would help us?' asked Gamache. 'Something that would convince us your daughter didn't kill Madeleine, because it certainly looks like it.'

'She didn't do it. I know that. She couldn't have.'

'Madeleine was given ephedra. Sophie had ephedra, and she was there.' Gamache spoke very slowly and clearly though he doubted much of this was going in.

'I can't go on much longer,' she whispered. 'And I can't lose Sophie too. If you arrest her I'll die.'

Gamache believed it.

Jean Guy Beauvoir looked at Hazel. The exact same age as Madeleine though you'd never know it. She now seemed a fossil, something coughed up by the mountains around Three Pines. One of Gilles Sandon's murmuring stones. No, not a stone. They were strong. This woman was more like what they'd been trying not to step on during their walk. And were about to crush now.

'When the ephedra was found on Sophie you said, "Sophie, you promised,"' said Beauvoir. 'What did you mean?'

'I said that?' Hazel thought, trying to remember what she could possibly have meant. 'Yes, I did. Madeleine had found a bottle of ephedra pills in Sophie's bathroom a couple of years ago. It was just after one of the athletes had

died and it was all over the news. Probably what gave Sophie the idea of using diet pills.'

It was like dragging a memory from the bottom of the
sea, yanking it up with great effort.

'She sent away for them from some Internet company.
Madeleine found the bottle and took it away.'

'How did Sophie react?'

'Like any nineteen-year-old. She was angry. Mostly angry she said about her privacy being violated, but I think
she was mostly embarrassed.'

'Did it affect their relationship?' Gamache asked.

'Sophie loved Madeleine. She could never kill her,' said
Hazel. She had one message left and she'd say it over and
over. Her daughter was no killer.

'We won't talk to Sophie just yet,' said Gamache. He
reached out and lifted Hazel's head so that she was looking
him in the eyes. 'Do you understand?'

Hazel looked into his deep brown eyes and willed him
never to look away. But, of course, he did. And she was
alone again.

They called Clara to collect Hazel, to keep her company for
the day. Clara showed up and led Hazel back to the Morrows' house where she listened to her then asked if Hazel
would like to lie down. Hazel had never felt so tired and
gratefully she put her head on the sofa. Clara raised her
legs, got a blanket, tucked her in and watched until she was
certain the suddenly old woman, younger actually than herself, was asleep.

Then Clara walked slowly back to her studio and started
painting again. More slowly now, the lines firm and delib-
erate. An image was appearing, but more than the features,
something else was coming to life on the canvas.

'Sophie Smyth is well liked at Queens. Even volunteers at
the help center. She works part time at the bookstore on
campus and seems like a regular student.'

Yvette Nichol had returned. She sat at the conference table sipping the Double Double coffee she'd bought for herself.

'Grades?' asked Beauvoir.

'Decent, not phenomenal. I was too late to speak to the office but I talked to her roommates and some classmates and they said Sophie's a solid student.'

'Illnesses?' asked Gamache. He noticed Agent Lemieux was uncharacteristically silent, his arms crossed tightly, almost violently, across his chest.

'None,' said Nichol. 'Not a sore throat, not a bruise, not a limp. Never visited the infirmary or the Kingston Hospital. As far as her friends know she never even took a day off school, unless she was skipping class for fun.'

'Perfectly healthy,' said Gamache, almost to himself.

'So that Landers woman was right,' said Nichol. 'Sophie put on an act when she was home, trying to get Mom's attention away from Madeleine.'

'You dropped the pill bottle off?' asked Beauvoir.

'Of course,' said Nichol, eating her cream-filled doughnut, oblivious of the hungry stares around her.

'Could you call and see if they have the results yet?' Gamache asked Beauvoir.

While he did, Gamache handed out assignments and then walked to his desk. All eyes were on him, he knew. Watching, he supposed, in case he exploded or dissolved. Instead he looked at them. Lacoste, Lemieux, Nichol. So young. So eager. So human. And he smiled.

Lemieux smiled back. Eventually Lacoste did too, though not very happily. Nichol looked as though she'd been insulted.

Gamache found what he was looking for. Whoever had gone into the B & B and taken the yearbooks hadn't taken them all. The most important one was still on his desk. The one Nichol found at Hazel's home. Madeleine's graduation yearbook. He sat and read it, going immediately to the back of the book and the grad photos. But it wasn't Hazel or even Madeleine he wanted to see. It was another girl. A cheerleader.

'I have the results,' said Beauvoir, throwing himself into a seat at the conference table and slapping his notebook down. 'The ephedra from Sophie's pills is probably not the stuff that killed Madeleine.'

Gamache leaned forward and put the yearbook down. 'No?'

'The lab isn't totally sure yet, they want to run a full spectrum analysis, but it seems Sophie's contained another material, what the lab called a binding agent. Since ephedra's really a plant, a kind of herb, the companies need to distill it then put it in pill form. Different companies use different binding agents. This one was different from the chemicals found in Madeleine.'

Gamache was bright-eyed now. 'What a fool I've been. Did she say anything about the chemicals used to kill Madeleine?'

He waited, almost holding his breath.

'She said the ephedra was from a generation back. More natural but less stable.'

Gamache nodded. 'More natural. They would be.'

He called Lemieux over, asked a few questions, then turned to Beauvoir.

'Come with me.'

Odile Montmagny was just opening when Beauvoir and Gamache arrived.

'Come to hear more poetry?'

Beauvoir couldn't tell whether she was serious. He ignored the question.

'Have you ever heard of ephedra?'

'No, never.'

'I asked you about it after Madeleine died. You know it was used to kill her,' he said.

'Well, yes, I heard about it from you, but never before.' They were in the musky store now. It smelled of too many teas and spices. And herbs.

Gamache walked over to the bins with labels like *Devil's Claw*, *St John's Wort*, *Ginkgo biloba*. He took a plastic bag, but instead of using the scoop provided he reached into his pocket for tweezers then carefully dropped some in the bag. He then labeled it.

'I'd like to buy this, *s'il vous plaît*.'

Odile looked as though she could have used a Ruth-sized drink.

'It's so small you can just take it.'

'No, madame. I need to pay.' Gamache handed the small sample to her to weigh.

The label said Ma Huang.

'The Chinese herb Lemieux told us about that first morning,' said Beauvoir when they were back in the car. 'It's ephedra.'

'Used for hundreds, maybe thousands of years for other purposes,' said Gamache. 'Until the pharmaceuticals found it and turned it into a killer. Ma Huang. The coroner, Dr Harris, told me about it too. Every time we discussed ephedra with someone who actually knew anything they talked about it being an herb. Used in Chinese medicines and others. But I was so focused on the diet supplements I barely heard. It was here all along.'

'Well, you're ahead of me,' said Beauvoir, trying to avoid a frog on the wet road, though Gamache wasn't sure if he was trying to avoid it or swerved to get it. 'I had visions of Sandon boiling down a ginkgo tree.'

'The caul doesn't always work, I guess.'

'Seems to slip over my eyes, it's true,' said Beauvoir. 'What does this Ma Huang mean? Did Odile use it to kill Madeleine? And what about the psychic? Is it just a coincidence she has the same name as those magical caves in France? I'm confused.'

'We see through a glass darkly,' said Gamache. 'But soon we'll see all.'

'I know that one,' said Beauvoir, as though he'd won a game show. 'First Corinthians. We read it at our wedding. It's the one on love. But it's not the same passage Ruth read last night. What should we do with that?' He gestured to the bag of Ma Huang.

'I'll take it to the lab when I go into Montreal,' said Gamache.

'Careful. The media sees you with that they'll think you're Daniel's best customer.'

Beauvoir shut up, appalled at himself for making a joke like that.

'On days like this I wish that was true,' Gamache laughed.

'I'm sorry.'

'Don't be. It'll all work out.'

'Through a glass darkly,' said Beauvoir, almost to himself. 'What a great description. You really think that window will soon be clear?'

'I do,' said Gamache. But he also knew St Paul wasn't talking about a window, but a mirror.

CHAPTER 40

The conference room on the top floor of the Sûreté headquarters was familiar to Gamache. How many coffees had turned cold as he'd struggled with the ethical and moral issues facing the Sûreté? The constant barrage of questions that finally reduced to one: how far to go to protect a society? Safety versus freedom.

He had great respect for the people in this room. Except one.

A wall of windows looked out over east end Montreal and the thrusting arm of the Olympic stadium, like some prehistoric creature come to agonizing life. Inside, the oblique wooden table was surrounded by comfortable captain's chairs. Each equal.

That was the conceit.

Though seats were never assigned each man knew his place. A few of the senior officers looked at Gamache, a couple shook his hand, but most ignored him. He'd expected nothing more. These were people he'd worked with all his life, but he'd betrayed them. Gone public with the Arnot case. He'd known even as he did it what it meant. He'd be cast out. Sent from the tribe.

Well, he was back.

'*Alors*,' said Superintendent Paget, their titular leader. 'You've asked us here, Armand, and we've come.'

He sounded so matter-of-fact, as though they were about to discuss vacation schedules. Gamache had seen this moment coming from a long way off, like a storm at sea. He'd been an anxious mariner, waiting. But the wait was finally over.

'What do you want?' Superintendent Paget asked.

'This must stop. The attacks on my family must stop.'

'That's nothing to do with us,' said Superintendent Desjardins.

'Of course it is,' said Brébeuf, turning to the man beside him. 'We can't stand by while a senior officer is attacked.'

'The Chief Inspector has always made it clear he doesn't need our advice or help.' The voice was deep and reasonable. Calming even. Most of the men turned to look at the speaker, a few stared down at their notes.

Superintendent Francoeur sat next to Gamache. As Gamache knew he would. It was, after all, Francoeur's place, and Gamache had chosen the seat right next to him. He hadn't come this far to hide. He was damned if he'd cower in a corner or behind Brébeuf.

He'd taken the seat right next to the man who wanted him gone. Preferably right off the planet. Pierre Arnot's best friend, confidant, protégé. Sylvain Francoeur.

'I'm not here to fight old battles,' said Gamache, 'I'm here to ask that these attacks stop.'

'And what makes you think we can stop them? The press has a right to print what it wants and I can't imagine they'd actually print anything they haven't thoroughly researched,' said Superintendent Francoeur. 'If they've done something wrong maybe you should sue them.'

A few guffaws were heard. Brébeuf looked furious but Gamache smiled.

'Perhaps I will, though I don't think so. We all know they're lies—'

'How do we know that?' Francoeur asked.

'*Voyons*, what are the chances Armand Gamache would prostitute his daughter?' demanded Brébeuf.

'What were the chances Pierre Arnot was a killer?' asked Francoeur. 'But according to the Chief Inspector, he is.'

'According to the courts, you mean,' said Gamache equably, leaning in to Francoeur's personal space. 'But perhaps that's a part of our system you're not familiar with.'

'How dare you?'

'How dare you attack my family?'

Both men stared at each other. Then Gamache blinked and Francoeur smiled, throwing himself back comfortably in his chair.

Gamache looked steadily at Francoeur. 'I'm sorry, Superintendent. That wasn't called for.'

Francoeur nodded as a knight might to a peasant.

'I haven't come here to fight with any of you. You've all read the papers, seen the television reports. And it'll only get worse, I know. As I said before, they're lies, but I don't expect you to believe me or trust me. Not after what I did in the Arnot case. I crossed the Rubicon. There's no going back.'

'Then what do you expect, Chief Inspector?' Superintendent Paget asked.

'I'd like you to accept my resignation.'

Those not already sitting up did so now. All chairs tipped forward, some so quickly they threatened to spill their distinguished contents onto the table. Now all eyes were on Gamache. It was as though Mont Royal had begun to subside, to sink into the earth. Something remarkable was about to disappear. Armand Gamache. Even those who loathed him recognized he'd become legend, had become a hero both inside and outside the Sûreté.

But sometimes heroes fall.

And they were witnesses to that now.

'Why should we?' asked Francoeur. All eyes swung to the Superintendent. 'Wouldn't that let you off the hook? It's what you want, isn't it? You want to run away just as you did from the Arnot decision. As soon as things get difficult that's what you do.'

'That's not true,' said Brébeuf.

'You believe one of us is responsible for planting those

stories in the paper, don't you?' Francoeur said, comfortable and in command, the natural, if not assigned, leader of the group.

'I do.'

'*Voilà.* See what he thinks of us?'

'Not all, only one.' Gamache stared back at Francoeur.

'How dare you—'

'That's the second time you've asked me that and I'm tired of it. I dare because someone has to.' He looked around the room. 'The Arnot case isn't over, you all know that. Someone in this room is continuing his work. Not quite to the murder stage, but it won't be long. I know it.'

'Know it? Know it? How can you?' Francoeur shot to his feet, leaning over Gamache now. 'It's ridiculous to even be listening to you. A waste of time. You don't have thoughts, you have sentiments.'

A few chuckles were heard.

'I have both, Superintendent,' said Gamache. Francoeur towered above him, one hand on the back of Gamache's chair, the other on the table, as though to imprison the man.

'You're fucking arrogant,' Francoeur yelled. 'You're the worst sort of officer. Full of yourself. You've created your own little army of underlings. People who'll worship you. The rest of us choose the best of the police grads for the Sûreté, you deliberately choose the worst. You're a dangerous man, Gamache. I've known it all along.'

Gamache stood up too, slowly, forcing Francoeur to back away.

'My team has solved almost every murder it's investigated. They're brilliant and dedicated and courageous. You set yourself up as judge and you toss out those who don't conform. Fine. But don't blame me for picking up your garbage and seeing value in it.'

'Even Agent Nichol?' Francoeur had lowered his voice and now the rest had to strain to hear the words, but not Gamache. They were loud and clear.

'Even Agent Nichol,' he said, staring into the cold, hard eyes.

'You tossed her back once as I remember,' said Francoeur, his voice almost a hiss. 'Fired her and she landed in my division. Narcotics. She took to it.'

'Then why send her back to me?' Gamache asked.

'What is it you like to say, Chief Inspector? There's a reason for everything. Very deep. There's a reason for everything, Gamache. Figure it out. Now I have a question for you.' His voice lowered even further. 'What was in that envelope you were passing so secretively to your son? Daniel's his name, I believe. Daughter, Florence. Wife. Did I hear she's pregnant?'

Now no one else in the room could hear, the words were spoken so softly. Gamache had the strangest impression Francoeur hadn't even spoken out loud, but had inserted them directly into his head. Sharp, stabbing, intended to wound and warn.

He inhaled sharply and tried to contain himself, to not bring his fist up and smash the leering, smug, wretched face.

'Do it, Gamache,' hissed Francoeur. 'To save your family, do it.'

Was Francoeur inviting him to attack? So that he'd be arrested, imprisoned? Exposed to any 'accident' that might happen in the cells? Was that the price Francoeur was proposing for backing off his family?

'Fucking coward.' Francoeur smiled and stepped back, shaking his head. 'I think the least Chief Inspector Gamache can do is explain himself,' he said in a normal voice. The faces, strained and nervous, relaxed a little now that they could hear again. 'I think before we can even consider acting on his behalf, or accepting his resignation, we need to know a few things. Like what was in the envelope he was passing to his son. *Voyons*, Chief Inspector, it's a reasonable question.'

Around the conference table there were nods of agreement. Gamache looked over at Brébeuf who cocked his brow as though to say it was a strangely benign request. They'd get off easy if this was all the council wanted.

Gamache remained silent for a moment, thinking. Then he shook his head.

'I'm sorry. It's private. I can't tell you.'

It was over, Gamache knew. He bent down and placed his papers in his satchel, then made for the door.

'You're a stupid man, Chief Inspector,' Superintendent Francoeur called after him, smiling broadly. 'You walk out of here now your life will be in ruins. The media will keep picking at you and your children until even the bones are gone. No careers, no friends, no privacy, no dignity. All because of your pride. What was it one of your favorite poets said? Yeats? Things fall apart. The center cannot hold.'

Gamache stopped, turned and deliberately walked back. With each step he seemed to expand. The officers around the table, wide-eyed, leaned out of his way. He walked to Francoeur, whose smile had disappeared.

'This center will hold.' Gamache pronounced each word slowly and clearly, his voice strong and low and more menacing than anything Francoeur had ever heard. He tried to recover himself as Gamache turned and walked through the door, but it was too late. Everyone in the room had seen fear on Francoeur's face and more than one wondered whether they'd backed the wrong man.

But it was too late.

As Gamache strode down the corridor, men and women on each side smiling hello and nodding to him, his mind settled. Something Francoeur said had jogged something loose. Some piece of information had twisted in that instant and he'd seen it in a different way. But in the stress of the moment Gamache had lost it. Was it to do with Arnot? Or was it the case in Three Pines?

'Well, that went well. For Francoeur,' said Brébeuf, catching up with him as they waited for the elevator. Gamache said nothing, but stared at the numbers, trying to recall what had struck him as so significant. The elevator came and the two men stepped in, alone.

'You could have told him what was in the envelope, you

know,' said Brébeuf. 'It can't possibly be that important. What was in it anyway?'

'I'm sorry, Michel, what did you say?' Gamache brought himself back to the present.

'The envelope, Armand. What was in it?'

'Oh, nothing much.'

'For God's sake, man, why not tell him?'

'He didn't say please.' Gamache smiled.

Brébeuf scowled. 'Do you ever listen to yourself? All the advice you give others, does any of it penetrate your own thick skull? Why keep this secret? It's our secrets that make us sick. Isn't that what you always say?'

'There's a difference between secrecy and privacy.'

'Semantics.'

The elevator door opened and Brébeuf stepped out. The meeting had gone better than he'd dared dream. Gamache was almost certainly out of the Sûreté, but more than that, he was humiliated, ruined. Or soon would be.

Inside the elevator Armand Gamache stood rooted like one of Gilles Sandon's trees. And had Sandon been there he might have heard what no one else could, Armand Gamache screaming as though felled.

Behold I show you a mystery.

The haunting words of St Paul's letter to the Corinthians swirled around Gamache's head. The words had been prophetic. In the twinkling of an eye his world had changed. He could see clearly something that had been hidden. Something he never wanted to see.

He'd stopped at the high school in Notre-Dame-de-Grâce and just caught the secretary as she left for the day. Now he sat in the parking lot staring at the two things she'd given him. An alumni list and another yearbook. She'd wondered why in the world he needed so many, but Gamache had mumbled apologies and she'd relented. He thought she might assign him lines. I will not lose another yearbook.

But it hadn't been lost. It'd been stolen. By someone who'd been at school with Madeleine and Hazel. Someone who'd chosen to keep their identity secret. Now, looking at the alumni list and the yearbook, Gamache knew exactly who that was.

Behold I show you a mystery. Ruth's crumbling voice came to him as she'd read the magnificent passage. And hard on that another voice. Michel Brébeuf. Accusing, angry. *It's our secrets that make us sick.*

It was true, Gamache knew. Of all the things we keep inside the worst are the secrets. The things we are so ashamed of, so afraid of, we need to hide them even from ourselves. Secrets lead to delusion and delusion leads to lies, and lies create a wall.

Our secrets make us sick because they separate us from other people. Keep us alone. Turn us into fearful, angry, bitter people. Turn us against others, and finally against ourselves.

A murder almost always began with a secret. Murder was a secret spread over time.

Gamache called Reine-Marie, Daniel and Annie, and finally he called Jean Guy Beauvoir.

Then he started his car and turned it toward the country. As he drove the sun went down and by the time he arrived in Three Pines it was dark. In his headlights he saw the dirt road thick with bouncing frogs, trying to get across the road for a reason he knew would remain a mystery to him. He slowed right down and tried not to run over them. Up they jumped into his headlights as though joyfully greeting him. They looked exactly like the frogs on Olivier's rather silly old plates. For a moment Gamache wondered whether he might buy a couple of them, to remind him of the spring and the dancing frogs. But then he knew he probably wouldn't. He'd want nothing that would remind him of what happened today.

'I've called everyone,' said Beauvoir as soon as Gamache walked into the Incident Room. 'They'll be there. Are you sure you want to do it this way?'

'I'm sure. I know who killed Madeleine Favreau, Jean Guy. It seems right that this case that started with a circle should come full circle. We meet at the old Hadley house at nine tonight. And we find a murderer.'

CHAPTER 41

Clara's heart was in her throat, in her wrists, at her temples. Her whole body was throbbing with the pounding of her heart. She couldn't believe they were back in the old Hadley house.

In the darkness, except for the puny candlelight.

When Inspector Beauvoir had called and told her what Gamache wanted she'd thought he must be kidding, or drunk. Certainly delusional.

But he'd been serious. They were to meet at nine in the old Hadley house. In the room where Madeleine died.

All evening she'd watched the clock creep forward. At first excruciatingly slowly, then it had seemed to race, the hands flying round the face. She'd been unable to eat and Peter had begged her not to go. And finally her terror had found purchase, and she'd agreed to stay behind. In their little cottage, by the fire, with a good book and a glass of Merlot.

Hiding.

But Clara knew if she did that she'd carry this cowardice for the rest of her life. And when the clock said five to nine she'd risen, as though in someone else's body, put on her coat, and left. Like a zombie from one of Peter's old black and white movies.

And she'd found herself in a black and white world. Without street lamps or traffic lights, Three Pines became bathed in black once the sun set. Except for the points of light in the sky. And the lights of the homes around the green that tonight seemed to warn her, beg her not to leave them, not to do this foolishness.

Through the darkness Clara joined the others. Myrna, Gabri, Monsieur Béliveau, the witch Jeanne, all trudging, as though they'd given up their own will, toward the haunted house on the hill.

Now she was back in that room. She looked at the faces, all staring at the flickering candle in the center of their circle, its light reflected in their eyes, like the pilot light for the fear they carried. It struck Clara how threatening the simple flicker of a candle can be when that's all you have.

Odile and Gilles were across from her, as were Hazel and Sophie.

Monsieur Béliveau sat beside Clara and Jeanne Chauvet took her seat beside Gabri, who was festooned with crucifixes, Stars of David and a croissant in his pocket. Myrna asked because it looked like something else.

But still their circle was broken. One chair was on its side, having tumbled into the center almost a week ago, and there it sat like a memorial, though in the uncertain light it looked like a skeleton with its wooden arms and legs and ribbed back throwing distorted shadows against the wall.

It was a calm and tranquil night, outside the old Hadley house. But inside the house had its own atmosphere, its own gravity. It was a world of groans and creaks, of sorrow and sighs. The house had taken another life, two if you count the bird, and it was hungry again. It wanted more. It felt like a tomb. Worse, thought Clara, it felt like limbo. In stepping into the house, into this room, they'd walked into a netherworld, somewhere between life and death. A world where they were about to be judged, and separated.

Out of the dark a hand reached into their circle and grabbed the skeletal chair. Then Armand Gamache joined them, sitting silently for a moment, leaning forward, elbows on his legs, his large powerful hands together, his fingers intertwined as though in prayer. His deep brown eyes were thoughtful.

She heard an exhale. The candle flickered violently, from the force of their stress released.

Gamache looked at them. At Clara he seemed to pause and smile, but Clara thought everyone probably had that impression. She wondered how he managed to make time disobey its own rules. Though she also knew Three Pines itself was like that, a village where time seemed flexible.

'This is a tragedy of secrets,' said Gamache. 'It's a story of hauntings, of ghosts, of wickedness dressed as valor. It's a story of things hidden and buried. Alive. When something not quite dead is buried it eventually comes back,' he said after a moment's pause. 'It claws its way out of the dirt, rancid and fetid. And hungry.

'That's what happened here. Everyone in this room has a secret. Something to hide. Something that came alive a few days ago. When Agent Lacoste told me about her interview with Madeleine's husband I started to get some insight into this murder. He described Madeleine as the sun. Life-giving, joyous, bright and cheerful.'

Around the circle the glowing faces nodded.

'But the sun also scalds. It burns and blinds.' He looked at each of them again. 'And it creates strong shadows. Who can live close to the sun? I thought of Icarus, the beautiful boy who with his father made wings to fly. His father gave him one warning, though. Do not fly too close to the sun. But, of course, he did. Anyone with children will understand how that can happen.'

His eyes flickered to Hazel. Her face was blank. Empty. Where once there'd been anxiety, pain, anger, now there was nothing. The horsemen had ridden through, leaving nothing standing. But Gamache thought maybe they hadn't brought grief. The horsemen Hazel had been desperate to keep at bay carried something far more terrifying. Their burden was loneliness.

'The most obvious suspect is Sophie. Poor Sophie, as everyone calls her. Always getting hurt, always getting sick. Though things started to get better when Madeleine arrived.'

Sophie stared at him, her brows low and glowering.

'The house that had been so full of things and yet so empty was suddenly full of life. Can't you just imagine?'

Suddenly they were transported to a day in their imaginations when the drab home of Hazel and Sophie was visited by sunshine. When the curtains were thrown open. When laughter stirred the decay in the rooms and sent it twirling into the rays of light.

'But the price you paid was that your shadows were revealed. You fell in love with Madeleine, didn't you?'

'Love isn't a shadow,' said Sophie defiantly.

'You're quite right. Love isn't. But attachment is. Myrna, you talked about the near enemy.'

'Attachment masquerading as love,' nodded Myrna. 'But I wasn't thinking of Sophie.'

'No, you were thinking of someone else. But it applies here.' He turned back to Sophie. 'You wanted Madeleine for yourself. You went to her university, Queens, to impress her. To get her to pay more attention to you. It was bad enough to share Madeleine with your mother, but when you returned home recently and found Madeleine in a relationship with Monsieur Béliveau, that was too much.'

'How could she? I mean look at him. He's old and ugly and poor. He's just a grocer for God's sake. How could she love him? I'd gone all the way to fucking Queens for her and when I come back she's not even around. She's at a séance with him.'

She jabbed her crutch at Béliveau, who seemed beyond the insults.

'When the next séance came you saw your chance. You've fought your weight all your life, even taking ephedra a few years ago, until it was found and taken away. But eventually the weight crept back and you ordered more pills from the Internet. This photograph shows a plump girl, just two years ago.' Gamache handed round the picture from the fridge. Each person looked at it. It seemed to have been taken on another planet. One where people laughed, and loved, and celebrated. One where Madeleine was still alive.

'You found the pill bottle. You knew your mother threw

nothing away. Inspector Beauvoir described the cupboard filled with old pills, most long out of date. We know from the lab that you didn't use your current ephedra pills. Instead, you found the old ones. You knew Madeleine had a heart damaged by her chemotherapy treatments—'

A small murmur went around the circle.

'—and you knew a high enough dose, combined with the bad heart, could kill her. All you needed was a scare. Something to challenge her heart, to get it pounding and racing. And one was handed to you. A séance in the old Hadley house.'

'This is stupid,' said Sophie, though she was looking far from confident.

'You made sure you sat beside Madeleine at dinner, and you slipped the pills into her food.'

'I didn't. Mom, tell him I didn't.'

'She didn't,' said Hazel, finding the energy to come, feebly, to Sophie's defense.

'Of course, everything I've said about Sophie applies to Hazel as well.' Gamache turned to the woman beside Sophie. 'You loved Madeleine. Have never tried to hide it. A platonic love, almost certainly, but a deep one. You probably loved her since you were children together. And then she comes to live with you, recovers from her chemo, and your lives start again. No more dullness. No more loneliness.'

Hazel nodded.

'If Sophie could find the ephedra, so could you. You were on Madeleine's other side at dinner. You could have slipped it to her. But one nagging question was why not kill Madeleine at the first séance? Why wait?'

He let the question sink in. There seemed now to be no world beyond their circle of light. The known world had disappeared over the edge of the darkness.

'The séances were different in three ways.' Gamache counted them on his fingers. 'The dinner at Peter and Clara's, the old Hadley house, and the Smyths'.'

'But why would Hazel kill Madeleine?' Clara asked.

'Jealousy. That picture?' He gestured to the photo, now in

Gabri's hand. 'Madeleine was looking with great affection at Hazel and Hazel was looking with even more open affection. But not at Madeleine or Sophie. She was looking off camera. And I remembered something Olivier said. He said how kind Hazel had been to Monsieur Béliveau after his wife died. He was invited to all celebrations, especially the big ones. The hat Hazel wore was white and blue, the cake had blue frosting. It was a man's birthday. It was yours.'

He turned to Béliveau, who looked perplexed. Gabri handed him the photograph and the grocer studied it for a few moments. In the silence they heard more creaks. Something seemed to be coming up the stairs. Clara knew it was all in her mind. Knew what she'd felt before had only been the baby bird, not the monster of her imagination. That bird was dead now. So nothing could be coming up the stairs. Nothing could be on the landing. Nothing could be creaking along the corridor.

'Hazel's always been very kind,' Monsieur Béliveau finally said, looking over at Hazel who'd all but disappeared.

'You fell in love with him,' said Gamache. 'Didn't you?'

Hazel shook her head slightly.

'Mom? Did you?'

'I thought he was nice. I once thought maybe . . .'

Hazel's voice petered out.

'Until Madeleine showed up,' said Gamache. 'She didn't mean to, almost certainly had no idea how you felt about him, but she stole Monsieur Béliveau from you.'

'He wasn't mine to steal.'

'We say that,' said Gamache, 'but saying and feeling are very different. You were two lonely people, you and Monsieur Béliveau. In many ways a much more natural match. But Madeleine was this magnificent, lovely, laughing magnet and Monsieur Béliveau was mesmerized. I don't want to give the impression Madeleine was malicious or mean. She was just being herself. And it was hard not to fall in love with her. Am I right, Monsieur Sandon?'

'*Moi?*'

At the sound of his own name Sandon's head jerked up.

'You loved her too. Deeply. As deeply and totally as un-requited love can be. In many ways it's the deepest because it's never tested. She remained the ideal for you. The perfect woman. But then the perfect woman faltered. She fell in love with someone else. And worse. The one man you despise. Monsieur Béliveau. The bringer of death. The man who allowed a venerable old oak to die in agony.'

'I could never kill Madeleine. I can't even cut down a tree. Can't step on a flower, can't crush an earwig. I can't take a life.'

'But you can, Monsieur Sandon.' Armand Gamache grew very silent and leaned forward again, staring at the huge lumberjack. 'You said so yourself. Better to put something out of its misery than allow it to die a long and painful death. You were talking about the oak. But you were prepared to kill it. Put it out of its misery. If you knew Madeleine was dying, perhaps you'd do the same for her.'

Sandon was speechless, his eyes wide, his mouth wide.

'I loved her. I couldn't kill her.'

'Gilles,' Odile whispered.

'And she loved someone else.' Gamache moved in closer, thrusting his words home. 'She loved Monsieur Béliveau. Every day you saw it, every day it was in your face, undeniable, even for you. She didn't love you at all.'

'How could she?' He rose from his chair, his massive hands clenched like mallets. 'You don't know what it was like, to see her with him.' He turned to look at meek Monsieur Béliveau. 'I knew she couldn't care for someone like me, but . . .'

He faltered.

'But if she couldn't love you, she couldn't love anyone?' said Gamache softly. 'It must have been horrible.'

The lumberjack collapsed into his chair. They waited for the crack as the wood gave way, but instead it held him, as a mother might a hurt child.

'But the stuff that killed her was in the Smyths' medicine cabinet,' said Odile wildly. 'He couldn't get it.'

'You're right. He didn't have access to their home.'

Gamache turned to Odile. 'I mentioned the lab report. It said the ephedra that killed Madeleine wasn't from a recent batch. It was much more natural. I'd been a fool. Over and over people had told me and it never registered. Ephedra's an herb. A plant. Used for centuries in Chinese medicines. Maybe Gilles didn't need access to their home. Maybe you didn't either. You know what I took from your store?'

He stared at Odile, who stared back, frantic and frozen.

'Ma Huang. An old Chinese herb. Also known as Mormon's tea. And ephedra.'

'I didn't do it. He didn't do it. He didn't love her. She was a bitch, a horrible, horrible person. She tricked people into thinking she cared.'

'You spoke to her, warned her, as you were walking here that night, didn't you? You told her she could have anyone, but Gilles was the only man you ever wanted. You pleaded with her to stay away from him.'

'She told me not to be so stupid. But I'm not stupid.'

'By then it was too late. The ephedra was already in her.' Gamache looked at the circle of staring faces. 'You all had reason to kill her. You all had the opportunity to kill her. But there was one more necessary ingredient. What killed Madeleine Favreau was ephedra and a fright. Someone had to provide the fright.'

All eyes turned to Jeanne Chauvet. Her own were hooded, sunken and dark.

'You were all trying to get me to consider Jeanne a suspect. You told me you didn't trust her, didn't like her. Were frightened of her. I'd put it down to a kind of hysteria. The stranger among you. The witch. Who else would you want to be guilty?'

Clara stared at him. Gamache had put it so simply, so clearly. Had they really thrown this mousy woman to the inquisition? Turned her in? Lit the pyre and warmed themselves by it like smug Puritans, confident the beast wasn't one of them. No thought for the truth, no thought for the woman.

'I'd all but dismissed her as being too obvious. But dinner last night changed my mind.'

Clara thought she heard creaking again, as though the house had woken up, could sense a kill. Her heart thudded and the candle began flickering as though trembling itself. There was something about in the old Hadley house. Something had come to life. Gamache seemed to sense it too. He cocked his head to one side, a puzzled look on his face. Listening.

'Ruth Zardo was talking about the burning times and called you Joan of Arc,' he said to Jeanne. 'And I remembered that Jeanne is French for Joan. Joan of Arc becomes Jeanne d'Arc. A woman burned for hearing voices and seeing visions. A witch.'

'A saint,' corrected Jeanne, her voice detached, far away.

'If you prefer,' said Gamache. 'That first séance you thought was a joke, but the next one you took seriously. You made sure it was as atmospheric, as frightening, as possible.'

'I'm not responsible for other people's fears.'

'You think not? If you jump out of the dark and say boo, you can't blame the person for being frightened. And that's what you did. Deliberately.'

'No one forced Mad to come that night,' said Jeanne, then stopped.

'Mad,' said Gamache quietly. 'A nickname. Used by people who knew her well, not by someone who'd only just met her. You knew her, didn't you?'

Jeanne was silent.

Gamache nodded. 'You knew her. I'll come back to that in a moment. The final element for murder was the séance. But no one here was going to lead one, and who'd expect a psychic to show up for Easter? It seemed far too fortuitous to be chance. And it wasn't. Did you send this?'

Gamache handed Gabri the brochure for the B & B.

'I've never sent these out,' said Gabri, barely looking at the brochure. 'Only made them to satisfy Olivier who said we weren't doing enough advertising.'

'You've never mailed any out?' Gamache persisted.

'Why would I?'

'You're a B & B,' suggested Myrna. 'A business.'

'That's just what Olivier says, but we get enough people. Why would I want more work?'

'Being Gabri is work enough,' agreed Clara.

'It's exhausting,' said Gabri.

'So you didn't write that across the top of the brochure?' Gamache pointed to the glossy paper in Gabri's large hand. Leaning into the candlelight Gabri strained to see.

'Where lay lines meet—Easter Special,' he read, guffawing. 'As if. Is that what you meant when you said I wouldn't get laid?' he asked Jeanne, shifting his croissant.

'I didn't say that. I said ley lines don't meet here.'

'I thought you said they don't work here,' said Gabri, relieved. 'But I never wrote that.' He handed the brochure back to Gamache. 'Don't even know what it means.'

'You didn't type those words and you didn't send it. So who did?' It was clear he wasn't expecting an answer. He was talking to himself. 'Someone who wanted to lure Jeanne to Three Pines. Someone who knew her well enough to know talk of ley lines would pique her interest. But someone who doesn't themselves know enough about ley lines to spell it correctly.'

'I'd have to say that means all of us,' said Clara. 'Except one.' She looked at Jeanne.

'You're thinking I wrote it myself? So that it only looks as though someone tried to trick me into coming? And even misspelled the word? I'm not that clever.'

'Maybe,' said Gamache.

'That first séance, Gabri,' said Clara, 'you put up posters saying Madame Blavatsky would be contacting the dead. You lied about her name—'

'Artistic license,' explained Gabri.

'It must be exhausting being him,' said Myrna.

'—but you knew Jeanne was a psychic. How'd you know?'

'She told me.'

After a moment Jeanne spoke. 'It's true. I keep telling

myself not to say anything, and of course it's the first thing out of my mouth. I wonder why?'

'You want to be special,' said Myrna, not unkindly. 'We all do. You're just more open about it.'

'Well,' said Gabri, in a voice uncharacteristically small, 'I did kinda wheedle it out of her. I ask all my guests what they do. What passions they have. It's interesting.'

'And then you put them to work,' said Sandon, still smarting from the time he lost two hundred dollars to Gabri's poker champ guest.

'A village gets quiet,' Gabri explained to Gamache with dignity. 'I bring culture to Three Pines.'

No one chose to mention the shrieking opera singer.

'When Jeanne checked in she read my palm,' Gabri continued. 'In my past life I was the Keeper of the Light at the Acropolis, but don't tell anyone.'

'I promise,' said Clara.

'But before that I walked around the village,' said Jeanne. 'Sensing the energy of the place. The funny thing is, whoever wrote that,' she pointed to the brochure in Gamache's hand, 'was almost right. There are ley lines here, but they run parallel to Three Pines. It's quite unusual to have them so close together. But they don't meet. You don't actually want them to meet. Too much energy. Good for sacred places, but you notice no one actually lives in Stonehenge.'

'Not that we can see anyway,' said Gamache, to everyone's surprise. 'Whoever sent the brochure knew that Gabri would find out that his guest was a psychic, and from there it was a guarantee he'd put her to work. A séance was a sure thing.

'At Peter and Clara's last night you brought me a book, Myrna. *The Dictionary of Magical Places*. I looked at it and do you know what I found?'

No one spoke. He turned to Jeanne. 'I think you know what I found. You looked upset when the book was produced, especially since it was the latest edition. Olivier asked if they were finding new magical places. He was joking, of course, but it turned out to be quite true. They did find a new magical place in the last twenty years. In France. A series of caves named after the region they were found. The Chauvet caves.'

Another creak was heard and Gamache knew time was running out. Something dark and personal was approaching.

'Jeanne Chauvet. A psychic and self-proclaimed Wicca with the name of a medieval woman burned for witchcraft and a magical cave. There was no way it was your real name. But something else happened last night. Inspector Beauvoir and I couldn't sleep for the frogs. We were in the living room looking at yearbooks from Hazel and Madeleine's high school when Jeanne showed up. This morning the books were gone. There was only one person who could have taken them. Why did you, Jeanne?'

Jeanne stared off into the darkness then after a moment she spoke.

'Something's coming.'

'*Pardon?*' Gamache asked.

She turned to him, her eyes finally catching the candle-light. They were glowing now. It was unnatural, unnerving.

'You can feel it, I know. It's the thing I warned you about that morning in the church. It's arrived.'

'Why did you take the yearbooks, Jeanne?' Gamache needed to remain focused, to not let his mind wander to the other thing. But he knew time was short. He needed to finish this now.

She stared openly at the door and remained silent.

'I stopped at the high school on my way back this after-noon and picked up two things. Another yearbook and an alumni list. I'd like to read something from Hazel and Madeleine's grad book.' He reached down and brought a book onto his lap. He opened it to a spot marked by a Post-it. 'Joan Cummings. Cheerleader. Joan of Arc plans to set the world on fire.'

He softly closed it.

'You're Joan Cummings?' said Hazel, rousing herself. 'From school?'

'Didn't recognize me, did you? Mad didn't either.'

'You've changed,' said Hazel, sputtering a little in embarrassment.

'But Mad hadn't,' said Jeanne.

Gamache turned the yearbook round and showed them the picture of the cheerleaders. In the uncertain light they saw a young woman, toned arms straining to the skies, a huge smile on her pretty face.

'This was almost thirty years ago. But for all the make-up and smiles they still called you Joan of Arc, and talked about burning.'

Jeanne's eyes flicked to the door then back again.

'I knew Madeleine from the cheerleading squad. You were right about the sun, you know. She was all that and more. She was genuinely nice and that made it worse. After years of being teased and tormented for being different all I wanted was to fit in. I wore make-up, did my hair, learned to talk nonsense, and finally made the cheerleading squad. I wanted to be her friend, but she was oblivious. Not cruel, really, but dismissive.'

'You hated her?' asked Clara.

'You've probably always been popular,' snapped Jeanne. 'Pretty, talented, lively.' Clara heard the words but didn't recognize herself in them. Jeanne continued, 'I was none of those things. I just wanted a friend. One single friend. Do you have any idea how horrible it is to be on the outside, all the time? And finally I made the squad. The place where all the cool girls were. And do you know how I did it?'

Jeanne was almost hissing now.

'I betrayed everything I was. I made myself silly and superficial. There's a reason they call it "make-up." I literally made up myself every day. I locked all the things I cared about inside and turned my back on people who might've been my friends. All in the pursuit of the one, perfect girl.'

'Madeleine,' said Gamache.

'And she was perfect. The worst moment of my life was when I realized I'd betrayed everything I cared about, for nothing.'

'So you changed your name to Chauvet. You made up yourself yet again.'

'No, I finally accepted myself. Changing my name to Chauvet was a celebration, a declaration. For once I wasn't hiding who I am.'

'She's a witch,' whispered Gabri to Myrna.

'We know, *mon beau*. So am I.'

'I knew who I was, but not where I belonged. I felt a stranger everywhere. Until I came here. As soon as I drove down that road into Three Pines I knew I'd found home.'

'But you also found Madeleine,' said Gamache.

Jeanne nodded. 'At the séance that Friday night. And I knew she'd steal my light again. Not because she was greedy, but because I'd hand it to her. I could feel it. I'd found myself, I'd found a home and the only thing missing was finding a friend. And as soon as I saw Mad I knew I'd do it all over again. Try to be her friend, and be rebuffed.'

'But why kill her?' asked Clara.

'I didn't kill her.'

There were murmurs of disbelief around the circle.

'She's telling the truth,' said Gamache. 'She didn't kill Madeleine.'

'Then who did?' asked Gabri.

Jeanne stood up, staring into the darkness at the door.

'Sir?' The voice at the door was young, tentative, but that made it more frightening somehow, like discovering the devil was a family friend.

Gamache rose too and turned to the door. He could see nothing but black, then eventually an outline appeared. He'd run out of time. He turned back to the circle. All eyes were on him, their faces round and open like searchlights, probing for reassurance.

'I'll be back in a few minutes.'

'You're not leaving us?' said Clara.

'I'm sorry. I have to, but nothing bad will happen to you.'

Gamache turned and walked away from the flickering light, disappearing over the edge of the world.

CHAPTER 42

Agent Lemieux led him to the very end of the corridor and into a dim room where someone sat cross-legged, a flashlight cradled in his lap.

'Hello, Armand.'

The voice was so familiar. The body, even in the struggling light, immediately recognizable. Beloved over the decades. Sneaking into bars underage, double-dating, cramming for exams, long walks as young men picking apart the world's problems. And putting it together again, perfect. Smoking together. Quitting together. They'd been each other's best man. Stood for each other, chosen each other to be godparent to a precious and beloved child.

Suddenly Armand Gamache was back at home, his cheek resting on the back of the rough sofa, eyes trained on the road. Waiting for Mom and Dad. Every other night they'd come home. But tonight a strange car drove in. Two men got out. A knock on the door. His grandmother's hand finding his, the suddenly strong scent of mothballs from her sweater as she shoved his head into her side, to shield him from the words. But still the words found him and washed over him and clung to him for the rest of his life.

A terrible accident.

And his little friend Michel Brébeuf had been there for him even then. It had been somehow comforting as he grew to know that almost certainly nothing would ever be that devastating again.

Until now.

Now he stood facing the man he loved most in the world. The horsemen were loose and pounding down the slope, horses screaming, weapons raised. There would be no prisoners.

'*Bonjour, Michel.*'

'You knew, didn't you? I saw it in your face as I left the elevator this afternoon.'

Gamache nodded.

'How?' Brébeuf asked.

Gamache looked round and found Agent Lemieux standing by the door.

'He stays, Armand.'

Gamache stared at Lemieux, searching his face. But all he found was a cold, hard stare.

'It's not too late,' said Gamache.

'It's way too late,' said the young man. 'For both of us.'

'I didn't mean you,' said Gamache.

'How did you know?' Brébeuf stood up.

'Secrets,' said Gamache, surprised to hear his own voice so normal. It seemed like so many conversations he'd had with Michel. Reasonable, thoughtful, gentle even. 'It's our secrets that make us sick. You said that to me in the elevator.'

'So?'

'You said it's one of the phrases I tell trainees. But that's not true. I've only ever said it once and that was here, in the old Hadley house. I said it to Agent Lemieux.'

Brébeuf thought for a moment.

'You knew then that he was working for me?'

'I knew he was working for someone other than me. I knew he was the spy.'

'How?' Despite himself Brébeuf was curious.

'It's how Arnot worked. Simple and effective. Put someone trusted into a situation and let them do their worst. *Un agent provocateur.* I realized if Arnot's people were going to try to bring me down, it would be from the inside. Put someone on my own team. But Arnot used thugs. You're much more clever. You chose someone engaging, someone designed to insinuate himself easily.'

Gamache turned to Lemieux.

'You're easily liked. The whole team took to you. You're smart and nicely self-deprecating. You fit in. Far more insidious than a thug. You kill with a kiss.'

Agent Robert Lemieux's cold eyes never left Gamache's. Gamache stared back. 'Be careful, young man. You're playing with things you can't begin to understand.'

'You think not?' Lemieux stepped forward. 'You think I'm young Agent Lemieux, naïve, unsophisticated, slightly stupid? You think I've been led astray perhaps with extravagant promises by the Superintendent? You think I've been seduced?'

As he spoke he walked closer to Gamache, deliberately, slowly, his voice smooth and honeyed, enticing. Enchanting. But the blush of youth was falling away and what approached Gamache was growing older and more decayed by the step until he stopped within inches of the Chief Inspector's face. Gamache had the impression this thing was going to lick him, with a rancid, slimy tongue. It was all he could do not to fall back, gagging.

'You think I'll regret this one day, don't you?' Lemieux's foul breath was on Gamache's cheek. 'You're predictable, Chief Inspector. You need to save people, just as you've been saved. Given a second chance. The Superintendent here's told me about your parents. That would have scarred most boys, but somehow you survived and even flourished. But the deal you made was that you'd help others. No one drowns on your watch. Quite a burden.'

Gamache could feel his heart pounding.

'The things boys share with each other. I can see you, Gamache. A solid, strapping, earnest boy telling his best friend of his solemn oath to help people. And Brébeuf here pledged to help you, didn't he? Like Lancelot and Arthur. And in the end, the one betrays the other. What was it your first chief taught both of you? Matthew 10:36. You didn't think I was paying attention, did you?' he asked Gamache.

'Oh, I always knew you were paying attention.' Gamache turned to Brébeuf. He could feel himself losing control, and if he lost that, all was gone. 'I can see attacking me, but my family, Michel? Why Daniel? Annie, your own goddaughter?'

'I was sure you'd know it was me then. Who else knew so much about your family? But still you were blind. So loyal.' Brébeuf shook his head. 'You never suspected, did you? Kept thinking it was Francoeur.'

Gamache made a move toward Brébeuf but Lemieux stepped between them. Gamache couldn't remember Lemieux being so large. He stopped, but just, and his eyes never left Brébeuf.

'I knew something had changed between us,' said Gamache. 'You were distant, polite but no more. It was small things, nothing I could quite put my finger on. Nothing worth mentioning, but it was one tiny thing after another. A birthday forgotten, a party missed, a flippant remark that seemed designed to insult. But I couldn't believe it. I chose not to believe it.' *I was afraid to believe it,* thought Gamache. *Afraid it was true and somehow I'd lost my best friend. Like Hazel lost Madeleine.* 'I thought you were preoccupied with family problems. I never dreamed . . .' He ran out of words. But one last one formed and fell from his mouth. 'Why?'

'Do you remember right after Arnot and the others were sentenced? The case was over, but you were in disgrace. Tossed out of the council. Catherine and I invited you and Reine-Marie for dinner, supposedly to cheer you up. But you were in fine spirits. We went into my study for a cognac and you told me then you didn't care. You'd done what you had to. Your career was in tatters, but still you were happy. After you left, I sat reading. Some obscure book you probably gave me. In it I found a quote that devastated me. I copied it out that night and put it in my wallet, so I'd never forget.'

He brought out his wallet. From the billfold he withdrew a folded piece of paper, softened and worn as a love letter might be. He unfolded it and started reading. 'It's from AD 960. Supposedly said by Abd-er-Rahman the Third, of Spain.'

He sounded like a nervous schoolboy in front of the

class. Gamache almost gasped with the pain of it. Brébeuf cleared his throat and read on.

'*I have now reigned about fifty years in victory or peace, beloved by my subjects, dreaded by my enemies, and respected by my allies. Riches and honors, power and pleasure have waited on my call, nor does any earthly blessing appear to have been wanting. In this situation I have diligently numbered the days of pure and genuine happiness which have fallen to my lot: they amount to fourteen.*'

Robert Lemieux laughed. But Armand Gamache's heart broke.

Brébeuf carefully refolded the paper and placed it back in his wallet.

'All our lives I've been smarter, faster, better at tennis and hockey than you,' said Brébeuf. 'I got better grades and found love first. Had three sons. Five grandchildren to your one. I won seven commendations. How many have you?'

Gamache shook his head.

'You don't even know, do you? I beat you out for Superintendent and became your boss. I watched as you ruined your career. So why are you the happy one?'

The question pierced Gamache, thrusting through his chest and through his heart, and burst into his head forcing him to close his eyes. When he opened them again he thought he was seeing things. Standing slightly behind Lemieux was someone else. In the shadows.

Then the one shadow separated from the whole and became Agent Nichol, like a ghost caught between worlds.

'What do you want?' he asked Brébeuf.

'He wants you to resign,' said Lemieux, still apparently unaware of Nichol. 'But we both know that won't be enough.'

'Of course it's enough,' Brébeuf snapped. 'We've won.'

'And then what?' asked Lemieux. 'You're a weak man, Brébeuf. You've promised to sponsor my rise through the ranks, but how can I trust a man who'll betray his own best friend? No, my only guarantee is to hold something so hideous over you there'll be no going back.' He took out his gun and looked at Gamache. 'You told me right here in this house never to draw my gun unless I mean to use it. It's a lesson I took to heart. But I don't mean to use it. You do.'

He thrust the revolver at Brébeuf. 'Take it.' Lemieux's boyish voice was smooth and reasonable.

'I will not. You're telling me to shoot my friend?'

'Your friend? You've already killed that relationship. Why not the man? He won't let you go, you know. Look at what he did to Arnot. There's no way even if he resigned he'd let this drop. He'd spend the rest of his life trying to bring you down.'

Brébeuf dropped his hands to his sides. Lemieux sighed and cocked the gun.

'Lemieux,' called Gamache, starting forward, trying to keep his eye on both Lemieux and Nichol behind him. He saw Nichol reach for her hip.

'Stop.'

A gun walked out of the darkness, with Jean Guy Beauvoir attached to it. He held it steady, his eyes hard and staring at Lemieux. Nichol dissolved back into the shadows.

'You all right?' he asked Gamache without losing his focus.

'Fine.'

Like ancient enemies Beauvoir and Lemieux stared at each other, their guns thrust forward, pointing. Beauvoir's at Lemieux and Lemieux's at Gamache.

'You know I have nothing to lose, Inspector,' said the reasonable young voice. 'There's no way I'm going to walk out of here your prisoner. If you don't lower your gun by the count of five, I'll kill Gamache. If you even breathe, if I get the faintest hint you're preparing to shoot, I'll shoot first. In fact, what the hell.' He turned his head slightly to Gamache.

'No! No, wait!' Beauvoir dropped his revolver.

'Weak.' He shook his head. 'All your people are weak.'

He turned to Gamache and fired.

CHAPTER 43

Clara Morrow jumped to her feet at the sound of the shot. For the last fifteen minutes they'd heard muffled voices sometimes raised in argument, though at least they were human. But the gunshot was something else. Something most Canadians never ever hear. It was grotesque and signaled death was again loose in the old Hadley house.

'Should we see?' she asked.

'Are you nuts?' asked Myrna, her eyes wide with terror. 'What're we going to do? Someone has a gun, for God's sake. We should get out of here.'

'I'm with you,' said Gabri, already on his feet.

'We should stay,' said Jeanne. 'The Chief Inspector asked us to.'

'What's that supposed to mean?' Sandon demanded. 'If he asked you to jump from the window would you?'

'But he didn't and he wouldn't,' said Jeanne. 'We need to stay.'

Armand Gamache was on the floor, scrambling for the gun. Beauvoir was on his hands and knees desperately trying to find his own gun and calling to the chief.

'You all right? What happened?'

'Get the gun,' yelled Gamache, straining against Lemieux who was writhing to get away. In the darkness on the floor every foot, every hand, every chair leg felt like a weapon. Gamache's hand closed around a rock.

'You can stop now.'

Above them a young voice spoke. All three men, writhing on the floor together, looked up. Agent Yvette Nichol stood with a gun in her hand.

Slowly the men got up. Lemieux brought his hand to the back of his head. It came away with blood.

'Give it to me.' He put his hand out for her gun.

'Oh, I don't think so,' said Nichol.

'Listen, you stupid bitch, give it to me.'

But Nichol stood stock-still, her gun steady. Lemieux shifted his gaze to Brébeuf, who'd slunk into the shadows.

'What's your game, Brébeuf? Call her off.'

'I can't.' The voice high, almost squeaking, as though suppressing hysteria.

'I'm warning you, Brébeuf.'

From the shadows came a brief eruption of laughter before it was strangled.

'I'm not his to call off,' said Nichol, her eyes cold and hard.

'Francoeur,' Lemieux hissed at Brébeuf. 'I thought you had him under control.'

'Give me the gun, Agent Nichol.' Gamache stepped forward, his hand out.

'Shoot,' yelled Lemieux. 'Shoot him.'

Just then her cell phone rang. To their astonishment, she answered it, her eyes never leaving them.

'Yes, I understand. He's with me now.'

She thrust the cell phone at Gamache. He hesitated then took it.

'*Oui, allô?*'

'Chief Inspector Gamache?' the heavily accented voice asked.

'*Oui.*'

'It's Ari Nikolev. I'm Yvette's father. I hope you're looking after my daughter. Every time I call she tells me she's solving the case for you. Is that true?'

'She's a remarkable young woman, sir,' said Gamache. 'I must go now.'

He handed the phone to Nichol. She handed him her gun. Lemieux watched, slack-jawed.

'What is this?' He turned once again to Brébeuf, the sputtering in the shadows. 'You said she's with us.'

'I said she served a purpose.' Brébeuf's voice was strained, fighting to control the hysteria that gripped him. 'When Francoeur transferred her back to homicide I knew Gamache would suspect she was a spy for Francoeur. Why else would he send her back? But Francoeur was never anything but a bully and a fool. He dropped Arnot as soon as things got difficult. Nichol was our scapegoat. The obvious suspect, if Gamache got suspicious.'

'Well you were fucking wrong,' snarled Lemieux.

'Yes, Dad, I think he'll say yes now.' She turned to Gamache. 'He's been bugging me to invite you for tea sometime.'

'Tell your father I'd be honored.'

'Yup, Dad. He says he'll come. No I don't have a gun on him.' She raised her brows at Gamache. 'Now. No, I didn't fuck up, but thanks for asking.'

'Did you know?' Lemieux asked Beauvoir as his hands were yanked behind him and cuffs clamped on.

'Of course I knew,' Beauvoir lied. He hadn't known until he'd confronted the chief on the side of the road. Until they told each other everything. Then it had come out. Nichol was working for them. He was glad he hadn't thrown her into the spring-bloated Rivière Bella Bella, as all his instincts had told him to do. That caul really couldn't be completely trusted.

'I knew she wasn't Francoeur's spy. Too obvious,' said Gamache, handing the gun to Beauvoir. 'I spoke to her almost a year ago, told her my plan and she agreed to play along. She's a courageous young woman.'

'Don't you mean psychotic?' asked Lemieux.

'Not likeable, I'll grant you, but that's what I was counting on. As long as you thought I suspected her, you were free to do what you wanted. And I was free to watch you. I told Nichol to be as annoying as she could to everyone, but to focus on you in particular. To rattle you. Your armor's your likeability. If we could keep you off balance you might say or do something stupid. And you did. That day here you sneaked up on me. No agent of mine would ever draw his gun on me. You did it to shake me up. Instead you put beyond doubt that you were the spy. But I made a massive mistake.' Gamache turned to Brébeuf. 'I thought the near enemy was Francoeur. It never occurred to me it would be you.'

'Matthew 10:36. A man's foes shall be they of his own household,' quoted Brébeuf, softly. The hysteria gone, the anger gone, the fear gone. Everything gone.

'But so shall his friends.' Gamache watched as Beauvoir and Nichol herded Brébeuf and Lemieux to the door.

Fourteen days, thought Michel Brébeuf. *Fourteen days of happiness*. It was true. But what he'd forgotten until this very moment was that most of them had been with this man.

'What the hell did you hit me with?' Lemieux demanded.

'A rock,' said Nichol, preening. 'One fell out of Inspector Beauvoir's coat the other day and I picked it up. I threw it at you just as you fired.'

Armand Gamache walked down the dim corridor. Something odd was happening to the old Hadley house. It was becoming familiar. He could move about without turning on his flashlight. But he stopped partway along.

Something very large was coming toward him.

Reaching into his coat he took out his flashlight and flicked the switch. There in front of him was a multi-headed creature.

'We've come to rescue you,' said Gabri, from behind Myrna. Jeanne was in the lead followed by Clara and the rest.

'Onward pagan soldiers,' said Jeanne with a relieved smile.

The candle was burning low. They took their seats, the same ones they'd always taken, as though this was an old and comfortable ritual, a rite of spring.

'You were about to tell us who killed Madeleine,' said Odile.

Gamache waited until everyone was settled then he spoke.

'*How bitter a thing it is to look into happiness through another man's eyes.*'

He let the terrible words sink in.

'Someone here had grown bitter looking at the joyous world Madeleine had created for herself. Do you know where that quote comes from?'

'Shakespeare,' said Jeanne. '*As You Like It.*'

Gamache nodded. 'How'd you know?'

'It was the school play our final year. You produced it.' She turned to Hazel. 'And Madeleine starred.'

'Madeleine starred,' repeated Gamache. 'Always. Not because she tried but because she couldn't help it.'

'She was the sun,' said Sandon, softly.

'And someone flew too close,' agreed Gamache. 'Someone here is Icarus. Too close to the sun for too long. Finally the sun did what it always does. It sent this person plunging to the ground. But it took time. It took years. It actually took decades.

'The murderer had created a fine life. Friends, a comfortable social life circle. It was a rich and happy time. But the ghosts of our past always find us. In this case the ghost wasn't a person, but an emotion, long buried and even forgotten. But it was potent. Blinding, staggering, scorching jealousy.' He turned to Jeanne. 'If you thought it was hard being on Madeleine's cheerleading squad, imagine being her best friend.'

All eyes turned to Hazel.

'According to the yearbooks, you were a fine basketball player, Hazel, but Mad was better. She was the captain. Always the captain. You were on the debating team, but Mad was the captain.'

He picked up the yearbook and found their grad pictures.

'She never got mad,' he read the caption under young

Hazel's photograph, then closed the book. 'Never got mad. I took that to mean you never got angry, but it meant something more, didn't it?'

Hazel's eyes were on her hands.

'She never got Madeleine. Never caught up. And never understood. Never "got it". Kept trying and kept failing, because you started seeing it as a competition and she never did. You were dogged by a best friend who was slightly better at everything. Once high school was out you broke away and the friendship faded. But years later, after a bout of breast cancer, Madeleine wanted to find old friends. By then you'd made a good life for yourself. A modest home in a lovely community. A daughter. Friends. A potential romance. You were involved in the ACW. But you'd learned something from high school. This afternoon at a meeting in Montreal a colleague said something to me. It was about . . .' Gamache hesitated for a moment, 'another case.'

Gamache heard the voice again, deep, commanding, authoritative. And accusing Gamache of only taking in the weak, the waste, the people no one else wanted. So that he'd always be better than them. To boost his own ego. He knew that wasn't true. Not that he didn't have an ego, but he knew that the people on his team were the best, not the worst. They'd proved it time and again.

But still Francoeur's accusation had resonated. Driving back to Three Pines it clicked. It wasn't the Arnot case. It was this case. It was Hazel.

'You surround yourself with people who are wounded, handicapped in some way. Needy. You befriend people who are sick, or in bad marriages, alcoholics, the obese, the troubled. Because it makes you feel superior. You're kind to them, in a condescending way. Did you ever hear Hazel refer to anyone other than "Poor" so-and-so?'

They looked at each other and shook their heads. It was true. Poor Sophie, Poor Mrs Blanchard, Poor Monsieur Béliveau.

'The near enemy,' said Myrna.

'Exactly. Pity for compassion. Everyone thought you

were a saint but it served a purpose for you. Made you feel needed and better than all the people you helped. When you met up with Madeleine again, she was still ill. You liked that. Meant you could nurse her, look after her. Be in charge. She was sick and needy and you weren't. But then she did something you hadn't counted on. She got better. Better than ever. A Madeleine not only shiny and bright and alive, but full of gratitude and the desire to grab life. But the life she grabbed was yours. Little by little she was taking over again. Your friends, your job at the ACW. You could see it coming, the day when you again faded into the background. And then Madeleine crossed the line. She took the two things you cherished most. Your daughter and Monsieur Béliveau. Both turned their attentions to her. Your enemy was back and living in your home and eating off your plates and feeding off your life.'

Hazel was slumped in her chair.

'What was it like for you?'

She looked up.

'What do you think it was like? All through high school coming second in everything. I was the best volleyball player on the team, until Mad joined.'

'But second best is still great,' said Gabri, who'd have loved to come in the top ten in any athletic event, even the Wellington Boot Toss at the fair.

'You think so? Try it all the time. At everything. And having people like you saying exactly that, all my life. Second best is good. Second best is fine. Well it isn't. Even in the school play. I was finally in charge. The producer. But who got all the credit when the play was a success?'

She needn't tell them. A picture, bright and brutal, was forming. How many condescending smiles could one person take? How many fleeting glances as the person searched for the real star?

Madeleine.

How bitter a thing it is, thought Clara.

'Then out of the blue Madeleine called. She was ill, she wanted to see me. I searched my heart and couldn't find any more hatred. And when we met she looked so tired and pathetic.'

Everyone could see the reunion. The roles finally reversed. And Hazel making the one, spectacular mistake. Inviting Madeleine to live with her.

'Madeleine was wonderful. She brightened up the house.' Hazel smiled at the memory. 'We laughed and talked and did everything together. I introduced her around and got her involved in committees. She was my best friend again, but this time an equal. I started to fall in love with her again. It was the most wonderful time. Do you have any idea what that feels like? I didn't even know I was lonely until Mad was there again, and suddenly my heart was full. But then people began calling just for her, and Gabri asked her to take over the ACW, even though I was vice-president.'

'But you hated the job,' said Gabri.

'I did. But I hated being left out more. Everyone does, don't you know that?'

Clara thought of all the wedding invitations she hadn't received and how she'd felt. Partly relieved at not having to go to the party and bring a gift they couldn't afford, but mostly offended at being left out. Forgotten. Or worse. Remembered but not included.

'Then she took Monsieur Béliveau,' Gamache said.

'When Ginette was dying she'd often say he and I would make a good couple. Keep each other company. I began to hope, to think maybe that was true.'

'But he wanted more than just company,' said Myrna.

'He wanted her,' said Hazel, the bitterness seeping out. 'And I started to see I'd made a terrible mistake. But I couldn't see how to get out of it.'

'When did you decide to kill her?' Gamache asked.

'When Sophie came home for Christmas, and kissed her first.'

The simple, devastating fact sat in their sacred circle, like the dead little bird. Gamache was reminded of the one thing they were told over and over: don't go into the woods in spring. You don't want to get between a mother and her baby.

Madeleine had.

Finally Gamache spoke. 'You'd kept Sophie's ephedra from a few years ago. Not because you planned to use it then, but because you don't throw anything away.'

Not furniture, not books, not emotions, thought Gamache. Hazel let nothing go.

'According to the lab, the pills used were too pure to be the recent manufacture. At first I thought the ephedra was from your store,' he said to Odile. 'But then I remembered there'd been another bottle of pills. A few years ago. Hazel said Madeleine had found it and confiscated them, but that wasn't true, was it, Sophie?'

'Mom?' Sophie sat wide-eyed, stunned.

Hazel reached for her hand, but Sophie quickly withdrew it. Hazel looked more affected by that than anything else.

'You found them. And you used them on Madeleine for me?'

Clara tried to ignore the inflection, the hint of satisfaction in Sophie's voice.

'I had to. She was taking you away. Taking everything.'

'You first tried to kill her at the Friday night séance,' said Gamache, 'but you didn't give her enough.'

'But she wasn't even there,' said Gabri.

'No, but her casserole was,' said Gamache, turning to Monsieur Béliveau. 'You said you couldn't sleep that night and thought it was because you were upset by the séance. But the séance wasn't all that frightening. It was the ephedra that kept you awake.'

'*Est-ce que c'est vrai?*' Monsieur Béliveau asked Hazel, astonished. 'You put that drug in the casserole and gave it to us? You could have killed me.'

'No, no.' She reached out to him but he quickly leaned away. One by one everyone was backing away from Hazel. Leaving her in the one place she most feared. Alone. 'I'd never take the risk. I knew from news reports that ephedra only kills if you have a heart condition and I knew you didn't.'

'But you knew Madeleine did,' said Gamache.

'Madeleine had a bad heart?' asked Myrna.

'It was brought on by her chemotherapy,' confirmed Gamache. 'She told you about it, didn't she, Hazel?'

'She didn't want to tell anyone else because she didn't want to be treated like a sick person. How'd you know?'

'The coroner's report said she had a bad heart and her doctor confirmed it,' said Gamache.

'No, I mean how'd you know that I knew? I didn't tell anyone, not even Sophie.'

'Aspirin.'

Hazel sighed. 'I thought I'd been clever there. Hiding Mad's pills in among all the rest.'

'Inspector Beauvoir noticed them when you were looking for something to give Sophie for her ankle. You have a cupboard full of old pills. What struck him was that you didn't give Sophie the aspirin. Instead you kept searching for another bottle.'

'The ephedra was hidden in the aspirin bottle?' asked Clara, lost.

'We thought so. We had the contents analyzed. It was aspirin.'

'So what was the problem?' asked Gabri.

'Its strength,' said Gamache. 'It was low dose. Way below normal. People with heart conditions often take a low dose aspirin once a day.'

There were nods around the ring. Gamache paused, staring at Hazel.

'Madeleine kept something a secret. Even from you. Perhaps especially from you.'

'She told me everything,' said Hazel, as though defending her best friend.

'No. One last thing, one huge thing, she kept from you. From everyone. Madeleine was dying. Her cancer had spread.'

'*Mais, non,*' said Monsieur Béliveau.

'But that's impossible,' Hazel snapped. 'She'd have said something.'

'Odd that she didn't. I think she didn't want to, because she sensed something in you, something that fed on, and created, weakness. Had she told you, though, you wouldn't have killed her. But by then the plan was in motion. It started with this.'

He held up the alumni list he'd gotten from the school that afternoon.

'Madeleine was on the alumni of your old high school. So were you.' Gamache turned to Jeanne, who nodded. 'Hazel took one of Gabri's brochures, typed "Where lay lines meet – Easter Special" across the top and mailed it to Jeanne.'

'She stole one of my brochures,' Gabri said to Myrna.

'Big picture, Gabri.'

With a struggle he accepted that maybe he wasn't quite as aggrieved as Madeleine. Or Hazel.

'Poor Hazel,' said Gabri, and everyone nodded. Poor Hazel.

CHAPTER 44

A kind of shell shock settled over Gamache in the week that followed. His food tasted dull, the paper held no interest. He read and re-read the same sentence in *Le Devoir*. Reine-Marie tried to engage him in discussions of a trip to the Manoir Bellechasse to celebrate their thirty-fifth wedding anniversary. He responded, showed interest, but the clear, sparkling colors of his life had dulled. It was as though his heart was suddenly too heavy for his legs. He lugged himself around, trying not to think about what had happened. But one evening when he was out for a walk with Reine-Marie and Henri, the shepherd had suddenly tugged free and raced across the park toward a familiar man on the other side. Gamache called after him and Henri stopped. But not before the man on the far side had also spotted the dog. And the owner.

Once more, and for the last time, Michel Brébeuf and Armand Gamache locked eyes. In between so much life happened. Children played, dogs rolled and fetched, young parents marveled at what they'd produced. The air between the men was ripe with lilac and honeysuckle, the buzz of bees, puppies barking, children laughing. The world stood between Armand Gamache and his best friend.

And Gamache longed to walk across and hug him. To feel the familiar hand on his arm. The smell of Michel in his nostrils: soap and pipe tobacco. He yearned for his company, his voice, his eyes so thoughtful and full of humor.

He missed his best friend.

And to think for years Michel had actually hated him. Why? For being happy.

How bitter a thing it is to look into happiness through another man's eyes.

But today no happiness could be found there, only sorrow and regret.

As Gamache watched, Michel Brébeuf raised one hand then lowered it and walked away. Gamache was just raising his, but his friend had already turned away. Reine-Marie took his hand, and he picked up Henri's leash and the three of them continued their walk.

Robert Lemieux had been charged with assault and attempted murder. He faced a long prison sentence. But Armand Gamache couldn't bring himself to lay charges against Michel Brébeuf. He knew he should. Knew he was a coward for backing away. But every time he approached Paget's office to lay the charge he remembered little Michel Brébeuf's hand on his arm. Telling him in his little boy voice it would be all right. He wasn't alone.

And he couldn't do it. His friend had saved him once. And now it was his turn.

But Michel Brébeuf had resigned from the Sûreté, a broken man. His house for sale, he and Catherine were leaving their beloved Montreal and all they knew and loved. Michel Brébeuf had placed himself beyond the pale.

Armand Gamache was invited to take tea with Agent Nichol and her family one Saturday afternoon. He pulled up to the house, tiny and immaculate. He could see the faces at the picture window overlooking the road, though they disappeared as he came up the walk. The door was opened even before he knocked.

He met Yvette Nichol for the first time. The person, not the agent. She was dressed in simple slacks and a sweater, and he realized it was also the first time he'd seen her without a stain on her clothing. Ari Nikolev, small and thin and worried, wiped his palms on his pants then held his hand out.

'Welcome to our home,' he said in broken French.

'It's an honor,' said Gamache, in Czech. Both men must have spent the morning practicing the other's language.

The next hour was taken up with a cacophony of relatives shouting at each other in languages Gamache couldn't even begin to recognize. One old aunt, he was sure, was creating it as she went along.

The food kept coming, the beverages. Then the songs. It was a joyous, even riotous, event. And yet, every time he looked for Nichol he found her standing just outside the living room. Finally he approached her.

'Why don't you come in?'

'I'm fine here, sir.'

He watched her for a moment. 'What is it? Do you ever go in?' he asked in amazement, standing next to her on the threshold.

She shook her head. 'I've never been invited.'

'But it's your own home.'

'They've taken all the places. There's no room.'

'How old are you?'

'Twenty-six,' came the sullen reply.

'Time you made your own place. Insist. It's not their fault you're standing here, Yvette.'

Still she hesitated. The truth was, it was comfortable there. Cold, lonely sometimes, but comfortable. What the hell did he know? Everything was easy for him. He wasn't a girl, he wasn't an immigrant, his mother hadn't died young, he wasn't mocked by his own family. He wasn't a lowly agent. He'd never understand how hard it was for her.

As Gamache left, full of sweet cakes and strong tea, he asked Yvette Nichol to walk him to his car.

'I want to thank you for what you did. I know how painful it is to deliberately put yourself outside the group.'

'I'm always outside,' she said.

'Time to come in, I think. I believe this is yours.'

He reached into his pocket and pressed something into her hand. Opening it she found a warm stone.

'Thank you,' he said.

Nichol nodded.

'Do you know, in the Jewish faith when someone dies, loved ones put stones on top of the grave marker. I gave you a piece of advice a year or so ago, when we first discussed the Arnot case. Do you remember it?'

Nichol pretended to think, but she remembered clearly.

'You said I should bury my dead.'

Gamache opened his car door.

'Consider it.' He nodded to the stone in her hand. 'But just make sure they're really dead before you bury them. Otherwise you'll never get rid of them.'

As he drove away he thought, maybe, he should take his own advice.

Armand Gamache ascended to the top floor of Sûreté headquarters, walking along the corridor to the impressive wooden door. He knocked, hoping no one was in.

'Come in.'

Gamache opened the door and stood before Sylvain Francoeur. The Superintendent didn't move. He stared at Gamache with undisguised loathing. Gamache reached into his pants pocket, instinctively looking for the charm he'd carried most of his life. But his pocket was empty. A week ago he'd placed his father's dented and damaged crucifix in a simple white envelope with a little note, and given it to his son.

'What do you want?'

'I want to apologize. I was wrong to accuse you of spreading stories about my family. You didn't do it. I'm sorry.'

Francoeur's eyes narrowed, waiting for the 'but.' None came.

'I'm prepared to write an apology and send it to all the members of the council who were there.'

'I'd like you to resign.'

They stared at each other. Then Gamache smiled wearily. 'Is this going to be it for the rest of our lives? You threaten, I retaliate? I accuse, you demand? Do we really need to do this?'

'I've seen nothing to change my opinion of you, Chief Inspector. Including how you've handled this. Superintendent Brébeuf was a far better officer than you'll ever be. And now, thanks to you, he's gone too. I know you, Gamache.' Francoeur stood and leaned over his desk. 'You're arrogant and stupid. Weak. You rely on instinct. You never even saw that your best friend was working against you. Where was your instinct then? The brilliant Gamache, the hero of the Arnot case. Blind. You're blinded by your emotions, by your need to help people, to save them. You've brought nothing but disgrace on the force from the moment you got into a leadership position. And now you come sucking up. It's not over, Gamache. It'll never be over.'

The word splashed into Gamache's face, no longer smiling. He stared at Francoeur, who was trembling with rage. Gamache nodded then turned and left. Some things, he knew, refused to die.

A few days later the Gamaches, including Henri, were invited to a party in Three Pines. It was a sunny spring day, the young leaves in full bloom and turning the trees every shade of fresh green. As they bumped and thumped along the dirt road, the canopy of lime green overhead shining like the stained glass in St Thomas's, they noticed unusual activity off to one side. Though they couldn't quite see it yet, Gamache knew it was at the old Hadley house and wondered if the villagers were finally tearing it down. A man stepped into the center of the road and waved them to the side. Monsieur Béliveau, in overalls and a painter's cap, was smiling.

'Bon. We all hoped you'd come.' The grocer leaned into the open window, patting Henri who'd climbed over Gamache to see who was there so that it appeared a dog was driving the car. Gamache opened the door and Henri bounced out to great yells of recognition from villagers who hadn't seen him since he was a puppy.

Within minutes Reine-Marie was up a ladder, scraping flaking paint from the old house, and Gamache was scraping trim around ground floor windows. He didn't like heights and Reine-Marie didn't like trim.

As he scraped he had the impression the house was moaning, as Henri did when he rubbed his ears. With pleasure. Years of decay, years of neglect, of sorrow, were being scraped away. It was being taken down to its real self, the layers of artifice removed. Had that been the moaning all along? Had the old house been moaning for pleasure when company finally arrived? And they'd thought it sinister?

Far from tearing it down, the villagers of Three Pines had decided to give the old Hadley house another chance. They were restoring it to life.

Already the place seemed to preen in the sun, shining where the new paint had been applied. Teams were installing new windows and others were cleaning inside.

'A good spring clean,' as Sarah the baker said, her long auburn hair falling out of the bun at the back of her head.

A barbecue was fired up and the villagers took a break for beer or lemonade, burgers and sausages. Gamache took his beer and stood staring over the hill, into Three Pines. It was quiet. Everyone was here, old and young; even the ill had been helped up and given lawn chairs and a brush so that all souls of the village touched the Hadley house and broke the curse. The curse of anguish and sorrow.

But most of all, loneliness.

The only people not there were Peter and Clara Morrow.

'I'm ready,' Clara sang from her studio. Her face was streaked with paint and she rubbed her hands on an oil rag, too soiled to do any good.

Peter stood outside her studio, steadying himself. Breathing deeply and saying a prayer. A begging prayer. Begging for the painting to be truly, unequivocally, irredeemably horrible.

He'd given up fighting the thing he'd run from as a child, hidden from as the words chased him through his

days and into his dreams. His disappointed father demanding he be the best, and Peter knowing he'd always fail.
Someone was always better.

'Close your eyes.' Clara came to the door. He did as he
was told and felt her small hand on his arm, leading him.

'We buried Lilium on the village green,' said Ruth, coming
up beside Gamache.

'I'm sorry,' he said. She leaned heavily on her cane and
behind her stood Rosa, growing into a fine and sturdy duck.

'Poor little one,' she said.

'Fortunate one, to have known such love.'

'Love killed her,' said Ruth.

'Love sustained her,' said Gamache.

'Thank you,' said the old poet then turned to look at the
Hadley house. 'Poor Hazel. She really did love Madeleine,
you know. Even I could see it.'

Gamache nodded. 'I think jealousy's the cruellest emotion. It twists us into something grotesque. Hazel was consumed by it. It ate away her happiness, her contentment.
Her sanity. In the end Hazel was blinded by bitterness and
couldn't see that she already had everything she wanted.
Love and companionship.'

'She loved not wisely but too well. Someone should
write a play about that,' said Ruth, smiling ruefully.

'Never work,' said Gamache. After a moment's silence
he said almost to himself, 'The near enemy. It isn't a person, is it? It's ourselves.'

Both looked at the old Hadley house, and the villagers
working to restore it.

'Depends on the person,' said Ruth, then her face changed
to surprise. She pointed to the woods at the back of the old
Hadley house. 'My God, I was wrong. There are fairies at
the end of the garden.'

Gamache looked round. There at the very back of the
garden the brush moved. Then Olivier and Gabri emerged,
dragging cut bracken.

'Ha,' laughed Ruth, triumphant, then her laughter died

and she was left with a small smile on her hard face. '*Behold, I show you a mystery.*' She nodded toward the villagers working on the old house. '*The dead shall be raised incorruptible, and we shall be changed.*'

'*In the twinkling of an eye,*' said Gamache.

'Ready?' Clara asked, her voice almost squeaky with excitement. She'd worked non-stop, racing the arrival of Fortin. But then it had become something else. A race to get what she saw, what she felt, onto the canvas.

And finally she had it.

'Okay, you can look.'

Peter's eyes flew open. It took him a moment to absorb what he saw. It was a huge portrait, of Ruth. But a Ruth he'd never seen. Not really. But now, as he looked, he realized he had seen her, but only in passing, at odd angles, in unsuspecting moments.

She was swathed in luminous blue, a hint of a red tunic underneath. Her skin, wrinkled and veined, was exposed down her old neck and to her protruding collar bones. She was old and tired and ugly. A weak hand clasped the blue shawl closed, as though afraid of exposing herself. And on her face was a look of such bitterness and anguish. Loneliness and loss. But there was something else. In her eyes, something about the eyes.

Peter wasn't sure he'd ever be able to breathe again, or need to. The portrait seemed to do it for him. It had crawled inside his body and become him. The fear, the emptiness, the shame.

But in those eyes, there was something else.

This was Ruth as Mary, the mother of God. Mary as an old and forgotten woman. But there was something those old eyes were just beginning to see. Peter stood still and did as Clara had always advised and he'd always dismissed. He let the painting come to him.

And then he saw it.

Clara had captured the moment when despair turned to hope. That instant, when the world changed forever. That's

what Ruth was seeing. Hope. The first, new-born, intima-
tion of hope. This was a masterpiece, Peter knew. Like
Michelangelo's Sistine Chapel. But while Michelangelo
had painted the instant before God brought Man to life,
Clara had painted the moment the fingers touched.

'It's brilliant,' he whispered. 'It's the most wonderful
painting I've ever seen.'

All the artsy descriptive words fled before the portrait.
All his fears and insecurities vanished. And the love he felt
for Clara was restored.

He took her in his arms and together they laughed and
wept for joy.

'The idea came to me that night at dinner, when I watched
Ruth talk about Lilium. If you hadn't suggested the dinner,
this never would've happened. Thank you, Peter.' And she
gave him a huge hug and kiss.

For the next hour he listened as she talked a mile a
minute about the work, her excitement infecting him until
they were exhausted and exhilarated.

'Come on.' She poked him. 'Up to the old Hadley
house. Grab a six-pack from the cold room; they'll probably need it.'

As he left he peeked into Clara's studio once more and
was relieved to feel just a hint, just an echo of the crippling
jealousy he'd felt. It was going, he knew. Soon it would
disappear completely and for the first time in his life he'd
be able to be genuinely happy for someone else.

And so Peter and Clara made their way to the old Hadley
house, Peter carrying a case of beer and a tiny shard of jealousy, which started festering.

'Happy?' Reine-Marie slipped her hand into Gamache's.
He kissed her and nodded, pointing his beer down the
lawn. Henri was playing fetch with an exasperated Myrna,
who was trying to get someone else to throw the ball to the
tireless dog. She'd made the mistake of giving him a soiled
hot dog and now she was his new best friend.

'*Mesdames et messieurs.*' Monsieur Béliveau's voice

bellowed over the gathering. The eating stopped and everyone gathered at the porch of the old Hadley house. Beside
Monsieur Béliveau stood Odile Montmagny, looking very
nervous, but sober.

'I read *Sarah Binks*,' Gamache whispered to Myrna,
who joined them just as Ruth sidled up. 'It's delightful.' He
withdrew it from his jacket pocket. 'It's a supposed tribute
to this Prairie woman's poetry, except the poetry's awful.'

'Our own Odile Montmagny has written an ode to the
day and to this house,' Monsieur Béliveau was saying as
Odile shifted from foot to foot, as though she suddenly
needed to relieve herself.

'But *Sarah Binks* was my book. I was going to give it to
her.' Ruth grabbed it from his hand and used it to gesture
toward Odile. 'Where'd you get it?'

'It was hidden in Madeleine's bedside table,' said
Gamache.

'Madeleine? She stole it from me? I thought I'd just
lost it.'

'She took it from you when she realized what you were
going to do with it,' hissed Myrna. 'When you told Odile
she reminded you of Sarah Binks she thought it was a compliment. She worships you. Madeleine didn't want you to
hurt her, so she hid it.'

'This is a little something I wrote last night while
watching the hockey game,' said Odile. Nods greeted this
insight into the creative process, this natural affinity between poetry and the playoffs.

She cleared her throat.

> *A cursed duck pecked off his ear,*
> *And his face grew peaked and pale;*
> *"Oh, how can a woman love me now?"*
> *Was his constant and lonely wail;*
> *But a woman came and she loved the man,*
> *With a love serene and clear –*
> *She loved him as only a woman can love*
> *A man with only one ear.*

A silence greeted the last word. Odile stood uncertainly on the porch. Then, to his horror, Gamache saw Ruth move through the crowd, the Sarah Binks book clutched in her hand and Rosa quacking behind.

'Make way for the duck and the fuck,' yelled Gabri.

Ruth hauled herself onto the porch and stood beside Odile, taking the younger woman's hand. Gamache and Myrna held their breaths.

'I have never heard a poem that moved me so much. That speaks so clearly of loneliness and loss. Using the man as an allegory for the house was brilliant, my dear.'

Odile looked confused.

'And like the blighted man the old Hadley house will be loved again,' Ruth continued. 'Your poem brings hope to all of us who are old and ugly and flawed. Bravo.'

Ruth slipped the book into her tattered sweater as she embraced Odile, who looked as though she'd found heaven on the battered porch of the old Hadley house.

Peter and Clara arrived, carrying a welcome case of beer. But they stopped just short of the house. Gamache watched and wondered what they'd do. More than any villager the old Hadley house had haunted Peter and Clara. And now the two stood outside the buzz of activity, and stared. Then Clara bent down and lifted the 'For Sale' sign. Using her sleeve she wiped the worst of the mud and dirt from its face, then she handed it to Peter, who thrust it into the ground. The sign stood upright, clean and proud.

'Do you think anyone will buy it?' Clara asked, wiping her hands on her jeans.

'Someone will buy it and someone will love it,' said Gamache.

'*But a woman came and she loved the man, With a love serene and clear—She loved him as only a woman can love A man with only one ear,*' Ruth quoted, joining them again. 'Ridiculous poem, of course. But still . . .' She limped off to join Odile, giving kindness another chance. Little Rosa waddled behind.

'At least Ruth now has an excuse for the quacking,' said Clara.

In the bright sunshine Armand Gamache watched as the old Hadley house was brought back to life, then he put down his beer and joined them.

A RULE AGAINST MURDER

PROLOGUE

More than a century ago, the robber barons discovered Lac Massawippi. They came with purpose from Montreal, Boston, New York, and burrowing deep into the Canadian wilderness, they built the great lodge. Though, of course, they didn't actually dirty their own hands. What clung to them was something else entirely. No, these men hired men with names like Zoétique, Télesphore, Honoré to hack down the massive and ancient forests. At first the Québécois were resistant, having lived in the forest all their lives. They balked at destroying a thing of such beauty, and a few of the more intuitive recognized the end when they saw it. But money took care of that, and slowly the forest receded and the magnificent Manoir Bellechasse rose. After months of cutting and stripping and turning and drying, the huge logs were finally stacked one on top of the other. It was an art, this building of log homes. But what guided the keen eyes and rough hands of these men wasn't aesthetics, but the certainty that winter's bite would kill whoever was inside if they didn't choose the logs wisely. A *coureurs du bois* could contemplate the stripped trunk of a massive tree for hours, as though deciphering it. Walking around and around, sitting on a stump, filling his pipe and staring until finally this *coureurs du bois,* this man of the woods, knew exactly where that tree would sit for the rest of its life.

It took years, but finally the great lodge was completed. The last man stood on the magnificent copper roof, like a lightning rod, and surveyed the forests and lonely, haunting lake from a height he'd never achieve again. And if that man's eyes could see far enough he'd see something horrible approaching, like the veins of summer lightning. Marching toward not merely the lodge, but the very place he stood, on the gleaming metal roof. Something dreadful was going to happen on that very spot.

He'd laid copper roofs before, always with the same design. But this time, when everyone else had thought it was finished, he'd climbed back up and added a ridge, a cap along the peak of the roof. He had no idea why, except that it looked good and felt right. And he'd had the copper left over. He'd use the same design again and again, in great buildings across the burgeoning territory. But this was the first.

Hammering the final nail he slowly, carefully, deliberately descended.

Paid off, the men paddled away, their hearts as heavy as their pockets. And looking back, the more intuitive among them noticed that what they'd created looked a little like a forest itself, but one turned unnaturally on its side.

For there was something unnatural about the Manoir Bellechasse from the very beginning. It was staggeringly beautiful. The stripped logs were golden and glowing. It was made of wood and wattle and sat right at the water's edge. It commanded Lac Massawippi, as the robber barons commanded everything. These captains of industry couldn't seem to help it.

And once a year, men with names like Andrew and Douglas and Charles would leave their rail and whiskey empires, trade their spats for chewed-leather moccasins and trek by canoe into the lodge on the shore of the isolated lake. They'd grown weary of robbery and needed another distraction.

The Manoir Bellechasse was created and conceived to allow these men to do one thing. Kill.

It made a nice change.

Over the years the wilderness receded. The foxes and deer, the moose and bears, all the wild creatures hunted by the robber barons crept away. The Abinaki, who often paddled the wealthy industrialists into the great lodge, had receded, repulsed. Towns and villages sprung up. Cottagers, weekenders, discovered the nearby lakes.

But the Bellechasse remained. It changed hands over the generations and slowly the stunned and stuffed heads of long-dead deer and moose and even a rare cougar disappeared from the log walls and were tossed into the attic.

As the fortunes of its creators waned, so went the lodge. It sat abandoned for many years, far too big for a single family and too remote for a hotel. Just as the forest was emboldened enough to reclaim its own, someone bought the place. A road was built, curtains hung, spiders and beetles and owls were chased from the Bellechasse, and paying guests invited in. The Manoir Bellechasse became one of the finest auberges in Quebec.

But while Lac Massawippi had changed, Quebec had changed, Canada had changed, almost everything had changed in over a century, one thing hadn't.

The robber barons were back. They'd come to the Manoir Bellechasse once again, to kill.

CHAPTER 1

In the height of summer, the guests descended on the isolated lodge by the lake, summoned to the Manoir Bellechasse by identical vellum invitations, addressed in the familiar spidery scrawl as though written in cobwebs. Thrust through mail slots, the heavy paper had thudded to the floors of impressive homes in Vancouver and Toronto, and a small brick cottage in Three Pines.

The mailman had carried it in his bag through the tiny Quebec village, taking his time. *Best not to exert yourself in this heat*, he told himself, pausing to remove his hat and wipe his dripping head. *Union rules.* But the actual reason for his lethargy wasn't the beating and brilliant sun, but something more private. He always lingered in this village. He wandered slowly by the perennial beds of roses and lilies and thrusting bold foxglove. He helped kids spot frogs at the pond on the village green. He sat on warm fieldstone walls and watched the old village go about its business. It added hours to his day and made him the last courier back to the terminal. He was mocked and kidded by his fellows for being so slow and he suspected that was the reason he'd never been promoted. For two decades or more he'd taken his time. Instead of hurrying, he strolled through Three Pines talking to people as they walked their dogs, often joining them for lemonade or *thé glacé* outside the bistro. Or a *café au lait* in front of the roaring fire in winter. Sometimes the villagers, knowing he was having lunch at the bistro, would come by and pick up their own mail. And chat for a moment. He brought news from other villages on his route, like a traveling minstrel in medieval times, with news of plague or war or flood, someplace else. But never here in this lovely and peaceful village. It always amused him to imagine that Three Pines, nestled among the mountains and surrounded by Canadian forest, was disconnected from the outside world. It certainly felt that way. It was a relief.

And so he took his time. This day he held a bundle of envelopes in his sweaty hand, hoping he wasn't marring the perfect, quite lovely thick paper of the top letter. Then the handwriting caught his eye and his pace slowed still further. After decades as a mail carrier he knew he delivered more than just letters. In his years, he knew he'd dropped bombs along his route. Great good news, children born, lotteries won, distant, wealthy aunts dead. But he was a good and sensitive man, and he knew he was also the bearer of bad news. It broke his heart to think of the pain he sometimes caused, especially in this village.

He knew what he held in his hand now was that, and more. It wasn't, perhaps, total telepathy that informed his certainty, but also an unconscious ability to read handwriting. Not simply the words, but the thrust behind them. The simple, mundane three-line address on the envelope told him more than where to deliver the letter. The hand was old, he could tell, and infirm. Crippled not just by age, but rage. No good would come from this thing he held. And he suddenly wanted to be rid of it.

His intention had been to wander over to the bistro and have a cold beer and sandwich, chat with the owner, Olivier, and see if anyone came for their mail, for he was also just a little bit lazy. But suddenly he was energized. Astonished villagers saw a sight unique to them, the postman hurrying. He stopped and turned and walked briskly away from the bistro, toward a rusty mailbox in front of a brick cottage overlooking the village green. As he opened the mouth of the box, it screamed. He couldn't blame it. He thrust the letter in and quickly closed the shrieking door. It surprised him that the battered metal box didn't gag a little and spew that wretched thing back. He'd come to see his letters as living things, and the boxes as kinds of pets. And he'd done something terrible to this particular box. And these people.

Had Armand Gamache been blindfolded, he'd have known exactly where he was. It was the scent. That combination of woodsmoke, old books and honeysuckle.

'*Monsieur et Madame Gamache, quel plaisir.*'

Clementine Dubois waddled around the reception desk at the Manoir Bellechasse, skin like wings hanging from her outstretched arms and quivering so that she looked like a bird or a withered angel as she approached, her intentions clear. Reine-Marie Gamache met her, her own arms without hope of meeting around the substantial woman. They embraced and kissed on each cheek. When Gamache had exchanged hugs and kisses with Madame Dubois she stepped back and surveyed the couple. Before her she saw Reine-Marie, short, not plump but not trim either, hair graying and face settling into the middle years of a life fully lived. She was lovely without being actually pretty. What the French called '*soignée.*' She wore a tailored deep blue skirt to mid-calf and a crisp white shirt. Simple, elegant, classic.

The man was tall and powerfully built. In his mid-fifties and not yet going to fat, but showing evidence of a life lived with good books, wonderful food and leisurely walks. He looked like a professor, though Clementine Dubois knew he was not that. His hair was receding, and where once it had been wavy and dark, now it was thinning on top and graying over the ears and down the sides where it curled a little over the collar. He was clean-shaven except for a trim graying moustache. He wore a navy jacket, khaki slacks and a soft blue shirt, with tie. Always immaculate, even in the gathering heat of this late June day. But what was most striking were his eyes. Deep, warm brown. He carried calm with him like other men wore cologne.

'But you look tired.'

Most innkeepers would have exclaimed, '*But you look lovely.*' '*Mais, voyons, you never change, you two.*' Or even, '*You look younger than ever,*' knowing how old ears never tire of hearing that.

But while the Gamaches' ears couldn't yet be considered old, they were tired. It had been a long year and their ears had heard more than they cared to. And, as always, the Gamaches had come to the Manoir Bellechasse to leave all that behind. While the rest of the world celebrated the New Year in January, the Gamaches celebrated at the height of summer, when they visited this blessed place, retreated from the world and began anew.

'We are a little weary,' admitted Reine-Marie, subsiding gratefully into the comfortable wingchair at the reception desk.

'*Bon*, well, we'll soon take care of that. Now.' Madame Dubois gracefully swiveled back behind the desk in a practiced move and sat at her own comfortable chair. Pulling the ledger toward her she put on her glasses. 'Where have we put you?'

Armand Gamache took the chair beside his wife and they exchanged glances. They knew if they looked far enough back in that same ledger they'd find their signatures, once a year, stretching back to a June day more than thirty years ago when young Armand had saved his money and brought Reine-Marie here. For one night. In the tiniest of rooms at the very back of the splendid old Manoir. Without a view of the mountains or the lake or the perennial gardens lush with fresh peonies and first-bloom roses. He'd saved for months, wanting that visit to be special. Wanting Reine-Marie to know how much he loved her, how precious she was to him.

And so they'd lain together for the first time, the sweet scent of the forest and kitchen thyme and lilac drifting almost visible through the screened window. But the loveliest scent of all was her, fresh and warm in his strong arms. He'd written a love note to her that night. He'd covered her softly with their simple white sheet, and then, sitting in the cramped rocking chair, not daring to actually rock in case he whacked the wall behind or banged his shins on the bed in front, disturbing Reine-Marie, he'd watched her breathe. Then, on Manoir Bellechasse notepaper, he'd written,

> *My love knows no—*
> *How can a man contain such . . .*
> *My heart and soul have come alive—*
> *My love for you—*

All night he wrote and the next morning, taped to the bathroom mirror, Reine-Marie found the note.

I love you.

Clementine Dubois had been there even then, massive and wobbly and smiling. She'd been old then and each year the Gamaches worried they'd call for a reservation to hear an unfamiliar crisp voice say, '*Bonjour, Manoir Bellechasse. Peux-je vous aider?*' Instead he'd heard, 'Monsieur Gamache, what a pleasure. Are you coming to visit us again, I hope?' Like going to Grandma's. Albeit a grander Grandma's than he'd ever known.

And while Gamache and Reine-Marie had certainly changed, marrying, having two children and now a grand-daughter and another grandchild on the way, Clementine Dubois never seemed to age or diminish. And neither did her love, the Manoir. It was as though the two were one, both kind and loving, comforting and welcoming. And mysteriously and delightfully unchanging in a world that seemed to change so fast. And not always for the better.

'What's wrong?' Reine-Marie asked, noticing the look on Madame Dubois's face.

'I must be getting old,' she said and looked up, her violet eyes upset. Gamache smiled reassuringly. By his calculations, she must be 120.

'If you have no room, don't worry. We can come back

another week,' he said. It was only a two-hour drive into the eastern townships of Quebec from their home in Montreal.

'Oh, I have a room, but I'd hoped to have something better. When you called for reservations I should have saved the Lake Room for you, the one you had last year. But the Manoir's full up. One family, the Finneys, has taken the other five rooms. They're here—'

She stopped suddenly and dropped her eyes to the ledger in an act so wary and uncharacteristic the Gamaches exchanged glances.

'They're here?' Gamache prompted after the silence stretched on.

'Well, it doesn't matter, plenty of time for that,' she said, looking up and smiling reassuringly. 'I'm sorry about not saving the best room for you two, though.'

'Had we wanted the Lake Room, we'd have asked,' said Reine-Marie. 'You know Armand, this is his one flutter with uncertainty. Wild man.'

Clementine Dubois laughed, knowing that not to be true. She knew the man in front of her lived with great uncertainty every day of his life. Which was why she deeply wanted their annual visits to the Manoir to be filled with luxury and comfort. And peace.

'We never specify the room, Madame,' said Gamache, his voice deep and warm. 'Do you know why?'

Madame Dubois shook her head. She'd long been curious, but never wanted to cross-examine her guests, especially this one. 'Everyone else does,' she said. 'In fact, this whole family asked for free upgrades. Arrived in Mercedes and BMWs and asked for upgrades,' she smiled. Not meanly, but with some bafflement that people who had so much wanted more.

'We like to leave it up to the fates,' he said. She examined his face to see if he was joking, but thought he probably wasn't. 'We're perfectly happy with what we're given.'

And Clementine Dubois knew the truth of it. She felt the same. Every morning she woke up, a bit surprised to see another day, and always surprised to be here, in this old lodge, by the sparkling shores of this freshwater lake, surrounded by forests and streams, gardens and guests. It was her home, and guests were like family. Though Madame Dubois knew, from bitter experience, you can't always choose, or like, your family.

'Here it is.' She dangled an old brass key from a long keychain. 'The Forest Room. It's at the back, I'm afraid.'

Reine-Marie smiled. 'We know where it is, *merci*.'

One day rolled gently into the next as the Gamaches swam in Lac Massawippi and went for leisurely walks through the fragrant woods. They read and chatted amicably with the other guests and slowly got to know them.

Up until a few days ago they'd never met the Finneys, but now they were cordial companions at the isolated lodge. Like experienced travelers on a cruise, the guests were neither too remote nor too familiar. They didn't even know what the other did for a living, which was fine with Armand Gamache.

It was mid-afternoon and Gamache was watching a bee scramble around a particularly blousy pink rose when a movement caught his attention. He turned in his chaise longue and watched as the eldest son, Thomas, and his wife, Sandra, walked from the lodge into the startling sunshine. Sandra brought a slim hand up and placed huge black sunglasses on her face, so that she looked a little like a fly. She seemed an alien in this place, certainly not someone in her natural habitat. Gamache supposed her to be in her late fifties, early sixties, though she was clearly trying to pass for considerably less. Funny, he thought, how dyed hair, heavy make-up and young clothes actually made a person look older.

They walked onto the lawn, Sandra's heels aerating the grass, and paused, as though expecting applause. But the only sound Gamache could hear came from the bee, whose wings were making a muffled raspberry sound in the rose.

Thomas stood on the brow of the slight hill rolling down to the lake, an admiral on the bridge. His piercing blue eyes surveyed the water, like Nelson at Trafalgar. Gamache realized that every time he saw Thomas he thought of a man preparing for battle. Thomas Finney was in his early sixties and certainly handsome. Tall and distinguished with gray hair and noble features. But in the few days they'd shared the lodge, Gamache had also noted a hint of irony in this man, a quiet sense of humor. He was arrogant and entitled, but he seemed to know it and be able to laugh at himself. It was very becoming and Gamache found himself warming to the man. Though on this hot day he was warming to everything, especially the old *Life* magazine whose ink was coming off on his sweaty hands. Looking down he saw tattooed to his palm *EFIL*. Life. Backwards.

Thomas and Sandra had walked straight past his elderly parents, who were lounging on the shaded porch. Gamache marveled yet again at the ability of this family to make each other invisible. As Gamache watched over his half-moon glasses, Thomas and Sandra surveyed the people dotted around the garden and along the shore of the lake. Julia Martin, the oldest sister and a few years younger than Thomas, was sitting alone on the dock in an Adirondack chair, reading. She wore a simple white one-piece bathing suit. In her late fifties, she was slim and gleamed like a trophy as though she'd slathered herself in cooking oil. She seemed to sizzle in the sun, and with a wince Gamache could imagine her skin beginning to crackle. Every now and then Julia would lower her book and gaze across the calm lake. Thinking. Gamache knew enough about Julia Martin to know she had a great deal to think about.

On the lawn leading down to the lake were the rest of the family, the youngest sister, Marianna, and her child, Bean. Where Thomas and Julia were slim and attractive, Marianna was short and plump and unmistakably ugly. It was as though she was the negative to their positive. Her clothes seemed to have a grudge against her and either slipped off or scrunched around awkwardly so that she was constantly rearranging herself, pulling and tugging and wriggling.

And yet the child, Bean, was extremely attractive, with

long blond hair, bleached almost white in the sun, thick dark lashes and brilliant blue eyes. At that moment Marianna appeared to be doing Tai Chi, though with movements of her own making.

'Look, darling, a crane. Mommy's a crane.'

The plump woman stood on one leg, arms reaching for the sky and neck stretched to its limits.

Ten-year-old Bean ignored Mommy and continued to read. Gamache wondered how bored the child must be.

'It's the most difficult position,' Marianna said more loudly than necessary, almost throttling herself with one of her scarves. Gamache had noticed that Marianna's Tai Chi and yoga and meditations and military calisthenics only happened when Thomas appeared.

Was she trying to impress her older brother, Gamache wondered, or embarrass him? Thomas took a quick glance at the pudgy, collapsing crane and walked in the other direction. They found two chairs in the shade, alone.

'You're not spying on them, are you?' Reine-Marie asked, lowering her own book to look at her husband.

'Spying is far too harsh. I'm observing.'

'Aren't you supposed to stop that?' Then after a moment she added, 'Anything interesting?'

He laughed and shook his head. 'Nothing.'

'Still,' said Reine-Marie, looking around at the scattered Finneys. 'Odd family that comes all this way for a reunion then ignores each other.'

'Could be worse,' he said. 'They could be killing each other.'

'They'd never get close enough to manage it,' laughed Reine-Marie.

Gamache grunted his agreement and realized happily that he didn't care. That was their problem, not his. Besides, after a few days together he'd become fond of the Finneys in a funny sort of way.

'*Votre thé glacé, Madame.*' The young man spoke French with a delightful English-Canadian accent.

'*Merci,* Elliot.' Reine-Marie shaded her eyes from the afternoon sun and smiled at the waiter.

'*Un plaisir.*' He beamed and handed a tall glass of iced tea to Reine-Marie and a perspiring glass of misty lemonade to Gamache, then went off to deliver the rest of his drinks.

'I remember when I was that young,' said Gamache, wistfully.

'You might have been that young, but you were never that—' She nodded toward Elliot as he walked athletically across the manicured lawn in his tailored black pants and small white jacket snugly fitting his lithe body.

'Oh, God, am I going to have to beat up another suitor?'

'Maybe.'

'You know I would.' He took her hand.

'I know you wouldn't. You'd listen him to death.'

'Well, it's a strategy. Crush him with my massive intellect.'

'I can imagine his terror.'

Gamache sipped his lemonade and suddenly puckered, tears springing to his eyes.

'Ah, and what woman could resist that?' She looked at his fluttering, watering eyes and face screwed into a wince.

'Sugar. Needs sugar,' he gasped.

'Here, I'll ask the waiter.'

'Never mind. I'll do it.' He coughed, gave her a mockingly stern gaze and rocked out of the deep and comfortable seat.

Taking his lemonade, he wandered up the path from the fragrant gardens and onto the wide verandah, already cooler and shaded from the brunt of the afternoon sun. Bert Finney lowered his book and gazed at Gamache, then smiled and nodded politely.

'*Bonjour,*' the elderly man said. 'Warm day.'

'But cooler here, I notice,' said Gamache, smiling at the elderly couple sitting quietly side by side. Finney was clearly older than his wife. Gamache thought she was probably in her mid-eighties, while he must be nearing ninety and had that translucent quality people sometimes got, near the end.

'I'm going inside. May I get you anything?' asked Gamache, thinking yet again that Bert Finney was both courtly and one of the least attractive people he'd ever met. Admonishing himself for being so superficial, it was all he could do not to stare. Monsieur Finney was so repulsive he was almost attractive, as though aesthetics were circular and this man had circumnavigated that rude world.

His skin was pocked and ruddy, his nose large and misshapen, red and veined as though he'd snorted, and retained, Burgundy. His teeth protruded, yellowed and confused, heading this way and that in his mouth. His eyes were small and slightly crossed. A lazy eye, thought Gamache. What used to be known as an evil eye, in darker times when men like this found themselves at best, cast out of polite society and at worst, tied to a stake.

Irene Finney sat next to her husband and wore a floral sundress. She was plump with soft white hair in a loose bun on her head, and while she didn't glance up, he could see her complexion was tender and white. She looked like a soft, inviting, faded pillow, propped next to a cliff face.

'We're fine, but *merci.*'

Gamache had noticed that Finney, alone among his family, always tried to speak a little French to him.

Entering the Manoir the temperature dropped again. It was almost cool inside, a relief from the heat of the day. It took a moment for Gamache's eyes to adjust.

The dark maple door to the dining room was closed and Gamache knocked tentatively, then, opening it, he stepped into the paneled room. Places were being set for dinner, with crisp white linen, sterling silver, fine bone china and a small arrangement of fresh flowers on each table. It smelled of roses and wood, of polish and herbs, of beauty and order. Sun was streaming through the floor-to-ceiling windows that looked onto the garden. The windows were closed, to keep the heat out and the cool in. The Manoir Bellechasse wasn't air-conditioned, but the massive logs acted as natural insulation, keeping the heat in during the bitterest of Quebec winters, and the heat out on the most sizzling of summer days. This wasn't the hottest. Low eighties, Gamache figured. But he was still grateful for the workmanship of the *coureurs du bois* who raised this place by hand and chose each log with such precision that nothing not invited could ever come in.

'Monsieur Gamache.' Pierre Patenaude came forward smiling and wiping his hands on a cloth. He was a few years younger than Gamache and slimmer. All that running from table to table, thought Gamache. But the maitre d' never seemed to run. He gave everyone his time, as though they were the only ones in the auberge, without seeming to ignore or miss any of the other guests. It was a particular gift of the very best maitre d's, and the Manoir Bellechasse was famous for having only the best.

'What can I do for you?'

Gamache, slightly bashfully, extended his glass. 'I'm sorry to bother you, but I need some sugar.'

'Oh, dear. I was afraid of that. Seems we've run out. I've sent one of the *garçons* to the village to pick up some more. *Desolé.* But if you wait here, I think I know where the chef hides her emergency supply. Really, this is most unusual.'

What was most unusual, thought Gamache, was seeing the unflappable maitre d' flapped.

'I don't want to put you out,' Gamache called to Patenaude's disappearing back.

A moment later the maitre d' returned, a small bone china vessel in his hands.

'*Voila!* Success. Of course I had to wrestle Chef Véronique for it.'

'I heard the screams. *Merci.*'

'*Pour vous, Monsieur, c'est un plaisir.*' Patenaude picked up his rag and a silver rose bowl and continued his polishing while Gamache stirred the precious sugar into his lemonade. Both men stared in companionable silence out the bank of windows to the garden and the gleaming lake beyond. A canoe drifted lazily by in the still afternoon.

'I checked my instruments a few minutes ago,' said the maitre d'. 'A storm's on the way.'

'*Vraiment?*'

The day was so clear and calm, but like every other guest at the gracious old lodge, he'd come to believe the maitre d's daily weather reports, gleaned from his home-made weather stations dotted around the property. It was a hobby, the maitre d' had once explained, passed from father to son.

'Some fathers teach their sons to hunt or fish, mine would bring me into the woods and teach me about the weather,' he'd explained one day, while showing Gamache and Reine-Marie the barometric device and the old glass bell-jar with water up the spout.

'Now I'm teaching them.' Pierre Patenaude had waved in the direction of the young staff. Gamache hoped they were paying attention.

There was no television at the Bellechasse and even the radio was patchy, so Environment Canada forecasts weren't available. Just Patenaude and his near-mythical ability to foretell the weather. Each morning when they arrived for breakfast, the forecast would be tacked outside the dining room door. For a nation addicted to the weather, he gave them their fix.

Now Patenaude looked out into the calm day. Not a leaf stirred.

'*Oui.* Heat wave coming, then storm. Looks like a big one.'

'*Merci.*' Gamache raised his lemonade to the maitre d' and returned outside.

He loved summer storms, especially at the Bellechasse. Unlike Montreal, where storms seemed to suddenly break overhead, here he could see them coming. Dark clouds would collect above the mountains at the far end of the lake, then a gray curtain of rain would fall in the distance. It would seem to gather itself, take a breath, and then march like a line of infantry clearly marked on the water. The wind would pick up, catching and furiously shaking the tall trees. Then it would strike. Boom. And as it howled and blew and threw itself at them, he'd be tucked up in the Manoir with Reine-Marie, safe.

As he stepped outside, the heat bumped him, not so much a wall as a whack.

'Find some sugar?' asked Reine-Marie, stretching out her hand to touch his face as he leaned down to kiss her then settle back into his chair.

'*Absolutement.*'

She went back to reading and Gamache reached for *Le Devoir*, but his large hand hesitated, hovering over the newspaper headlines. ANOTHER SOVEREIGNTY REFERENDUM POSSIBLE. A BIKER GANG WAR. A CATASTROPHIC EARTHQUAKE.

His hand moved to his lemonade instead. All year his mouth watered for the homemade Manoir Bellechasse lemonade. It tasted fresh and clean, sweet and tart. It tasted of sunshine and summer.

Gamache felt his shoulders sag. His guard was coming down. It felt good. He took off his floppy sun hat and wiped his brow. The humidity was rising.

Sitting in the peaceful afternoon, Gamache found it hard to believe a storm was on its way. But he felt a trickle down his spine, a lone, tickling stream of perspiration. The pressure was building, he could feel it, and the parting words of the maitre d' came back to him.

'Tomorrow's going to be a killer.'